Erica Hayes was a law student, an air force officer, an editorial assistant and a musician, before finally landing her dream job: fantasy writer. She writes dark paranormal romance, urban fantasy and romantic science fiction, and her books feature tough, smart heroines and colorful heroes with dark secrets. She hails from Australia, where she drifts from city to city, leaving a trail of chaos behind her. Currently, she's terrorizing the wilds of Northumberland.

First published in 2012 by Momentum
Pan Macmillan Australia Pty Ltd
1 Market Street, Sydney 2000

A CIP record for this book is available at the National Library of Australia

Dragonfly

EPUB format: 9781743340998
Mobi format: 9781743341001
Print on Demand format: 9781743341681

Cover design by Bree Mateljan
Edited by Sarah Hazelton
Copyedited by Nicola O'Shea
Proofread by Glenda Downing

Macmillan Digital Australia: www.macmillandigital.com.au

To report a typographical error, please email
errors@momentumbooks.com.au

Visit www.momentumbooks.com.au to read more about all our books and to buy books online. You will also find features, author interviews and news of any author events.

Dragonfly

Erica Hayes

1

"What's the emergency?" I took a seat before the director's shiny black desk, adjusting my plasma pistol so it wouldn't dig into my ribs.

Director Renko didn't look up from her glowing 3D workspace.

I fidgeted, impatient. My reflection gleamed in the sanctum's polarized black windows, and I tried to smooth the creases from my forehead, wishing I'd tied my hair up more neatly or revitalized my make-up tints to make it look like I wanted to be here. I was frustrated that she'd dragged me in. I needed that vacation.

My most recent mission—bleeding out a rebellion in a backwater star system, a new Imperial conquest whose poor and hungry hadn't learned to keep their mouths shut yet—had been a quiet but definite success. The rebel leaders died a slow and conspicuous death, the poor and hungry got a tough lesson in Imperial citizenship, and I got a pat on the head and a long-awaited week off. I'd worked without rest for months on end and I was exhausted. I'd booked a swim-out bungalow at the pleasure resorts on Vostok Four: UV-filtered sunshine, cocktails by the pool, an anti-gravity combat gym and twice-daily deep-tissue massages from a blue-eyed underwear model named Antonio.

But you're never really on vacation from Axis, the Imperial secret intelligence service. Especially not from counter-insurrection division. They know exactly what you've done, where and to whom. They could screw you to the wall in an instant. So if they whistle, you jump, and you do it right away, no matter what Antonio's doing.

At last, Lyudmila Renko, my boss, director of Axis's counter-insurrection division, flicked her workspace away and reclined in her transparent chair, resting pointed elbows on its arms. Today she wore a black silk flight suit, same as mine, belted around her greyhound-thin waist, her blonde hair pulled tightly back.

"Aragon. You're late."

Aragon's my codename. I doubted she remembered my real one: Carrie Thatcher, ex-lieutenant of marines, one-time military intelligence officer, now Imperial secret agent extraordinaire with a license for mayhem.

"Sorry, ma'am. I got here as fast as I–"

"Three days ago, a rebel colony in sector five surrendered." No small talk. No apology for interrupting my rest. "In eleven days, that colony is joining our Empire. The negotiation teams are meeting at a neutral space station as usual, but surveillance reports have uncovered an insurrection problem in the area. I want you to stop it before it interferes with Imperial business."

Translated: before it makes us look weak in front of our new subjects. Weakness breeds rebellion, that's the Axis motto. Still, I wasn't sure what it had to do with me.

"Eleven days from now? Doesn't sound like much of an emergency. What's their target?"

Director Renko studied her clipped fingernails. "The neutral space station is a casino called Casa de Esperanza. The criminal's target is the vault, on the day the surrender pact will be signed."

I swallowed to stop my jaw from dropping. A heist at a glitzy mob-infested gaming palace? She'd dragged me in from vacation to stop a petty thief?

Granted, the Esperanza vault reputedly held enough cash to buy a few minor planets, and to have it whipped out from under our noses in the middle of the surrender negotiations would splat egg on some important Imperial faces—but still.

"With all due respect, ma'am, you've got dozens of people for work like this. Why me? I'm on vacation."

A sly eye-twinkle. "This particular criminal may interest you. Our source agent suggests the thief is Dragonfly."

I sat up, my pulse leaping, my exhaustion forgotten. Dragonfly. Not just a thief with a grand reputation for audacity and skill, but an insurrectionist with a following. He stole to finance his bloody little wars, and rebels and malcontents all over the galaxy loved him for it.

I'd crossed him before, though I'd never seen his face. My guts heated at the memory.

Three years ago; Urumki City burning, night air filled with smoke, gunfire and dying screams. Our troops under fire, running and hiding like vermin, armor glinting, lasers flashing. My counter-insurrection team, armed to the hilt, searching dark streets and crumbling towers for the enemy cell, the leaders. My point sharpshooter, her rifle arm ripped bare to the muscle by an acid bomb; my comms tech with bioware torn loose from his skull and his shoulder blackening from a poison dart; and sweet Mishka, my second-in-command, his long black braid singed, urban camouflage darkened with sweat, one brown eye seared shut from atomflash. It was fluid, knife-edge work. One moment we were cleaning up a row of tenements with smart plasma rounds. The next, liquid shatterfire descended in burning streams, flames and deadly molten glass fragments erupting like lava. I ducked for cover, and never saw my team alive again.

Dragonfly killed six Axis agents that night. All of them my friends. All my responsibility. And one, the love of my life, the man I was going to marry. Mishka's codename was Ariel, after the nebula cluster, and maybe the angel too, but in private we'd long gone beyond codenames. I didn't even get to weep over his body, because nothing was left. I'd returned to base alone, my heart bleeding cold with fury and vengeance.

A hole still festered there, where my friends—and especially Mishka, my silent, loyal soldier—once lived. A tortured, broken Dragonfly would fill it nicely.

This was the assignment I'd dreamed of. I'd done well in my recent mission, but I still needed to prove myself. I always needed to prove myself. If I could pull this off, maybe I'd finally be back on Renko's go-to list.

I inched forward in my seat. "When can I start?"

Renko smiled thinly, her narrow cheeks creasing. "You will travel to Esperanza station and meet our source. Your mission is to foil Dragonfly's plan using whatever means necessary—*short* of termination." Her red lips tightened even further. "Dragonfly irritates my superiors. He makes them itch, and they want him squashed—but in full view of any disgruntled idiots who might be thinking about emulating him. The further his little expedition gets, the more satisfying and spectacular the squashing will be. Understood?"

"Yes, ma'am."

My stomach tightened with relish. They wanted an agent provocateur. Someone to whisper in Dragonfly's ear, guide him softly into the trap, and crunch it closed at the last second, when he'd have no escape. Renko knew this was personal for me. It was part of the test. And I wouldn't fail. I'd give them Dragonfly with his sticky little fingers on Esperanza's money, and I'd laugh as our interrogators took him away.

The director returned to her glowing desktop projection, golden datastreams reflecting in her eyes. "I want full reports on schedule. Collect your preliminary briefing from intelligence as usual. You'll get the rest from our source when you get there."

I stood, eager to get on with it. Esperanza lay a good two days in slipspace away. "Understood. What's the rating?"

"The mission is classified omega blue." Impatience sharpened her tone.

Excitement rippled warmer in my blood. Blue meant a dire security risk. Omega meant no one knew about the mission except me, Renko, and our source. Axis wasn't messing around on this one. This source had better be someone good, with the proper clearances. Someone who wouldn't get in my way.

"Who's the source?"

"Your source is Malachite."

My heart thudded into my guts, and I flushed, my palms damp.

Renko's thin blonde brows rose. "Is there a problem?"

Damn right there was a problem.

"No, ma'am, not at all."

Taking on Dragonfly had just gotten less enticing. And a whole lot more dangerous.

***

I walked out of Renko's office, past potted green ferns and into the dim blue lobby, where brightly colored fish cruised up and down in a wall aquarium, among rocks and swaying plants. Swirling lights glowed in columns lining the pale walls. Calmlights are a randomized display designed to soothe savage nerves, and they weren't outside the director's sanctum by accident. But tension still ached in my fingers as I touched the silver contact to call the elevator.

The gleaming black door dissolved, and scarlet sunlight poured in through the elevator's clear plastic walls. I stepped inside, an infuriating wobble in my legs, lemon-scented airborne antivirals making my head ache.

"Thirteen," I mumbled automatically, and the elevator shot silently down the side of the Axis building toward intelligence division, where I'd get my briefing.

New Moskva, the Empire's capital city, glittered to the horizon, sharp metal and glass towers shining like needles spiking into the red-stained midday sky. Glinting silver flyers flitted to and fro, and a few bulbous passenger transports cruised by at higher altitude, windows flashing golden as stray electrical storms crackled in the dusty air. But I couldn't concentrate on the view. Ideas bounced around in my head like shrapnel, and I wanted to duck for cover.

First, if Renko had put Malachite in charge, she was taking the Dragonfly threat very seriously. Malachite was her top agent, and she didn't waste him on trifles. There was more to this mission than she'd let on.

Second, I was targeting like a smartbomb toward making an abject idiot of myself, and I didn't know what to do about it.

Malachite had been my mentor when I first transferred to Axis from military intelligence, way before I'd met Mishka or even heard of Dragonfly. Even back then, Malachite was a legend. The perfect operative, skilled, effortless, suave, the one everyone wanted to be. I was young, awe-struck, desperate for his approval. He'd said everything I'd ever dreamed he'd say, and I was starry-eyed enough to believe he meant it. We ended badly, and for the last six years I'd avoided him. If I never saw Malachite again, I'd die a happy woman.

I laughed. I'm an Axis agent. I can't expect to die happy anyway.

The elevator glided to a halt and the door phased open. I stepped out, and the black floor glared at me, my own reflection sharp in white icelights. The smell of gunfire coated my tongue, hot metal and salt. No white corridor, no laserglass security screen or pale blue orchids. Just a black vault door, silvery shatterbolts gleaming.

My spine prickled. This wasn't floor thirteen.

The elevator phased shut behind me with a sizzle. Alarm stung my body into action and I lurched backward, my hand flashing upwards for my pistol.

The hard, hot edge of an atomflash barrel jabbed into the base of my spine, and a warm male voice caressed my ear. "Think again."

I froze, my hair springing tight. But I flushed, angry at myself. All very well to pay attention now. Slowly I eased my hand from my holster, fingers twitching. No need to ask who this was.

"I already told your boss *no.* What do you want?"

"Get inside."

The shatterbolts cranked aside, and the vault eased open in a puff of warm darkness. A hand pressed me forward. I swallowed dryness and did as I was told.

2

Inside, a corridor stretched black under reddish ice-lights, glaring and uncomfortable. No calmlights here. They wanted you on edge. At the end, a fireproof black ultraglass door whisked open. My escort shoved me through, and the glass slammed shut with an echo straight from a bad prison-colony movie.

The man behind the desk looked up, and his green lasersight eyes slitted in the light like a cat's. My stomach rippled. Arkady Surov, director of black ops division, the shady cousin no one talks about at Axis parties.

At counter-insurrection, we infiltrate, spy, collect information, do the odd elimination if necessary. We're all a little angry and maladjusted, but we're basically normal. Black ops agents just kill people for a government salary, and to get assigned there, you need to have something seriously wrong with you. They've been trying to poach Malachite for years, only he won't go. It's too anonymous for him. He likes the spotlight.

Apparently, I was now on Surov's headhunting list. I wasn't flattered.

I folded my arms, ignoring the atomflash still pointed at me and the warning tingle in my spine. Black ops agents think we at counter-insurrection are soft. We think they're gung-ho freaks. Some things never change.

"You guys are such drama queens," I said. "Slam this and crunch that. How about some blood dripping down the walls? That'd be a nice touch."

"Aragon. So nice to see you."

Surov flexed to his feet and slinked around the desk to drape himself on the front edge like a twitchy feline. He wore a standard black combat suit: tight, bullet-retardant armor that hugged his long muscles. A cortex stimulator flattened his dark hair over suspiciously sharp-pointed ears, and a plasma pistol lay half-stripped on his desk, like he'd just come in from the virtual range. He gestured to a black velvet lounge, and slick gunmetal claws gleamed in his fingertips.

I wrinkled my nose in distaste. I mean, we've all had work done, some plastic hyper-extending joints or a nose job or some superconductor filaments to spice up your reflexes. But metalcore biotech enhancements and weaponised gene splicing are illegal. It messes you up, everyone's known that for four hundred years since the Kovalev Six Mutant Massacre. The fanatics at black ops just don't care, and when you shoot people in the back for a living, you want every advantage you can get.

They say that Surov the cat-man can leap two stories high and shoot a man's eyeball out in the dark from two thousand meters. I don't doubt it. Hope it makes all the raw fish dinners worth it. And at least no one can say the folk who hand out codenames don't have a sense of humor: Surov's designation is Felix.

"Hear you've got a tasty new mission," he said, licking his chops.

So much for omega blue.

I ignored the lounge and stayed standing, tossing my braid back over my shoulder. "Sorry, comrade. Can't confirm or deny. You know the rules."

"Dragonfly, mmm-hmm. How gratifying for you. Pity Renko won't let you loose."

Curiosity itched, and I squirmed. Damn it. "What do you mean?"

"You know. *Short of termination* and all that. Hardly revenge, is it?" He twitched one ear.

I bristled, because he was right. "Look, I already told you—"

"We at black ops want Dragonfly dead." Surov's pupils slitted wide. "No reason you can't be the one to do it. No more than you deserve, the way Renko's sidelined you since ... Well, you know."

I flushed, and there was no use hiding it. Ever since Mishka and my friends died, Director Renko hadn't trusted me. She was always checking up on me, setting other agents to watch over me in case I lost my nerve. My most recent assignment was the first time she'd let me out on my own since Urumki City. And even now, with the Dragonfly mission, she'd crippled me with restrictions. Not to mention with Malachite, who'd graduated academician *cum laude* in Renko's class at New Moskva Tech and probably still bought her drinks and let her beat him at chess whenever he was in town.

Since Mishka died, my job was all I had. If I stopped fighting for the Empire, he'd have died for nothing. But until Renko let me off the hook, my career was going nowhere.

And I couldn't deny that the thought of killing Dragonfly—of being the one who pressed the atomflash to his smug forehead and jammed my thumb on the contact—ignited a spark of anticipation in my flesh that wasn't entirely professional.

But I wasn't dumb enough to imagine Surov the cat-man was doing me a favor.

They say that back on Planet Zero, before humans had ventured into space, the Old Russiyans had a vast military empire, the largest on the planet, bristling with holocaust weapons and backed up by iron-cast ideology and the spirit of revolution. Only they lost their nerve, and it all fell apart and gangsters took over. Not much had changed in a thousand years, except Planet Zero was a smoking ruin, and now the gangsters wore uniforms again.

I eyed Surov coolly. "So what's in it for you if I kill him?"

Surov shrugged, his armor flexing like thick black skin. "Dead insurrectionist, well and good. But this Dragonfly has a dangerous mind. Exceptional mathematician, you may have heard. There are certain ... concepts we'd rather he didn't pursue."

I shrugged. Whatever. I was good at math too, and self-appointed rebel geniuses were common as space junk. I didn't care if Dragonfly was a concert pianist. He'd still melted my friends. And from what I'd heard, he mostly used his fancy number-theory tricks to crack bank vaults and cheat at cards. Not exactly a model citizen. "No, I mean what's really in it for you?"

"You'll come and work for us." Surov's sharp teeth glinted. "You're wasted on Renko, Aragon. She's lost her way. She'll be peeved, certainly. I'll personally cover you. And I've got a little vacancy here I think you'll like."

I snorted. "Cannon fodder in the Great Renko–Surov War? Thanks very much, comrade, but I think I'll pass—"

"Assistant director operations," he interrupted, scratching behind one ear. "It's a step up for you, but I've every faith you'll manage."

I caught my breath. Assistant director was the promotion I'd dreamed of since I'd joined Axis, that I'd worked even harder for since my friends were murdered. The one I'd never get, so long as Renko was my boss. If I defied her and Dragonfly died on my watch, she'd stick me behind a dusty desk in Analysis and I'd never see an active mission again. That's if she didn't decide I was an unacceptable security risk and send her goons around to slit my throat.

But black ops? Was I cut out to be an assassin? Hell, I'd killed people; it was an occupational hazard. But black ops was different. Colder. More premeditated.

I swallowed. "Umm. I see. Well, I'll have to ... A vacancy? What happened to the last assistant director?"

I remembered him. He'd bought me a vodka or six once. Sharp smile, great hair, the planet's cleanest shower. An okay guy. I mean, sure, he was a compulsive killer with laser-sparked reflexes and a twitch, but he was fun to talk to.

"He disappointed me." Surov folded his long legs beneath him on the desk, and I swear that mentally he coiled a tail. Gene splicing, boys and girls. Don't try it at home. "I'm sure you won't. Kill Dragonfly, and the job's yours."

"And if I refuse?"

"You're a big girl, Aragon. You figure it out." He retrieved his pistol and stripped out the depleted energy rod, dismissing me with a twitch of his nose.

The atomflash prodded me in the spine again and Surov's silent minion ushered me back out to the elevator.

I stepped inside, and that warm whisper brushed my neck once more. "Watch your back. You're not the only one who wants the job."

My nerves jumped. I whirled, but he was gone.

The door phased shut, and I cracked itchy knuckles, annoyed. Black ops prima donnas and their games.

"Thirteen," I ordered again, and this time I paid attention.

3

Floor thirteen houses Axis's information and intelligence branch. It's where everything we bring in gets collated, indexed and analyzed, disseminated to those who need to know, and hidden from those who don't. They have the latest neural supercomputers, ninth generation quantum cryptography, and people with neurotech grafted to their cortexes, loaded with analysis algorithms that would melt their brains if they didn't already have high-orbit IQs. Even their coffee boy is so smart he can barely talk.

My postgrad degree was algebra, and I spent months in military cryptanalysis before I came to Axis, but at intel division, I feel like the village idiot. Mishka used to say they kept brains in jars and dribbling savants chained in steel cells. I couldn't swear he was wrong. In any case, floor thirteen gives me the creeps.

I dropped in quickly to collect my briefing, which I planned to study on the trip to Esperanza station, and fidgeted as I waited by the orchids while the spooks collected my material. I hadn't decided what to do about Surov the cat-man's offer. Tempting though it was to kill Dragonfly and get a promotion for it—assistant director, a stellar achievement for a girl from the galactic backwaters like me, perks and privileges ahoy and out from under Renko's pointy thumb at last—being a pawn in the perennial squabbles between Surov and Renko could end stickily and painfully. A director's promises counted for nothing when the safeties came off.

I'd have to assess the situation when I got there. Weigh up the pros and cons, analyze the intelligence and all that.

Or, I could just blow Dragonfly's murdering head off and chance the consequences. Suited me. Playing it Renko's way had gotten me nowhere. Maybe it was time I took matters into my own hands. Lost my nerve, had I? We'd see about that.

The slim, dark-haired agent behind the intel security desk glanced up at me, a half-smile dimpling his smooth cheeks. It took me a moment to realize I'd seen him here before. No doubt I'd had the same reaction last time, and the time before. He was cute but nondescript, unremarkable. Like me, he'd had all distinguishing marks removed, anything that made his face memorable or unusual altered by cosmetic surgery. Axis call it *normalizing*, and most of us in counter-insurrection have had it done. It makes it easier to infiltrate, provoke, destroy. Not Malachite, though. No one dared to suggest it, and he was audacious enough not to need it. Normalizing Malachite would be like jimmying the jewels off a Fabergé egg.

An unsettling tingle shot through my torso as the invisible security system took its molecular core sample. A diode flashed on the agent's console, the computer confirming that I was me. Lucky for me, or that sweet young thing would have vaporized me in an instant. He smiled wider, and slid an oblong security case of clear hardened plastic and a silver chip across the counter with a weapon-callused hand.

"My pleasure," he said, giving me a swift, sexy undress with his eyes that said he was interested in more than my core sample.

Cheeky. My skin sparkled in response. Cute, and smart too—my favorite combination. I could use an hour or two of indulgence; I was still weary from my interrupted vacation.

Axis encourages casual liaisons between agents. It's an efficient way to get natural frustrations out of the system; quick, easy, and no lying about what you do for a living, and let's face it, most of us don't have a clingy personality type. On any other day I might have thought seriously about it, but I was too shaken up. I kept thinking about Mishka, Dragonfly, Surov's proposition, Malachite and his goddamn lies. Too many ugly relics from my past unearthed in one day.

I just mumbled, "Sure," and took the case and the chip.

The plastic case—*Aragon*, the tiny black letters said—stayed cool in my hand as I descended in the elevator. It contained my omega briefing, and was keyed to my body chemistry. If anyone but me tried to open it, or held it for too long, it'd self-destruct. The chip was my equipment requisition, and I took it down to hardware straight away to have it filled.

The basement hangar where our hardware people work is always littered with spaceship parts and dismantled weapons, blackened metal gleaming under long rows of white xenon icelights. Technicians and white-suited inventors slouched around, banging metal cases with spanners and splicing plastic-coated wires together.

The head tech, Onyx, threw me a grin, her curly black hair swept back under a dented vis-helmet. "Heard you be coming down, *señorita*." Her Rus was flat with that Espan accent she'd never managed to shake. Like me, she had an unfashionable heritage. Unlike me, she didn't try to hide it. "Thought you were on vacation."

I handed her the chip. "So did I."

Onyx wiped greasy hands on her blue fireproof boilersuit and jacked the chip into her vis-helmet, slotting the hexagonal glass display down over one eye. "*Está bien.* I get this one *prioridad* this morning—I got your ship stocked already. *Un fénix,* beat to shit."

I wrinkled my nose. Director Renko's rotten sense of humor strikes again. "Nothing like traveling in style."

"You got that right. Who you piss off to get these lousy missions? At least your kit inside got some class."

Onyx led me through the hangar and out into the massive spaceport, past lines of shiny Sliver-class fighters and two square Monolith transports, their radshields crusted black with decay. A half-dismantled Starshine cruiser lay like a giant fossil being unearthed, its shiny parts scattered, techs climbing around in its skeleton with theodolites and laser cutters.

In the corner near the blast doors, half in the Starshine's shadow where the setting sun shone onto the hardstand, stood my new ship. An old Phoenix-class dart, about as big as a hovertrain carriage, with a sharp nose and twin side fins sweeping back to a scalloped stern. The Phoenix was swift, reliable, simple and responsive to fly. But the nose on this one was flattened, its dented bodywork patched together from a dozen different ships in a dozen different shades of filthy. The stealthplate tiles designed to hide the ship from unwanted sensor sweeps were mostly missing, and dark corrosion patches stained the fins and cracked the anodized surface. Someone had blown a hole in one fin, just for realism, and the energy exhaust vents at the back were chipped and seared with atomflash.

Whoever I was pretending to be got shot at a lot. I just hoped the inside was better than the outside, or it'd be a long ride to Esperanza.

Onyx grinned, pleased with her handiwork. "Aragon, meet the starship *RapidFire.* She fly true, even if she look like shit."

My home for the next eleven days. Excellent.

4

RapidFire turned out to be better than she looked. The main cabin was neat, the white plastic walls a bit dented but clean, and the separate sleeping cabin at the back smelled fresh. The navset wasn't the latest, but it was new, hardly a scratch on the glass console, and the ion drives ran smooth as air.

I spent an hour or two testing everything, flashing the arc rockets and disinfecting the air scrubbers and running diagnostics on the life-support computers. All systems functioning. I checked the weapons cache too, making sure the plasma charges were full, no expired atomflashes or dirty contacts on the shock grenades. Our hardware people were competent; I didn't expect problems. But if I'd learned one thing from Malachite, it was *trust no one but yourself.*

Once I had everything the way I liked it, I grabbed my stuff from the locker room, sealed the airlocks and prepped the console for departure. No need to hang around. I was still packed from my trip to the pleasure resort—could be I'd need a thong bikini at Esperanza—and it wasn't like I had anyone waiting for me at my apartment. Besides, I didn't fancy another visit from Surov's black ops goons, and the longer I stayed, the more perilous my position became. Renko could find me out any moment, and if she even suspected I was thinking about defying her, I'd be doing the filing in a dusty vault with my clearances revoked before the day was out.

I strapped myself into the carbonsteel command chair, the three-point harness tight over my shoulders. The glass console glowed silver and blue as I manipulated the controls. Propulsion, fuel, gravity, life support, nav sensors. Datastreams climbed like columns of green fireflies, showing me engine sensors, tactical schematics, slipspace equations.

I selected control frequency on the etherwave comms, and thumbed the contact. "Axis Arclight, this is *RapidFire*, Phoenix on platform six-five, flightplan delta one epsilon. Request departure vectors."

A crackle of etherstatic, and a deep male voice came on. "*RapidFire*, this is Arclight, affirm. Cleared on vector one-seven-five, departure pattern theta."

Sexy voice. I resisted the temptation to ask him what he was wearing. "One-seven-five theta, Arclight. Have a nice day."

The blast doors ground aside, scarlet sunlight pouring in, and I kicked the arc rockets alight and speared out into the traffic. Wind buffeted the ship as I climbed on my assigned departure trajectory, rockets howling. Particle coolants hissed as the ion stardrive accelerated to escape speed. My clearview windows dimmed, polarizing to block out UV and sunflash. The thinning atmosphere gave one last golden glimmer and broke to black.

My butt lifted in the chair as the console chimed the escape velocity warning, and I killed the rockets and spiraled sunward on stardrive, the smoky red globe of New Russiya receding in the rear clearview.

I'd seen the view a hundred times. Normally I didn't think much of it, but today it invigorated me, the stars misting into sight beyond that dusky twinkling planet I now called home. Here I was, just a girl from some grotty farm world, off on another mission to save the Empire. It seemed naive, but I couldn't deny the thrill sparkling through my body, the nav-set's static-charged warmth under my fingertips, the excitement pulsing in my blood. I was alive. I was making a difference. And that's more than anyone else on that grotty farm world could say.

Not that they talked to me any more. The last conversation I'd had with my father, right before I ran away to join the marines, had involved yelling and tears and the words *traitor* and *collaborator.* I just wanted a decent life, proper food and an education. But my parents were separatists, opposed to Imperial expansion, and they'd disowned me.

I still missed my family: Mom, Dad, Janey and little chubby-cheeked Will, who'd be grown into a young man by now and breaking hearts with his big brown eyes. For all I knew, they were dead, starved or frozen or killed in a food riot. But they were the ones who wouldn't return my calls. I'd given them the chance to support me, and they'd thrown it back in my face. I was sorry they were gone. But I wasn't losing any sleep over it.

I glanced out the clearview again, where stars glittered golden in fading sunset swirls, and smiled.

Once I'd cleared Moskovi space and passed the last departure beacon, I set an evasive course for Esperanza. Straight lines had landed me in trouble before, and even though it was difficult to track a ship through slipspace, if anyone was watching for my arrival I didn't want it to be too obvious where I'd come from.

Besides, to say I wasn't keen to see Malachite again would be a cosmic understatement. Damn it if he wasn't already in my mind, in the way my sweaty fingers slipped as I entered the course coordinates. I'd avoided thinking about him for six years, but now the memories came flooding back to swamp me. Malachite has gentle, precise fingers, a lilting voice I could listen to all day, a smile that weakens my knees. He smells of something exotic and mysterious that drives me wild. He's funny, charming, a good listener, embarrassingly good in bed. The bastard can even cook.

It's ironic how attraction blinds us to the bleeding obvious. When Malachite left me to burn on that dying prison hulk, my oxygen depleted and my rifle's last laser charge half-empty, the only one left wondering why was me.

I dragged the last coordinate across the glass a little too hard, scorching my fingertip. The past didn't matter any more. I was smarter now. I'd be frosty, professional, detached. I wouldn't fall for his lies. We'd bring Dragonfly down and I'd walk away. Right?

A trigger on my console flashed, indicating transition velocity, and I confirmed the nav course equations and engaged slipspace drive. The air in the cabin glowed momentarily red like sunset, and in the clearview window the stars winked out.

Bumps prickled my arms, and I turned up the heating. Slipspace is dark and motionless. There are no streaking stars or swirling mist as you hurtle on, faster than light, through the slit you've made in space–time. No visible light, no color, no sensation of movement. It's an in-between place, a wacky warpassed dimension where relativity doesn't ruin all the fun. But stay there too long and you'll lose your mind.

I rolled down the clearview shutters—all that *nothing* gives me the shivers—locked on to the nearest navnode and hit the automatics.

Long ago, the first slipspace travelers left beacons to find their way, and, with a bit of Imperial maintenance, their ancient tech still works. These days, slipspace navigation is like following the strands of a four-dimensional cosmic spider's web. You can't always travel the shortest route, and straying too far from the beacons is asking for trouble. It's a bit tedious, but it's the only way. Get disoriented out here and you could disappear forever.

Corporations will pay millions to get an exclusive on a new streamlined slipspace trade route, and if you're the suicidally reckless type, you can make a very good living mapping out new beacons. But beacon jockeys don't usually get to enjoy their riches for very long. They strike off into the black unknown and don't come back. Some say that slipspace is a dimension humans were never meant to navigate.

Bullshit, if you ask me. There's nothing out there. Maybe they get lost, disoriented, too far from any beacon to recover. Maybe their ships malfunction or their fuel depletes beyond return. Or maybe their minds crack, out there all alone in endless silent darkness.

Sometimes, death just happens.

With the nav neurospace keeping *RapidFire* safely on the slipspace web, and drive coolant humming softly beneath the floor, I opened a bottle of fruit juice—you can tell when the galley's been stocked by a woman—and slouched back into the command chair to read my omega briefing and get my mind off what I'd say to Malachite.

Curiosity itched me about this mission. Something had tasted odd when I'd swallowed Director Renko's story. I'd visited Casa de Esperanza before: a glitzy space station on the Imperial fringe, run by Empire-sanctioned mob bosses with freightloads of cash. Gambling, guns, drugs, black biotech—anyone with enough imagination who wants something done away from the spotlight goes to Esperanza. It's a luxury pleasure palace for high rollers, a place where if you have to ask how much, you can't afford it. Many negotiations, legitimate or otherwise, go on there. First, it's nominally neutral. And second, Esperanza's security is notoriously infallible. The vault has one of the nastiest reputations in the galaxy for impregnability, and the mob aren't known for mercy toward those who piss them off. Attempting a heist there is a suicide mission.

It didn't sit right with me. I knew how Dragonfly's mind worked. The man was a coward with an inflated opinion of his own importance, surrounded by sycophants and brainwashed disciples. The night my team was massacred, he'd burned Urumki City and murdered hundreds of people so he could get away. As much as he loved to embarrass the Empire, I didn't think he'd be prepared to kill himself to do it. He had plenty of people ready to kill themselves for him.

More likely, Dragonfly wanted to muscle in on the mob action the Empire took such a large piece of, and Renko wanted it stopped. I guessed I'd see when I got there.

I brushed my hand above the little projected display and text scrolled. The surrendering rebel colony in sector five was called Santa Maria, a tiny system of agricultural and mining worlds a long way from anywhere, headed by a politician named Alvarado. I'd never heard of either of them. No apparent connection to Dragonfly.

Intelligence division fixed me up with a false identity for the mission. My name, apparently, is Lazuli. Sounds like a showy parody of an Imperial codename, which makes me either a rebel or a smart-ass. I'm a young thief with a growing résumé of impressive jobs, itching to get in on something bigger. I'm ex-military, probably where I learned my tricks, but I don't like telling people because it makes me look uncool. No insurrection history yet, but I lost friends in the marines, and my parents died in our colony's forced surrender. So sad.

I'm Rus by birth and my Brit sucks, so I'd better remember to speak it with an accent. I'm a crypto expert, they say, which means I'm probably too smart to have much common sense and not too hot at the physical stuff, like getting in and out. Could be handy. Rumor has it Dragonfly has a histrionic gallant streak, thinks he's some hero in ultraglass armor. Maybe I could use a bit of rescuing from time to time.

I'm hetero, a non-smoker, a vegetarian. My favorite drink is the Lvov martini, and I use oblivion crystals, but only when I'm not on the job. I'm right-handed—good thing Aragon is too—and I'm a quick shot with my favourite weapon, the Molokovsky SK-195X, better known as shatterfire junior or the shatterjay, a delightful little close-range fingergun that slots minuscule slivers of hot ultraglass into the target's blood vessels. I've killed four people in the course of my career, and I'm only just getting started.

Charming, aren't I?

5

Forty-four hours later, I docked *RapidFire* at Casa de Esperanza.

The station—Esperanza for short—is two great sparkling spires laid end to end, spearing through the centre of a shining ring that holds the spaceports. The whole thing spins slowly, three and a half revolutions a day, and in space you can see its lights from eight hundred spacials away.

The briefing told me to be at the Spire North tarocchi room at twenty-two hundred local, so I only had a few hours to adjust to the gravity, shower, and get my bearings. I could have checked into a suite—the rooms at Esperanza are palatial, and normally only the owners of the most luxurious space yachts would want to stay on their ships—but I wanted to prepare for a swift departure if necessary, so I remained aboard *RapidFire* and ordered up a ridiculously expensive meal of real shellfish on company cash.

My new wardrobe was tailored to my new identity. I whipped my hair up in a twist, squeezed into a tight black evening dress that ended a hand's-breadth shy of my knees, and slipped on a pair of black stilettos. My permanent make-up tint is only light, and I figured Lazuli for a glamor girl, so I chose a sparkling silver shadow for her eyelids and a lipstick called Frosted Mocha Plum. Someone had thoughtfully slipped a little suite of diamonds into her kit—a choker and a pair of teardrops, nothing too flashy—so I put those on too.

I wasn't usually nervous before heading into the field, but tonight my mouth felt dry, my guts twisted up. I checked my flushed face in the mirror, trying not to hyperventilate, and washed a couple of beta-blockers down with OJ so my hands wouldn't shake. I hated both Malachite and Dragonfly more than ever for making me like this.

Now, I lounged stiffly at the bar in the tarocchi room, where crystal chandeliers shone like sun clusters over the black carpet. Players in tuxedos and cocktail dresses leaned over the velvet-edged card tables, gaudy jewelry dripping. Metal chips flipped back and forth, the black-suited croupiers spreading and collecting the bets almost too rapidly for me to follow the game. When the smallest chip is ten thousand sols, time really is money.

The glass shatterjay lay warm in its strap holster around my thigh, my pulse thudding against it. A glowing blue Lvov martini sat untouched before me on the copper counter. Already, three men and a woman had tried to buy me another one, their gazes roving over me, but none had caught my eye as useful or attractive. Still, I should flirt a bit. I was a thief on the make, after all.

I cocked a three-inch heel into my stool's rung and sipped the blue martini. It burned my throat like acid-fuel, tart and strong, the fumes rising into my nose. A few more of these and I'd be on my much-admired ass. But I needed the courage. I felt unprepared, and I hated it. There'd been next to nothing in my brief about Dragonfly himself; just a bunch of anecdotes and aliases and some poorly educated guesses that passed for analysis. I still didn't know what he looked like, what he was planning, if his people had even arrived on Esperanza yet. I didn't even know his real name.

I downed the rest of the martini and plonked the glass back on the bar. I didn't want to know his name. The idea of getting that intimate with him made me cringe. Distance is what codenames are for. He was Dragonfly, the rebel asshole who'd murdered my friends. End of story.

"Care for another, beautiful?"

A shiver spidered down my spine.

Warm blue eyes, deep as space. Perfect lips turned up in a seductive smile, cheekbones like chipped ice, pale blond hair, crisp and crushable. He wore an immaculate black suit, and moved like a dancer, elegant and deliberate. I knew for a fact he was built like one as well.

My thighs tingled, and I wanted to press them together. He didn't look a day older. If anything, he looked even better than I remembered. So perfect, the kind of man who'd bring your mother flowers on your first date. Hard to believe so much was so dangerously wrong with him.

I faked a smile, fighting to stay in character while my pulse raced. "Sure. Why not?"

Malachite leaned toward me, and his hair brushed my cheek, his familiar smell evoking those warm starlit nights in New Moskva, before I'd realized what he was.

"We can talk here," he murmured, "the room is iced. It's good to see you, Aragon."

Liar.

I flushed. I thought I'd forgotten my anger. I thought I'd forgotten how he'd humiliated me. But I wanted to hit him, and my fingers itched as I pictured the shatterjay tight around my sweating thigh. I clenched my fist, shaking. Calm down, Aragon. Remember it's not his fault. They make drugs for what he's got, only Axis won't let him take them, even if he wanted to.

There's a note in his security clearance data, under "Personality" where most agents have "prone to stress" or "borderline obsessive" or "poor anger management". I know, because six years ago I bribed someone in records to let me see it. What's wrong with Agent Malachite is called *antisocial personality disorder with extreme psychological violence.* That's the fancy term for a charming psychopath. It means that he has no conscience. Everything is an act, every word a lie designed to catch you out. He can't help it, and wouldn't if he could. You can never, ever trust him.

Axis like him that way. It makes him such an effective agent.

The bartender brought my martini. I leaned away so Malachite couldn't touch me, wouldn't feel the heat in my skin.

"My omega brief wasn't all there. Where's the rest of it?"

He sipped his vodka tonic, leaning back on the bar to show off, and a few wisps of blond hair fell in front of his eyes. It looked unintentional, but wasn't. He does that when he wants to look harmless. When he wants some woman to take pity on him.

"Charmed to meet you, Lazuli," he said, ignoring my question. "I'm some rich asshole who's trying to get up your skirt, and it'll take me about two minutes to piss you off so badly you'll walk away to join the tarocchi table on the left." He grinned at me, in full disarm mode.

Despite myself, a smile tempted my own lips. He loved this playacting stuff. It came naturally to him. "So what's at the table, then?"

"The rest of your omega brief. Dark hair, blue silk suit, platinum rings on his right hand."

I didn't need to turn around; I'd catalogued all the players already. Blue suit hadn't tried to hit on me yet, though I'd hoped he might. Hypnotic dark eyes, long deft fingers that made me stare, sinful lips that put dirty thoughts in my head. He sat alone, no jeweled woman or handsome boy draped over his shoulder, and barely said a word. He drank top-shelf scotch and water, spoke Rus with a faint Espan accent, and had won a couple of hundred thousand sols while I'd been sitting here. A smart player. Cute.

My skin prickled. I hadn't known I'd be dealing with yet another agent. "I thought you were my source."

"I am. He's Dragonfly."

I choked on a mouthful of martini.

Blue suit was Dragonfly? He couldn't be. He was too ... normal. Too soft. I'd expected hardness, scorn. A monster. Surely, you'd recognize a callous killer like that. He'd be different.

I studied him again from the corner of my eye, alcohol still burning my throat, but now my skin burned too, out of embarrassment that I'd thought him attractive. He looked harmless, insouciant, younger than I'd imagined. Not the vicious anarchist who'd murdered Mishka. Scorn stung my heart. No doubt he paid others to do his dirty work. I'd make him regret I'd ever laid eyes on him.

Malachite tucked a stray curl behind my ear, his fingertips leaving a warm trail on my cheek. "He's played here six nights running," he said absently, as if I distracted him. "Games of skill. Tarocchi, baccarat. Never dice or faro. Sometimes he wins, sometimes not. If he's cheating, he's careful at it."

He gave a wistful smile, his fingers lingering on my lips, and I remembered the night we'd cheated the poker game at New Smolensk of two million sols to expose their crooked pit bosses. We'd made love that night in a heap of crisp plastic cash, high on winning and oblivion crystals, his fingers clenched around mine, our bodies slick ...

I flushed, and pushed his hand away, every breath of air shivering my skin. "Do Esperanza security know he's on the station?"

"Those clueless idiots? They've got no idea. They don't even have imagery to facematch him. You'd think he'd been flying the spaceways with a bag over his head."

"But what's he doing here? He can't check vault security from the tarocchi room."

Malachite grinned knowingly. "That's the question, isn't it? He's alone, no lovers, never the same friends two nights running. His ship's in dock, epsilon five. Old Nebula class, new biochemical security."

Curiosity scratched my nerves. The latest biochem had likely cost more than the ship. "Why? What's he keep in there?"

He shrugged, dismissive, as if such a menial job were beneath him. "I thought you might like to look. If you really think you can get in." His wicked eyes flashed a challenge.

I tried to stay cool, but the old excitement bubbled inside me, the way we'd teased, challenged each other to impossible games. My pulse quickened, and I wanted to lick my lips, my mouth watering. I wanted to tease him back, say yes, compete the way we used to. Say his name, flirt like old lovers, taste that lost thrill.

He knew what he was doing, the bastard.

I hesitated. I could call Director Renko, tell her I couldn't do this, that she should send someone else. The last carefree piece of my heart had shattered along with my fiancé's skull, but Malachite—his real name is Nikita, if you've got the misfortune and the security clearance to be properly introduced, and it's one real name I sure wish I'd never learned—had made the first and biggest crack. Did I really want anything to do with him?

Did I want to return to the time before I'd gotten old and cynical? When I'd loved my life, when the Empire I served was beautiful and exciting and worth the struggle, when every daybreak brought a new adventure?

Hell, yes.

I gulped my martini, fire engulfing my belly from the heady mix of alcohol and danger. I didn't care if Malachite was still the sexiest man I'd ever met. I'd give him his challenge. Damned if I'd give him me.

"You think I can't get in?"

"I know you can't. I'd just love to see you try." He flicked his deep blue gaze down my body, and it burned over every curve.

My spine tingled warm, even as my indignation rose. "Fine. Watch me."

"With pleasure. Your two minutes are up, by the way. You can slap me if you like."

"Don't tempt me."

I slid my glass onto the bar and walked away before he could say *too late.*

A thin woman in furs and diamonds was folding her hand, leaving a place open at the tarocchi table. I sauntered up and sat down, crossing my legs conspicuously, the soft leather chair warm beneath my thighs, and waved at the waiter for another martini. Dragonfly glanced at me, those hot brown eyes giving me a swift once-over, and glanced away again. Was he impressed? I couldn't yet tell.

I nodded at the cashier, and he pushed a short stack of shiny chips my way across the merlot baize. The old man opposite me was dealing, his ancient fingers heavy with alabaster rings. I tasted my icy drink and watched him, half a sultry eye on Dragonfly.

The game was seven-card tarocchi, four in the kitty. You bid for how many tricks you thought you could take, then whoever won the bid got the kitty and called a suit for the king, and whoever held that king became their partner for that game. You could bet on who'd win which tricks with which cards, where the kings would end up, how many tricks would get trumped, who'd win the most or the least points. Pretty much anything.

Dragonfly glanced at his cards, dark chocolate strands of hair falling over his cheekbones, and bid four cups in his soft Rus.

I studied my cards, keeping my face blank. I had the queen and prince of cups. If he wasn't careful we'd be partners.

I sipped my martini. "Five."

The fat Espan man to my right snapped his hand closed and passed, his damp jowls wobbling.

The dealer peered at his cards, bony fingers quivering, and bid five swords in a wavering voice.

Dragonfly flipped a chip between those talented fingers. "Pass."

A gambit, for sure. The dealer bid swords, and the remainder of my hand was a washout. The rest of those cups had to be somewhere. Dragonfly must surely have the cards for six, yet he'd forgone. Was he tempting me to call cups for the king, which would no doubt make him my partner? Was he flirting with me?

My stomach clenched. In my work, I'd cozied up to murderers, lowlifes and guys who turned me off—who hadn't?—but never to such a personal enemy. I steeled myself, imagining the needling I'd get from Malachite if I couldn't go through with it. Dragonfly wasn't repulsive to look at, at least. On the contrary. My gaze took in those soft dark lashes, melting brown eyes, that maddening mouth.

Two-faced little bastard.

I shifted in my seat, my nerves writhing. "Six."

The ancient dealer shook his head.

I reached for the kitty and swapped a four of coins for the queen. "The king is cups," I said, and the betting started.

I put two chips on my team winning all the kings, and another on winning the last trick with the king of cups, four to one each.

Dragonfly sipped his scotch and slid four chips across the table. He was betting on valat, which meant he and his partner—surely me—had to win every trick. The payout on valat was sixteen to one. As he withdrew, his fingers brushed mine, accidentally or not. My palm tingled, and I wanted to yank my hand away.

I led the fat red queen, and the game was on.

***

When Dragonfly led the last trick with the king of cups, I tossed my queen of coins on top, my fingers damp. His gaze came to rest on mine, and heat crept over my skin from somewhere below my waist. I'd been certain he held that king. We'd just won nearly eight hundred thousand sols. Most of it was Dragonfly's, of course, since he'd made the chancy bet. But valat etiquette demanded he award a portion to me. I didn't want his money. I didn't want anything his bloodstained hands had touched. I averted my eyes, feigning modesty, hoping the color hadn't reached my face.

The cashier collected the bets and measured chips into four stacks without needing to look.

Dragonfly flipped my tricks over, totaling the points at a glance. "Twenty-four for the lady, and another martini, if you please."

Before I could protest, the cashier slid nearly a quarter of Dragonfly's chips across to me, and the waiter whisked away my glass and placed a fourth shimmering blue drink before me with a flourish. I swallowed half in a single gulp. I'd need it to spend much more time in this murdering bastard's company without punching in his sweet choirboy face.

The fat Espan to my right was broke and leaving the game. As the cashier collected, Dragonfly watched me, flipping a chip over his knuckles. He was left-handed, a thick platinum chain gleaming on his wrist. "A clever game, miss."

I smiled at him over my glass's rim, my vision refusing to focus. Four Lvovs in twenty minutes was probably a bad idea. So he'd caught me off guard with his cute-and-harmless act, but I was wise to him now. I could handle him. "A dangerous one, if you give away too much. Do you always twirl that chip before you bluff?"

"Only when the stakes are so enticing." He showed me his smile for the first time, charming, confident, attractive.

I just wanted to punch him harder. "What a pity. Your winnings must so rarely live up to your expectations."

"But tonight I've already won what I desire."

I eyed his pile of chips with disdain. "Eight hundred new? How dull of you."

"Your curiosity, miss. That's a different game entirely."

His candid gaze fixed on mine, and I flushed. Damn him for being right. I ached to know what he was up to, who and where his people were, why he sat here playing tarocchi and flirting with me when the vault lay seventeen stories below us. Why a man who had everything he could ever want—money, looks, brains, lifestyle—was an insurrectionist at all.

"You should stick to cards, then," I said coldly. "It's what you're good at." I tossed back the last of my drink. Damned if I'd listen to his bullshit any more.

"I say, do you mind frightfully if I join you?" A smooth hand descended on my shoulder, pressing me down in my seat so I couldn't get up.

Dragonfly's warm gaze frosted over at last. "Not at all. So long as the lady doesn't object."

I smiled sweetly and gazed hotly up through my lashes, inwardly cursing both of them. "Of course not."

Malachite winked. "Smashing. I so love a good game." He took the empty seat next to me, grinning broadly like the filthy rich idiot he was pretending to be. He waved airily at the waiter. "Another round, if you'd be so kind. Capital. I say, who's dealing?"

Dragonfly gathered the cards into two piles and riffled them together with his thumbs. He offered me the deck coolly, and I cut it, aware of two pairs of eyes fixed on me, one sending shivers of distaste along my spine, the other a hot caress that surely didn't need much more help from alcohol before I'd do something stupid.

Malachite smiled smugly, and yet another glowing blue martini appeared before me. For my own sake, as well as the mission's, I shouldn't drink too much more. I could already see how this night would end. We'd take Dragonfly for everything he had, Malachite would hit on me, I'd tell him to get lost and then I'd go back to *RapidFire* alone and take a long cold shower.

I raised my glass to toast the table and chugged.

Sure I would. Right?

6

Sure enough, two hours and half a million sols later, I was back on *RapidFire*, flushed with victory and alcohol. Dragonfly had taken the loss well on the outside, with a brilliant smile and a promise to win it back with interest next time. I sure hoped the slimy bastard was seething inside. He'd been charming, I'd give him that. Attentive. Engaging. After a while I'd found it difficult to remember who I was supposed to be flirting with.

Time for bed.

My vision wobbling, I tugged off my stiletto heels and swayed toward my cabin, wishing I hadn't downed quite so many martinis. I hadn't realized I was this drunk. Lvovs creep up on you. They're one of those evil drinks where you think you're sober until you try to stand up.

"Easy," said Malachite, gripping my waist, steadying me and caressing me at the same time.

Was he still here? Shit.

I slid my arm over his shoulder for balance, but only succeeded in pulling him closer. He brushed his lips across my hair, tempting me. Damn, he smelled fantastic. I wanted to taste him, kiss him, forget what a pathological liar he is and ravish him senseless.

"I can take it from here. God, Nikita, you smell good ... I mean ..."

"Uh-huh," he murmured, playing with a loose curl. "First, tell me what you've learned about Dragonfly."

"What?" I didn't want to think about Dragonfly. All I could think about was the man in my arms and how good his tongue would feel in my mouth. I hadn't had a real lover, one who knew me, since Mishka. And Nikita ... *Did I just say his name? Shit* ... Nikita knew everything.

"Dragonfly," he prompted, pulling hairpins out one by one and dropping them, teasing my hair free.

It didn't help me concentrate. "What, is this a test?"

"Of course. Isn't everything?"

"Umm ..." I tried to ignore him stroking my lips. I wanted to whisper his name, suck his fingers into my mouth. "He's clever, confident. Not afraid to bluff. Thinks highly of himself."

"So?" He leaned closer, pinning me against the wall. Longing stabbed me, deep and delicious, painful. His gaze focused on me, the hot blue of summer sky, and his breath came deep and quick. He was doing a damn good impression of a man who wanted me, and a hot ache blossomed between my legs.

"So ... he doesn't like to lose. His plan will be meticulous, whatever it is."

"Which means?" He pressed his hard thigh between mine, which made the ache worse.

"Which means ... he's not played tarocchi six nights running for no reason ... There's something in that room he needs."

I couldn't help inhaling his scent, pulling my fingers through his crisp hair to make him kiss me.

But he pulled back, teasing me. "Go on."

"Umm ..." I tried to imagine how I'd do it. I thought of Dragonfly, sitting there with his scotch and water and those ridiculous rings, so heavy on his narrow fingers. He hadn't been paying attention to much except the game and my legs ...

"Shit," I said suddenly. The rings. Nikita had clued me in first thing, but I hadn't listened. Those rings weren't platinum. They were stealthplated. Like one-way glass for transmissions, hiding him from view but transparent from his side. The bastard was collecting data the whole time. "It's the ice. He's probing the comms-jamming system to get the frequency map."

"Very good," Nikita murmured, and our mouths met, tasted, explored. The desire in his kiss felt real enough. His hot, dangerous taste made me drunk with memory and anticipation. In my mind, I tied him to my bed and devoured every sculpted inch of him, hot and sweet and wet on my tongue ...

He slid tempting fingers into my hair. "Make love to me, Carrie. You know you want to."

My insides melted, hot and aching. It was so long since I'd heard my real name, since I'd wanted anyone like this. He knew by heart all the things that moved me, and he was doing them, one by one. He kissed me deeper, tilting my head back, his tongue teasing me into response. He made me feel wanted. It was a lie. I didn't care.

Don't do it. Don't say his name.

I turned my head away, testing the urge to throw him down on his back and take him. "This is a bad idea."

But he'd trapped me, giving me nowhere to go. He teased me, brushing hot kisses across my throat. The cool plastic wall did nothing to soothe my burning skin, and I shivered.

His lips curled on my collarbone as he smiled. "But

I've missed you. You were never like the others."

I murmured, arching my back to lean into his kisses, and for a long, sweet moment I believed him. He's that good.

Sweat trickled between my breasts, and he tugged my hair back so he could lick my throat, spreading delicious kisses downward, heat crawling over me. He crept hot fingers under my skirt, and I longed to draw him to me, feel him inside me.

His fingertips brushed my tender flesh, teasing, and it felt so horribly good. I wanted his tongue there, on me, in me. When he felt how wet I was he slid his fingers into me, one long, smooth stroke, and my breath caught.

I fought through swimming senses to think about something else, anything that would give me the presence of mind to make him stop. Much as I wanted him, much as I longed to pretend I was young and carefree again, just for a few hours, I couldn't let him manipulate me like this.

I pictured my shatterjay, pressed against his perfect throat, deadly ultraglass spearing into his bloodstream. But much as I loathed how he'd betrayed me, I didn't wish him dead.

I thought of Mishka, wounded and gentle, the last man I'd had a chance at loving before Dragonfly blew him to bits, but remembering Mishka only made my longing worse.

Instead, I brought Dragonfly to mind, cool and smug, flirting with me, nothing but hate in his cold, murdering heart. I imagined they were his lips burning my throat, his dark hair brushing my skin, his elegant fingers sliding into me ...

I caught Nikita's wrist, tugging his hand away.

"Don't."

He grazed my collarbone playfully with his teeth. "Don't what? I haven't started yet."

I pushed his face away. "Then don't start."

He groaned theatrically, wrinkling his nose, but he planted a fond kiss on my forehead and let go. "You're wasted on these other men, Aragon. You'll realize that."

"No doubt. Go away."

He lingered at the top of the gangway, ruffling his blond hair, seductive. "Sure you won't change your mind?"

"Good night." I thumbed the door shut behind him before I could.

Nikita isn't one to force when things don't go his way; he just lies a little harder next time. Next time, I'd be ready for him.

Sure I would.

I walked unsteadily to the bathroom and peeled my sweaty dress off, stepped into the white plastic cubicle. "Shower," I mumbled, "cold."

Water sprayed in four directions, and I closed my eyes, letting the bitter fluid wash over me. Gradually, the fire in my blood cooled, and Nikita's delicious, poisonous fragrance sloughed off. But the imagined caress of Dragonfly's hands didn't, and I crawled into bed feeling cold and sick.

***

I woke with a distant headache to the mouth-watering smell of frying eggs and tomatoes. My stomach rumbled. I sat up, bewildered.

Nikita grinned at me from the galley. "Afternoon."

I was glad I'd pulled the quilt up with me. "How did you get back in here?" I mumbled, before I realized it was a stupid question. He's worked for Axis all his life. The security system on a Phoenix wouldn't give him even a moment's pause.

He sliced tomatoes with a flick of practiced fingers, knife blade glinting. The nerves and muscles in his hands are nano-tuned for precision. I'd seen him cut an enemy's throat with that same easy gesture.

"Thought you might be hungry," he said.

Like he actually cared. All he knew was that I used to like it when he cooked for me.

He wore dark pants and a pale blue shirt that set off his eyes. He was fresh and gorgeous, effortlessly elegant, one of those rare men who looked equally as good in clothes as out of them. I felt doubly glad I'd gotten rid of him last night before anything humiliating happened.

I suddenly wondered why he'd want me back, after the way we broke up. Apart from the fact that he wanted everything. I shivered, on my guard. Maybe something more sinister was going on here. Did he know about my conversation with Surov the cat-man? Was he bribing me to stay on Renko's team?

With the quilt still tucked around me, I climbed out of bed and thumbed the door closed. I pulled on my black flight suit and boots, tugged my hair into a black velvet shrinkband. When I emerged, he'd set the little table with my breakfast: two golden-fried eggs on cheese toast with tomatoes, topped with pepper, and a glass of fruit juice. I sidled into the metal chair opposite him, uneasy. I was ravenous but didn't want to show him appreciation he didn't deserve.

"Thanks," I muttered, and started to eat.

He put on a wounded look, his big blue eyes wide. "Why scowl at me? I didn't do anything. Nothing you didn't want, anyway."

I stabbed at the toast with my fork. "This isn't about what I want. It's about you."

"So I wanted it too. I missed you, Carrie."

"Give up, okay? Stop calling me that."

"It's true. I've never forgotten you."

My fingers itched to claw that earnest expression from his face. But I knew he didn't understand the problem. He thought this was how real people acted.

I didn't want to have this conversation. Didn't want to drag up past stupidity. But it was too hard not to argue, with all those years I'd hated him washing back over me like a cold ocean. My fingers tightened around my knife. "Really? How about on Volkus Sept? That prison hulk? You sure as hell forgot about me then. You were my backup and you deserted me."

"You know how that happened. It was an operational imperative."

His soothing tone raised my hackles, and I forgot I was supposed to be keeping cool.

"You were screwing one of your operatives, Nikita. Doesn't sound very fucking imperative to me."

I hacked into my eggs, spilling yolk on the white plastic table, and shoved a forkful into my mouth before I could say anything else. The fact that he'd cheated wasn't the issue. It wasn't even that he'd abandoned me on a shattered station with two hundred misogynistic Empire-hating mutants and no weapons because he simply couldn't be bothered.

It was that I'd believed him when he said he loved

me.

The eggs tasted fantastic, which only made me angrier. I glared holes in the table and ate until the plate lay empty.

When I looked up, he was sitting at my console, flicking through a data chip, the display flashing colored diagrams in three dimensions.

"Vault specs," he said, like we'd been chatting about the weather. "Take a look."

Curious despite myself, I slouched over and peered at the display. Esperanza aren't coy about their security. It's one of their biggest selling points, and they want every petty criminal and slime-dwelling terrorist in the sector to know exactly how hard it would be to pull any stunts there.

For starters, the physical security is imposing. The vault itself is built from fusion-grade septurium, which means you can't blow it apart without taking the entire station and the loot with it. Guards patrol seamlessly around the clock, and state-of-the-art visual, audio, infra-red and chemical surveillance systems pick up anything they miss. And quantum anti-jamming systems—ice—blanket the entire station except for the spaceport. They stop dead not only transmissions that might fool with the security systems, but any unauthorized transmissions at all.

Even if you do get lucky and reach the vault alive, and somehow get inside, there's no way you're leaving with the loot. Everything going into the Esperanza vault is not only chemically coded for a specific person, but quantum coded for a specific date and time window when it can be removed. If you don't have the cipher key, there's no way to crack it open, and in a thousand years no one has come up with a reliable way to break quantum crypto. The rules of physics don't allow it. It simply can't be done.

In my professional opinion, the vault probably couldn't be cracked. But Dragonfly obviously thought it could. He'd found a weakness. And it had something to do with six nights of tarocchi and a handful of stealthplate rings.

I jammed my butt into the command chair next to Nikita. "Any idea what his plan is?"

He shifted over to give me room, the display frosting his perfect face with silver light. His eyes shone, fascinated. He was as captivated by this as I was. "None. That's why you're here. You're the security expert. How would you do it?"

I chewed on my lip as I scrolled the data. "Well, let's assume that whatever he's doing with the ice has worked. No ice means the electromag security systems are vulnerable, so let's count them out as well. Assume he can bribe the guards, fool them, distract them somehow. He might even be able to fool the biochem with the right samples. But there's still the crypto." I stabbed my finger at the display, and a glowing blob popped up around one box in the flow diagram. "He can't get in or leave without it."

"And it's unbreakable," Nikita said cheerfully. "Unless you own it. Maybe he's going to impersonate Santiago Esperanza."

Heat spread up from my guts. "What did you say?"

"I said, it's unbreakable—"

"Unless you're the one transmitting it." I flipped back to the navigation page. "Where do they generate their cipher key?"

"What?"

He hadn't caught on, but I was too excited to enjoy his puzzlement. "The key that deciphers the code. You just encode a bunch of digits with a cipher key, same as any single-use code. Then you send your friends the cipher key in a quantum-encrypted transmission. It's secure because it's impossible to intercept that transmission without garbling it—"

"I know what the uncertainty principle is, Aragon. I read it on the back of a cereal box."

"Then you should know that it means Dragonfly can't steal the encrypted key without giving himself away. But if he's the one sending the key in the first place—"

"—and fools the other end into thinking he's Esperanza?"

"Exactly. He's not going to break the code. He's going to write the key himself."

"But if it's a single-use cipher," Nikita mused, "it'll only be used to protect a single deposit."

"Then he must know exactly what he's aiming for. Something big, that's leaving the vault during the surrender negotiations?"

He laughed. "How about the rebel colony's entire tithe? They're joining the Empire, remember? You don't do that for nothing."

"Which is how much?"

"Everything they own plus change." He shrugged. "Cash, stocks, mining rights, the idents to a bunch of secure deposits. A billion sols, give or take."

A billion new rubles. Holy shit. With that, the insurrection could build themselves an army.

I clenched my fists on my knees, my palms damp.

"Okay. So he fakes the deposit code, and the colonists think their deposit is secure until surrender day. But he gets there a few minutes early and steals the loot."

"Cocky little shit." A mixture of contempt and admiration. "So assuming it's even possible, what's his next move?"

"He'll have to generate their crypto ... What's the surrendering colony called again?"

"Santa Maria." Nikita gave me a *read-the-damn-briefing* glare.

"Yeah, them. He'll have to generate Santa Maria's crypto at the time they make the deposit. So either he'll need to build a quantum emulator—"

"Something that'll look like Esperanza from the colonists' end when they receive the cipher key? Sounds chancy."

"It is," I said. "Too chancy for our careful friend. Quantum emulators almost never work. The other way would be to intercept the key inside the Esperanza neurocomputer, before it gets transmitted."

Nikita cocked a perfect blond eyebrow. "Can he do that?"

"I've never seen it done. But assume he can. He'll have to do it from within the Esperanza security system. That's what he's hacked the ice for." I thought hard, my brow furrowing. "But unless he's already studied the schematics for their neurospace, it'll take hours to integrate his own interception algorithm. Days, maybe."

"He won't want to sit there for hours. He'll get caught."

"So, first steal the schematics for study. Right?" I pursed my lips. "Unless he's already done that."

Nikita shook his head. "He got here six days ago,

and since then he's spent every evening playing tarocchi and every night on his ship, alone. If he'd broken the ice already, he'd have stolen the schematics and gone."

"So it could be tonight." I glanced up at him, mischief burning bright, happy holes in my composure. "He'll have to download the schematic data on-site. There's no outside access. Think he could use some help?"

"From a sexy crypto expert who just took him for half a million sols?" Nikita dropped his arm around my shoulder and kissed my forehead softly. "You bet he could."

7

At twenty-three hundred local, I crouched over the Esperanza neurospace console in warm green light, waiting for Dragonfly. A neurospace is a living computer, brain tissue embedded with circuitry, and bio-diodes glowed on the console's soft living skin, casting colored shadows over my hands as I worked. Glowing white streams of maintenance data flowed in columns. The thick air, laced with neuroplasma, made my skin clammy, and water dripped from the low plastic ceiling. Sweat trickled down my neck and between my breasts, soaking into my tight black scoop-necked top. I'd chosen tight shorts too, with my shatterjay strapped on the outside, and black combat boots. Lazuli, brazen little thief-whore. I liked her already.

I flipped through surveillance files, hunting for something juicy enough to be worth stealing. I wasn't here to attack the vault; that was way too audacious for small-time scum like me. No, as far as Dragonfly was concerned, I worked for some faceless mob client who wanted the dirt on his enemies, and there was dirt enough here to bury half the sector. The amount of money flowing through the place meant that the Esperanza family needed to keep strict tabs on comings and goings. They had their own little intelligence service bubbling beneath their respectable surface, and from what I could see, they coerced, cheated and blackmailed with the best of us.

I'd hooked my own virtual display into the loop—only a few photons thick so nothing would show on their monitors—and the stuff that flashed up was little short of macabre. These guys had the filth on everyone: three-star generals, top-flight civil servants, glitterati, the mob, even legit business tycoons and ordinary billionaires. Images, audio, bank account records, credit history, along with the usual juicy details about who was screwing what, for how much and to whose detriment.

The security footage from last night was there. Even some snaps of me and Dragonfly at the tarocchi table. Not Nikita, though. He had some guy from casino security in his pocket; the same guy who'd be making our escape so interesting in a few minutes' time.

I peered closer, dragging through the pictures one by one. There we sat, Dragonfly and I, playing cards, drinking, me smiling and glancing sidelong, him leaning toward me to whisper, his fingertips brushing my arm. The pictures made me cringe. I'd done a pretty good job of flirting with him. We looked about ready to drag each other out the back and get on with it.

If I hadn't known he was an ice-blooded killer with shit for morals, I might have considered it. I'd been pretty drunk, and even sober I had to admit he was good-looking and charming. Good thing for me that Nikita and I had won the game, the easiest way to get rid of Dragonfly. The loser never gets the girl.

"Well, if it isn't the delectable Lady Curious."

My heart thudded, and my head whipped around before I could stop it.

Dragonfly slouched against the open hatchway, his hands shoved in his pockets, a sweet little smile turning his lips. He wore a grey silk suit, cufflinks glinting, dark hair tumbling about his shoulders, his tie loose like he'd wandered in from the bar.

Flushing, I turned back and flicked away from the pictures so he wouldn't see. I should shoot him right now, get his irritating face off my radar. Suited me. Only I wasn't convinced Nikita would let me live if I defied my orders, and I had to admit Dragonfly's murky plans intrigued me.

"Go away, I'm working."

"As it happens, so am I. And on the same thing, judging by that set-up of yours."

He sauntered up to peer over my shoulder, and I squirmed. Scented soap, whisky, a hint of spice. Damn.

He pulled a golden hyperchip from his pocket and flipped it over his knuckles. "You're full of surprises, Lady Curious. I'm captivated. Now move over, you're in the way."

"Stop calling me that. It's Lazuli, if you must know."

"Enchanted, Lazuli. You're still in the way."

I split the display contacts, and the projection vanished. I stuffed the slim set away into my thigh pocket, but didn't step aside. "Be my guest. I've got what I came for."

"By grace of my icebreaker, if I'm not mistaken. Leaving now, are you?"

He leaned past me over the neurospace, running his fingers delicately over the bio-skin, probing for the right receptor for his chip. My own skin shivered warm in sympathy, and inwardly I cursed. This was no time to get distracted.

"Dragonfly, right? The insurrection's favorite armed robber?" No way was I asking his real name. I didn't care. Vermin didn't have names. "Kinda thought you'd be taller."

He grinned, careless, but color brightened his face in the green light. "You've heard of me. I'm flattered."

"Don't be. They say it's the vault you're after, and that makes you either a genius or an idiot. I know which one I'm betting on."

"Can't argue with your betting skills after last night."

He slotted the chip, and all the bio-diodes flickered out.

I gasped. He'd just put the entire autonomous portion of the neurospace to sleep. "How did you do that?"

Static crackled and popped, and above our heads the laser security grid snapped off. Dragonfly studied the data columns, flicking his gaze up and down. "Wouldn't you love to know? Okay, we're on our way. You want to keep an eye on this?"

"What?"

He slipped a smooth hand around my arm and pulled me closer. My skin burned. I tensed, my throat tight, but he just pointed at the glowing column. "If you're going to stand there, you might as well help. See that synapse voltage? Anything below twelve nano is bad."

I glanced at him, intrigued despite myself. "How bad?"

"Alarm-screeching, tear-gas-up-your-nose, laser-rifle-in-the-face bad."

He pulled a glittering plastic cube from his pocket and twisted it in half. Faint yellow light speared up a hand's-width wide, a remote display. Keeping half an eye on the data column, I sneaked a look. He fingered lightly through encrypted directories and hidden files, flicking what he wanted onto his hyperchip. I had to admit he impressed me. He worked swiftly, confidently, without pause, not a bead of sweat on his smooth face.

I craned my neck, resting my hand on his shoulder, trying to see what he was taking. "What good is that?" I asked as he copied yott after gibberish yott. "It's still encrypted."

"What do you care?" he retorted, his eyes on the display. "Numbers, please."

Quickly I scanned the shifting data column. "Fifteen three. Volts are dropping quickly. Get on with it."

"Patience." He flipped through a couple more screens, pushing his hair from his eyes.

"Fourteen." I glanced at the sweating neuroconsole, my pulse urgent even though I knew what would happen. "Thirteen. They'll be onto us. Time to go."

On the console, a bio-diode flickered blue, and another, and another. I couldn't hear the alarms, but I didn't need to. "That's it. It's awake."

"Too bad for them. I'm done." Dragonfly crunched the cube closed, shutting the display off, and shoved it into his pocket. "It's been fun, nice knowing you, all that. See you around."

He reached for the golden hyperchip, but I got there before him and pulled it from the slot with a sharp pop.

His gaze hardened like glass, reflecting the flashing diodes, and he took a step toward me. "We don't have time for this. Give it to me."

Scarlet security lights snapped on in the corridor, and in the distance above someone shouted.

The chip felt warm in my fingers, and I gripped it tightly. "I can't do that."

"Give." He flashed out his hand to grab my wrist.

He was quick. But I was quicker. My shatterjay dug into the pulse in his throat.

He swallowed, and slowly let me go, holding his hands away. Now sweat gleamed on his face. "What do you want?"

His body was tense, hard, only a whisper away, but I didn't have time to think about that now. I slipped the chip down the front of my shorts into my underwear—he'd die before he got his hand down there—and jabbed the shatterjay in tighter. Feeling him squirm heated my skin, my damp hair sticking to my neck. "You'll take me with you."

He laughed. "You've got to be kidding."

"No way. I was doing fine until you got here. Thanks to you, my exit strategy is toast. We go together or we don't go at all."

He looked ready to argue, but the crack and sizzle of the laser security grid recharging overhead must have changed his mind. Nikita couldn't have timed the recharge more perfectly.

Dragonfly spun around with no regard for my weapon and pulled his own, a short-range plasma pistol. "*Está bien.* Are you any good with that thing?"

I switched the jay to projectile mode and took cover beside the hatchway. "Want to wait here to find out?"

"No." He gripped his pistol two-handed and led with it into the corridor, poking his head out to clear to the right. He moved smoothly and efficiently, without wasted motion. "Come on. We'll finish this conversation later."

"Whatever you say."

I slipped out behind him and cleared the left. Green neuroplasma glimmered in hardened plastic conduits beneath the white mesh under my feet. Dragonfly put a burning red shot into the krypton light overhead. It arced and melted in a shower of purple sparks, leaving us in near darkness, and we were on our way, me in the lead, stepping lightly but quickly through a sharp ozone haze.

The security matrix had activated when the neurospace awoke, but we were in the deepest of two neurolevels and the response hadn't made it down to us yet. As we danced along the steaming corridor, our weapons covering alcoves and corners, violet sparks raining from the burning lights, the thrill of pursuit quickened my pulse, my skin alive with excitement. I smiled to myself. Nikita had been right, as usual. Explosives and poison were out, because they'd harm the neural circuits. Esperanza's security was limited to good old-fashioned guys with guns, and they'd have to catch us first.

"This way." Dragonfly nudged me, and we ducked behind a row of cylindrical plastic cooling tanks, their wet white surface stretching up through a gap in the ceiling to the next level. He gestured with his pistol over my head, to where narrow access steps molded into the tank's side. "Up."

I'd kind of figured that, but I didn't say anything. He was supposed to be rescuing me, after all. I didn't like the idea of disarming. Nikita might be running this escape, but the goons with guns wouldn't know that. But I needed two hands. I snapped the jay back onto its clip around my thigh and swung myself up onto the first rung, my sweaty hands slipping on slick plastic.

On the next level, footsteps clanked, and that yelling voice still hadn't shut up.

"Back," snapped Dragonfly, twisting the heat up on his pistol, and I ducked just in time.

He seared a small round hole into the ceiling, and the four-inch-thick ultraplastic vaporized, the hole widening until it grew large enough to climb through. The brown polymer smell wrinkled my nose, but I didn't waste any time. I sprang and gripped the hole's warm edge, folding first one leg and then the other through. Times like this, I was thankful for all those hours in the combat gym. Especially as I could feel his gaze glued to my ass, enjoying the view.

Soft green neon greeted me. Aerated oblivion crystals stung fruity in my nose, making my head ache. Sinuous music coiled, the bass thudding under laughter, clinking glass and bubbling smokewater. Still on my knees, I peered into an array of soft white couches, well-dressed bodies sprawled across them, languid in pairs or threes. Glass shisha pipes lay uncoiled on the shiny floor, their dangerous sweet smoke drifting. Next to us, a guy and a girl were already at it clumsily in a corner, spit shining on her neck, her painted eyes glazed. We'd come up in a dropout den, and no one had noticed.

I rose cautiously, and clunked my head on the underside of a long table. Dragonfly climbed up beside me and tucked his pistol away under his jacket.

To my surprise, he grinned. "Wonder what we could be up to down here?"

Before I could make a sharp retort, he grabbed my hand and dragged me to my feet. A few dopers blinked curiously at us, and I puffed hair from my face, wishing I wasn't sweating so much.

Dragonfly flung his arm around my shoulder and planted a kiss on my cheek, his lips lingering. "Well, my dear, shall we go on back to the ship and freshen up?"

Was he going out of his way to provoke me? If that hand went anywhere, he'd be sorry. I slid my arm around his narrow waist and gave him an infatuated smile, slurring my voice to sound spaced out. "What a good idea."

We wove our way through the bar and out onto the main terrace, where soft red carpet lined the floor under bright green pot plants, and massive oblong viewing windows looked out over the mighty blue Irkutsk nebulas. Behind us in the den, voices raised, furniture crashed, glass broke. The goons had found our escape route.

Dragonfly leaned his head on mine, his arm still draped around my neck. His lean body pressed against me, and he smelled of warmth, excitement, healthy sweat. "Shall we get on with it, my love?" He dropped his voice to a murmur. "You'd better still have my chip, hellcat."

The thrill of danger still heated my blood, and his closeness wasn't helping. I needed to pull away, to keep my distance, but I just smiled for the audience as we strode past the awe-inspiring view toward the spaceport ring, trying not to look in a hurry.

As we stepped under the square-cornered archway into the massive curved metal tube of the epsilon docking ring, the bright white icelights in the ceiling faded to red.

"That's alert phase," I whispered. It was after midnight local, but if any docking crew remained, they'd be armed. "Any plan?"

"Yes. Don't alert anyone. Slot five, quick."

A ribbed steel catwalk with a handrail stretched inside the tube to our left and right, seven slots on each side. We turned left and walked past some trapezoidal blast doors, through a bulkhead, past a storage alcove stacked with metal crates and provisions, another set of doors, another alcove.

Booted feet clanged on the catwalk ahead of us, and charging laser pistols buzzed, high-pitched, at least two. My fingers tensed on his hip, my throat tightening. I didn't want to have to kill anyone. "Shit. You got a plan B?"

"Sure," whispered Dragonfly. "Look too dumb to be a threat. Don't hit me, okay? I'm sorry."

And he pushed me into the bulkhead's shadow and covered my mouth with his. His kiss was hot, alive, arousing, his lips demanding my response. My back smacked against the wall, sharp bolts digging in, and breathless fury blazed through me. No fair. I understood what he was doing, but I wanted to hurt him, to jab my fingertip into that nerve centre in his cervical spine and watch him pass out. He wasn't pretending, though, if the urgent press of his body was any guide. Hard, muscular, unyielding, just like I'd imagined ... Okay, so when did I start imagining his body?

I struggled to keep my mind on the mission as the docking crew's footsteps clanged closer. Looking convincing wouldn't be easy if we didn't both play. So I slid my wrists around his neck and wrapped my leg around his thighs, opening my mouth a little, letting him in. He groaned into my mouth, and our tongues entwined, unwelcome pleasure burning to my core. He was a damn good kisser, and he tasted pretty good for a murdering psycho.

He slid his strong hand up my thigh and pulled me onto him, his fingers digging in, and damn it if I didn't start to ache. It was only natural, considering the danger. From the feel of what pressed into my groin, he was getting off on it too, and I thought about touching him, unzipping him, guiding him into me. Sinking onto him, deep and hard, crushing his hair in my fists ...

Metal clunked against the bulkhead, and I realized someone was talking.

Dragonfly broke our kiss, leaving his hand planted on my ass and giving me a cheeky squeeze. I gasped, trying to control my breathing, and the bastard winked at me, his lips still shining from our kiss. "*Un momento, cara.*"

He turned his head, the picture of exasperation. "I'm sorry, what?"

One of the two young docking trolls stared, grease smeared in his straw-colored hair. That laser pistol looked useless in his gangly hand. From what I could see he'd be more likely to shoot himself than anyone else. The other one hefted his pistol above a thick-veined forearm, vein-ridged latissimus muscles bulging under his sleeveless grey coverall, sweat gleaming in his bristle-cut hair. Clearly he worked out too much.

"Security check. Let's see your ident."

The shatterjay lay warm and ready against my sweating thigh, and tension curled my fingers.

Dragonfly grinned at him. "Is that necessary, craftsman? We were just on our way back to her … that is, our ship, and we got a bit distracted."

RoidBoy stretched his fingers around the silver pistol grip. "Ident."

Dragonfly let me go and walked up to him, and I slouched, sulking, playing along. He bent his face close to RoidBoy's, making him blush, the poor sweetie. "I'd really rather you didn't sec-log this, my friend. It's … delicate for me. And, well, it's pretty obvious who she is, don't you think?"

I slung one hand on my hip, tossing my hair over my shoulder. "Yeah, and time is money, so can we get on with it?"

The skinny blond one tugged RoidBoy's shoulder. "Come on, let 'em be. Alarm's going off."

Not too bright, these kids. That's why they worked on the docks.

RoidBoy hesitated, and Dragonfly stroked a speculative finger down the kid's tight coverall, his gaze hot and half-lidded. "You want to come along, handsome? We've got space for three."

RoidBoy watched, fixated, and Dragonfly drifted his hand down toward the kid's groin.

I sauntered up, curled my arm around Dragonfly's neck and added my hand to the mix. Seemed what they said about steroid use was true. "Tricks for three, too."

RoidBoy stumbled backward, sweating. "Get off me, freak."

"Baby doesn't want to play," I said, pouting, and laughed when he and his goggling friend made a quick exit.

"Good," murmured Dragonfly as we slipped past the bulkhead. "I was having fun with just us two."

I almost punched him before I remembered he didn't know who I really was. My flesh still burned from kissing him, my breasts still ached, my thighs were still damp, and I hated him for it.

"I'm still awake, I suppose," I retorted. "Barely."

"I did say I was sorry."

He twisted the red steel hinge and wrenched the lever out and down, and the foot-thick blast doors parted with a clunk. At the end of a short corridor, through a clear plastic airlock, his ship's tubular gangway gleamed, the dull metal fluorescing green and yellow with rabid biochemical security. He strode down the corridor, leaving me to seal the blast doors while he typed his code into the console studded to the wall. The plastic slid aside, and we scrambled on board.

As soon as the airlock sealed, chemically induced nausea gripped me like a magclamp. I choked and doubled over, plastering my hand over my mouth.

"Hold it in, can't you?" He grabbed my other hand, dragging me around a corner and up the few ladder steps into the ship proper, the sickening luminescence crawling over me. Tears seeped out, a fist of pain squeezing my guts. I skidded around a metal workbench bolted to the deck and collapsed onto a sunken black sofa littered with tools and fragments of electromag kit.

He hopped up the steps into the cockpit and slid into the padded grey command chair, the bright display igniting in the air at the brush of his finger. He tapped a couple of commands, cancelling the biochemical security precautions, and the luminescence died.

I swallowed and wiped my mouth, the sickness subsiding but the sour taste lingering. He was already arcing the short-range propulsion, and with a lurch the ship rolled to starboard and darted away from Esperanza.

8

The main deck of Dragonfly's ship smelled of plastic and burned solder, like a workshop. By the time the security goons realized their mistake, we'd skipped traffic clearance, and Dragonfly gave a sharp arc-rocket boost to the ion drives and we were gone. Once the course was set and the drives accelerated us into slipspace, he shut the glass console down and stretched from the command chair with a sigh.

I watched him from the sunken lounge in the saloon, rubbing angry hands on my thighs, his golden chip jabbing warm into my belly beneath my shorts. We were alone, Dragonfly and I. In my dreams, I'd waited for this a long time. I could kill him now and no one would care. Except Director Renko, and I could deal with that later. Claim he'd attacked me, that it was an accident.

He stripped off his jacket and unholstered his pistol, tossed it wearily onto the console. He looked young and harmless, scraping soft hair from his dark-ringed eyes. Yes, I could kill him all right. Slide that shatterjay under his chin and blow his artery apart.

But I wasn't sure I wanted to sell my soul to Surov and black ops just yet. There was still the question of what Dragonfly was up to. I could blow his little ruse wide open, stab the insurrection in the heart and score even more points with Axis. There'd still be time to kill him later.

He hopped down the steps and planted himself on the worktable before me, shoving aside a half-built gammaspace commlink and a bunch of colored wire. "Welcome to *Ladrona*," he said, but he didn't sound pleased to have me here. "Now give me my chip."

Ladrona. Lady thief. It figured.

I crossed one leg over the other—here, have another eyeful—and folded my arms. "I don't think so."

Challenge glinted in his eyes. "I could search you for it."

I couldn't help glancing at his fingers. Remnants of desire lingered in my hot skin and skipping pulse, and my guts tightened. I flashed him a glare, daring him. "Not without that pistol."

He watched me, dark because he knew I was right. "So what, will you just sit there?"

"Only for as long as it takes. I want in."

He laughed, pleasant and melodic. It made me remember kissing him, the way he'd tasted, how he'd made me ache for him.

Anger boiled, and I glared at him. I should never have let him get away with that. "What's so funny?"

"*Señorita*, you have no idea what you're asking." He stood and walked back toward the cockpit, dismissing me. He really knew how to hack at my nerves.

I tried to tame my indignation with slyness. "Think not? I know you're planning to break the vault the day they sign the Santa Maria pact."

He paused.

I checked my fingernails airily. "I know you're faking the deposit crypto, and I know that what's on your chip is the operator schematic for the neurospace."

He tried not to show his surprise, but when he turned his eyes had narrowed. "How do you figure that?"

"Because that's how I'd do it. Look, you can have your chip once we get to where we're going. I just want in. I'm good with crypto, I can help you."

He looked unconvinced, suspicion creasing his brow.

I tried flattery. "I've seen you on pirate newscasts. That thing with the plasma futures, ripping off the Luvanenko mob? That was priceless. And I'd give my left arm to know how you broke those guys from the supermax at Bin Guska." I let my gaze flicker away, like I was embarrassed. "Believe it or not, you're kind of my hero. This is the biggest game of my life, my dream job. I can't just walk away."

He eyed me for a moment longer, his expression dark, then silently he climbed back to the cockpit and lit the console, plasma veins glowing violet inside the glass.

I leaped up and followed, trying to peer over his shoulder. "So where are we going?"

"Don't touch that." He jabbed at the contact that set the local biochem, stimulating it to tolerate his chemistry and his alone, and the field glowed bright over the entire console like festering green fungus.

I snatched back my hand. "Watch it, why don't you?"

He ignored me, retrieving his pistol and holstering it, sidestepping me, around the console toward the narrow plastic spiral steps leading to the accommodation deck. "I need to sleep. You do whatever you want. Shower and food are upstairs, blankets under the bench. But touch anything else and you'll do worse than vomit."

I watched him climb, poison bubbling in my heart. Perhaps he'd live through the night, perhaps not.

He paused with his hand on the ladder rail, and gave me that sweet little smile. "Oh, and if I have an accident and don't wake up? You'll never get off this ship."

***

I stood in the glow of flickering green fluorescence, listening to his footsteps as he crossed overhead, waiting for him to stop moving. Water gushed, drumming on plastic. He was undressing, getting in the shower. Shaking hot water through his hair, letting it run over his face, into his mouth, down his body …

Damn it. I needed to call Nikita, report on what had happened before we got too far apart to have a real-time conversation. I glared at the slot on the console where the hyperchip would fit. It was shrouded in crawling green bugs and inaccessible, at least to me. The biochem would make me dangerously sick, but it also meant the controls wouldn't respond to anyone but Dragonfly.

Thanks to his paranoia, I didn't have much to tell, but there was a strong chance that he'd figure out we were on to him and shoot me dead. I needed to send as much information as I could before that happened. A harsh assessment, maybe. But I worked for Axis, not for someone who gave a shit about me. My own safety wasn't important.

I slipped my finger into my shorts' seam for my sub-ether transmitter—a shiny clear oblong the size of a fingernail—and swiftly quartered the saloon, snapping pictures from four angles. I walked my fingers through the gadgetry on his worktable: tools, silicon-flecked components, ragged stealth-plate filings, a couple of synapses still in wet plastic wrapping, the remains of a mocha in a black plastic flask. Stuffed down the back of the black sunken lounge I found a handful of Esperanza casino chips and an old digital proton decay meter. I imagined him crouched here late into the night, enthralled, his deft fingers twining wire and arcing plasma contacts. It looked like a mad scientist's laboratory, but if he'd built something that had left these scraps behind I couldn't figure what. Maybe he was just tinkering.

Above, the shower stopped running. His footsteps crossed the corridor, and after a moment all was quiet. In bed, then. Warm, fragrant, relaxed after his shower, sleepy ...

Nope. Not going there.

Beneath the sick green glow, the console operated in power-down mode, everything shut off but the basics. He was clever enough to hide that much from me. The slipspace field showed voltage, and the navset diodes glimmered red and yellow. We were moving, on some course. Big deal. I photographed the console anyway. Better too much information than missing that all-important detail.

His grey suit jacket hung over the command chair. I checked the pockets and seams. Nothing. He'd strolled into the neurospace with nothing but a loaded hyperchip, a shielded virtual display and a plasma pistol. Gutsy.

My fingers tingled in the soft fabric. I put the jacket back, trying not to notice that it smelled of him, subtle but human. Dragonfly had always been just a name to despise for me, never a person. I wouldn't let him become one now.

I crept up the flimsy spiral stairs, white plastic creaking under my boots. The upper deck was long and narrow, split down the middle by a passageway barely wide enough to walk front on. On the left, past the shower, hid a galley, similar to *RapidFire*'s with a shallow stainless sink, a tiny electromag cooker and plastic storage bins. Spotless, meaning he was fastidious, or more likely didn't eat here much.

On the right, a tiny room was taken up almost entirely by his bed, and there he slept, wet dark hair spilling onto his pillow, the white sheet crumpled over his hip, his hand curled next to his cheek. A broad, shallow atomflash scar striped his lean shoulder. Interesting. Scars were easy to fix these days, if you had the cash. Which made him either poor—um, that's a no—or sentimental—hardly—or stubbornly making a point.

His chest shifted slowly as he breathed, and for a moment I imagined slipping into bed beside him, his body warm on mine.

I fidgeted, my guts twisting. As far as my mission went, sleeping with him wasn't out of the question as a way of mining information. Never mind that I hated him, that he was an Imperial enemy. I should consider this rationally. Weigh up the pros and cons, disregard my personal inclinations.

Yeah. Because it wasn't like I wanted him or anything.

I watched him, compelled and disgusted at the same time. He looked weary, troubled, isolated. I wanted to stroke that soft hair away from his forehead, feel his skin again under my fingers, soothe his trouble into peace.

I turned away, injustice burning in my soul. Why should he sleep when Mishka and my murdered friends no longer breathed? I wouldn't even need to make a mess with the shatterjay. I could press my finger into that lethal place in his throat and he'd be gone without a sound, back to the soulless realm of names and myth.

And I'd be stuck in slipspace in a ship full of gut-rotting biochem, flitting from navpoint to arbitrary navpoint until I dehydrated to death or the air scrubbers backed up. That ignobility was enough to give me pause, but another more pressing itch nagged at my insides, and I realized it was professional jealousy. I wanted to see him crack the vault. There was so much about his plan I still didn't understand, and it riled me that he might be cleverer than I was. I needed to know exactly how he'd do it before he died.

Dragonfly stirred, twitching as if he dreamed something unpleasant, and I crept down the stairs before he could wake.

I plopped onto the sunken sofa, flicked on my virtual interface to slipspace comms mode and pinged the sub-ether frequency Nikita had given me. Slipspace comms aren't instantaneous, but they're pretty damn fast, and the beacons boost the signal so it won't degrade over the vast distance. So long as you're close enough, you can talk back and forth like regular etherwave comms. Normally I'd have to worry about the ship's active sensors detecting my transmission, but *Ladrona*'s console wouldn't pick this up. No one can detect sub-ether, in slipspace or out. It's too new.

For a moment Nikita didn't pick up, and I felt only cold cosmic hash, but then his voice slipped into my head, smooth and warm but tinged with icy calculation that prickled my spine.

"Wasn't expecting you so soon. Finished with him already?"

"He's sleeping." I kept my voice low and flicked him the image bundle.

I tried not to sound irritated, but normal lying techniques are useless over sub-ether, which breathes your emotions down the line as easily as it sends your voice. Axis developed it last year from some experimental prototype interrogation kit. You hear a lot of rumors about the latest techgasm from our hardware people—everything from personal teleporters to space folding and antigravity—but this one, they actually came through with. It's still classified, and it's the latest craze at Axis.

"I bet he is." Nikita laughed, and bumps broke out on my skin. People who say emotive sub-ether is a technological marvel obviously never had to use it to talk to a sociopath.

I swallowed, sweating. "It's not like that, okay? I'm on the ship, I've got his chip. What more do you want? Any clues to what he downloaded?"

"None. His algorithm sidestepped the neurospace access log. Last record is you looking at some pictures." Dark amusement, like a warm whisper on my cheek. "Any luck with the encryption?"

I scrubbed my hand over my face. "Not yet. The console's still germed up, and the chip looks like a special hybrid, I can't jack it. But he got awful bashful when I mentioned faking deposit crypto—"

A shuffle from upstairs. Was he waking up?

I lowered my voice even further. "Look, I've gotta go. Renko wanted a sitrep—"

"Taken care of. Forget it."

Fine with me. Nikita was the expert at telling directors what they wanted to hear, and I didn't have time to spin this up. "Thanks. Anything new from your end?"

"Just this." A tiny data package drifted down the line and slotted into my interface, with a twinge of Nikita's careless malice that made my pulse skip. "I thought you might be interested. Seems you've still got friends in high places."

"What is it?" I asked, but empty hash flowed in like fresh air.

I felt cleaner already.

Nikita's data popped up on my display, and I peered at it with a hint of trepidation. A military action message, classification violet, time a few days ago. Addressed to a bunch of inscrutable Imperial acronyms, heading GCQ-A: ANNEXATION COLONY SANTA MARIA.

The personnel authorization for the Empire's negotiation team.

I scanned the list, and stopped short. The first line read: OIC O9 SHADRIN VY K47757D9E.

I'd worked for Lieutenant General Valodyi Shadrin when I was military. He'd chosen me as his aide when I'd only just been promoted to major, and I'd served a full tour with him in Expansion directorate, organizing his diary and making his arrangements and fielding ideas as he bounced them off me. He'd inspired me to transfer to Axis, back when my idealism still burned fresh and his words about honor and pride still meant something. He was that rare beast: a hard man with a conscience. A good man. People like him made the Empire worth fighting for, even if I now knew that to beat dirty rebels we had to play dirty ourselves, and honor wasn't exactly an Axis buzzword. If Shadrin was officer in charge of the negotiations, these ex-rebel Santa Marians might even escape with their self-respect.

An uneasy ripple made me swallow. First Malachite and Dragonfly, now Shadrin. So much of my past resurfacing, so many familiar faces. Something strange was going on here. If I wasn't such a trusting girl, I'd suspect someone was setting me up.

Why did Nikita want me to see this? An ugly thought struck me cold. Did he think I needed extra motivation? Everything in Axis is a test of some sort. Maybe he was warning me I was risking a flunk. Maybe he knew about my meeting with Surov the cat-man, and this was a threat to keep me on edge.

Maybe he was just screwing with my mind.

I slipped the ESE back into my shorts and stretched, vertebras popping. My skin felt grimy with sweat after the neurospace. My hair stuck to my neck, and salt flecks ringed my black top. I could use a shower and a night's sleep. But the idea of stripping off weaponless to shower with Dragonfly right there made my stomach tighten. And the only decent place to sleep was his bed. Which had him in it. Naked.

This train of thought was getting me nowhere.

I stretched out on the sofa with a sigh, but my nerves twinged, tense. When I finally slept, I dreamed of Mishka and me at the infra-red range in that ultra-green forest, white rabbits scampering in the snow between black tree trunks.

It's the first time we kiss, and frigid pine-scented air sparkles fresh in my nose. Frost crusts his black hair as he folds me in his massive arms, gentle, ever holding back, afraid of his own strength. We're the same height, Mishka and I, and our pistol holsters clunk together as we embrace. He tastes of snowmelt water, pristine, and I can feel his heartbeat.

In my dream, I slide my hand inside his shirt, caressing tight scarred muscle, and fire shatterglass into his warm body over and over until the clip empties.

9

When I woke, Dragonfly was sitting at the console, studying a stream of equations on the projected display, the blackness of slipspace stark in the clearview window beyond. He was dressed casually, a loose grey shirt over black combat trousers.

He heard me get up and tossed a smile over his shoulder. "Sleep well?"

I nearly didn't hear him. My shatterjay was missing, and jacked into the glass console by his left hand sat his golden hyperchip.

An angry flush crept up my body, and I risked a quick glance down at my clothes. Everything was still there. "How did you get that?"

He shrugged, watching the display. "It's what I do. You didn't even move. You should be more careful."

Light fingers, then. Impressive. I imagined those fingers slipping down the front of my shorts, searching ...

My skin tingled, and my fist clenched in fury. "Don't ever do that again."

"If you behave, I won't have to, will I?"

I whirled and stomped up the stairs before I could punch him. I clipped the plastic bathroom door shut, still swallowing my rage, and swiftly examined the turned-up seam at my thigh. Relief cooled me. At least he hadn't found my ESE.

I stripped off and endured a two-minute cold shower, washing off sweat and indignation. I had no clean clothes to put on, but it was better than nothing. I studied myself in the mirror, grey circles showing under my eyes, and took a few deep breaths to focus. He got under my skin, this Dragonfly, I could admit that. But if I wanted to play his game and win, I'd have to do better. I couldn't let my temper—or my hormones—jeopardize the mission. I had to make him trust Lazuli, respect her. Not think her foolish, hotheaded, intemperate.

I watched him from the bottom of the stairs while he studied the display, entering decryption parameters on the console by touch, reflected equations glimmering in his dark eyes. He was cracking crypto, no doubt the data he'd stolen from the neurospace.

I wandered over, casual. "What's that, a Zykovski space?"

He flicked me a cool glance. "Want to try?"

"Me?"

He shrugged and stood, swinging the chair toward me. "You said you wanted in. It's Zykovski six-gen, or maybe four. Recalcitrant son of a bitch."

Excitement clinched, and I sat down, the padded seat warm from his body. I studied the math he'd done so far, and unease glimmered inside. There were abbreviations, incomplete fractal sketches, leaps of deduction I couldn't follow, and the first half of it baffled me completely, but the whole thing fit together perfectly. Elegant, efficient, intuitive.

Exceptional, Surov the cat-man had said of Dragonfly. He hadn't exaggerated. I was impressed, and I didn't want to be. Damn it. Did the scumbag have to be clever as well?

I bit my lip and concentrated. He'd stopped partway through a rapid factoring construct, the kind of thing that etherwave hackers would wet their pants over, and that sent cold sparks of terror down the biotech-riddled spines of the infosec creeps at intelligence division. Since Petrova and Solitsin at New Moskva Tech discovered the new math, even neural circuits couldn't codebreak as quickly as a human brain. Cryptosystems are based on one-way functions—arithmetic that's simple to do, but impossible (or at least violently impractical) to undo. For instance, it's much easier for a computer to multiply two numbers together than it is to figure out from the answer what those numbers were.

Even neural computers still factorize by brute force, starting at one and trying every prime number on the way up. When you're talking million-digit numbers, that takes a lifetime, unless you can take a short cut by eliminating sets of options.

That's the sort of thing hyperalgebra is for, and when you consider that everything we do is based on information security, it's the scariest mathematical discovery of the millennium. The upside is that almost no one understands it. But coupled with black-art intuition, it can wreck a cryptosystem in record time, so long as you've got a genius on hand.

Luckily for me, my new pet genius had already done most of the work. It took me twenty clumsy minutes of guesswork to complete his construct and execute. Error. I transformed a variable and ran it again. Still an error.

Dragonfly watched, tapping the console's glass edge softly. "So what's your name?"

"I told you already." I added an imaginary constant and tried again.

"No, I mean really. *Lazuli* sounds like an Imperial codename." He watched me for a reaction. "But it wouldn't be yours, would it?"

I kept my face blank. "What do you mean?"

He reached over me to point, pressing against my shoulder. "Try seven alpha *i* there."

I couldn't see the connection. I shifted my thighs, warmth creeping over me. His damn smell was all over the place, along with my concentration. "Sorry, what?"

"I said, your left-hand side there reduces to an isomorphic field. Try seven alpha *i*."

He glanced at me, his gaze flicking downward, then he flushed faintly and glanced away. Now I was getting somewhere. I wasn't above dirty tactics—why should I be, if he and his rebels weren't?—and if he wanted me, we might as well get it over with. I could take it. I'd just pretend he was someone else. And then he'd tell me what I wanted to know. They always did.

I licked my lips and leaned closer. "You can't run seven alpha without transforming the whole thing."

He swallowed and shifted away, his gaze returning to the display. "So transform it."

I sighed. "Can I have the matrix calculator, then?"

"Do you need it?"

"What is this, a test?" Frustration hacked at my nerves. I didn't understand his game. He had nothing to gain by teasing me.

"Just seeing if you're who you say you are. Lazuli's an awfully noble name for a thief, Lady Curious. Axis names criminals after vermin. What's your name really?"

I picked my way through the difficult Qiao transform, and for a moment I considered actually telling him. But it was too intimate, too close. If I told him mine, he'd tell me his, and I didn't want to know.

"So I thought it'd be funny to steal one of their precious codenames," I said. "They can call me whatever they want. It's what I go by. It goes with the reputation. Surely you understand that."

There. Done. I entered seven alpha *i* as the last term. The construct calculated for a second or two, and started spitting out sets of potential prime factors, page by page.

Dragonfly stared at the screen. "I'm impressed."

"Really?" I played the bashful acolyte, dropping my head as if I was blushing.

"Don't give me 'really'. I don't meet many people who can run a four-variable field transform in their heads. Especially not a woman as delicious as you. I'm practically in love."

He reached across me to re-seat the hyperchip, his hair almost brushing my cheek. To my chagrin, a real blush burned my skin. Was this an invitation or a tease? Did I win by accepting or rebuffing? And how had that smell become so familiar so soon?

I didn't wriggle away, though the warmth swelling inside made me want to. "Guess you don't get out much."

He glanced up at me, his smile flickering. "You'd be surprised."

I held my breath as he straightened, not wanting to inhale any more. I couldn't figure what he was playing at. Too inscrutable, this Dragonfly.

The display switched to a larger aspect ratio, and at last the decrypted data flashed up. I stared. Schematic diagrams, all right. But for the station, not the neurospace. I bit my lip, confused. They looked the same as the ones Nikita had given me on *RapidFire*. What was Dragonfly up to, if it wasn't stealing circuit diagrams so he could hack the neurospace later?

He laughed, and saved the plaintext version to his console. "Nice work. Well done. Take the rest of the day off."

"But those plans are practically public domain," I retorted, his casual attitude riling me. "You can get them anywhere."

He arched his eyebrows. "Really? You don't say? Guess I've wasted my time, then."

I squinted, zooming in on the display for a closer look. He was right. They weren't the same. Stress lines were marked along diagrams of station components, with relativity field equations and geodesics in the margin.

The artificial gravity schematic. Most definitely not public domain.

Because it showed how, theoretically, you could take Casa de Esperanza apart.

My mouth dried. He wanted to break the station open to steal the money?

He scraped his hair back, mischief twinkling in his eyes. "Intrigued yet, Lady Curious?"

All right, so I was. "You're going to weaken the vault integrity somehow? How does that help with the crypto?"

He chewed his lip. "Is that what you'd do?"

"Excuse me?"

"With top-secret grav schematics for a strategically vital space station. Weaken the vault integrity?" His brow creased as he flicked the display off.

My heart skipped. "What?"

He leaned close. "Maybe you should use a little imagination."

I remembered the feel of him between my thighs in the docking ring, his lips hot and sure on mine, his hand sliding up my thigh. My blood heated. I was using my imagination, all right, and it made me shiver. "And what would I see?"

"What's right in front of you." He traced the corner of my mouth, his dark gaze following his finger.

My mouth watered, pleasant tension twisting in my abdomen. "I don't think I'm missing much right now."

He smiled, wicked, and caressed my bottom lip with his fingertip. "You know your algebra's a real turn-on?"

"You're not so dumb yourself."

I parted my lips, inviting, and his taste flooded my mouth. My skin hummed with anticipation, my thighs tingling. Damn it. I actually wanted to kiss him.

He leaned even closer, and his whisper burned my ear, delicious. "Then it's too bad you think so small. Now get off my console. I'm bored."

10

After that, the journey stretched interminably. Dragonfly sat there in silence, tinkering with his half-built gammaspace link or flicking through reams of data on his console, making occasional adjustments on the navspace. I had nothing to do but huddle on the sofa and stare at the walls. He avoided looking at me, which was just as well, because I was so furious that if he said another word to me I'd rip his presumptuous throat out.

My mission wasn't going well, no matter what I'd told Nikita. I'd come no closer to finding out what Dragonfly was really doing. I'd merely achieved a juicy bruise to my pride.

I'd imagined this for years—finally getting close to the man who'd murdered my friends—and in my vision I was cool, focused, deliberate as I tore him apart mentally and morally.

But the reality was different. He wasn't the stupid, callous, mechanical killer I'd expected, even if he was a terrorist and a criminal. He hadn't killed those docking trolls to escape from Esperanza, though that would have been the easiest thing to do. He'd used his imagination instead, even if it resided somewhere other than his brain. He was the sweet, quiet, clever kid from algebra class, and I liked him. Fuck.

Time crawled, and I fidgeted and paced, more irritable by the minute. Dragonfly fetched crackers and fruit juice, and I ate sullenly. I climbed upstairs to use the bathroom. I came back down. I sat. I paced. I stretched. It must have been nearly midnight by ship's reckoning before the drives buzzed and eased off, and we dropped out of slipspace with a swift, inertial jerk.

I jumped up from a bored doze, my muscles creaking. The clearview shimmered blue for a moment as the visible wavelengths compressed, then star clusters shone red and gold like scattered jewels. A fresh supernova swelled bright, blotting the starfield around it black.

I blinked sleepy eyes and walked up to the console, where he sat fiddling with a crystal datacube. I retied my hair, smoothing loosened curls. "Where are we?"

"The place we're going." He flicked up the micronav controls and finessed the arc rockets fore and aft, and *Ladrona* began a graceful lateral turn.

I peered out the clearview, but I couldn't see anything except shifting space—and then above us, a corroded space station drifted into view, its battered rad-shields ragged like rust. Not a shining pleasure palace like Esperanza. This was a working dockyard.

Long arms of flashburned septurium scaffolding stretched in nine directions from a central dodecahedral hub, and spacecraft in varying stages of repair hung from the docking ports, ranging from bare metal skeletons to shiny corrosion-stripped vessels awaiting new stealthplate. I saw fighters, small freighters, an Imperial cruiser, a couple of passenger transports, a scattering of private runabouts and commerce ships. Junk fragments littered the surrounding space, twisted waste metal coated in fractal ice crystals that splintered the station's spotlights to tiny rainbows.

Snatches of control comms crackled on the etherwave as ships darted back and forth, docking and departing.

Dragonfly flipped open the datacube and held it out to me, circuitry flickering green and blue inside. "Put your finger here."

"Why?"

He sighed and grabbed my hand, pressed my finger to the contact. Static zinged.

"Ouch! What was that?" I yanked back, sucking at a bloodspot on my fingertip.

"You're welcome. It's a security ident."

He snapped the cube closed and tossed it to me. I fumbled the catch, the crystal warm in my cold fingers.

"I realize that. What's it for?"

"Did you really think I'd leave you on my ship by yourself?"

He flicked a switch and a pink-tinted gammaspace filter snapped over the clearview. The station's approach grid sprang into view, sharp red lines from outside the visible light spectrum slicing the space into corridors, approach vectors, holding patterns.

I peered closer at the station. It didn't look familiar, but Imperial space was littered with repair-and-refuel outposts like this. "So what are we doing here? Slipdrive refuel? Your arc rockets sound a bit corroded too. And we could do with some real food."

"You'll see." Red gamma-lasers reflected in Dragonfly's eyes as he tilted the ship closer by touch. "Your name's Ekaterin, and you're my co-pilot. A fine upstanding Imperial citizen. Ever worked in short-range freight?"

"No."

"You do now. Just think trash-hauling and keep your pretty mouth shut." He thumbed the etherwave comms. "Vyachesgrad, this is Red Sunday, Nebula on zero-one-three arc four. I have clearance sigma one omicron, confirm." He drawled his vowels like a back-lane freight shyster and it made me smile.

The comms crackled, some distant arcweld fighting for bandwidth. "Affirm, Red Sunday, cleared dock nine as you find it, all vectors open on visual."

Typical lazy R&R control: *everything's on visual, park where you like, and if you have a collision, don't come whining to us.*

"Dock nine, Vyachesgrad, thanks so much." He flicked off the comms and kicked the arc rockets, sending the ship hurtling on a showy sweeping curve up toward the vertical docking arm.

I eyed him archly. "Red Sunday? What are we, Imperial ass-lickers?"

Red Sunday is an Imperial holiday from eight-hundred-odd years ago, when the first Imperial Court ratified the Charter of Cultural Expansion. The soldiers still hold parades and fly-bys. Even at Axis, we sink an ironic vodka or two.

Dragonfly shrugged. "Flattery never hurts."

"And pre-approved clearance? Did you hack the traffic database?"

"In all that spare time I've got? No. I filed a flight plan."

"What?" I laughed, uneasy. "Are you trying to get caught? What kind of thief files a flight plan?"

That gentle smile. "You watch too many movies. Be practical. This is a borderlands outpost, not New Moskva spaceport. The ship is *ordinaria* ... sorry, what's the word? Nondescript. We're nondescript. We could be anyone. No one here cares so long as we pay. Don't sweat it."

I bristled that he'd think me afraid. "So what are the false idents for, if you're so cocky?"

"I said practical, not stupid."

He glided the ship into place at the dock, his fingers sliding confidently over the console. Heavy magclamps clunked hard against the external airlock at starboard and we jolted to a halt, the drives spinning down to silence. He closed the clearview shutters, flat strips of blackmetal radshield folding tight, and shut down his console. The diodes flickered dark, and luminous green biochem crawled across the glass like fungus.

"Besides, I still don't know your name," he said. "What was I supposed to do?"

I opened my mouth, and shut it again.

He grinned at me. "Speechless. There's a first."

Obviously he was pretending he'd forgotten I'd been speechless all afternoon, thanks to his smart-ass tricks. Prick. "Hope you enjoyed it while it lasted."

"Best fun I've had all day." He filled his pockets, selecting another couple of data crystals, the golden hyperchip, his newly-built gammaspace link. He holstered his plasma pistol and slipped on a dusty grey jacket. Suddenly he looked ordinary, harmless, just a guy about his business like everyone else. The perfect monster.

I smoothed my tight black top, wishing I had something to collect, something to prepare. Without weapons, information, all the trappings of my Axis identity, I felt naked. But I wasn't me right now, I reminded myself. I was Lazuli, cool, competent, ready for anything.

I tightened my braid with a nonchalant tug. "You ready?"

He studied me and grimaced. "Wait here," he said, and disappeared upstairs. He soon came back down and tossed me a shiny black combat jacket. "Wear this."

I caught it, the silken fabric smooth in my fingers. A woman's jacket. Whose? "Why? It's not cold."

He avoided my gaze. "Not the point. You're too conspicuous. Much as I like the view, you make people look."

I flushed, and slipped the jacket on. It fit me well, short and tight, hugging just above my hips. I thrust my hands into the pockets, and the nails of my right hand clinked on glass.

My shatterjay.

I glanced after him, but he'd already hopped down the stairs to the airlock.

11

Vyachesgrad station stank of burned fuel and rust, and half the lights in the docking lane were broken. We walked along a corroded corridor past scratched glass viewholes showing workmen crawling up and down the scaffolding in dirty spacesuits, half-repaired ships laid open to space. The air scrubbers buzzed and rattled, and beneath my feet the cracked metal floor rumbled distantly with overstressed gravity accelerators.

We joined the entry line behind a bunch of dirty freightbugs who looked like they'd been in slipspace far too long, their reddened eyes sunken and their flight suits stained with sweat and grease. They sniggered and scratched their mangy hair and harangued each other in Brit so fouled up with pungent Rus cursewords that even I could barely understand them. Not a classy place.

I wanted to cross my arms and fidget. I felt underdressed, over-young, over-smart. Normally when I go undercover like this, I pick less conspicuous clothing, try to go unseen and unremembered. But Lazuli dressed like this all the time, and it wasn't like she'd had the chance to pack a change.

One of the freightbugs made some crude joke about my legs, and all his friends chortled like hungry jackals.

Dragonfly gave the guy a dirty stare, and I clutched my shatterjay tight in my jacket pocket, my cheeks burning. Yeah, they sure would wrap around your neck, asshole. Right before I tear your greasy head off with them. What was this, the twentieth century?

Dragonfly's fingers tightened on my elbow, his murmur barely audible under the screeching aircon. "Don't make a scene. It isn't worth it."

My jaw clenched. I wasn't used to sucking up insults any more. Flash some Axis rank and the knuckle-draggers back off faster than you can say *kiss my ass.* It's one of the perks of Imperial service. But I couldn't pull rank now. What would Lazuli do? Probably punch the guy in the face. But if I started a fight and we got kicked off the station, I'd ruin Dragonfly's plans and he'd cut me loose.

I forced a smile, razors in my cheeks. "Whatever you say, dear."

A grimy little blonde girl scuttled up, holding the crate of smokes and crystals she wasn't supposed to be selling tight to her chest. The freight-bug slipped her some crumpled plastic for a little pack of orange glitter, and sent me a leering smile. His bloodshot eyes gleamed, one green, one blue. In a dizzy instant, I was back on Port Victoria, a little girl just like this one, scavenging in the grubby spaceport streets, too hungry to say no when a strange-smelling man with one green eye slid cold fingers over my shoulder and promised me apples. Just another sordid day in a crappy childhood, forced to scrap and simper for a living while the Imperial kids had everything they wanted.

Not the same guy. Couldn't be, not after so many years.

I hadn't thought about those days in a long time, and the force of my reaction shocked me. I wanted to vomit. I wanted to crawl into the corner and cry, like I'd done then, my mouth bleeding and the taste of bruised apples sick in my throat.

I swallowed, and shook off Dragonfly's hand. Focus, Carrie. Forget it.

We reached the front of the line, and the Imperial soldier at the security checkpoint looked me up and down with sleepy blue eyes. Young, untidy, his strawberry hair too long, his glossy black uniform gleaming under dirty orange atomglow tubes. The poison pistol in his holster looked dusty and unloved, and he stifled a yawn as he held out a gloved hand for my ident.

I handed the cube over with a sigh, trying to look bored, but my pulse jumped faster, and sweat beaded on my scalp. I didn't even know what was on the damn thing. I could only hope Dragonfly had done his job properly. For all I knew, he'd set me up. Ekaterina, freight pilot. For the rest, I'd just play dumb.

Corporal Redhead flicked my cube open and slotted it into his viewscreen. Beside me, Dragonfly had already slipped his finger into the blood sampler that would verify his chemistry, calm and unruffled as always.

I thought of Nikita, all those missions we'd done together, all the people we'd lied to. Deception had always been a thrill, a game. I'd snuck past security undercover dozens of times, but the truth had always been on my side. Imperial soldiers wouldn't shoot an Axis agent if she screwed up and her cover slipped. This time, I was pretending to be a criminal pretending to be a different criminal; more than one layer of lies that could crack. If I got found out, these guys would fight with Dragonfly over who got to blow my head off.

Still, as Redhead copied my details into his dusty console with one finger and carelessly pushed the blood scanner across for me to use, I felt like giving him a good dressing-down worthy of any company sergeant. He was lazy, slow, careless. Wasn't paying attention. Hadn't even really looked at me. If this was New Moskva, he'd be court-martialed.

The fiber optic pierced my fingertip, taking its sample—not as sophisticated as Axis's lightscan, and sporadically unreliable—and my finger itched as I handed back the scanner. Small lazinesses added up to big holes. With outpost security like this, no wonder Dragonfly and his petty rebels did as they pleased.

Diodes on the camera overhead flickered green as it recorded my image. Redhead glanced dully at my imprint, and my heart skipped. If either of our samples rang alarms, we'd be toast.

But Redhead just yawned and tapped a couple of commands. "Weapons?"

"Can I have any?"

Redhead shrugged. "Course not. All weapons confiscated. Unless you got the proper permit."

I glanced at Dragonfly, and then I understood. He'd emptied his pistol and particle chargers onto the desk next to an innocent-looking pile of silverplastic cash. My indignation fumed. Imperial soldiers taking bribes. I'd seen it before, but never this blatant. They practically had a sign out. Lying to trick the enemy was one thing. This was just sordid graft. I liked to think the Empire still had some honor.

I plucked out the jay and held it up. I could have had a laser cannon up my shorts and another one down my cleavage and Redhead wouldn't have noticed or cared. "Just this. And my friend's got the permit."

"No weapons." Redhead made another agonizingly slow entry in his console and tossed me back my data crystal without looking up. "Welcome to Vyachesgrad. Next."

The dented steel security door crunched aside, motors whirring, and Aragon, a.k.a. Lazuli, a.k.a. Ekaterina the Red Sunday freight pilot, walked right in.

Just like that.

***

The corridor opened into a wide steel walkway that ringed a vast atrium, lit in the centre by a glowing white column that stretched down into the station's bowels. Opposite, a cluster of shops offering packaged ship supplies and circuitry components were jammed in beside a rowdy snack bar that stank of burned candy floss and a sparkle-lit parlor of virtual shooting games. Engine noise and thudding machinery from the docking arms echoed in the metal walls, and the low iron ceiling shuddered.

People strolled or hurried: mechanics and space-jocks in flight suits and coveralls, a woman and her two ratty kids, a fat greasy guy in an ill-fitting suit. I couldn't see my new caveman friends. Pity. I could use a good ass-kicking to calm my nerves.

A pair of patrolling marines sauntered by, green

laserlight glinting from the tubular accu-sights each wore slotted over one eye. They carried shiny-barreled laser rifles slung low across their tight-molded black combat suits. Looked like Imperial security had a heavy presence here, even if they were corrupt and half asleep.

Dragonfly leaned against a bulkhead waiting for me, hands stuffed in pockets and that annoyingly sweet little smile. “Still alive?”

I scowled, just to make myself feel better. “I didn’t start a fight. Happy?”

“So far. Come on, we’re late.”

I followed him down the metal steps to the next level, where a dirty crowd milled around a bar furnished in dented plastic. Vapid electronic music burbled in a mist of apple-scented shisha smoke and colored lights. Voices and laughter in three languages blurred to hash. We sidled through the crowd, to a dim-lit corner where a grotesquely fat shaven-headed guy sat stuffed into a metal alcove, the table cutting into the smeared khaki flight suit stretched over his belly.

FatBoy saw us, and raised his half-empty beer glass with a sloppy grin. Already two or three empty jugs littered the table. “Ahoy there, ya rotten anarchist scumbag,” he boomed in Brit-mangled Rus, his damp jowls shaking. “Don’t you got a watch? Happy hour’s over.”

“Drinks are on you, then,” Dragonfly said.

He stood aside for me, and I squeezed into the booth on the bench opposite FatBoy. The greasy vinyl stuck to my bare thighs, bacteria no doubt multiplying with glee on my sweaty skin, and I spared a moment’s regret for my lost flight suit.

I concentrated on the fat guy, cataloguing him for future reference. Older than Dragonfly, hands big and scarred from manual work, a dent in the side of his skull from some old wound. A fighter, not a thinker, even if he was past his prime. My anticipation sharpened. Was it time for action? Would I find out what Dragonfly was up to at last?

FatBoy shot a glance at me, his beetling brows merging in a frown. "Who's your new girlfriend?"

I swallowed an indignant snort.

Dragonfly just shrugged. "She's okay."

FatBoy rubbed stained hands on his stretched flight suit. "I can see she's okay, kid. She looks more than okay to me. But I don't recall a threesome in our discussions. Not that I'm complaining, mind." He leered at me, a harmless wink ruining the effect.

I didn't care. Enough with the crude remarks. I grinned back, sharp. "You know how sometimes it's your lucky day?"

"Ha, ha. Capital. I like her already." FatBoy gave a happy snort.

I leaned forward, the shatterjay ready in my hand. "Today isn't your day."

Dragonfly's hand came down on mine, squeezing. "Calm, children. Lazuli, meet Sebastian Fouchon, known to his alleged friends as Little Bastie the Trash-Hauler. He has a dirty mind and a dirtier mouth and means absolutely nothing by either. Bastie, this is Lazuli. I picked her up ripping off the Esperanza mob's database, and if you don't keep it in your pants, she *will* blow it off. There. Now can we act like grown-ups, just for a few minutes?"

Bastie rolled heavy shoulders, sweat spraying, his

washed-green gaze merry. "Certainly, old chap. Any friend of yours and all that. No offense, miss. Care for a drink?"

He grabbed his jug and a couple of smeared glasses and poured us each a frothy beer.

I shook Dragonfly's hand off and jammed the jay back in my pocket, scowling. But my mouth watered. I hadn't slept properly for what seemed like an age, and my stomach grumbled for lack of real food. A beer would sure go down well.

Dragonfly and Bastie clinked glasses and chugged. Bastie's went down fastest, but not by much. He smacked his lips, broken teeth shining. "Showing your age, kid. You not drinking, miss? He never said you were one of *those*."

Dragonfly gave that annoyingly handsome, smack-his-face-in smile. "If only I'd known. It's hard to get good help these days."

I flipped him off and gulped down my beer. The cool malt liquid sparkled down my throat and settled happily in my stomach. My eyes watered. Yum. Almost as good as food. I wiped froth from my lips, burping.

When Bastie refilled all three glasses with a laugh, I stifled a groan. I needed to keep my wits about me. The last thing I needed was another heavy night. But Dragonfly just sipped a mouthful, then pulled a smeared glass notescreen from his pocket. He scribbled swiftly on it.

"This is what I want." He slid the screen across the table.

Bastie took it before I could see, and inwardly I cursed.

Bastie glanced at it and his florid face paled. "Kid,

your handwriting sucks."

Dragonfly just waited.

Bastie took a swallow of beer, his fat throat bobbing. "So it's on, then," he said, and his voice rang quieter, his thick Brit accent less pronounced. Like he'd forgotten to keep up his act in the face of what Dragonfly was planning.

My curiosity itched. Even a billion-ruble heist hardly seemed worthy of that. Maybe it was what he planned to do with the money that turned Fat Bastie so pale.

Dragonfly shrugged. "Talking doesn't get the job done."

I resisted squirming in my seat. Talking hadn't done the job on Urumki Mor either, the night he'd massacred Mishka and my friends without so much as a surrender-or-die. The prick was too calm, too offhanded. I wanted to smash his face into the table.

Bastie sighed and erased the writing with a swipe of his thumb. Damn. Maybe I could recreate it later with a magnetic probe, but unlikely. Dragonfly was too paranoid. He'd probably burn the glass to molten dribbles with atomflash before I had the chance.

The fat man pushed the blank screen back across the table. "Well, I don't wish to say I told you so, old boy—"

"Then shut up. Can you get them?"

Bastie snorted. "Of course I can get them. This is me you're talking to. Know a chap who knows a chap and all that." He tapped the side of his fat nose with a conspiratorial wink in my direction. "Know a lot of chaps, me. You ever want a chap, I'm the man to see."

I smirked. "I'll bear that in mind."

Dragonfly finished his beer. "*Está bien.* Can you bring them by? You know my timeline."

"Es-tah beeyen. No pro-bleemo, ya ratty Espan moo-chacho. But it'll cost ya extra, and it'll be a day or two. I gotta pick up some crew while I'm here."

Dragonfly twisted his little finger in his ear with a grimace. "Can I have it without the rotten accent? Would that be cheaper?"

"To the core, my friend." Bastie mimed stabbing himself in the heart. "I'll have you know I learned your annoyingly pronoun-challenged language from the best."

"A toothless lady of the night in a street brothel on Sevilla Nueva is not the best."

Bastie winked. "Al contray-rio, kid. You should get out more. So, are you excellent fellows on for a capital evening of frivolity and excess? Somewhere in the galaxy it's Friday night, after all."

"Tempting." I smiled, thinking hard.

Bastie was the only person I'd met who had any idea what Dragonfly was planning, and though he acted like a blustering idiot, a beady glint in his eyes said he wasn't so dumb as to let anything slip while he was sober. But I eyed his imposing bulk and florid nose and thought twice about a drinking contest. He had to weigh two hundred kilos. It was hard to fake drinking that many rounds of beer, and my chances of wheedling anything out of him before I lost consciousness weren't good. Maybe I could rifle his ship later, once Dragonfly slept, see what I could find.

A thought sparked danger along my nerves. If only one person knew Dragonfly's plans, then where had Axis found their intel? *Surveillance reports*, Director

Renko had said, but I'd bet an agent could watch Dragonfly for a month and not learn anything more than I'd already gleaned, which was a big fat nothing.

Maybe Bastie was the leak. Maybe his jolly plump exterior hid a traitorous streak, or at least a mercenary one. Maybe I could buy information from him, or bribe him with a saucy flash of cleavage.

Or maybe Renko had lied. That had happened before. Perhaps I should pick Nikita's brains about it before I did anything foolish. Not that I trusted him to tell me the truth for its own sake—"truth" is a fluid, self-serving concept for him. But emotive sub-ether cuts both ways. If he glibly told me Renko was on the level, I'd know it was bullshit.

Dragonfly shrugged. "You two go right ahead. I have to deal with replenishment."

"Good luck," Bastie teased. "This has gotta be the worst R&R station in the quadrant. Half the techs don't know a slipspace bearing from an arc rocket transducer. Last time I was here, they put radfuel in the coolant tanks and I had to flush the whole thing out with polymers before it went critical. Cost me a mint."

"Well, you don't get—"

"—what you don't pay for. I know. That's why I charge you a fortune. Nothing but the best." Bastie turned to me, green eyes twinkling. "Well, pretty lady, shall we get started? Poster Boy here can pay. I trust you've got his credit?"

But I couldn't let Dragonfly out of my sight. I didn't put it past him to leave me here, and if he had any other visits to make I didn't want to miss them.

I sighed, faking regret. "Think I'll give it a miss. But

thanks. Maybe tomorrow, if you're still here?"

A sly glint in his grin, almost imperceptible. "We'll have to wait and see about that, won't we?" He turned back to Dragonfly. "Kid, consider it done. Since you didn't ask how much, I'll assume you're desperate enough to pay whatever they charge. I'll even do cash on delivery, but only because I know you're too dumb to rip me off."

"In that case, I take back everything I said about you." Dragonfly stood and offered his hand. "An unsavory pleasure, as always."

Bastie clasped his hand, and raised a glass to me with a lascivious wink. "All yours, by the look. Don't keep him up too late, miss."

12

We weaved through the bar crowd to the walkway's edge. I unclipped my jacket, the beer and the overheated air making me sweat.

"So, are we really refueling?"

"Sure." Dragonfly dug in his pocket, counting plastic cash chips. "But also avoiding another sore head. That bar better have some serious *cerveza* on tap. Bastie could drink a small ocean dry." He saw my expression and shrugged. "He's okay. Not as dumb as he pretends."

"And he gets you stuff." I tucked my thumbs in my belt as we walked along beside the carbonsteel railing.

"Yes. He does a freight run from here to the Leonov cluster every few weeks. Slow and inconspicuous."

Vyachesgrad to Leonov. Long way. Could be going anywhere.

I fished a little deeper. "Yeah? What kind of ship does he run?"

"A rusty one with radfuel in the coolant, apparently. *Tiene hambre*?"

"Excuse me?" Paranoia never slept. I'd try again later.

"Hungry. Food. You want some?" He dragged me up to a high plastic counter, where a crazy-eyed Espan guy in a blue apron was slashing greasy slabs of flesh off a carcass that rotated on a spike in front of a bright orange flashspit.

I didn't like the idea of Dragonfly buying me anything. I didn't want his bloodstained charity, and I remembered Lazuli was supposed to be a vegetarian. Any cyberthief worth the name would already have his console fishing out information about me, and the false identity Axis had cooked up for me was there ready for him to find. But my stomach rumbled, and my mouth watered at the juicy aroma. I had to eat something or I'd lose efficiency.

"That's not sub-meat," I argued for show. "That's a real animal. It had fur once. You want me to eat that?"

"Are you kidding? I live on this stuff." He paid for two piles of spicy dead beast wrapped in thin bread with what looked like shredded red cabbage and cream, and squirted them with a generous flood of garlic sauce. He handed me one. "Come on, try it. Your mouth will love you."

"I don't eat meat, okay?"

"Do you see anything else?"

"I guess not." I took it. Warm sauce dribbled from the paper over my hand. I wrinkled my nose, but had to admit it smelled fantastic. I closed my eyes and took a bite. Mmm. Hot, spicy, flavorsome. I chewed, the stringy texture filling my mouth, salt and juice tingling my tongue.

I swallowed, smacking my lips. "Okay, you win. But only because you starved me all day."

"All part of my plan to buy you dinner."

He grinned, and we stuffed ourselves. Crackers and juice for lunch just didn't cut it.

I wiped my mouth and licked the last tasty drops from my fingers, but my mood clouded dark. This made me think of Mishka, the one time we ever got to go away together, a sultry summer planet with endless beaches and cobalt skies.

Him and me, eating weird food with our fingers in a crowded marketplace full of rickshaws. Lazing in the green saltwater until our skins shriveled, diving to the coral reef in a cascade of rainbow-scaled fish. Choking on sweet-smelling shisha pipes in a dusty velvet bar, with a piper wheedling his snake from a basket in the corner. Hunting each other through a fragrant maze of overgrown jungle flowers at the laser range. He beat me, like he always did, never one to suck up to a superior, even when he was courting her like the old-fashioned gentleman he did his best to be. We slept under red summer stars on a wicker-lined rooftop, his body hard and warm next to mine and my head nestled in his massive shoulder amid the woody scent of his long black hair, and he woke me in the middle of the night when the meteors rained crimson fire and asked me to be his wife.

Two weeks later, we landed on Urumki Mor.

Now my lover was dead, and the man who'd killed him had just bought me dinner.

My eyes ached, and the empty place in my heart swelled like an icy abscess. My sweet, silent soldier. I missed him. But most of the time, I just got on with life. Filled that empty space with hunger for vengeance while he faded to a distant dream.

Wounds heal, right? Memories wash thin. Broken hearts mend. That's how it's supposed to be. How we survive.

It didn't make me feel better. Only more like a traitor.

My stomach creaked, satisfied in spite of me, and I made an effort to sound cheerful above jangling nerves. "Meat *and* beer in the same day. Great. You owe me a week in the grav gym to get my ass back into shape."

"Your ass looks just fine to m— Hold up." Dragonfly touched my shoulder, a warning.

I spun around, tense, but too late. The cavemen had already seen me.

My special friend sauntered up, a shit-eating grin on his crusty mouth. "Hey, baby. Still ain't ditched your pretty-face boyfriend? Why don't ya come with us? We'll show ya what a real man can do."

Bad smell. Bad hair. Bad teeth. Zero on the hygiene scale, pal. But Dragonfly ignored him, so I did too, even if I itched to smack the guy's nose from his face. We didn't need a fight right now.

But the guy wouldn't give up. He squeezed my butt with one greasy hand. "Tasty. What's it worth?"

My cheeks warmed. Those odd-colored eyes made my guts churn. Would Lazuli put up with that? Hell, no. And neither would I.

I shoved him back into his pile of Neanderthal friends. "Kiss my ass, pencil dick."

He stumbled and righted himself, and they all advanced on me like a pack of one-track-mind jackals.

His face twisted. "I'll do something to your ass, bitch. So hard you'll scream like a baby."

Dragonfly gripped my arm. "Leave it. Let's go."

But fury rippled in my blood, washing away caution. I should be keeping a low profile. Security could kick us off the station for fighting ... but I couldn't forget that image of the hungry little colony girl. I wasn't her any more, scrapping for favors in alleyways. I didn't have to take this shit and run home crying afterwards. I'd disgraced my family and joined the marines so no one would have to take this shit again.

I shook Dragonfly off. "Yeah, you're right. Wouldn't want this moron to get his ass kicked by a *girl*."

The guy swung at me, and I grinned. Idiot.

I grabbed his wrist and twisted it behind his head, ramming the heel of my hand into his kidneys. There was muscle under that lazy fat, harder than I'd expected. Still, he oomphed and buckled. I kicked his legs from under him, jammed his throat to the floor with one knee, and crunched my shatterjay deep under his chin where his pulse thudded.

My hand shook, adrenaline pumping, but I forced it steady. "Go on, dickhead. Move, and see what happens."

And that's all I had time for before the rest of them crashed into me.

I thudded into the hatchway bulkhead and bounced off, bones jarring. My chin hit the floor, and salty blood squirted in my mouth. A kick slammed into my side. Blindly, I jabbed the jay into flesh and fired. Anonymous blood spurted. A hand grabbed my hair and yanked hard, and my neck whiplashed back. And then the harsh slide and clunk of a weapon being cocked, and I was free.

I clambered up, still clutching my jay. One guy lay limp and groaning on the metal floor. My guy howled on one knee, gripping his other kneecap. Dragonfly stood over him, hair falling in his eyes and blood staining his mouth, pressing the sawn-off barrel of a ballistic metalgun into the guy's forehead. Not his own weapon; he'd taken it from someone. It was corroded, the trigger housing bent out of shape, but it still worked.

"Back it off." Tone soft but steely, that cold determination I'd noticed on Esperanza gleaming darkly in his eyes. "We don't want a fight."

Unassuming to scary in five seconds flat, and I still didn't know which was the real him. Still, he'd jumped in to help me when he could've walked away. That was promising.

The other two guys cursed and pulled out weapons. My pulse leaped. This could get nasty.

But marching boots clanged on the floor, and someone shouted in that clipped, formalized Rus you only ever learn in the military. Imperial marines, displeased with our breaking the peace.

Dragonfly looked over his shoulder and swore in Espan. The cavemen hesitated, their dull eyes glinting.

Neanderthal and his friends looked like Vyachesgrad regulars. No guarantee the marines would take our side, even if we didn't start it. I bit my lip. How had I gotten myself into this? My buttons were way too easy to press right now. Port Victoria was a long time ago. Forgotten, I'd thought, just one lousy day among a host of lousy days. Maybe Director Renko was right not to trust me. Maybe it was true that I'd been twitchy since Mishka died ...

No. I felt fine. At the top of my game. I had a bunch of successful missions to prove it, even if Renko no longer gave me the responsibility she used to.

So why couldn't I prise the memory of that dirty

little girl from my mind?

The bootsteps came closer.

Dragonfly gnashed his teeth in frustration. "Don't say anything," he hissed, and dragged me by the arm across the hatchway threshold.

He jammed his palm on the button and the bronze hatch spiraled shut with a clunk. Sparks showered as he smashed the electric controls with the metalgun's grip. We could only hope the marines didn't care enough to come after us.

The curving black corridor was dim, old icelights flickering, and he pulled me into a swift walk, past locked instrument panels and storage bins and iron-clad doorways.

I bristled, and he let me go, but we kept walking. "What are you—"

"What were you thinking?" He uncocked the metalgun and stripped it, his gaze focused ahead. "Can't you hold your ego in even for a few minutes?"

I flushed, because I knew he was right. I'd made a mistake. What would Lazuli say?

"Don't give me a hard time, okay? It wasn't your ass he grabbed. You're not the one who has to listen to that shit."

"You don't think so?" He dumped the barrel into a storage bin with a resounding clang and kept dismantling. "Look at me, Lazuli. I'm not exactly a poster child for Russiyan genetics. You think no one's ever called me names?" Crunch: the firing mech in pieces into a trash receptor. "You have to be smarter than that if you want to play this game."

I wiped blood from my lip and spat copper. He was

right, about me and Lazuli both, and it stung.

"What the hell does it matter? So we punch a few guys. I can handle myself. You didn't do too badly yourself—"

"We nearly got arrested!"

"So? You said our idents are solid. And you've got freightloads of cash. Plastic a few palms and we're out."

Crash: the trigger and the magazine behind a pile of crates. We rounded a corner and he glared at me, exasperated. "Yeah. Right. Tomorrow, maybe, if we're lucky. More like next week, after they process our asses via carrier pigeon."

"What the hell's a carrier pigeon?"

"Never mind. But do you think I've got that sort of time? Think I need that kind of attention right now?" He saw my scowl and pulled me to a stop in the shadow of a low bulkhead, his hand hesitant on my shoulder. "Look. I'm sorry that idiot said those things. And I'm sorry you got hit in the face. But you have to prioritize if you want to make a difference. You can't let little things get in the way of what matters."

Little things. Like melting my fiancé, maybe? Like tiny Carrie crying in the snow?

Anger shattered my reason to glassy shards. I really didn't need Freedom Fighting 101 from him. I'd learned enough of his lessons on Urumki.

I shook him off, my pulse aflame. "Fine. Next time, don't go out of your way, okay? I didn't ask for your help. You really shouldn't let little things get in the w—"

A footstep clunked, and I whirled, my hand flashing to the warm glassgun in my pocket. No one. Shadows thickened. Sweat trickled down my neck. Behind me I heard Dragonfly's pistol charging, a sharp buzz. "Watch it—"

Clang.

Not good. I spun and aimed, left eye squinting in the dark. Too late.

Two people pinned Dragonfly to the metal wall, disarming him. But not the cavemen. Not Imperials. This guy and girl were lean, ravenous, muscles and scars shining under mismatched, spaceworn clothes. The girl was tall and boyish, pale face under white buzz-cut hair, dull steel piercings sharpening her brow. The guy was just a kid, skinny and pimple-cheeked with porcupine brown hair, but his eyes were hard, his mouth twisted tight. And their atomflashes looked hard-used, grips worn, contacts polished shiny from endless cleaning.

Dragonfly closed his eyes and sighed. He looked convinced. Not good.

I switched my aim from one to the other, backing off to get a better shot. "Let him go."

"Not a chance." A low voice, musical, resonating so my ears couldn't pinpoint the source.

And a third figure ghosted from the shadows. Tall, black hair in four-inch dreadlocks, dark urban combat trousers and boots under a molded black armored vest that probably could have fit two of me inside. Muscular dark brown arms, glistening with sweat. Buckled wristguards, no gloves, thorny artwork on one forearm. Pistol strapped to one massive thigh. Big son of a bitch.

He sauntered up to Dragonfly, careless of my arc of

fire, and flashed a crooked white grin. "You're a hard man to find, said the spider to the fly. Let's have a chat."

Cocky. Who the fuck were these people?

Dragonfly spat blood, insolent. "I already told you *no*."

Shades of me and black ops. What did these guys want from him?

"That was then. You haven't heard my latest offer."

I circled, all three enemies in my sights. The shatterjay worked better at intimate range. And the big guy wouldn't go down easy. With shatterglass, I probably couldn't take all of them before they jumped me. Or killed Dragonfly. That'd save me the trouble. But better the devil you've already sold your soul to.

Inwardly, I cringed. Me protecting *him*. What a joke.

But I didn't have time to laugh at myself. His plasma pistol lay on the floor where they'd forced it from his hand, and I started calculating how far I'd have to dive, the best trajectory and attitude to come up firing.

"Let him go," I repeated.

"Do I know you?" The big black guy turned, a frown creasing his brow. Diamond earstud, colored glass beads glinting in his dreadlocks, sharp green eyes flecked gold with crazy. He studied me, cocking his head. "I don't think I know you. I don't think I like you, either."

His gaze flicked over my shoulder, and my reflexes jerked a sharp warning. But before I could react, something hard thwacked into the back of my skull, and everything flashed white.

13

I awoke groggy, fumbling for my aching head. Hard floor, uncomfortable under my side. I squinted, ice-lights glaring. My hand came away bloody. I wiped it on my shorts and wobbled unsteadily to my feet.

The corridor was deserted, red guidelights pulsing softly in the floor. No sprays of blood or vomit. Dragonfly could still be alive. But my shatterjay lay crushed, a pile of splintered glass, like some big black guy (for instance) had crunched it under his boot. And Dragonfly's pistol was gone.

Fuck.

I stumbled for the nearest instrument panel, flicking the screen alight. Smugly, it denied me access. I fumbled in my shorts for my ESE and slotted it. The system blinked and opened, just a simple password that the ESE's processor chewed up in moments. Diagrams and text glowed green as the station's logistics logs came online. The clock in the top corner blinked red station time: 0126. Obviously those marines hadn't bothered to hunt for us once the fight broke up. I'd been out for twenty minutes or more.

Twenty minutes in slipspace. They could have taken him anywhere.

I took a breath, calming. Not too late. Just think ...

I found the maintenance logs and flicked through. My finger slid too fast on the glass, skipping a few menus, and I forced myself to slow down. There.

Docking lane six, near the entry gate. Magclamps still activated. All slots taken. A quick glance at the video security monitor confirmed it. *Ladrona* was still there.

Which meant Dragonfly probably hadn't left of his own accord. But I didn't know which was his captors' ship. If they even had a ship. For all I knew, they were still here.

My thoughts raced ahead. I didn't know who these guys were, what they wanted. The only person I knew on the station was Bastie, and for a moment I considered finding him. But I'd already suspected him of treachery, and for all I knew he was in on this. I couldn't risk giving myself away.

Nothing for it then.

I yanked my ESE from the console and thumbed the sub-ether contact before I could change my mind. "Malachite, you there?"

Black-matter interference howled like wind for a few empty seconds, then Nikita's voice chimed in my head, distorted faintly with the distance. "Aragon, sweetheart. How are you getting along with Algebra Geek?"

Deep breath. "I've lost him."

"You what?"

The delay didn't blunt that razor-edged tone and my spine crackled cold.

I shivered, sweating. "I lost him. We're on an R&R outpost called Vyachesgrad. He bought some stuff—it's a long story, I'll tell you later. But we got ambushed and it wasn't Imperials. D'you know this guy?"

I pictured Dreadlock Boy's face and the ESE flashed my mental image down the line. Not very accurate, but better than nothing.

Nikita laughed, and shadows flitted across my heart. "It really is your lucky day, isn't it? Search the dataspace under 'lunatic fringe'. His Imperial codename is *Spider*. Angry malcontent, stole a navy battleship a while back. Cruises around blowing shit up and getting himself on the news. He and Dragonfly'll have a nice little rebel reunion."

I remembered Dragonfly's eyes, heated with defiance or disgust. *I already told you no.* "They didn't seem like friends."

"They're not, any more. I'll send you the file. They had some kind of falling out. It's better than a soap opera."

"So what's this Spider want him for?"

"Screwed if I know. That's your job, isn't it?" Short, tinged with hot disdain that prickled my cheek.

My stomach sank. "Look, can you do me the favor and not tell Renko? I'll get it under control. I promise. I just need a little time."

The two-second delay killed me, but he came back smooth and smug like a cat's purr. "I suppose I can lose Lyudmila's commcode for a few hours. But you owe me, Carrie."

I sighed. Like I had a choice. "Yeah, okay. Thanks."

"I like it when you owe me."

The sultry suggestion in his voice warmed my skin. "I bet you do."

"Would you like to know how I'm going to make you pay?"

Invisible fingers stroked my thigh, and I jumped. Damn it.

"Get a girlfriend," I said, and snapped the link before he could get any more creative.

Well, that could have been worse. At least he hadn't cut me loose right away. But I only had a few hours to put this right.

My ESE buzzed and, true to Nikita's word, a data package dumped itself on my chip. I flipped through it, my eyes glazing over as text and images jumped into my optic nerves. Spider was Dreadlock Boy all right, the rebellion's typical angry young man who'd lasted beyond his youth with guile and ruthlessness. Brit by birth, joined the rebel militia young. Urban warfare, fought the Imperial occupation, lifetime grudge, blah blah whine, so sad. Some kind of musician, apparently, and I grimaced. Great. Another self-appointed genius. Thwarted artistic pretensions meant a vicious and fragile ego.

I skimmed through his record: a catalogue of bombings, kidnappings, armed assaults. Much more conspicuous than Dragonfly. He'd evaded capture so far through strike-and-run tactics. Strange that I'd never heard of him, but the galaxy was a big place and insurrection festered everywhere. He cruised around in a stolen Imperial battleship—how the hell did you steal a battleship?—with his crazy-ass crew, kicking heads and breaking things. Shock tactics, mass destruction with maximum terror, civilian casualties an optional extra. Nice guy. He and Dragonfly were welcome to each other.

But I couldn't let my prey get away that easily. And face it, if I lost Dragonfly, I was screwed. Renko and Surov could have a sideshow to their little war, fighting over who got to kill me first.

I snapped the ESE off and let my lazy eyes refocus. I hadn't seen a battleship docked as we approached, and Spider would be even madder than he looked to bring it in here. He must be standing off somewhere at a safe distance, and came here in a shuttlecraft or something. If he'd made it to his ship, I was in trouble. No way I could track him through slipspace when he had such a big headstart, even if I could fly *Ladrona*, which I couldn't, not with Dragonfly's biochem crawling green death all over the console.

I couldn't second-guess them. I had to start with what I knew, which was that I wasn't even certain they'd left the station yet.

I switched the maintenance console off. It was useless without access to any surveillance cameras or entry records. For that, I needed the Imperial dataspace, and that prickly cybercreature would notice if I tried a remote uplink to station security. I needed to access a console the marines used. But how?

I wiped my nose, blood smearing sticky. No time to waste. If I'd had my Axis ident, I could've dropped my cover and pulled rank. But I had nothing except my ESE. Not even a weapon.

I thought of Dragonfly's stolen metalgun, and brightened, then I remembered he'd dropped the firing mechanism in the trash compactor. Even if I found the rest of it and bluffed, it wouldn't look functional, not even to the idiots who passed for Imperial security around here.

Guess I was left with lies and attitude then.

I grinned, buoyant. No problem. They're what I'm good at.

***

I eased my head past the steel bulkhead's edge, stilling my breath. It was late, and the young marine sat at the security desk alone, his black diagonal jacket unclipped, playing a virtual lasergame on his little touchpad. He was doing okay too, kicking horned-alien ass in a razorcut maze of death. His cap lay folded on the desk, and his pistol sat snug against his blackclad hip, the holster clip fastened. No doubt he was better at the laser game than the real thing.

You'd think these repair-and-refuel stations would run around the clock, but the maintenance crews had manning issues like everyone else and worked a reduced night shift. After local midnight, the workshops and entry stations pretty much shut down, unless you'd scheduled them at extra cost, and everyone went to the bar. This guy had obviously drawn the short straw tonight. He'd have backup on etherwave, but for the moment he was alone.

I watched him for a while longer, but he didn't lift his gaze from his game. I could hardly blame him. This place was like the grave. Unluckily for him, his night was about to spring alive.

I raked my hair half-loose from its braid, palmed my eyes to make them wet and red, and let my jacket slide off one shoulder, pulling my top down to show a bit more flesh. I sucked my cut lip hard to make the blood flow, and smeared my mouth, leaving a fat scarlet stain.

Ready? Deep breath. Ready.

I stumbled around the corner, panting and catching my fall against the bulkhead. The marine jumped up, dropping his game.

I staggered. "Please, help me. That man, he attacked me, I don't know what ..."

I fell toward him like a proper damsel in distress. He ran forward, trying to hold me up. "What? Where?"

I pointed wildly behind me. He looked up. I clocked him in the temple with my elbow, and he crumpled without a sound. Quietly, I eased him to the floor. He'd have a bruise and a sore head, nothing more.

I unclipped his pistol and stuffed it into my jacket, and hurried to the desk. Only a few minutes until he woke. I prodded his console alive. He was already logged in. Too easy. I flipped to the entry logs and accessed video. A bunch of images, headshots of everyone who'd alighted at Vyachesgrad this week. I jacked my ESE, downloaded them with a data-ripper and ran them through face recognition with Spider's picture from the Axis file. Handy little kit, this ESE.

It only took a second or two. There he was, dreadlocks and diamonds and that crazy-ass grin. A terrorist who kidnapped bank robbers. Fascinating.

I retrieved his entry log data from the console. Spider was calling himself Lukas Radjevich, and he must have bribed the guards with some pretty gifts, because he'd been here since yesterday morning and security hadn't lifted a finger.

Interesting. We'd arrived only a few hours ago on *Ladrona*. Either this abduction was a spur-of-the-moment thing, or Spider had known Dragonfly was coming.

I thought again of Fat Bastie and his laughing eyes. Maybe they hid something more sinister. In my urgency, I'd forgotten to ask Nikita about him.

Behind me, the marine groaned and shifted. Hastily, I pulled up accommodations and searched. On-ship lodgings weren't permitted on a R&R station, because the maintenance crews didn't want idiots getting in their way while they sprayed toxic fuel around and messed with the oxy pressure.

Lukas Radjevich was staying at some place called Madame Tulip's, sixth level, room 181. Good enough for me.

I exited back to the menu, dimmed the screen, and hurried away around the corner, shoving the marine's gamepad into my pocket. At least now I'd have something to do for all those dead slipspace hours on *Ladrona*. If I ever made it back to *Ladrona*.

I hopped into the empty elevator and pressed six. As motors whirred and the galvanized cage jerked upwards, I checked my new pistol's charge and cleaned the crusted contacts with two flicks of a fingernail. The overhead lights flickered, and the cage stopped, the door grinding open onto a dimly lit corridor.

I gripped the pistol lightly in both hands, cleared left and right, and stepped out, my pulse hot but steady.

I'd make it back to *Ladrona*, all right, and Dragonfly with me. And then I was going to kick his pretty Espan ass for making me care if he lived or died.

14

The corridor was warm, and stank of sweat and stale takeaway food. To the left, a little shopping mall, closed, the stores dark and barred in steel. To the right, it opened into a dim red-lit lobby. Low-hanging fiber optics sparkled from the ceiling, a waterfall of garish purple, and in the lobby's center stood a huge plastic flower arrangement in vivid scarlet, proclaiming this as the place I was looking for. Tacky, lowlife, deserted.

Swiftly, I padded across the lobby and into Madame Tulip's. Red lightbulbs gleamed sickly above the row of cracked plastic doors on each side, and nylon carpet crunched under my feet like it hadn't been cleaned this century. No one in sight.

Closest to the lobby was room 100. I stalked quietly down the corridor, eyeing each door for movement. Sweat trickled down my midriff and into my shorts. 120. 125. Snatches of sound: a sports vidcast, a porn movie, someone snoring. 150. A horde of monstrous roaches scuttled by my feet, their feelers brushing my ankles. 178. 180. 181.

Light seeped under the broken-edged door, and with it muffled conversation. I paused. Breathed. Listened. I couldn't make it out.

I inched closer, my trigger finger tightening. Male voices, more than one. A crack split the plastic near the doorframe, and I leaned forward and peered inside.

Light dazzled me, and I blinked until my eye adjusted. An old orange atomglow lamp, a broken chair, the edge of a crumpled bed. Someone crossed—a glimpse of faded pink shirt, dirty trousers, cropped white hair. The woman from the pair who'd attacked Dragonfly. That made three in there at least. I jerked back, but she didn't come closer.

"Listen to me." That was Spider. I recognized that melodious voice, like a musical instrument. Accent round and singsong, from some working-class Brit hellpit like my home planet. "It's simple. All we do is—"

"No, you listen to me." Dragonfly. Tense, pissed off, like he'd sounded when I started that fight. "Are you listening? The answer's *no*."

"I'm not asking you to stay. Like I'd want your sorry ass on my ship again, god help me. I just want to borrow some snotty blackshirt's kid for a while. No harm done."

"Kidnapping the admiral's daughter? Sure you haven't popped a few more synapses since we last met? Come on, Lukas, you know I don't do the personal grudge stuff."

"Then what the fuck do you do? You used to be more useful. What's wrong with you, Sasha? All that slipspace math turned you soft?"

I winced. Sasha. Way too much information. Hell, it probably wasn't even his real name, but it still stung.

"Think what you like," he said. "You may have heard I'm a little busy at the moment, so if you don't mind—"

"Yeah. I heard." A dark Spider chuckle, hot chocolate and cream. "So noble of you. What's it gonna take for you to realize they can't be reasoned with? How many friends you got left to lose?"

I imagined Dragonfly doing that tense, angry thing with his jaw. "Not enough. But I'll have fewer if I start snatching innocent girls for ransom."

I mimed a retch. Listen to him, coming over all precious. Bet he didn't step on roaches either. Murdering bastard.

Spider snorted. "Hey, we play with the toys we're given. You trick it out of them, I kick it out of them. What's the difference?"

A laugh, stripped of all Dragonfly's warmth. "As if you'd get it if I tried to explain."

"Whatever, hero. I just want you to work your magic on the security system. Locks and latches. A five-minute window, that's all I'm asking."

"Not in a million years."

"So that's a yes?"

"Is there some part of *screw you* that you don't get?"

A sigh. "I'm disappointed, Sash. I thought we were friends."

"You're breaking my heart. Really. Is this the part where you threaten me?"

"Will it work?"

"It never did before."

"I never wanted it this bad before." Metal clicked, and atomflash hissed, and Spider strode into my field of view, the weapon aimed steady in one big hand. "Last chance. Yes or dead?"

The smell of hot steel tightened my breath, and my fingers tensed, damp on the pistol's grip. Weigh up the risks, assess the percentages. Stay here, or jump in?

A hiss, like flesh burning, and Dragonfly's voice snapped tight. "Go right ahead. Melt me to mist. I'm not changing my mind."

Current zapped, and my heart clenched. Spider really was going to kill him.

Adrenaline pumped through my muscles. and I tensed, ready to spring. Spider's chin jerked upward. His gaze swiveled, searching, and came to rest on me.

Shit. He'd heard me. How the hell did he hear me?

I flung myself backward and dragged up my pistol to fire. But before I could find my aim, Spider flashed forward and ripped the door open.

Fucking fast for a big guy. Ultra-hearing. Ultra-reflexes. He was wired up. Had to be.

His fingers clamped my elbow like steel. I tried to fire, but my forearm went numb and the pistol dropped from my nerveless fingers. He dragged me inside and threw me on the floor, and before I recovered from my sprawl, I was on my knees with a hot atomflash jammed against my temple.

Dragonfly swore and scrambled from his bench, but the white-haired girl shoved him back down.

My hair sizzled, stinking. I jerked away. But Spider twined his hand in my braid and forced the atomflash to my head.

He chuckled, rich with satisfaction. "Let's try this again, Sasha. Yes or dead?"

One little mistake. Just one, and now I was helpless. My guts watered, and I closed my eyes and cursed my own stupidity. Leverage in some bickering rebel crossfire. What a shitty way to die.

15

"Okay."

My pulse flip-flopped. I squinted one eye open. What the hell?

Spider yanked my hair tighter, and hot metal singed my brow. "I'm sorry?"

"I said, okay." Dragonfly banged his head back into the wall, his jaw clenching. "Whatever you want, I'll do it. Just get off her."

"Aww." Spider cuffed me over the head—not that hard, mind you—and shoved me away. "Ain't that sweet? Knew you'd come around."

I picked myself up, confusion and stupid relief burning holes in my composure. Why would Dragonfly change his mind for me? As if a killer like him gave a spit about a woman he didn't even know. He was ready enough to get his own head blown off to thwart Spider. What was he trying to prove?

Maybe he'd known Spider was bluffing. But from all accounts, when Spider pointed a weapon, he fired it, probably until the clip was empty.

Either way, I'd somehow contrived to owe this smug murdering scumbag my life.

This night just kept getting stranger.

Dragonfly grabbed my hand and helped me up, but he didn't look pleased to see me. "You all right?"

I nodded, furious, not trusting my voice. Hell, I was happy to be alive. But damned if I'd be grateful. This asshole never did what I expected. Axis were supposed to be smarter than the rebels. How did he keep surprising me?

Spider laughed, and dealt Dragonfly a clap on the back that made him stagger. "It'll be just like the old days. Remember that time on Bin Guska? You and me and the sickos against a prison full of marine guards. Blew their optic nerves right out. No one fucked with us, that's for s—"

"We do it my way this time," Dragonfly said, his tone clipped. "Quick and quiet. No fuss. And keep your twitchy fingers off the trigger. *Entiendes*?"

Spider flexed his right hand. "More nerve-damage jokes. You're all class."

"Understand?" Dragonfly persisted, tense.

Spider grinned. "Whatever you say."

Dragonfly jerked his head at me. "And she comes with us."

"What?" Spider and I spoke at the same time.

We glanced at each other, wary. I could see him sizing me up, calculating what was in it for him. Not sexual speculation, nor one soldier examining another. This was pure predator's instinct. I suppressed a shiver. He was handsome in the same way as a tiger I'd once seen at New Moskva Gene Park: majestic, self-absorbed. A beast with no honor, only hunger. Stroke that lovely fur at your peril.

Dragonfly sighed. "What am I, a dating service? Lazuli, this is Lukas. What you see is pretty much what you get. Lukas, this is Lazuli. *Al contrario*. But she's good with Imperial systems. She can help."

Spider gave me another once-over, crazy eyes swirling gold. "As good as you?"

I glared back. I couldn't afford to get left behind again. Time to get involved, reassert some control. "Wow, I really love being talked about like I'm not here. I'm not too bad, thanks."

"She's good enough. She can back me up." Dragonfly grinned at Spider, sharp. "You know. In case you make a mistake and accidentally blow my head off?"

Spider shuffled a big hand through his dreads, unconvinced. "Can we trust her?"

I snorted. "You're the one who just tried to melt me, pal."

Dragonfly chuckled. "Good point. Of the people in this room? She's top of my list."

"Fuck you."

No heat in Spider's words. Like this was all a game between old friends, even if they no longer liked each other. My curiosity sharpened. A falling out, Nikita had said. And now Spider roamed the Empire carving a swathe of destruction in his battleship, while Dragonfly sneaked around stealing from casinos and kissing girls to avoid killing Imperial guards. Interesting.

Clearly they were butting heads on how to conduct this kidnapping, whatever it was. Moral qualms? Unlikely. Professional disagreement? Or just clashing egos? Either way, caught between bickering terrorists—amusing though it was to watch Imperial enemies fight amongst themselves—was the last place I wanted to be. The quicker we finished this and got away, the happier I'd get.

Dragonfly gave Spider his dangerous little smile. "Charming as ever. Can I have my pistol back?"

The skinny white-haired girl looked a question at

Spider. She wore dirty green braces and a faded pink T-shirt over combat trousers, her wiry shoulders hunched over a non-existent chest. She gazed at him with hard, adoring concentration, like the word of god might slip from his mouth any moment.

I squirmed. Spider's whole crew were probably just like her: fanatical, obedient and blindly loyal. I'd seen it before with insurrectionist leaders. They preyed on little people with crappy lives who were searching for something—anything—to believe in. They sought out the lonely ones who craved validation and dangled it just out of their reach, dishing out attention and praise like manipulative lovers, never going all the way. Just enough to make their victims long for more. To make them believe that one sweet day, if they tried hard enough, they'd earn what they craved. It was how guys like Dragonfly and Spider got people to die for them.

Spider shrugged, impatient. "Just give it to him, Foxy Lady. You can shoot faster than he can."

Starstruck warmth glowed in Foxy's tired eyes, and inwardly I sighed for her. He'll never sleep with you, baby. He'll never love you. Find someone else before he breaks your heart or gets you killed. But she never will. And one day she'll die, shot or tortured or blown away by Imperial torpedoes, and all she'll be thinking is *Maybe this time, he'll see me.*

Save me from ever wanting something that badly.

Foxy tossed Dragonfly his pistol, and he caught it and reholstered. "Thanks. Shall we get on with it?"

***

Ten minutes later, the three of us crouched in the dark around a battered black glass lensbox that projected a glowing green schematic map into the air. It was a 3D line diagram of the station, a meter or more in diameter with entries and exits marked. The station's body was a big twelve-sided blob with the docking arms spearing off like spikes, and the schematic showed levels and sub-levels arranged around the atrium with the gravity engine bays in the centre.

The old projector buzzed and flickered, the picture wavering. Not as swish a kit as Dragonfly's. Clearly Spider spent his cash on other things, like bombs and bullets and diamond earrings.

Spider pointed, and the display zoomed in on a hexagonal section of rooms and corridors. "Here's the Imperial quarters, level seven. The visiting admiral's name is Verenski. This is where his daughter, Natasha, sleeps. Two exits, front and side, marines guarding each one around the clock in threes. Visual and audio surveillance on a laser grid monitored from the front exit; no biochem, no infra-red. Lights at four-foot intervals, so no shadows or hides. The marine garrison are over here. Half-colonel in charge, three hundred fifty-two strong in three shifts, forty-three seconds away once they're mobilized. No etherwave obstructions, it's a clear call."

I was impressed. He'd done his research. Still, it made me grimace inside that he knew the girl's name. Kidnappers are supposed to objectify. It's one of the first things they teach you in hostage negotiation: make the hostages people, not objects. But Spider knew who this girl was. He just didn't care.

Dragonfly tapped his nails on the glass, thoughtful, green lines reflecting in his eyes. "Doors?"

"Magclamped. The girl has a codecard, so does her father. Everyone else has to ping for authorization, marines included."

"So we can't just roll them for it."

Spider snorted. "Think I'd need you if we could?"

"Where's the override?"

"That area's controlled from the garrison. Security, lights, life support, everything. It's quarantined from the rest of the station."

I nodded. The console I'd looked at had only covered security for its surrounding area too. "So how—"

"Lights," interrupted Dragonfly. "What kind?"

Spider scratched his nose, thinking. "Ice, I guess ... No. Conduits in the ceiling. Atomglow."

"You sure?"

"Of course."

I tried again. "So how are we leaving? Where's your ship?"

"Docking arm five, directly above her quarters. Ninety-five seconds, a hundred tops."

Dragonfly flicked him a dark glare. "Tell me you've got it sorted once we get inside. If this Natasha claws my eyes out, I'll blame you."

"Let me worry about clawed eyeballs."

"Was afraid you'd say that." Dragonfly considered. "So. Not only do we have to hack a security system that's surrounded by a company of marines, and break open a magclamped septurium door past three armed guards who don't have an entry code—do stop me any time if I'm wrong—"

"All good so far."

"—we also have to get an eye-clawing admiral's daughter out and off the station in forty-three seconds, in a ship that's nearly two minutes away."

"Yeah." Spider shrugged. "Sounds about right."

"Terrific," I said. "No problem then."

I wrinkled my nose, thinking hard. Maybe if we started a fight, created a diversion somehow ... Still. Not easy to distract a whole company.

But Dragonfly just tucked his hair behind his ears and sniffed. "Don't suppose you've got some gammaspace shades and a smoke grenade?"

An attractive Spider grin, shades of that personality cult showing. "Your wish is my 'hell, yeah'."

Dragonfly stood, dusting his hands clean. "Doesn't sound that hard to me. Let's go."

16

I strutted up to the garrison's front desk, my glossy black marine officer's uniform tight and smooth around my body. It felt strange to be back in uniform. The tight diagonal clips across the front pushed my breasts up, the firm high collar making me lift my chin. My hair was braided tightly under my cap, and the pins itched. I hadn't asked where Spider found the uniform. Better not to know. The one-piece was a bit big around the butt, but with my shorts on underneath—stripping off in Spider's seedy hotel room? Not an option—it fit okay. And the boots made me taller. It was nice to be tall.

Besides, I was the only one among us who could pass for military. Dreadlocks weren't exactly marine regulation, Foxy and the other kid were both too skinny or too insane, and the look I got when I suggested Dragonfly cut his hair could have melted ultraglass. Vanity. Who knew?

I halted in front of the desk sergeant, my breath tight. Dragonfly slouched beside me, bleary-eyed, his hair tousled like I'd dragged him out of bed. He wore a dusty grey coverall, and carried an armful of tangled techie tools, with wire and a welder and a pair of brass synapse colliders sticking out.

The young sergeant popped me a crisp salute. "Ma'am."

"Sergeant." My best ultra-Russiyan tone, clipped and efficient. "Major Kovalova, admiral's aide. Emergency repairs to climate control. Security grid access, please."

I flipped him my fake marine ident, trying to stay casual. Another Dragonfly creation, cooked up with Spider's rusty copykit. It even had my picture etched into the glass, just a still. I'd ignored Spider's gleeful suggestion that we make our own porn film while we had the lasercam out.

The sergeant glanced at it with swift blue eyes. "Ma'am, yes, ma'am. It's zero-four-fifteen. This isn't routine, ma'am?"

"I did say emergency."

"Ma'am, I'm sorry, but I'm going to have to call for authorization, ma'am."

He reached for his etherwave contact. Trust us to find the only efficacious Imperial soldier on the station.

I slapped my palm on the desk, impatient. "Look, sergeant, I commend your enthusiasm for regulations, but Miss Verenskaya called my direct line. The aircon's unserviceable in her apartment. She's freezing in there, and I think the scrubbers are malfunctioning. We don't have all night. You want to wake the admiral at zero-four-bloody-early to tell him you won't fix his daughter's airflow? Be my guest."

He hesitated, and I offered a tight Russiyan smile and leaned closer. "The admiral made Miss Verenskaya's comfort my responsibility. I'd like to resolve this quickly and quietly. You'd be doing me a personal favor, sergeant. I won't forget it."

He bit his lip and kept his gaze down. I did look good in uniform. "Ma'am. Who's the techgrub, ma'am?"

Dragonfly fidgeted, and I snickered inwardly. "The best I could find at 4 a.m., sergeant. Don't worry, I'll keep him on a tight leash."

At last, he cracked a smile. "Ma'am. Glad to be of service, ma'am."

He slid two fingers over the door control, lifting the metal security shield with an electromagnetic hiss, and we were in.

As the shield grated downwards and clunked tightly into the floor behind us, Dragonfly whispered, "If that kid says 'ma'am' one more time, I'll hit him. You liked that, didn't you?"

"It's no more than I deserve." Still, my pulse quickened. Had I been too convincing as a marine? Lazuli was a good actress, but ...

He leaned closer. "Can't blame him. You're sexy in uniform. I'm intimidated."

His gaze caressed my prominent chest and slipped lower. I tried not to notice the way my body reacted, my nipples tightening as though I were naked. It was just proximity and danger, the fight-or-fuck reflex. He'd be more than intimidated if I showed him my real rank. "Eyes on the job, tech-grub."

"Oh, they are."

I flushed and didn't reply. The way he flirted at inappropriate moments reminded me of Nikita. Except Nikita did it to test me, to put me off my guard when we were in danger, because he liked having the upper hand. Dragonfly ... well, he seemed to do it for fun. Like he meant it.

My fingers curled tight. He was a good liar. But so was I.

The consoles we needed lay along a short atom-lit corridor, the little orange globes glowing steadily. All seemed quiet, the majority of the marines on their rest shift.

I nudged him as we hurried along. "So why'd you change your mind?"

"About what?"

"Playing Spider's little game."

He glanced at me, inscrutable once more. "Should I have let him shoot you?"

"You don't know me."

He laughed, like I'd said something funny. "All the more reason. Yes, I've done my time as Lukas's conscience, and no, I don't want to sign up again. Doesn't mean it's worth a life."

Very convincing. He probably practiced those lies in front of a mirror.

I tried another angle. "So why am I really here?"

"Told you. Backup."

"You don't trust me, you mean."

"If I tricked my way onto your ship and kept asking too many questions, would you trust me?"

I snorted, and kept silent. But his sharp insight made my spine tingle. He'd been thinking about me then. About Lazuli, I corrected. About who she was, why she was with him, what she could possibly want. That was good. And he didn't seem fazed by how easily she'd slipped into Major Kovalova's skin, either. He was starting to think well of her. Even better.

We passed another soldier, and she and I exchanged salutes. The movement felt strange and natural at the same time, and nostalgia twinged my nerves. Military life was so simple. Orders to follow, schedules to meet, someone to tell you what to do. I missed that. At the same time, the idea of returning to it chafed at me. At Axis, you're allowed to use your brain, even if the chances of getting it blown out are high.

And this life of Dragonfly's was the same: fast, smart, on the edge. Counter-insurrection's warped reflection. Same tricks, different side, only the danger was greater because the enemy were everywhere. It excited me, like my job at Axis used to excite me before Mishka died.

Pity for Dragonfly he didn't have much of his life left.

The console room door had a glass eyescanner for entry. Dragonfly flipped out his golden hyperchip and slapped it against the scanner's metal edge. A little magnet clicked. Green light flashed over the curved glass, scanning an imaginary retina, and the hyperchip glowed white, spoofing the data. A red diode flashed, and the door popped open.

I quirked an appreciative eyebrow. "Nice."

He flashed a smile as he tucked the hyperchip into his pocket. "Isn't it? Beats emergency eyeball surgery, anyway."

"Is there anything that chip doesn't do?"

"Sure. Wind back time. Let's get on with it."

We hurried inside and I shut the door. We didn't have much time. Any moment, that helpful sergeant might decide he'd better call the admiral after all.

***

The narrow room was backlit with dim green spotlights to soothe the neural circuits, the air warm and damp. A bank of climate-control instruments lined one wall, the security console on the other: a flat, green-skinned neurospace panel with some old metal receptors and a cracked glass display. In the ceiling, the laser grid buzzed faintly, like the one on Esperanza except twenty years older, monitoring body temperature, movement, sound in the rooms below it, checking system-wide that all the doors were functioning, all the circuits lay unbroken, and no one was doing exactly what we were about to do. I could hear old contacts shorting out. Obviously they didn't update their kit very often. Good for us. Bad for them.

I wiped my damp face. Dragonfly had already untangled his tool bundle and was fiddling with the console, the security overrides flashing encrypted gibberish on the screen as he wired the receptors together with stealthcoated synapses.

The counter-crypto analyst in me was impressed. Hotwiring with pseudo-organics: nice way to fool an old neuroconsole like this one at short notice, seeing as he hadn't had time to re-code his hyperchip for the job. Crude, but effective, if your hands were steady enough.

"Where'd you learn to do that?"

"New Moskva Tech."

"You're kidding."

He swiped a loose lock of hair behind his ear. "Of course I'm kidding. Look like Imperial curriculum to you?"

My curiosity itched. You didn't learn hyperalgebra from pirate newscasts or terrorists' bomb-making manuals. "So where did you graduate, then?"

A laugh. "Study, yes. Graduate, not exactly."

"How come? Fail your exams?"

"Hardly." He twisted the end of another fleshy synapse and eased it into a metal receptor slot partly overgrown with pale green skin. "I got in trouble too much. They said, how about you finish your research in the navy and get re-educated, you separatist scumbag? I said, no thanks. Magically, I lost my place. They don't like troublemakers in their alumni."

"Who?"

"Everyone." A receptor zapped, sparks flashing, and he swore and ripped the burned synapse away. "Get me the atomglow potential, please."

"Sorry, what?" I'd been too busy watching his fingers move. So gentle and precise, soothing the neurospace into submission. I'd seen him do the same on Esperanza. What would it feel like, that thoughtful caress?

He pointed at the climate-control panels behind him, his gaze fixed on his synapses. "Screen on the left is the energy distributor for life support. Find me the atomglow channels so I can cut the current. A little slow, aren't you?"

Chastened, I popped the display on. Power grids and neuroplasma channels sprang into the air, projected in glowing green light. Space is dark, cold and empty, so a basic LSS has three functions: light, heat and air. Atomglow—it's a controlled fusion reaction—is more efficient than a straight photonic system because it makes both heat and light, and it's perfect for space stations because there's lots of room for fuel, and there's already plenty of radiation in space, so the byproducts don't matter. Just put the heater vents in line before the air scrubbers and you can't go wrong.

I fingered my way through the controls, lights flashing. "Atomglow channels? Are we gonna put the lights out?"

"Give the lady a prize. But we'll cut the emergency power and the laser grid first. When they go out, they'll stay out."

Glowing figures scrolled over my fingers. "Wait a sec ... got it. Uh ... there's a current differential here. The lights must already be turned down in the girl's quarters. But they're on in the corridor and at the guardposts."

"Won't wake her up then, will we?" He slotted his last synapse and bio-diodes flashed green. Now the console looked like an old etherwave exchange, connecting wires sprouting everywhere.

He scraped his hair back, sweating in the humidity. "Okay. Emergency power draining. Laser grid is checking ... Oops, the junction is hotwired. Emergency power looks fine, nothing to see here. Let's have a little radiation flood in the gammaspace band for later ..." He finessed a contact, stroking the neurospace skin gently, his voice mild and melodic like he was lulling a child to sleep. "There we go. Lazuli, if you wouldn't mind winding that atomglow current back a couple of dozen micros, *por favor.*"

I traced my finger along the glowing green power column, dragging it downwards. In the corner of the display, digits flickered, and the power column flashed orange.

"*Es perfecto.* Power's dropping. Laser grid thinks it's compensating ... *un poco mas,* thanks."

He still thought in Espan. Interesting. I dialed it back another notch or two, into the red zone.

"Not too much ... *está bien*. And ... we have collapse." He ripped out a synapse and tossed it away, and above our heads current popped and zapped silent. "Laser grid off. And magnetic field failure ... now. Time?"

I checked my counter. Five seconds until Spider's timecheck. Trust Dragonfly to be minute-perfect. "Three ... two ... one ... mark."

He severed another synapse. "Magclamp doorlocks open. And ... lights out. That's it."

He threw me a charming grin, dust drifting from his hair in the neurospace's green glow. "Nice job, techgrub."

"Yourself." I grabbed the boltcutters and cut the exposed power conduit with a bang and a shower of sparks. We'd already given ourselves away. No point making it easy for them to fix. "Let's get out of here."

"After you." He pulled his gammaspace shades down over his eyes, like ultrafine UV glasses with smoky lenses.

I did the same, blanketing the room in shadow, and we kicked our gear under the console and ran.

17

In the corridor, it was dark as space. Blindness swamped me. Shouts and orders rang out in the thick blackness, marines trying to get organized and figure out what had happened.

I stumbled over a jutting bulkhead, and Dragonfly fumbled for my arm. "Let there be light," he whispered, and snapped open the portable gammaspace link he'd spent all those hours building on *Ladrona*.

Static crackled blue on my shades as the remote interface lit up, and my vision glimmered red. Purple shadows loomed, the sharp edges of bulkheads and doorways glittering like bloody ice. Stray current arcing up from the gravity engines six stories below us flickered like tiny lightning strikes in the walls and floor, and the air sparkled with charged particles shedding their own tiny gammawave radiation. I grinned. It was the same as the station's approach grid, though not as sophisticated. Invisible ionized wavelengths revealed by gammaspace shades. Now we could see while everyone else fumbled blind. This was fun.

Dragonfly grabbed my hand and we ran. In the garrison entry corridor, soldiers stumbled in the dark, feeling their way. The security shield had opened when we switched off the magnetics, and we dashed through.

Somewhere behind me, a flashlight pierced the dark, and someone shouted. "There they are!"

Took them long enough.

I slotted Spider's smoke grenade into my marine regulation pistol, aimed high over my shoulder and fired. Crack. The ceiling splintered, charged metal edges glittering, and white smoke particles scattered, a diffuse cloud that made the flashlight useless. But in gammaspace, the charge in the smoke particles sizzled and faded like melting snowfall, leaving our way clear.

Muffled cursing rang out, and sweet smoke tickled my throat as we ran.

I'd asked Dragonfly why the marines wouldn't have gammaspace shades too, rendering our shelter ineffective.

"They're too dumb," he'd replied.

Seemed he was right, and for a moment I exulted in being on the better, cleverer, more efficient side.

Except this wasn't my side. We were the bad guys, and we were slipping past Imperial security with no more trouble than a kid playing hide-and-seek. The marines were well-trained and prepared, but they couldn't think of everything. Sometimes, all it took to be a criminal was the guts to try it.

Reluctant admiration warmed my blood. I'd thought maybe Dragonfly had tried to defy Spider because he was afraid. I was wrong. He'd talked as if this'd be simple as freefall, and it turned out the cocky son of a spaceworm could back it up. Damn.

Out in the corridor, Spider had already fired his smoke grenade, and the gammaspace radiation flood we'd made was doing its job. Glowing red metal edges guided us down the corridor like a shuttlecraft runway's lights, and we ran past looming bulkheads and storage compartments to the remote guardpost.

The door to the girl's apartment already stood half-open, magnetic locks broken and shiny metal clamps exposed. Spider loomed out of the smoke, dark shades gleaming across his eyes. On the red-glittered metal floor, three marines lay senseless or dead, degrading bio-current crackling like blue webs over their skin.

I swallowed, angry. I hadn't heard shots. Spider was clever enough not to give the other marines something to run toward. Too fucking clever. I wanted to punch his grinning face.

Dragonfly just looked at him and shook his head.

Together, we pushed the heavy steel door aside on its rollers and entered the apartment. White matte plastic walls decorated with flowers and bright-daubed art. A pile of glass books and a fluffy white teddy bear lay scattered on the low table, and beside the plastic autoclave in the kitchenette, take-out dishes lay untrashed. Fridge, mirror, dark glass movie display set into the floor, pink and white cushions on the sunken lounge, popcorn spilling from two creased boxes. A white daybed sat under an oblong clearview, stars shining steadily beyond the number three docking arm, the scaffolding stretching out into space. The heater was on high, warm air scintillating in gammaspace with the ionized scent of sweet perfume. A girl's room.

Spider hadn't mentioned she was such a *little* girl.

The side exit was half-open, its maglocks disabled too, and Foxy strode in through a cloud of smoke with a chunky black laser rifle slung low at her bony hip. Dragonfly dragged the main door shut behind us and jammed the shiny cylindrical plasma charge from his pistol between the locking contacts. Current flashed orange, and the contacts hissed and melted, welding together. He snatched his singed hand away and the electromagnets snapped on with a steely clunk that gripped the door tight. Temporary, but good enough.

I looked over my shoulder, alarmed. "What are you doing? How are we meant to get out?"

"Not that way, I guess. No point giving them options." He holstered his crippled pistol.

An open doorway led to the bedroom. Already Spider and Foxy had gone ahead, and I heard a thump and a muffled squeal before Spider strode out, dragging a girl in a white silk nightdress.

She kicked and struggled, her yells strangled by his hand over her mouth. Golden hair tumbled over her pretty young face, ionized blue eyes wide with shock. No gammaspace shades for her, and even the nightlights were out. She couldn't see, and she was terrified. She didn't look more than thirteen or fourteen. Her long slender legs were only half-covered by the sparkling static-charged nightdress.

She wriggled and kicked, but Spider held her like a doll, the ugly steel disruptor he pressed against her temple putting an end to any ideas she might have had of calling for help. I didn't like her chances of making it out of this unbruised. But if I acted squeamish, they'd just cut me loose. My mission was more important.

I shook my head, pretending disgust. "A little young for you, isn't she?"

The girl jumped at my voice. My words could have been more comforting, but at least now she knew there was another woman in the room.

"Old enough for what I want." Spider snapped his disruptor into its thighclip and pulled her to her feet, his big hand still plastered over her mouth. She stood, shivering.

Dragonfly waved his hand, irritated. "*Madre de dios.* At least let her put some clothes on."

But Foxy was already emerging from the bedroom holding a bundle. She swiftly wrapped the girl in a long brown coat and forced some shoes onto her feet.

Voices rang closer in the corridor beyond the side exit. Foxy shouldered her rifle, taking aim with her pierced lips thinned. "They're coming. Get on."

Spider pulled the girl backward against his chest in a rough embrace, and from a tiny pocket on his thigh he slipped a shimmering hypodermic clip. "Hang on now, Natasha." His whisper was musical, comforting, and all the scarier because of it. "We're taking a little ride. Sweet dreams."

And he stabbed her in the neck, glowing green fluid draining from the vial. She crumpled in his arms, asleep.

I shivered. I totally believed everything I'd read about Spider. His matter-of-fact carelessness gave me the creeps. Foxy, too, with her cold demeanor and vacant eyes, as if she felt nothing but adoration for Spider and hatred for everything else. On the whole, I preferred Dragonfly.

Great. What was this, terrorist aversion therapy? Now the murdering maggot was the nice one?

Dragonfly hopped up onto the low table and held out his hand to me. "Let's get out of here."

In a flash I understood. The docking arm lay directly above us. Spider's two minutes had just gotten shorter. I tossed him my plasma pistol, and swiftly he slashed a wide molten gash in the plastic ceiling and tore a section down. Current sputtered weakly like water, broken lasermirrors flashing in the cavity.

"Grid's still down," he said. "Can you make it through that hole?"

I skipped up beside him to look. He caught my waist to steady me, and the pistol's sharp edges jabbed into my ribs. It was still warm. His body was warm, too, where his hip pressed casually into mine, resulting in an unreasonable amount of thigh-to-thigh contact. I swallowed, his spicy scent drying my mouth. The smoky shades covered his eyes and I couldn't read his expression, but he still felt pretty good, even if he was faking the rest of it. "Huh? I mean, yeah, I can make it. Can you ... umm ..."

That annoyingly sweet smile. "After you, Major." He gripped my foot and heaved me upward.

I jumped and caught the edge of the hole. The mirrored edges of the deactivated laser grid slipped in my sweaty palms, but I held on and hauled myself into the ceiling cavity.

I rolled over to sit up, my biceps aching. Power conduits and glittering glass laser channels lined the plastic ceiling under my butt, and water pipes gurgled overhead, bolted to the steel girders of the station proper. Ahead, outlined in sparkling red gammaspace current, the vast docking arm connected to the station shell, with a huge array of welded scaffolding and safety bolts designed to split the docking arm off in an emergency, their charges coated in silvery stealthplate shields to ward off hackers.

I peered down just as Spider tossed Dragonfly a shiny metal cylinder as long and as thick as my arm. Dragonfly set it beneath me and popped the top off, and a fine steel ladder unfolded from inside, building itself joint by nanospliced joint until I could reach down and grab the top rung.

Bootsteps clunked outside the door, and a shout rang out. "Miss Verenskaya, ma'am? Sit tight. You're safe."

Wrong.

I hooked the ladder over a ceiling strut and the nanomachines aligned with a sharp click, snapping it rigid. "It's solid."

"Okay, let's skip it." Dragonfly held out his hands to take the girl.

Spider lighted up the ladder, nifty for such a big guy. I crawled aside and he squeezed through the hole, his massive shoulders scraping the sides. Once he was in, he reached down to drag up the insensible girl.

Foxy next, reaching down for Dragonfly to pass up her rifle. A red-hot shot sizzled, and halfway up the ladder, Dragonfly cursed.

I scrambled to the edge, risking a look. Another plasma round hit the ladder and flared, metal dripping, and Dragonfly hissed and let go, teetering a couple of meters above the floor. My heart lurched. I dived over, reaching down. Plasma flashed, singeing the hairs on my arm.

He grabbed my hand, fingers locking around my wrist. I pulled, muscles aching, and he scrambled up the last few rungs using me as a handhold. Just as he reached the top, the nanoladder shuddered and liquefied, hot metal pouring in globs to the floor.

He rolled over in my lap, panting. "Thanks. That's another one I owe you."

"Forget it."

I struggled to recover, my pulse still alight. His hair spilled over my thighs and I wanted to run my fingers through it. He felt warm, human, real. Not distant and faceless. My guts twisted. I didn't want his gratitude. I couldn't let his sweet façade fool me. It was all an act. It had to be. He wasn't a beginner at this. It was all too easy for him, fiddling old neurosystems and unlocking doors. Put him under pressure—more pressure than a few marines trying to shoot us in the dark—and he'd show his true colors.

It wasn't like I cared about him dying, or that him saving me from Spider was worth anything. If I let him get killed, I was screwed, and I didn't want to be alone on Spider's ship.

But no time to get pissy with him now. Already Spider had dragged the girl over one shoulder, her blonde hair bouncing, and was running toward the docking arm. I scrambled up and followed, not looking back. But Dragonfly was there behind me, I knew it. I could smell him. I could feel him, laughing at me.

Foxy kicked open a corroded maintenance hatch, and we hustled through one by one into the docking corridor. Icelights glared on a metal walkway that stretched for what looked like kilometers between rows of rad-burned airlocks capped with keypads. The starfield shone warped behind the dirty glass ceiling, tethered machinery hanging silent and still in space. I tore off my gammaspace shades and shoved them in my jacket as we ran, squinting in the harsh light.

More plasma shots hissed around us. Molten holes dripped in the metal walls, flames licking. Foxy vaulted the railing at the second airlock and stabbed in an access code. Air hissed and the soot-blackened glass groaned aside. She bolted in, and Spider followed, ducking his head.

The marines advanced, half a platoon of them, all armed with plasma. Dragonfly and I dived over the railing and rolled, molten shots arcing over us with that special *schllpp*! noise that meant we were well within lethal range.

Dragonfly crouched against the wall and reached up to rip the cover off the entry console. "Cover me."

"Oh, sure. With what?" I grabbed back the pistol he'd taken from me and aimed for just above the point guy's head, letting off a few quick shots in warning. Great. Shooting at marines. Hell, I'd done worse to keep my cover, but it didn't feel good. And the bastards just kept shooting back.

A bolt seared though the railing and slammed into the wall above my head. I ducked, red-hot metal dripping. "What are you doing?"

"Daisy-chaining the airlock system so they can't follow." Dragonfly tapped keys furiously. "At least not from this docking arm. Should buy us some time. There. Now burn it."

I whirled and fired at the keypad from point-blank range. Sparks showered, setting off a chain of exploding keypads along the docking arm, and together we dived through the airlock a second before the glass door slammed shut.

The equalizer hissed, but the pressure was already at equilibrium and the door at the other end popped open. We dashed through, first Foxy, then Spider and the girl, then me and Dragonfly.

I clipped my pistol and hopped up the rippled metal ladder, Spider's rear end in tight urban combat trousers right in front of my face. A not entirely unpleasant view. No doubt Dragonfly was getting a similar eyeful of my butt, again. Always the last to leave. How gallant. Hadn't stopped him killing hundreds to save himself on Urumki.

I shivered as I climbed, remembering how Nikita always acted strong and incorruptible until the moment it suited him to screw you over. Maybe Dragonfly had something wrong with his brain too. Something that made him think he was brave and self-sacrificing and always did the right thing, that the bad things that always happened around him weren't his fault. It's called narcissistic blindness, a pathological form of denial. The kind of sickness that makes you fit right in at black ops. A lot of really smart people have it to some degree.

But no time to pop-psych Dragonfly now. I pushed him from my thoughts as I scrambled through the hatch onto the warm metal deck of Spider's shuttlecraft.

It had a long cylindrical interior, ribbed metal walls and benches with dropship harnesses like a short-range Imperial troop transport. Already the arc rockets were charged, the stardrive humming. Spider dumped the senseless girl on a bench without breaking stride.

Foxy racked her rifle, fastened a steel-belted strap around the girl's waist, and grabbed a swinging handhold. "Grab on," she said. "It'll be a bumpy ride."

Dragonfly and I found a handle each and held on. Spider's pimple-cheeked accomplice with the porcupine hair was already strapped into the cockpit's starboard command chair, his pox-scarred hands alight on the controls. The ship tugged and rocked, waiting for release.

Spider took the port chair and clipped the harness tight. "Crack us off, Lux," he ordered.

Porcupine Boy punched a control with his fist. The magclamps banged open, and with a crackle of overheated arcfuel we hurtled away from Vyachesgrad.

My feet slipped, inertia dragging me backward, and I hung on tight. The station receded in the tiny rear clearview, the docking arm strangely silent and dark. No pursuit. Whatever Dragonfly had done to the keypad, it had worked.

We careened around a pulsing beacon on a screech of rocketfire and shot off into the starfield, missing an incoming minifreighter by meters. Porcupine Boy—Lux—was either expert or suicidal. No points for guessing which.

I peered out the clearview, watching for reaction. Blue lights pulsed along the adjacent docking arm, and two pairs of shiny Sliver fighters detached, their shardlike metal fuselages designed for slipspace precision and stealth. They also had hyperfueled ion drives and the arc rocket array from hell, maneuvering in four dimensions with ease, and direct neural contact between pilot and navset. Not to mention arclight torpedoes that crawled up your butt like hungry suckerfish. Nikita flew one—don't ask where he got it—and it ripped up the sky like a monster.

"They're coming," I yelled, so the cockpit could hear me over the howling arc rockets. "Four of them. Evasive maneuvers might be nice."

But we didn't change course. Just kept hurtling for the stars, a nice inviting straight line. The Slivers circled and spread in a tangential attack trajectory, splitting their arrival time by seconds to avoid crossfire, but all aiming for a single central point. Us. And we'd never reach slip velocity in time, not in this ship.

Dragonfly nudged me with his elbow, hanging on tight. "Don't sweat it. Just watch."

If he wanted to trust a bunch of lunatics, that was his funeral.

I ran up to the cockpit, the uncalibrated gravmotors pulling me left and right as we accelerated. Lux manipulated six arc rockets with his left hand to keep us on course, forcing the power past safe maximum with the right. Sweat ran from his spiky brown hair. I peered over his shoulder. The console showed empty space ahead. He didn't even have the attack sensors on.

"What, are you crazy?"

Spider ignored me and grabbed the etherwave, monitoring the seconds ticking over on the console timer. Thirty-nine, forty, forty-one.

"*LightBringer,* time four-nine, flash it," he ordered.

The ion drives shuddered, picking up speed. Forty-five, forty-six.

Ahead, a Sliver right-angled and hurtled toward us, stealthplate shining in the station spotlights. Our sensors weren't on, but I could almost hear the fighter's weapons powering up, torpedoes charging, targeting systems aflame.

Forty-seven. I swallowed, sweating. Forty-eight. Forty-nine.

And beside us, on a parallel trajectory almost close enough to touch, a monstrous black battleship dropped out of slipspace like a falling rock.

It dwarfed us, a curving hawk-like shell with massive black side fins underslung with torpedo tubes sweeping back from a sharp hooked nose to an angular stern crusted with radshield debris. A vicious bird of prey, built by the Empire to kill.

The Sliver jerked upward to avoid a collision, and hurtled off in a directionless arc like shining silver shrapnel. The battleship shuddered and course-corrected, speed dampers kicking in.

"Lock and load." Lux jammed his fist on the magnetics. Diodes flashed red. The shuttlecraft jerked sideways, and we slammed against the battleship's hull and stuck there. Current zapped, electromagnets holding us fast. My teeth shuddered, metal clanging in my ears.

"Contact," Spider snapped on the etherwave, and we yanked forward, propelled on the battleship's mighty acceleration.

I staggered back. Our stardrive howled and sputtered, unable to match such a vicious turn of speed. Transition velocity flashed on the console. The floor shuddered and warmed, the battleship's drives arcing hot. The air glowed scarlet as wavelengths warped and stretched, and, like a cosmic light switch, slipspace plunged the clearview into blackness.

18

Localized magnetics flipped our shuttlecraft into the nearest loading bay, where warm atomlights shone like suns, glaring off blackmetal walls hung with electric radshield scrubbers like giant welders and ammunition loaders the size of small houses. The massive airlock doors ground shut, blocking out the uncanny blackness of slipspace. The atmosphere equalized with a thump and a hiss, our ion-charged hull spitting sparks.

When the pressure alarm blinked out, I untwisted the steel-radial strap from my aching wrist and followed the others out. All six of us—Lux, Foxy Lady, Dragonfly, me, and Spider with the girl over his shoulder—crammed into one blackglass elevator, and Lux hit the flat red button for the battledeck.

The navy don't voice-activate as a primary on battlecraft any more. It's too unreliable. One dirty sensor or dented receptor and you lose functionality. But you can beat the shit out of those old metal buttons and they still work. Sometimes, simple is best.

Instinctively, I noted the shape of the doors as they hissed shut, memorized the configuration of levels on the schematic diagram, counted in my mind the rows of plasma fuel conduits I'd seen in the loading bay. A Raven-class battleship, third generation. The latest, deadliest Imperial hardware, worth five hundred million sols. I wondered how Spider replaced his coolants, where he found torpedoes and charges for his weapons. Half those plasma conduits had been drained, bare metal showing through the ultraplastic inspection ports. His crew didn't look well fed, let alone fully armed.

Stopping the rebels from provisioning is a core Axis strategy. It's not sexy, but it's effective, and we infiltrate more insurrectionist cells with dodgy supply deals than we do with any other tactic. Which made stealing a full-armor battleship either suicidally reckless or criminally insane. I swallowed, licking sticky lips. For me, the odds were still even between those two.

No one spoke as we ascended, motors whirring. Foxy fiddled with her rifle, eyes downcast. Lux flicked sweat from his porcupine hair. Spider hummed to himself, some melancholy melody that stretched my nerves, and Dragonfly flipped his hyperchip, his gaze dark, never a sign things were going well.

I wanted to pace, rake my hair loose, crack my aching neck. I was still wearing the major's uniform, tight and rigid around my chest. The air humidifiers were running on overdrive in here, and the thick hot-metal stink of stardrive maddened me. How in space did I get here? I was supposed to be luring Dragonfly to his doom, not kidnapping admirals' daughters. If this Natasha got hurt, I'd have to answer to Director Renko for it. But I couldn't let my cover slip now. If Spider found out who I was, I'd die slow and dirty. And I'd already used up my share of Dragonfly's goodwill.

Get a plan, Aragon. Nikita's voice stung in my memory, from long ago when he was my mentor and every word he spoke was gold. *Act, don't react. Take charge. Don't let the circumstances dictate your actions. Impose your plan on the circumstances. Act like you own the world and the world will fall into line.*

Resolution forged like steel in my spine. I'd do my best to keep the girl safe, but my mission came first. Get me and Dragonfly off this ship, back to *Ladrona* and on with the business. Dragonfly might be a mass murderer, but unlike Spider he wasn't psychotically violent from minute to minute, so if I could get Natasha off with us, so much the better. If not ...

The elevator door slipped open, and we walked onto *LightBringer*'s bridge.

It stretched in a wide black-and-silver curve around the ship's forward bulkheads, two decks high and as deep. Icelights shed a white chill on silvery septurium instruments and glossy black panels. A virtual viewscreen illuminated the entire length of the shuttered clearview, showing sensor imagery, a glowing green web of slipspace beacons, exit trajectories, frequencies. In full battle mode, the virtual display would cover all the walls as well as floor and ceiling, giving a 3D, 360-degree battlespace view far beyond visual range.

Engine data danced in flowing red columns from floor to ceiling, and the slipfield generators hummed quiet and smooth somewhere far below. We were hurtling through slipspace, untrackable and untraceable. No way the Slivers could pursue us with any precision now.

At the back by the elevators sat instrument banks with rows of tiny readouts: on the left, life support; on the right, engineering. Two rows of curved black consoles faced the front, split in the middle by the raised command walkway to form four workstations: comms, tactics, two for nav. Just like on any Imperial battleship.

The similarity ended there. Grime crusted the glossy black consoles, like they hadn't been cleaned for months, and the comms station was littered with food wrappers and someone's half-eaten lunch on a cracked metal tray. The place stank of junk food and hot steel. Stuff piled in the corners: stacks of weapon parts and atomcharges and crates of engine components I didn't recognize. Some of the readouts and a few icelights were smashed or melted, like there'd been a firefight, and a section of the flashscarred ceiling was missing. Beside the elevator, the crypto safe lay broken open, bolts sheared, the plastic capsules crushed and discarded on the floor.

LightBringer. A parody of an Imperial name. Spider had a twisted sense of humor.

A huge black-and-white cat crouched under the primary nav seat, its piebald coat twitching, and in the chair slouched a wiry red-headed kid in shorts and a ripped blue shirt, his long bare feet propped on the navspace console like he was sunning himself on a beach.

He glanced at Spider as we stepped from the elevator, still catching our breath. "Took you long enough," he said, and returned to his dented plastic book.

"Likewise. When I say 'flash it', I mean flash it, not show up next week." Spider dumped the admiral's daughter in the comms chair, dragging her lolling head upright.

"Bite me. Who's she?" Beach Bum jerked his pointy nose at me without looking up.

"Fresh meat," said Spider, grinning at me. "Sasha's got himself a *girlfriend.* Eww."

I cleared my throat. "It's Lazuli."

"You like cats?" Beach Bum said, still reading, flicking pages rapidly, his gaze jerking back and forth. Speed-reading. Obviously a quick mind. I committed his face to memory as best I could, filing it away with the others. Intel was never wasted.

"Sure." When I was a girl, cats were food, and the mangy critters skittered away whenever they saw us. And these days, my job meant I was never home. But Mishka had liked cats, and we'd talked about getting one. We'd talked about a lot of things that didn't end up happening.

"I'm Vish. This is Gus. You can rub his belly if you want." The kid tickled under the monster cat's chin, and the glaring beast meowed.

I sidled up to scratch the vast expanse of fur. Gus purred threateningly, sizing me up with one mean, scarred eye.

Vish grinned. "Gus says you're okay."

"What a relief." I glanced at the console, piled with books and discarded food packaging. A battleship's navspace was normally set up for two pilots. Single crew was difficult, unless you could do about eight things at once. It seemed Spider attracted the talented crazies. "You fly this by yourself?"

"Sure." Vish scratched his sharp red nose, bloodshot blue eyes rolling in opposite directions. "What you want I should do with the other hand?"

Lux mimed spewing with his finger down his throat, and Foxy snorted. "Who knew you could jerk off left-handed?"

Vish's florid face flushed even brighter, and privately I sighed. More shipboard heartbreak. Not in this universe, skinny boy. She's dreaming about a handsome, muscled-up terrorist asshole, and only half of those words describe you.

Spider shoved Vish's shoulder, artfully oblivious. "Stop showing off, Vishnayev. I told you, the new girl's taken, and Sasha's is way bigger than yours."

Vish giggled. "You mean his brain, right?"

"Not my ego, that's for sure." Dragonfly shook dust from his hair and stripped his boilersuit off, then rolled it and tossed it in the corner. He was still dressed in grey and black underneath—not that I was looking. "Hello, Vish. Now can we get on with this? I'm a little stretched for time."

I pulled the pins from my hair and unclipped my uniform, stretching my neck with relief as the tight collar peeled away from my throat. I hadn't actually thought about how we'd get back to *Ladrona* now that the whole station was on alert. In any case, what now? Spider had trapped his bait. Would he call the admiral for ransom? Or make the poor man suffer a while?

Spider poked the girl in the chest, but she didn't move. "Foxy Lady, come deal, can you?"

Foxy slung her rifle and pulled out another hypodermic clip. She yanked up the girl's coat sleeve and pressed the clip into her arm, and the girl spluttered and jerked awake, her face green like airsickness.

"Wh … what? Where am I?" She pushed herself up, staring around her and shivering, like the bridge was the jungle and we were the beasts.

"Hello, Natasha." Spider dragged her back down by one arm. "We're your new friends. Sit down and shut up, and I'll play nice. Piss me off and I'll forget the nice part. Okay?"

He snapped a smartcuff against her slender wrist. The flat metal coil unfolded and wrapped itself tight. He guided the other end around the console strut, and the metal melded itself seamlessly together, tough, flexible and unbreakable.

Natasha struggled, blonde hair tangling in her face. "You can't do this to me! Let me go, you dumb Britsky oaf!" Her accent was New Russiya boarding school, affected and snooty. Queen of the rich girls. Not in her favor on this ship.

Lux and Foxy grinned at each other. "Ten seconds to impact," Lux said.

At the nav console, Vish snickered, nose in his book. "Five, more like."

Spider rubbed his big palms together, dangerously calm. "I'm sorry, what?"

Natasha yanked at her cuff, furious. "I said, you can't do this to me! Let me go at once! Do you know who I am?"

"Huh?" Spider blinked, playing stupid.

I squirmed. *Look around you, girl. Shut your mouth before you get hurt.*

But she glared at him, girlish breasts heaving. No doubt she thought herself so brave and romantic. I wished she'd put all that skin away. Lesson one in talking down a crazy: don't get him thinking about his dick. Not unless you're prepared to follow through.

She tossed her haughty head. "I'll have you know my father is a very important man. You don't want to cross him. He won't stand for this—ugh!"

Spider caught her by the hair, dragged her face close. His thick biceps bulged, and that golden crazy-light swirled in his eyes. "Newsflash, Natasha Pyotrova Verenskaya. This dumb Britsky oaf won't stand for *his* shit." She whimpered and struggled, but he held her, staring into her eyes. "Wanna see? Want me to show you how I play, you snotty rich bitch? You ain't seen nothing like me before."

I stepped forward, alarmed. Clearly, she'd jammed her finger firmly on Spider's buttons. Was it just the accent, the stupid rich-girl attitude? Or something else? "Hey, look, don't harm the merchandise—"

But Dragonfly was quicker. He appeared at Spider's side—how did he move like that?—and grabbed one thick leatherbuckled wrist, light but firm. "Let it go, Lukas."

Spider snarled, trying to shake him off. "What the fuck do you care?"

Dragonfly held on, calm. "Let me handle it. She's nothing. A brainwashed kid. Break her now and you'll lose everything. Save your *loco* for *el almirante*, no?"

Spider gritted his teeth and stalked away. He vaulted up onto the command platform to plant his *loco* in the chair and glower.

Natasha giggled, terrified, and Foxy scowled and reached for her rifle. "Shut it, you stupid little tart."

"Relax, Foxy." Dragonfly leaned over the girl, resting his hands on her chair's arms. "Listen to me, *hija*. Are you listening?"

I held my breath. Time to show your colors, Sasha, or whatever your name is.

She shrank away, trembling. He didn't follow her. Just fixed her with a steady stare. "You're thinking you've landed on a ship full of dangerous lunatics, yes?"

She nodded, eyes wide.

"Well, you're right." His brown eyes glittered bright and hard. "Think you can figure us out? Make us play your game? You can't. You're dirt to us. A waste of space. Filth in our air scrubbers. So don't fuck with us. *Entiendes*?"

Unconsciously, she licked dry lips. "I—"

"Shut up." He jammed his finger roughly over her mouth, and there wasn't an atom of compassion in his tone. "Don't waste your brainwashing on me. I'm not the nice one. We don't have a nice one, get it? You know what I'd really like to do to you, you useless little bitch?"

She shook her head.

"Use your imagination, then." He thumbed her chin, his voice a velvety threat. "Are you using it?"

Tears sparkled in her eyes. She nodded, frantic.

"Good. Then you can imagine that I won't save you from him," he flicked a glance at Spider, "if he loses his temper. So enough with the attitude. Keep your mouth shut, and act like what you are—a means to an end, *es todo*—and you might make it out of here breathing."

Natasha swallowed, shaking, her face white. She believed him.

Hell, I believed him, and I'd spent the evening listening to him trying to persuade Spider that kid-napping her was a bad idea. If I hadn't known he didn't give a damn, I'd have thought he was trying to save her from herself.

Vish giggled, eyes rolling. "Well, you sure scared the shit outta me, Sash. Someone save me! I'm on a ship full of crazy people! When can I get off?"

Dragonfly stalked over to stand beside me, his expression dark. Spider just rocked in his chair, flexing his fingers like they hurt. I stood there, uneasy. You could taste the tension stretching the air. The sooner we got our ransom, the sooner we could get off this madhouse of a ship, return to *Ladrona* and get on with the mission.

I shivered. Imagine, actually wishing I was alone with *him*. But right now, it seemed a pretty good option.

Spider leaned over the command console and crunched a contact. "Let's talk to his holiness. Lux, give me unsecured etherwave. I want everyone to hear this."

Lux sauntered up to the comms and switched control, swiping in a frequency. "Open."

Spider lounged back in his chair, clasping big hands behind his head. "Hello, Vyachesgrad. This is *LightBringer*. Are we listening?"

A delayed hiss, just a fraction of a second—what was our slipspace trajectory then? were we circling?-—and a woman's voice clipped on, echoing on an open channel. "*LightBringer*. This is Lieutenant Colonel Boranova, Vyachesgrad security—"

"Don't waste time, lady. Put the admiral on. I know he's standing there, I can hear him shitting himself."

Etherwave crackled, another silence. Then: "Vice-Admiral Verenski here. State your name."

Natasha opened her mouth, and Dragonfly silenced her with a glare.

Spider laughed, stretching long legs. "You know who this is, Pyotr."

An intake of breath. "Lukas Nero."

I noted the alias. I didn't remember it from Spider's Axis file. But this admiral knew it. They'd met before. My spine crawled. More was going on here than I understood, and it itched my nerves raw.

"Close enough." Spider studied the ceiling, his big brown fingers locked in his dreads. "I've got something of yours, Pyotr. Just like you once took something of mine." He stretched out his right arm, clenching his fist—the tattoo and the wrist guard covered a scar, I noticed, a pale rope twisted between his veins—and his tone sharpened. "I'd say let's trade, but hey. Some things can't be returned, can they?"

Dragonfly shook his head, his eyes closing for a moment. I looked a question, but he just bit his lip grimly.

"Let me talk to her." Verenski's voice rippled with stress.

"Daddy!" Natasha called, trembling. "Daddy, I'm h—mph!"

Foxy slapped her hand over the girl's mouth and gave a female groan of pain. Lux laughed and muttered deep and dark, muffling it behind his hand, and Vish dropped his lunch tray with a clunk and clatter of metal. Nice bit of audio theatre, considering the admiral probably didn't know that Spider crewed *LightBringer* with three skinny-starved freaks and a cat. The stupid girl had played right into their hands.

But was it really just three? Surely he'd need more. I'd done tours on battleships as a marine. The flight crew was sizable. For all I knew, Spider had an army of brainwashed minions below decks. Memory scratched at the back of my mind, but I couldn't catch it. I chewed my lip. Lux, Vish, Foxy Lady. I hadn't seen anyone else.

Spider clicked his tongue. "Down, lads. Keep it clean. Listen, Pyotr, this is getting messy. How about we talk price?"

"Name it." Background scuffle, probably the security colonel protesting. "Name it! Tell me how much." This time, desperation hardened Verenski's tone.

I held my breath. How much would Spider ask for? A decorated officer like Verenski was worth a lot to the navy; even apart from his own personal fortune, which must have been substantial if the corruption I'd seen on Vyachesgrad was any guide. The Empire would pay a lot for him to save face, and he'd be able to pull strings at High Command to get his way. Spider was an idiot if he gave her back for anything less than ten million sols.

But Spider just grinned, wicked teeth shining. "Who says it's money I want?"

My pulse throbbed cold. Beside me, Dragonfly flipped his hyperchip over tense fingers.

Static noise, a pause. "Then what?"

"Oh, I'm so pleased you asked!" Spider twirled around in the command chair, and gripped the walkway rail to jerk to a stop. He leaned into the comms console until his mouth brushed the etherwave sensor, soft and intimate. "I want your filth off that station, Admiral. I want every marine, every soldier, every brainwashed Imperial flunky gone from Vyachesgrad and the civilian hierarchy restored by twelve hundred local, or your daughter dies. Simple enough for you?"

A cold crackle, and silence.

My throat corked dry. Verenski could never do it. High Command wouldn't let him, no matter how personal the threat. The Empire never ceded territory to rebels. Ever.

"Hear that, Admiral?" Spider whispered, his cheek pressed to the console, his fingers caressing the plastic like piano keys. "That's your heart breaking. Music, isn't it? Call me back when you've thought about it. I don't wanna see a single traffic movement from that station before you talk to me. But don't take too long. My boys are hungry, and so am I."

And he slammed his palm on the etherwave contact, severing the link.

19

Silence clanged around the battledeck, like that moment of quiet after a fusion bomb, before the sound rips your ears bloody. It was broken only by Natasha's harsh breathing and the urgent throb of my heart.

Vish giggled, breaking the spell. "That was fucking fantastic."

Spider levered himself from the command chair and stretched with a feline grin. Lux just shrugged, thoughtful, his gaze drifting. Foxy jumped up on the nav console beside Vish and swung her skinny legs. "Hell, yeah. Did you hear him shit himself?"

She elbowed Vish's bony ribs. He poked her back, laughing, and for a moment, they just looked like two shy young people who liked each other. A lunatic love scene. How touching.

Dragonfly slipped his chip into his pocket. When he spoke, his voice was dangerously smooth, like calm air before a sonic riptide. "Foxy, why don't you take this girl down to the galley and find her something to eat?"

Foxy stared. "But—"

"Just do it, please."

Dragonfly flicked her that cold, brown glare, and sullenly she slouched off the console. She dragged Natasha up, popping off the smartcuffs with a tiny electric disruptor that snapped the metal in two, and dragged her to the elevator. Apparently, Natasha was lost for words, because the elevator door hissed shut without any audible complaints from her.

Dragonfly whirled on the spot and hit Spider in the jaw. "You fucking liar."

Nice punch. Spider staggered, blood splashing his lip.

Lux goggled, his pimply nose quivering, and Vish's mouth dropped open. Dragonfly's stormcloud expression suggested he was too pissed off to care that Spider was a head taller than him and a third again his weight.

Spider spat a red stain and shoved him away. He was armed, his disruptor holstered at his thigh, and my pulse leaped as his fingers hovered dangerously.

But he didn't draw. His gold-flecked eyes glowed with relish. "Wanna take me on? We've tried before. You know how it turned out."

"The Empire never cedes territory!" Dragonfly's voice actually shook, something I'd never heard before, and my bones vibrated with it. Would this be the end? Would they finally kill each other? But his rage was quiet, festering, a starburst waiting to erupt. "You know Verenski can never do what you ask. What are you playing at?"

Spider shrugged, an evil little twist to his smile. "I'm only giving him the choice he never gave me."

Dragonfly stared, pale. "You always meant to kill her, didn't you? You never planned to give her back."

"Damn right. They don't hear us when we whisper, Sash. We have to scream in their fat fucking faces—"

"This is not about a message! It's about you. It's always about you! Why do you think I left?"

"You left because I kicked your sorry ass out. And don't change the subject. What about your little game at Esperanza? That's hardly impersonal."

"That's different."

Spider laughed. "Uh-huh. You just keep telling yourself that."

"It is and you know it." Dragonfly clenched his hands to keep them still. "What Verenski's people did to you can't be undone, okay? Get over it. *Madre de dios*, I should do us all a favor and put you out of your misery."

Spider's expression darkened, dangerous. "You know *nothing* about my misery—"

"We all know everything about your misery! It's splattered all over the fucking Empire! How much revenge is enough, Lukas? When will you be satisfied? Ever?"

Every muscle in Spider's body wound tight, like a tiger ready to spring, and his left hand darted for his weapon. But Dragonfly already had the jump on him, his little atomflash straight and level. Very sharp. I hadn't even known he had that.

"Try it," he snapped. "We'll both die. That what you want?"

My muscles jerked tight, but too late. Lux had already whipped his poisongun from nowhere, leveling it at Dragonfly with one eye tilted over the sights, and Vish snaked off the table and brandished an ugly nerve pistol.

Fuck.

If they shot Dragonfly, I'd be next. One weapon against four. Not good.

"Hell, why not?" Spider said. "God knows I've nothing better to do any more."

He advanced, pulling out his disruptor and switching it to his right hand. It quivered as he aimed, and he cursed and clenched his fingers tighter.

I didn't think. I just dived into the middle, arms outstretched. "Whoa. Chill on the testosterone, guys. Let's talk about this like grown-ups."

Dragonfly's aim didn't waver. "Lazuli, get away."

His stupid courage impressed me. It also pissed me off. Maybe just because I was standing on the bridge of a rebel battleship with four weapons simultaneously pointed at my head because of him. But for a kick-ass terrorist figurehead, he was dumbfuck careless with his own life.

"Yeah," I snapped, "because us all shooting each other is really going to help at this point."

Silence.

Then Spider laughed, dark and rich like coffee. "Keep this one, Sash. She suits you." But he didn't lower his weapon.

Dragonfly sighed and let his aim slip, and the creeping tension in the air melted away. "Fine. Torture that girl if it makes you feel good. Do whatever you want with her. I don't care. Just leave me out of it." And he pushed Lux's poisongun aside and stalked away along the battlebridge.

I didn't know what else to do but follow.

***

I caught up with him as he jammed his finger on the door switch at the far end, and his stormy mood swamped me like a thundercloud. He wouldn't look at me. Didn't speak. Didn't even acknowledge I was there.

I waited until the door ground shut behind us, and then I turned on him as we walked, the anger boiling tight in my chest finally exploding. "Are you insane? What did you say to me about little things? Are you *trying* to get yourself killed?"

He glared, hot and dark. "Why do you care?"

"Are you kidding? If they shoot you, I'll be next. I swear, if you die before we get off this ship, I'll bloody well bring you back so I can kill you again."

The emotion in my voice surprised me, and my throat caught as we stalked down the warm red-lit corridor, almost too fast for me to keep up. I'd been threatened, insulted, chased, shot at. Guess it'd been a tough day.

Dragonfly scraped back sweaty hair, muscles roping tight in his forearms. "Spider's like a child. He has to have his own way. Just let him do his thing, and when he's done he'll drop us off somewhere—"

"But what about Natasha?" I demanded. "You said yourself Spider will kill her. We can't just leave her here!"

"Why not?"

My mouth dried. "Excuse me?"

He flashed me a dark glance, and it chilled me. "Toughen the fuck up. Lukas is right. She's a snotty rich bitch who never wanted for a thing in her life. Why do you care if she dies screaming?"

I stopped, incredulous. This was a test, right? He was testing my loyalty to the rebellion? But he stopped with me, and there was none of that melting warmth in his gaze. His chocolate eyes had set cold and hard and empty, drained of every soft and giving gleam.

My hands twisted. "Umm …"

"Gotta hand it to Lukas—it's a good joke, yes? That admiral will have to sit on his fat, dumb hands while his daughter dies. Hell, we should just kill her now and get it over with." His mouth curled in a tiny smile, but no humanity lurked in it. Only sharp, animal hatred.

My stomach sickened. I opened my mouth, and nothing came out. And that's when it hit me. I'd actually believed it. I'd believed in him. The man who'd killed Mishka and my friends. For some stupid reason, I'd truly thought he might be different.

But he wasn't. He just did what he had to, no more and no less. He hadn't stopped Spider from killing me on Vyachesgrad because he gave a shit. He hadn't kissed me in Esperanza's docking ring because he didn't want to kill those trolls. He just had a hard-on for Lazuli in her cute tight shorts. He'd been trying to impress me and, like a naive rookie with stars in her eyes, I'd fallen for it.

Worse. I'd wanted to fall for it. I'd let him lead me on when all along I'd known he had ice in his heart.

My pulse thudded hot, and all the awkwardness I'd ever felt around him came spearing back like a poison dart. I tried a smile, but it misfired. "So all that about it not being worth a life was bullshit?"

"What did you think? That fighting the Empire is black and white? That you can keep the moral high ground and stay alive?" He laughed. "Grow up, little girl. This is the real world. If they won't see sense, we have to hit them where it hurts."

I edged away. "Then why did you punch Spider, if you don't care what he does with Natasha?"

"I don't like being lied to." He shrugged, careless, but his gaze stabbed a threat. "You might want to remember that."

Suddenly I was very aware of the atomflash just a quiver from his talented left hand.

Did he suspect me for an Imperial agent? I didn't know. But he could have killed me any time, only he'd spared me, for some dark and twisted reason of his own. I was damned if I'd wait around any longer to find out what it was.

I swallowed, tight. "You don't trust me."

"You've given me no reason to. You're soft, Lazuli. You talk a good fight, but when it comes to doing what's necessary, you cringe away. Frankly, I don't have time to walk you through this. Either you're in or you're out."

I nearly punched that smug little smile off his face. "Fine. Don't let me keep you. We're even, Sasha. Next time Spider tries to kill me, don't do me any favors."

And I stalked back toward the bridge, my eyes stinging warm.

20

I ignored the rest of the crew as I marched into the elevator and slammed my fist on the button. Vish giggled—when was that skinny redhead ever not giggling?—and Spider sent me a handsome smirk that hacked at my nerves. Even Gus the cat yawned and eyed me with disdain as the elevator door snapped shut. I half-expected them to stop me, and ask what I was doing, but they didn't. They probably thought we'd had a lovers' tiff.

I banged my skull back into the rippled metal wall, my nerves fraying. They could think what they liked. I was done listening to Dragonfly's bullshit. He was everything evil I'd thought he was, and worse. I didn't want to breathe air he'd touched for a moment longer than I had to.

I fumed, kicking the grated floor as the elevator sank to the sublevels, red digits flashing on the display. Director Renko could go to oblivion with *short of termination.* I'd kill the lying son of a spaceworm the next safe chance I got. Look him in the eyes as he choked to death on shatterglass. Win my promotion to black ops, get a set of telescopic cyber-retinas, and spend the rest of my career wearing tight black body armor and shooting insurrectionists in the back. They deserved it, the entire rotten-hearted lot of them.

Not that I was furious with myself, or anything.

Not that I was melting with embarrassment that I'd fallen for Dragonfly's lies even for an instant. Nikita would laugh his handsome blond butt off.

But I didn't have time to cringe about that now. I needed off this madhouse of a ship, and I wasn't leaving Natasha Verenskaya behind. Even if she was a snotty rich bitch, the kind of superior, self-obsessed whiner I'd always despised. Of no use to anyone. Part of the problem, with her stupid racism and thoughtless arrogance. That wasn't the point. I was an Imperial operative. It was my job to save her, even if she wasn't particularly worth saving.

But my skin itched, uncomfortable. I might have to kill Spider's crew to get her out. Four lives for one. And even I had to admit, some wildly creative minds lurked on this ship. Involuntarily, I recalled Dragonfly with glowing symbols reflecting in his eyes as he tossed off a string of math only a few hundred people in the galaxy were capable of. Carrot-headed Vish flashing a six-crew battleship on his own. Even Lux, the shuttle pilot from hell. How much waste was an ignorant teenager worth?

I shook my head, clearing my mind. That decision wasn't mine to make. I had standing orders, and they said *Protect the Empire at all costs.* A bunch of cocky rebels meant nothing.

At last, the elevator jerked to a halt, and I marched out into the mess hall, its rows of gleaming silvermetal benches neat and deserted in the dark. Only safety lights along the bulkheads shed any illumination, and pools of shadow hung close under the low ceiling. Spider and his ratty geniuses were smart enough to conserve power at least.

Metal scraped behind me, and I whirled. Shadows danced, empty. No one.

I breathed deep, calming my skipping pulse. Guess I was getting jumpy.

I headed for the galley at the far end, where arclights buzzed in the refrigeration system. I'd done enough time on battleships to know where everything was, at least as far as the enlisted marines' quarters, the armory, the dropship bays and the brig were concerned. Ask me for directions to the officers' wardroom and I'd be stumped. Briefly I wondered where Spider and his crew slept.

I ripped open the diagonal clasps of my marine uniform so I could pull it off my shoulders and tie the arms around my hips. It felt alien, too tight, and underneath my black top was plastered to my skin with sweat. The temperature in here wasn't helping. Whoever Spider had put in charge of climate control obviously came from a jungle planet, because the air hung hot and stifling, the smell of warm septurium alloy thick.

I rounded the corner into the galley to see Foxy Lady scraping some crumbling freeze-dried stuff from a plastic ration packet into a pot, her face a mask of concentration under her spiky pale hair. Her laser rifle lay within reach on the metal bench.

On the floor, Natasha crouched in her long coat, her wrists smartcuffed to a bolted-down table leg. Her gaze darted from me to Foxy, sizing us up. She swallowed, wiping hair from her face with a trembling forearm. "Please. Let me go. I haven't seen anything. I won't tell anyone. Just don't let them—"

"Shut up, bitch." I kicked at her ankles, hoping it looked harder than it was.

Maybe she thought I was on the good side. Maybe she thought she'd get sympathy from the women on the crew. Whatever it was, I didn't want Foxy thinking I had any pity for Imperials. I needed her to leave me alone with Natasha, just for a moment, so I could tell the girl what would happen next.

Problem was, I didn't know what to do next. Getting her off this ship was difficult. We were in slipspace, which made using a marine dropship a bad idea. As soon as we lost velocity, we'd pop out into real space, and depending on our trajectory that could be anywhere. Dropships had only arc-rocket propulsion and no slipspace drive, and drifting in space with a sullen teenager at the mercy of whatever horny, slipmad pirate happened to come by wasn't my idea of a rescue.

No, I needed a ship with its own slipdrive. A shuttlecraft or a fighter. Not the sort of thing Spider was likely to let me saunter off with. And not easy to steal alone. I didn't like my chances of luring any of his sycophantic crew turncoat. Except Dragonfly.

I shivered, warm with remembered wrongness. The less I thought about him, the better.

I pointed at the rations. "Mind if I share?"

Foxy shrugged lean shoulders, wary.

I peered into the pot as she dripped in water to make it go further. Rice and corn. I remembered the packaged food from my marine days, wrapped in flexible freezeplastic, designed to last for weeks in a soldier's kit. You ripped the packet open and a tiny atomflash went off inside, heating the food on the spot. But it always tasted better from a real cookpot.

Foxy sparked the arcburner on one of the stoves

and slapped the pot over the red-hot glow, and the salty smell made my mouth water. I hadn't eaten since that deadmeat kebab on Vyachesgrad, and it seemed like weeks ago.

"Got any grapefruit?" I asked.

"Huh?" Foxy poked at the grey mixture with her fork, doubtful.

"The fruit salad pack. They taste good together. Here." I rummaged in the half-empty ration bin and came up with a yellow packet, dented at the corners but unbroken. They hadn't changed in seven years. This one was out of date, but they often were. Hadn't killed me yet. I cracked the corner and squeezed the sticky fruit mixture into the pot.

Foxy stirred, licked the fork and grunted, flicking me an empty glance. "Not bad."

I nodded, careful not to smile. She didn't seem the sort to make instant friends. Still, she hadn't shot me yet. That was a promising sign.

I fetched three clean bowls from the big stainless dishwasher—it was nearly empty, with dirty dishes stacked head-high on the bench beside it—and Foxy dumped in our dinner with a big spoon: two large helpings and one small.

Natasha got the small one. Another promising sign.

The girl looked at her dinner bowl where Foxy had set it on the floor, away from her cuffed hands. "Can I have a spoon?"

Foxy didn't look at her. "No."

"But I can't reach. Can you—"

Foxy shoved the bowl toward her with one toe. "You want it or not?"

"Y—"

"Then shut up and eat. That's a week's bloody food where I come from."

Anger glimmered in Foxy's tired eyes, and for a memory-rich moment I tasted her rage.

Fucking Imperials, get everything while we starve. My father and his friends, whispering in our gaslit cabin while I lay behind the flimsy plastic wall wrapped in greasy blankets, me and my sister fighting over who got to sleep with the baby because he was always so warm. *Army parasites ... stealing our food ... send a delegation ... discussions ... talk to the council ...* It never did them any good. *They don't hear us when we whisper,* Spider said. He was right.

Foxy grabbed her rifle and walked out into the mess hall, and I followed. It looked strange with the rows and rows of empty benches, no noise or laughter. Shadows flittered in the far corner, and I jumped, searching for a weapon, but when I peered into the darkness, no one was there. I forced my pulse slower, breathing deep. This silent, empty ship was giving me the creeps.

I plonked down on a bench. Foxy waited to see where I sat before she chose her own seat, opposite me at a safe distance, her rifle beside her. I dug into my food—I rated a spoon, at least—and the familiar sweet-fruity flavor filled my mouth. We ate in silence, only whirring refrigerators and the slipspace drive's distant rattle keeping us company.

"So," I ventured, "you're pretty fine with that rifle, right?"

"You ain't seen me fire it yet."

"Well, yeah, but you don't miss nothing that's going down." Easy to slip into her mode of speaking. Not so different from my own a while ago. "I seen you on the station. You got everything covered while the big man does the doing. That why you're here?"

Foxy shrugged, but her gaze softened a little. "I help out."

"So how long you been at this? Here, I mean. On this ship."

She shrugged again, chewing. "A stretch."

"It's a pretty shady deal. I mean, I don't have nothing like this. I got me a little Phoenix, roll on my own mostly."

"You and Sasha."

Was that a twinge of envy? Maybe what Foxy-only-Lady-on-the-ship needed was some girl talk. I dropped my gaze and thought about *him* kissing me on Esperanza to work up a flush. Fucking prick. He'd deceived me from the start, and I'd walked right into it.

I squirmed, my face hot. "Oh, no. I mean, he's ... Well, you know how it is. You and Spider, right?"

Her mouth twitched. "Nope."

"You're stitching me. I seen him scope you out."

"You reckon?" She tried to look casual. It didn't work.

"Sure. His eyes and your ass, hello."

She jammed her mouth full of food, her gaze down. "In his dreams," she muttered.

Time for a change of subject. "So how's it go around here? You work long shifts?"

"We do our share."

"I mean, four doesn't seem a whole lot for a battleship. There's just four, right?"

Foxy snorted, scratching her rough-hacked hair. "You should know."

What did that mean? I'd only seen four. Was she trying to trick me?

I poked my chin toward Natasha, who, by the scraping and slurping coming from the kitchen, was taking lessons in how to eat from a bowl without her hands. Wouldn't do the spoiled little miss any harm. "What you think he'll do with her?"

Foxy scraped the last of her dinner into her mouth. "What do you care?"

"Will he kill her? I mean, would you, if he asked you to?"

"Enough with the questions, okay?" Her hand slid over her rifle's butt, a touchy threat.

I lifted my palms in surrender. "Hey, I don't mean nothing. I'm just ... Well, I'm on my own, like I said. I decide who lives and dies. Only now there's Sasha, and ... Well, you know men. Always wanna be in charge."

Foxy stared at me, her green eyes blank and hard. Testing me. I didn't look away. I'd stared down hard-ass marines. I could surely break a skinny girl.

At last, she spoke, and unexpected pain roughened her voice. "I don't think, okay? Spider does the thinking. I just do. If thinking's your game, you get out right now. Hear me?"

I swallowed. She made me think of Mishka, guiding my hand on some practice weapons test long ago. *You're thinking too much,* he'd murmured over my shoulder, his fingers strong and steady on mine. *It's making you hesitate. Just aim, breathe, fire.* Fact was, Axis did my thinking for me, at least as far as identifying the enemy was concerned, and until lately that had been just fine.

"But you didn't. Get out, that is."

Foxy shook her head, her stubborn chin set.

Unwanted sympathy warmed my skin. I knew what it was like when your heart screwed you over. "He's really worth dying for, huh?"

"And don't he know it." She shoved her plate aside, slung her rifle over one shoulder and walked away, her boots ringing cold in the empty mess hall. The elevator door crunched open, and she was gone.

I sighed, and pushed my unfinished dinner away. Wow, that was fun. But at least I got what I wanted. Swiftly, I wiped my hands on my unclipped uniform and went to talk to Natasha.

She was on her knees, licking the last scraps of rice from her bowl. Her hands were locked fast to the table leg beside her, and she had to crane her neck awkwardly over one shoulder to reach. Her loose yellow hair dangled, clogged with fruity rice. She heard me approach and jerked back, her face red.

I watched her, impassive. Her petty humiliation didn't please me. But it didn't move me to sympathy either.

I squatted, and she shrank away. I reached out an impatient hand. "You finished?"

She nodded, eyes wide.

I retrieved her bowl, dropped it with the others, and leaned on the bench, unclipping my pistol and clunking it onto the metal so she'd see I wasn't planning to shoot her. "You know why you're here?"

More nodding.

My fingers clenched. I had an irrational urge to slap her. So different from me at that age. So sheltered. So helpless. She hadn't even tried to break her cuffs while Foxy and I were eating.

"Tell me."

"Because they want my daddy to do things." Her voice sounded childish, like she'd regressed to a younger, safer place.

It happens. I've seen hard men suck their thumbs and beg for their mothers. Sometimes, the mind gives in before the body gives up. But usually it takes extreme torture. This little princess couldn't even take being tied to a table.

"That's right. Do you understand why your daddy can't do those things?"

"He will." Her lip quivered.

"Stop crying." I shoved her with my toe. "You're wrong. He won't rescue you, Natasha. Do you know why?"

"You're lying." Her eyes glittered bright with tears. "He'll rescue me. He'll come here and he'll rescue me and then all you horrid people will be sorry!"

I crouched and grabbed her chin, forcing her to look at me. "No, Natasha. He won't. Not because he doesn't love you. Because his superiors won't let him. You are in deep danger. Do you understand?"

She sobbed, shaking her head.

I squeezed her chin harder, nails drawing blood. "Do you understand?"

"Yes!" Spit and tears splashed my cheek. Her face twisted into a snarl and her little-girl shell broke. "Yes, you fucking bitch, I understand. You'll keep me cuffed here, and your stinking rebel friends will beat me up and rape me, and when they're done getting off, they'll send me back to my father in pieces. That make you feel good, you lump of shit?"

She actually snapped at me, teeth bared. I dodged. Good. A rise at last. Anger, I could work with.

"No, it doesn't make me feel good, Natasha. Listen to me." I whipped my arm around her shoulders, holding her tight. "Shh. I don't belong here either, okay? I can help you." She clawed at me, dragging my hair loose, scraping for my eyes. I pushed her hands down and held on. "I can help you. I promise. They won't hurt you if I can help it. But you have to calm down and keep quiet. Okay?"

Gradually her struggles subsided to quiet sobs, and she rocked in my arms, her face pressed to my chest like I was her mother. I sweated, uncomfortable. I wanted to tell her I was an Axis agent, that I had everything under control, that it would all be okay. But I didn't want her knowing the truth in case she spilled it. I might still need Dragonfly to get out of here.

"Okay," I whispered. "Listen, Natasha. Once I've found us a way home, I'll come for you. But until then you have to—"

Metal crunched, and the elevator door slid open. Fuck. I jumped up, shoving her backward onto the floor. "Remember what I said, bitch. Soon."

Lux's spiky brown head emerged from the elevator, his pierced brow shining with sweat. "Everything okay?"

I holstered my pistol and strode from the kitchen. "Sure. Why not?"

He shrugged, swinging from the doorframe on one hand, and glanced into the shadows, grey eyes sharp. "Just making sure."

I pushed into the elevator, shoving him aside. "Where do you guys sleep? I'm wasted."

"Level four. Officers' quarters. We got the LSS inactive down below to save juice." Lux leaned against the doorjamb to stop it closing, and scratched his ridiculous hair, studying me. "You really Sasha's girlfriend?"

I grinned, feral. "Wanna try something and see?"

"Maybe." An answering grin that transformed his face: angry boy to man on a mission. Bright, strong, hard. Older than he looked? "You don't seem his type."

"No? What's his type then?" I was curious despite myself. They all had history together that I knew nothing about. I didn't even really know Lux's job on *LightBringer*.

"Absent. Dead. Imaginary." He twisted a platinum earring, his lean forearms gleaming. "Shit, I don't know. Never seen her."

My belly warmed. A handsome liar like Dragonfly could have any girl he wanted, for a while. A loner? Or did he keep someone at home—wherever home was if it wasn't here. How recent was his famous falling-out with Spider anyway?

Not that I cared.

I twirled my loosened braid around my finger. "Maybe you still haven't seen her."

Lux wrinkled his nose in another grin—yeah, okay, that was kinda cute for a terrorist psychopath—and shoved his hands in his pockets. "Nearly two years."

"Huh?"

"That's how long since Sasha left. And yeah, he did leave of his own accord. That's what I do here, by the way, since you're wondering."

Now I was bewildered. "What?"

"You're wondering what Lux does here, if Vish flies the ship one-handed and Foxy Lady plays with guns. I tell Spider what other people are thinking."

I snorted. "What, you think you're psychic or something?"

All that mind-control crap is bullshit. Even ESE is just a window, not a doorway. We've split open a dozen dimensions since etherwave was discovered and we've never found anything resembling a psionic-capable medium. Unless you can stick an electrode in it, you can't control it.

"No. I just think like other people. Wanna come put the girl away?"

Put her away? Did he mean kill her? Or lock her up? Damn. A pair of cuffs was easy. A cell, not so much.

"I'm sorry?"

"The girl. We got rooms. Might as well lock her in so we can all get some zees." Lux's smile turned dark. "Unless you was thinking of letting her go."

Okay, so that was spooky.

I faced him down, lifting an unconcerned eyebrow. "What do you think, psychic boy?"

"I think you're hiding something, Sasha's-girl-or-not." Lux flipped a little disruptor like Foxy's from his pocket and flicked it on, gesturing toward the kitchen with a dark glint in his eyes. "That's what I think. Coming?"

21

Twenty minutes later, I was pacing in my room, the white plastic walls closing in on me. Icelights glared on the blue-quilted bunk, white storage lockers, the mirror in the tiny washroom. No window, no reflective holo to give the illusion of space. Junior officers' quarters—small and private and stifling like a coffin.

Lux and I had locked Natasha in a cabin the mirror image of this one, around the corner along the narrow white corridor. Everything in the officers' mess was white and it gave me the creeps. Deep down in the enlisted dorms, I knew, the black metal walls shone with condensation from the slipspace coolant and the air trembled with engine noise and stank of hot metal. The officers' quarters were pristine, plastic, pretend, like they'd covered up the real world so no one would see how dirty and noisy and rank it was. In the corps, we'd despised our officers with healthy fervor, no matter how competent they were, and it helped us band together, though they were likely just normal, decent men and women with a job to do.

Natasha had the good sense to keep her complaining mouth shut when Lux threw her on the bed and tightened the cuffs so she could barely roll over. Not even when he pulled her coat off and left her in her nightgown did she speak. She hadn't looked much at me. Either she was pretending so no one would find us out, or she hadn't believed me. I guessed I'd find out when I went for her.

If I ever got the chance.

Lux had locked her door with a voiceprint emergency lockdown code. I'd have to figure out how to bypass it. It was only thanks to Lux's whim that I wasn't locked in too. I had no idea where the rest of them slept. It could be across the ship. It could be next door.

Damn, it was hot in here. I looked around for a dimmer switch before I remembered where I was.

"Dim the lights," I ordered, feeling foolish.

Lights down, said the virtual valet in a soft female voice, and the harsh white light faded to soft yellow.

I tugged off my boots and stockings, my feet sticking to the plastic floor. I stripped off the uniform Spider had given me and tossed it in the corner, leaving only my shorts and tank top. Sweat soaked my body, trickling down my bare limbs and between my breasts, and I dragged my knotted hair from its ruined braid and tucked it up in a rough ponytail.

"Can we cool it down in here?"

Temperature is set to minimum for comfort, the valet advised.

Comfort, my ass. Maybe the system was malfunctioning. Or maybe I was just overwrought.

Without the uniform, I felt naked. I'd lost my Axis ident, my shatterjay, my backup weapon. I had only my ESE, still tucked into the seam of my shorts.

I unclipped the pistol in its holster from the discarded uniform and strapped it around my thigh, where the nano-elastic adjusted itself to my muscle movement so it fit perfectly and didn't slip. The pistol's charge was half-empty, the diodes along the cartridge glowing only dimly. I spent a few tense minutes rifling the drawers in the desk for anything useful, and finding nothing.

But all that was just to avoid thinking about the mess I was in.

I had to get a defenseless civilian off a hostile ship, and I had no way of breaking her from her cell, no transport, and only one weapon. Dragonfly already suspected me, and Lux was no idiot. And the admiral's deadline for action was only a few hours away. If Spider didn't come to kill her sooner, he surely would then.

I wiped my sweating face on my forearm. Would they rape her, as she feared? I suspected not. Spider had an ethical screw loose, but he wasn't random, and it was Admiral Verenski he wanted to torture, not his daughter.

I, on the other hand, had no such safety net if they found me out. And, of course, saving the girl meant abandoning my mission to entrap Dragonfly.

Unless I took him with me. Or killed him before I left.

My pulse quickened, and in my heart that black, vengeful creature stirred.

I could kill them all. Improvise a dampener for my plasma pistol to mask it from the battle sensors and shoot the evil-hearted pricks as they slept. Pick them off one by one. Rescue the girl, and return this stolen battleship to the fleet.

I'd be an Imperial hero. More importantly, I'd be assistant director of operations at black ops, and I'd never have to impress Renko or think about Dragonfly again.

Tempting. I was sick of moral ambiguity. These rebels were the enemy. End of story. Right?

But my chances of killing all five before I got caught were slim. I wasn't an infallible assassin. Not yet.

I straightened and addressed the valet. "Show me the crew."

Obediently, the valet flashed up a video projection divided into six oblong windows. Security camera footage, taken from high vantage points, the panoramic lenses distorting the images like a bubble. Foxy Lady, on a bench beside a blacked-out clearview, stripping her rifle across her knees. Vish on the bridge, the cat on his lap and his feet propped on the nav station, a stardrive diagnostic flickering green across the display. Lux at a mess hall table, his head resting on his forearm, pistol clasped loosely in his hand. He wriggled in his sleep, his lips moving. And Spider, drying himself in the hot-air draft after a shower, water beading on his naked body.

Uh-huh. I peered closer. Professional curiosity only, of course. Hmm. Very nice. Remind me never to get in an argument with those thighs. His skin was clear and smooth, his limbs long. Maybe he was younger than I'd figured.

A scar roped the length of his spine, angry and pale against his dark coloring. Too neat for an injury. More like a surgical wound poorly healed. I remembered Dragonfly's scarred shoulder, and frowned. You might keep a battle wound for sentimental reasons—I could understand that. Some kept them to remember fallen friends, or mull over their own mortality. But who didn't get their surgical scars erased?

Someone who ran out of cash for the cosmetic work?

Or someone who didn't get a say in it?

Someone, even, who fled before the surgery was finished?

I remembered how Spider had heard me outside the hotel room when I'd made no sound, how he'd jumped me ultra-fast. Dragonfly's words to him on the bridge repeated on me, ricocheting with extra meaning. *What they did to you can't be undone.*

I shivered. Maybe Spider's enhancements were more sinister than I'd thought.

He stretched, flexing long brown muscles, and I bit my lip and looked away.

The fifth screen showed white noise, and the sixth a dark empty corridor. So there really were only four in the crew.

"Where's Dragonfly?"

Unknown.

"You know. The other guy who came on board with us."

Unknown.

I cracked sore knuckles. Lux had said the life support was off in parts of the ship. Maybe some of the security was down too. "Okay. Turn that off. Can I access the lockdown from here?"

The screen dissolved and metal clamps clicked. *Door locked.*

I sighed. "No, idiot. Unlock the door."

Door unlocked.

"Thank you. I mean the voice lockdown across the corridor. Can I access it from my console?"

Lockdown is activated by authorized personnel only.

"Yeah, but from this console?"

Lockdown is activated by authorized personnel only.

I glared into the air. "Okay, I get that. Who's authorized?"

Lockdown is activated by authorized personnel only.

In other words, not me. "Thanks. You're a big help."

You're welcome.

I wiped my sweating face, frustrated. Some Imperial ident codes could be broken. Maybe I could fool the lockdown and get Natasha out. But maybe not. The doors were battlegrade septurium alloy. They couldn't be stormed with a plasma handgun. And I didn't have much time.

I needed Dragonfly's magic touch, or at least his magic hyperchip. And then there was the matter of stealing the shuttlecraft. If I killed him, I might get stranded here, and Spider would soon discover his pet was missing and come looking for me with a gun.

I scraped my hands through my hair, ruining my ponytail. Damn it. Escaping was a much surer thing with Dragonfly on my side. He wanted off as badly as I did—this ship wasn't big enough for two massive egos—and I could probably convince him to help me. But he'd never consider taking the girl with us. I knew that now. He despised all Imperials like the hate-blind monster he was. It was either Dragonfly or Natasha.

A laugh caught in my throat. The mission or the girl. A fine cliché I'd gotten myself into.

I swallowed, and made up my mind. Cliché or not, I was acting way beyond my orders here. I needed assurances. That there'd be a job for me when I got back. That whatever I did, Renko and Surov wouldn't take what I'd gained for them and kill me to cover it up. In any case, Dragonfly had screwed with my mind. I wasn't thinking straight. I needed fresh eyes on this mess, and I only had one person I could call.

"Is this cabin under video surveillance?"

There is no active visual surveillance.

"How about audio?"

In-room valet service is monitoring audio.

"Apart from the in-room valet."

There is no other active audio surveillance.

"Fine. Deactivate the in-room valet."

Deactivating.

A diode on the console blinked out. I rattled the door to be sure it was closed, and dug my ESE from the hole in my shorts. Sub-ether was theoretically secure, but it didn't hurt to be sure. I could only hope we weren't too far away.

"Nikita, you there?"

"Carrie." A stretch of warm muscles slipped down the sub-ether band, shivering silken heat down my spine. He'd been sleeping. "What's up? You're agitated."

Only a short delay, but noise filtered in and out. We didn't have much time before the comms broke up. "I need a sigma-level ident for a Raven Three. Can you do it for me?"

"I'm sorry, did I miss the part where a battleship got involved?"

"Long story. I got him back. You were right about Spider. But there's a problem." Quickly I recounted what had happened, leaving out my squabble with Dragonfly. Let Nikita think I'd kept my head all along. "So now I'm screwed," I finished. "They're gonna kill this Natasha, and I need the ident to get off the ship."

“What about Algebra Boy? Isn’t that his specialty?”

His suspicion sweetened the tip of my tongue. I swallowed. “He won’t come if I bring the girl.” Or even at all.

“Aragon, get a grip.” Cool disdain, like ice on the insides of my wrists. “Have you lost your wits in the last forty-eight hours?”

“No, I told you—”

“Then use them. Leave the girl behind and get Dragonfly the fuck out of there. He’s far too valuable to waste on this.”

My pulse leaped: either his urgency or my own. “But what about the admiral’s daughter?”

“A fourteen-year-old girl. I’m sure she’ll be a great loss. You’ll get over it. Dragonfly is your prize. Don’t give him up now.”

My mind shivered under his reason’s smooth caress. He was right, of course. Just what a good Axis agent would do. Assess the facts, weigh up the odds, make a rational decision. The mission, not the girl. But there was one fact Nikita didn’t have.

Without his help, I was screwed. I had no choice but to trust him.

Amusement feathered my spine, a breath of icy laughter. “Aragon? Is there something you’re not telling me? Say it’s not so.”

I sighed, and gave it up. “There’s one more thing,” and I told him about Surov the cat-man’s job offer.

An empty pause like space, devoid of emotion. “You do realize what you just said to me?”

“I know. Do me the favor, Nikita. I realize it’s a lot to ask. But this is my chance to get Dragonfly, don’t you see?”

"Carrie, if Dragonfly even breaks a nail, Renko's going to blame you. If you kill him, she'll have you gutted."

Probably by Nikita. I shivered. "Not if Surov comes to the party."

A chilly laugh. "I do adore your trusting heart, but once again it's screwed you over. Surov doesn't need an A-D Ops. He's already put someone in the job."

Stunned, I sat. On the table, my hand shook.

Watch your back, Surov's invisible, atomflash-wielding aide had told me. *You're not the only one who wants the job.* Seemed he was right. And if Surov no longer required my services ...

"Aragon? You still there?"

I swallowed. "Who? Who did he get?"

"Electra. Long-time black ops, already tested and cleared for mods. Better qualified than you."

My heart sank. Electra. I knew of her. Blonde, beautiful, aristo Russiyan, laser crystalsights cut into her irises and a reputation for ruthlessness. Not an enemy I wanted to make.

I sighed. "That cat-man is a lying bastard."

"Listen, if I'd known, I'd have had words with his pussy-striped ass, once I'd finished kicking yours. But you can't ... just because ..."

Static clouded in my mind like a stinging nanobug swarm. The bandwidth was fragmenting, the transmission torn apart by oblique slipspace velocity.

"I'm losing you. Nikita, please, give me a chance to sort this out. I'll call you."

Just a hiss of empty ether. He was already gone.

Shit.

22

I jammed my ESE away, my nerves itching. So much for fresh eyes. Now Nikita knew I'd been planning to defect, but I'd gained nothing in return. And someone already had my job at black ops, which meant Surov had no reason to protect me from Renko's wrath.

There was no profit for me in killing Dragonfly any more. Just personal gratification. Was it worth it?

I struggled, layers of complexity smothering me. Dragonfly had seemed so sensible, so driven. Like he had right and wrong all sorted out in little compartments in his head. Pity they'd turned out to be the wrong compartments.

Determination firmed in my heart. His kind didn't deserve to live. If he died, a hundred others who might get in his way—the way Mishka and my friends had got in his way, plus a thousand innocent others who never meant anyone any harm—might live. Killing him might mean my job, but Renko could stick me in a dustbin in Analysis for ten years for all I cared. Mishka would be avenged. There'd be one less murdering asshole terrorizing the spaceways, and at least I'd sleep with a clear conscience. And if Renko tried to have me killed, I wouldn't go down easy.

Fact was, Dragonfly had ruined my life. He'd taken my lover, my friends, my zeal for my career. Since Urumki, I'd drifted, stagnated, harboring no hope for anything but more of the same meaninglessness. I'd tried to lose myself in the job, tried to climb the Axis ladder like a good agent should, but it hadn't worked. Everything that was good and clean and pure in my life, I'd lost because of him.

Was killing him worth it? Hell, yes.

I jumped up, resolute. I'd give him one last chance: help me save the girl, or die. Either way, his life was in my hands. And he shouldn't be too hard to find. I knew he wasn't on the bridge or in the mess hall or in the shower with Spider. Hell, maybe I'd just ask someone.

Swiftly, I jammed my boots back on and slicked the chemical fastenings tight. Swiped my hair back into a tighter ponytail. Whipped out my pistol to check the contacts, and slipped out the door.

"Where you going with that?"

My breath crunched tight on that musical sound. Spider leaned against the opposite wall, one hand shoved in his pocket. The corridor lights shone dim for ship's night-time, and the red shadows clung to him. His knotted locks still glittered damp from the shower, jeweled beads sparkling.

Shit. Just a couple of fucking seconds to put the weapon away, Carrie. Wouldn't have killed you. But not taking the time might.

I swallowed. Spider had the disruptor strapped to his left thigh, ugly metal curves gleaming. Probably another weapon inside that bulky vest. And he was a hundred and twenty kilos if he was a pound. Verdict: I'd lose. My only chance was to talk my way out of it.

Casually, I clicked my pistol back into its clasp. "I could ask you why you're lurking outside my room."

"Never know what you'll hear." He jerked his head toward Natasha's cell. "Hope you weren't thinking of visiting her."

How much had Lux told him? I shrugged. "Nope. Just can't sleep. It's damn hot in there."

"And damn lonely. If you're looking for Sasha, he's sulking."

"So he fucking should be." No harm in keeping up the act. "What is it with you two anyway? Unrequited lust?"

"Does he look like my type to you?" Spider padded closer, catlike, and once again I was struck by the fluidity of his motion.

I shrugged. "Hey, I don't make assumptions."

"Neither do I." His eyes gleamed dark, dangerous, too close. "And that's why I don't buy you, lady. What you doing with him?" His melodious accent poured over my nerves like chili chocolate, hot and sweet but threatening. "Do you like him, hmm? Want to fuck him? 'Cause I know you aren't, not yet. Or are you just a new believer, come to poach off his reputation?"

Suddenly the corridor seemed very narrow. I had nowhere to back off to, the door hard against my shoulderblades. I licked dry lips. "It ain't that. We just kinda fell in together."

"Thieving his secrets, hmm? Trying to crawl under his skin? I'll tell you now, he's too clever for you, pretty. He's too clever for everyone."

He smelled of citrus bodywash, zingy and distracting. "Look, it's really none of your business."

"But it is. See, I've known Sasha a long time. I hate the wise-ass little weasel's entrails, but he's a diamond in this fucking cesspit of a galaxy and I swear to you, lady," Spider twisted my ponytail in his fingers, yanking tight, "if you screw him over, I'll come after you with everything I've got. And I mean *everything*."

My pulse thrummed, desperate to flee. But you didn't run from a tiger. You stared it down.

I tried what I hoped was a careless smile, though my throat ached under the pressure. "Well, hell, Lukas, I'd tell you that threats aren't your thing, but I gotta say you pull 'em off with style."

Amusement flickered in his eyes. "I practice."

"It's paying off."

"You think so? I'm making my point?" He loosened his grip on my hair, but his fingers lingered by my shoulder, a reminder.

"Admirably." I cracked my neck.

"You don't think I need to work on believability? Smack you around a bit, or something?"

"I'd say not necessary." I sucked in my bottom lip and gazed up at him through my lashes. Provocative, or merely considering? His choice. "Of course, you could always ..."

"I could always ...?"

"Show a little goodwill."

"Uh-huh." He stroked my shoulder, slight but definite.

I leaned closer. "You know. Give me a chance to prove myself?" If he told me where Dragonfly was, I'd save precious minutes. "Let me talk to Sasha. I could persuade him to stay. So long as I can stay too." I dared another smile. "You never know ... I could get to like it here."

His hand whispered across my thigh, caressing the corners of my pistol. "Think so?"

"Uh-huh." My throat dried. I'd surrendered. Rolled over and bared my belly. Only question was, did Spider give quarter?

His gaze drifted to my throat, and back up to my eyes ... And then he pushed the door open and shoved me backward into the cabin. My calves cracked against the bed's edge, and I landed hard on my butt on the mattress. And he still had my pistol in his hand.

For a moment, my muscles stung rigid. Another threat, or Spider's idea of foreplay?

But he didn't follow. He just watched me, that crazy golden swirl in his eyes. "For a rebel, you're a shocking liar."

I scrambled up, my pulse skipping. "Look, I only meant—"

"If you cared anything for Sasha, you wouldn't want him to stay with me." Spider jammed my pistol into his vest and cracked his big knuckles, one by one. "I was right, Lazuli, or whatever your name really is: I don't know you. And I definitely don't like you."

He slammed the door, plastic grating on metal, the unmistakable clunk of the four-armed lock twisting home, and his footsteps receded down the metal corridor.

23

I cursed and kicked the door. It didn't budge. Shit.

I forced myself to inhale slowly, calming my racing pulse. Any minute now, Spider could change his mind and come back to kill me. I had to get out of here. What happened after that was irrelevant. All that mattered now was escape.

Quickly I rifled again through the drawers and compartments, in case I'd missed a firearm, a knife, anything. No dice. The cabin was empty, uninhabited.

I wiped dripping hair from my face and punched the diode for the virtual valet. "Open the door."

Lockdown is activated by authorized p—

"Yeah, whatever. Shut up. Give me console command."

The control array sprang to life on the glowing glass touchscreen: channels and file systems and computer commands at my fingertips. I sat, thinking hard. I had no plasma pistol, and even if I did, the walls were alloy, not plastic, designed to withstand a torpedo barrage. I couldn't melt my way out. The aircon vents were only as wide as my hand. It was the doorway or no way.

I thumbed my ESE. "Nikita, you there?"

Just noise.

Shit. No hope of that fake ident.

I jammed the ESE away and poked at the comms channel on the control array. "Valet, let me talk to the bridge."

Communications available to authoriz—

“Lousy friend you are. Deactivate.”

Deactivating.

Guess I’d have to hack my way out. But the clock flashed in the screen’s corner, another minute ticking over. Nearly 3 a.m. ship time. Ten in the morning on the station. Only two hours left. And cracking codes took time.

I frowned at the fancy touchscreen display, each command in a nice neat colored box. Aircon. Lights. Comms. Duty schedules. Personnel records. Surveillance. Everything a competent young junior officer could want. And nothing that would help me. I poked one at random anyway. The security ident box came up. I tried another. Security ident. I wasn’t logged in, so nothing would work.

I jacked my ESE and ran the password generator. Should only take a second.

The screen flashed, and the diode on my ESE blinked out.

I tried again. Same thing. Rejected. Someone in Spider’s crew had overwritten the security system with their own voice protocols. I couldn’t get in.

Unless ...

A memory flashed, from years ago in the marine corps. Fifteen months in the bowels of a battleship, a protracted war with some gutsy rebel alliance, and our only shore time spent fighting our way along midnight streets in a storm of hot glass and lasers. Me and my friends copped three weeks’ extra duty for breaking into the officers’ gym for a splash in the swimming pool. The guy in the bunk next to me had wagered a red jellybar that I couldn’t break in, but I’d learned the trick stealing from the soldiers' food store on my home world, and we got a good hour in the hot tub before some early-rising lieutenant found us and kicked our dripping butts. After fifteen months of sweaty war, it had been totally worth it.

This was a third-gen battleship. The trick might not work. But it might.

I squeezed into the bathroom, searching the walls. What I needed was wire. I spied the soap dispenser, and levered the white box off the wall with a blunt plastic knife from the ration bucket. Citrus soap splashed my wrist, the scent an unsettling reminder of Spider. I wiped it away. A fastener popped on the lever and a silvery spring jumped into my hand. Perfect.

I sat at the console and untwisted the coils until the wire was as straight as I could make it. As long as my finger. That'd be enough.

With the knife, I pried off the white plastic casing on the side of the screen and felt along the bare metal edge with my fingertips. There it was, almost hidden by the rim. A keyhole, shaped round like the contact on a chip. The maintainer's reset switch.

I folded the wire in two and jammed it into the keyhole. The screen flashed blank, and relit, with only a letterboard and a blinking cursor in the top corner. Reboot to system prompt.

About twenty seconds. That's all I had until the core system realized there wasn't a real key in the slot and reloaded the touchscreen system. The commands I could access were the same, nothing special. But with luck, voice ident would be offline.

Swiftly I jacked my ESE and called up the security system.

Fifteen seconds.

The diode on my ESE blinked and a password spat up on the screen. Yes.

Ten seconds.

A list of security options flashed, and I sorted through them, my pulse thudding. Jeez. What was it with superconductor geeks and making up words?

Five seconds. Out of time. I sorted faster, my finger slipping.

There it was. Cabin security positive. Alter the attributes. Minus, zero, empty.

I hit enter, and the console screen blanked out.

Shit. Too late.

And then the doorlock clunked open.

I let out a breath, sweating. Just in time.

I retrieved my ESE, and pulled out the wire and dropped it in the toilet. It couldn't help me open Natasha's door; this console didn't have those commands. But at least I was free.

So what now?

I scraped wet hair off my neck. My top stuck to me, uncomfortable. I peeled it off, leaving only my tight cropped undershirt. I wriggled my hips to get some fresh air on my skin. Damn, it was hot in here, and I didn't smell good. I could really use a shower.

But it'd get hotter if Spider caught me, and Natasha was on borrowed time. She had to be my priority. Get her free. Hide her someplace so Spider couldn't find her, and worry about escaping afterwards. Raven-class battleships had a squadron of little Thorn fighter-skirmishers. Maybe we could scramble one and get away. They had a tiny slipspace burst and limited long-range nav, but it was better than nothing. And if I came across a weapon along the way ... Well, it still wasn't too late to settle that unfinished Dragonfly business.

I straightened. "Valet, show me the corridor outside."

The image flashed up: the narrow hallway dappled in red shadow, the row of doors silent and still. Three shifts of four junior officers on a Raven, with a cabin for each. No movement. I squinted. Something about the image looked odd. But I didn't have time to study it.

My heart thudding, I twisted the handle as silently as I could and eased the door open.

No reaction.

I peered left and right. Dim reddish light, same as before. No one.

I slipped out and closed the door. Nothing I could do about locking it. I'd just have to hope no one came to check on me for a while.

I stole up the corridor, my boots whispering on the energy-absorbent floor. My palms prickled, and sweat stung my eyes. The walls gleamed faintly in the red glow, the smooth plastic broken every now and then by tube-covered power conduits or safety strips in luminous blue indicating the exit route. Around the corner, where an emergency ladder led down to the next level. Another empty corridor. I'd counted the doors to Natasha's room when Lux and I put her there: third on the left. I tiptoed up to the door and listened. Nothing. Maybe she was sleeping.

Scrape.

Behind me.

I whirled, sweat dripping in my eyes, hands darting to defend. And something hard crashed into my ankles, sweeping my feet from under me.

24

My skull cracked onto the floor and bounced. Fingers plastered over my mouth and a hard body landed on top of me, pinning me down. A warm metal weapon jabbed under my chin.

I sucked in air through my nose, blinking. I couldn't move. Hair brushed my face, the smell of dust and spice, and inwardly I groaned. Only one long-haired asshole on this ship. And I was weaponless.

Dragonfly jammed a sharp knee into mine, holding me down. His body pressed against me, too familiar, and I wriggled but he wouldn't let me go and it only made my skin rub against his. By the smooth slide of the metal under my chin, I knew his gun was an atom-flash, and it was only warm. He hadn't armed it. More fool him.

He gazed down at me, inches away. "You gonna keep quiet?"

My pulse thudded. It hadn't escaped my notice that I was practically naked underneath him, and that the slide of his sweat on my skin made me think dirty thoughts, and it maddened me. Without blinking, I grabbed his hair, hurled my hips upwards and threw him over onto his back.

My shoulder slapped into the wall, but I held on. I landed on top of him with a thump and squeezed my thighs tight around his hips. I slammed his head into the floor with a fistful of his hair and forced one of his wrists down beside it. He'd changed his clothes, I saw. Flashy, for him; more like Spider in a black combat vest that left his arms bare, his hair loose and brushing his shoulders. Made him look bigger, edgy, more warlike. I didn't like it.

But my body insisted I did like it. My pulse wouldn't quit, and although it had a lot to do with the danger we were in, that wasn't all of it. My flesh ached inside, and my skin shivered, all soft and touchable. Like I wanted *him* to touch me. Like I wanted his hands on my body, his lips on mine, his kiss on my throat. I swallowed, dry. No reason involved here. No facts I could weigh up, no pros and cons to be considered. Something about him just made me all hot and girly, and I hated it.

I felt like screaming. There were a bunch of men on this ship. Lux had great hair and a supernova smile. Spider was bigger, stronger, more dangerous. Why did it have to be *him*?

Well, it wouldn't matter for much longer.

I leaned in harder. My breasts pressed against his chest, and it felt good for more reasons than one. "Yeah," I whispered, triumphant. "I'll be real quiet. It's you who'll scream."

He shifted slightly, and something warm and metallic jabbed into my bare midriff. His other hand, caught between us. With the atomflash still in it.

Shit.

He must have seen my expression, because he shrugged, as best he could with me on top of him. "I didn't know what you were doing here. Had to be sure. You gonna get off me?"

His finger moved against my belly, and I jumped as the flash armed, sizzling against my wet skin. Damn it. I let go and jumped up.

He hopped up with me, covering me with his weapon, and grabbed my wrist, tugging me into an empty cabin across the corridor. I struggled, but not hard enough to make him shoot me. Just enough to let him know I wasn't happy. But my skin burned as he clicked the door shut. I'd let him get the jump on me again, and again he hadn't killed me. One of these days, my luck would run out.

I folded my arms, all too aware of my bare midriff and his eyes on it. I had a taut midriff. He looked impressed. That wasn't the point.

"All right, you caught me trying to free her." I fought to keep my voice low. "Go on, shoot me if it'll make you feel good."

"What? No. I ..." He powered down the flash with a wet hiss, and I could have sworn he looked sheepish, that ironic twist to his lip. "I guess I thought you weren't coming. I'm sorry."

"You're sorry?" His words made no sense. My blood boiled hotter. I wanted to shove him into the wall, crack his head back into the plastic. "About what, your little speech to me up by the bridge? You should be fucking sorry after the lies you've spun. You want to leave her here, fine. You'll just have to stop me."

I pushed him aside and reached for the door.

"Please."

I halted, my heart thick.

He didn't grab me. Didn't aim his weapon. Didn't even move. Just that one little word, stressed to cracking with all the compassion I'd ever felt from him. And it stopped me like a steelplated wall. I didn't have to turn. The bathroom mirror showed me his face, and my stomach knotted.

He swallowed. "Those things I said … they weren't true. I guess I … Well, I thought you'd be better off here."

"You thought *what*?" Now I did turn, and I stared at him, bewildered.

"With Lukas. In the middle of the action. You're so young. So angry. You don't need lessons from me. You can go your own way."

"But—"

"No, Lazuli." He hushed me with a gentle finger on my lips. "Natasha is a suicide mission. You don't want to come."

"Bloody right I want to come!" I swiped his hand away, furious. Had he tricked me again? I didn't know what was real any more. He made me feel slow, and I hated it. I wasn't used to being the stupid one.

But it was more than that. Strange warmth flooded my heart, and I realized it was relief. I hadn't been wrong. There really was more to him. And that made me madder still.

If we survived this, I'd kill him for that alone.

"I don't care what you think," I snapped. "I'm not leaving her here. If that makes me soft, then just shoot me and get it over with."

I caught my breath, appalled. On the list of smart things to say right now, *kill me if you think I'm soft* didn't feature.

But he closed his eyes briefly and sighed, pressing one hand over his heart and dipping his head in old-fashioned apology. "*Lo siento, señorita.* I don't know what to say. I shouldn't have doubted you."

Bewilderment stuffed my head with cotton. "So … what was all that by the bridge? Trying to scare me off?"

"And for Spider's benefit. The ship hears everything."

"Even this?" I glanced around, agitated. We were keeping our voices low, but that meant nothing to a surveillance system.

He shrugged. "Maybe."

"Then how can I trust that you're telling me the truth?"

He checked the charge on his flash and primed the contacts. "Well, I'm about to go get myself killed saving an Imperial admiral's daughter from my best friend. That enough to convince you?"

"But …" I swallowed. I had to know, but I dreaded it. "Why?"

"Because Lukas's ego isn't worth her life. And because some ideas are worth dying for. It's up to us to decide which."

My guts knotted. Fancy words, but they pierced an aching spot deep inside. What did I have that was worth dying for? The Empire? Mishka? My promotion? I'd never thought of death as a satisfying end. More like a screaming injustice, with a curse on my lips and rage burning in my heart. Damn him for his convictions.

But it wasn't like I had a choice. If I stayed here, I was dead. Natasha was a means to an end, and so was he.

"If we get out of this alive," I said, "I'll give you a list."

"Thank you."

His gaze glowed warm.

I squirmed again. "Don't thank me yet. What's your plan?"

"You already saw it. Get her out of the cabin, hide, get off the ship."

"As good as mine, then. How exactly will we get away?"

"Shuttlecraft?"

"Can you steal it?"

He laughed. "Can you fly it?"

I gave him a lofty scowl. "Maybe not as flashy as Lux, but I can try, so long as you don't mind a few dents."

"Then I can steal it, so long as you don't mind a few burned bits."

"Okay." I thought hard, my head aching in the heat. "But how will we get back to Vyachesgrad? That shuttle only had a basic battlenav. What's to stop Spider chasing us down and blowing us to spacedust?"

Dragonfly flipped out his golden hyperchip and flashed it at me. "Didn't think I'd been admiring the scenery for the last hour, did you?"

"I figured you showered."

"You noticed."

I'd noticed, all right. Wet hair, bare skin, fresh clean scent ... "Don't flatter yourself."

He traced a lazy finger over the naked curve of my waist. "And here I was thinking you wore this for me."

I shoved him away, flushing. He never gave up. "You gonna tell me what that does or not?"

"I set up a little accident in the virtual navspace. To be instigated remotely from the chip when we're ready. They can't follow us if they're in real space."

"You'll leave them stuck without slip?"

"No. It'll only take Vish ten minutes to fix it. But in ten minutes, we'll be gone." That maddening little smile. "Have I impressed you yet?"

"We'll see if it works first." Hell, compared to my non-existent plan, it was fucking brilliant. "What about getting Natasha out of that cabin? And how do we reach the shuttlecraft bay without getting caught?"

"I was hoping you'd have a few ideas on those."

I chewed my thumbnail. "Well, I suppose we could just blast her out and run for it."

"Set a feedback in the atomflash? Could work. Might blow half the corridor away with it—"

"—and Natasha too. Okay, bad idea. What if …" A spark ignited in my mind. "Can you set that accident of yours off from anywhere?"

Dragonfly shrugged. "Sure. So long as there's a console."

"Right." I fidgeted on the spot, ready. "You go down to the shuttlebay and do what needs doing. I'll break her out. Give me a few minutes, then set your accident in motion, and I'll run her down there while they're still figuring out what's going on. Okay?"

"It's the worst plan I've ever heard. I'm in." He wristed his hair back. "How will you break her out?"

"I have no idea. I'll think of something."

"I could neutralize the voice recognition nodes. Give you a chance to … what's the word? Play a trick?"

"Spoof it?"

"That's the one."

"D'you think you can?"

A shrug. "I wrote the codes. I should be able to unwrite them."

"Figures. Give me your flash."

I tensed, ready for argument. If he wouldn't give me his weapon, it'd prove he wasn't really on my side. But he handed it over without pause.

As I took it, his fingers brushed mine. He hesitated. "Look ..."

I turned away. I didn't want apologies, explanations. I didn't want anything that made him human.

He held on. "Lazuli?"

I averted my face. "There's nothing to say, okay? Can we just get on?"

He touched my chin, warm, making me look. His gaze was guarded, shadowed so I couldn't see in. "Just so you know. If we live, this isn't over. If you come with me, you'll see my life. It's up to you if you learn from it."

I hesitated, unsure. Was that trust? Would he finally let me in on his secrets? I should be pleased my plan was working. And I was. But he scared me, this Dragonfly, with his sincerity and weary sorrow. It made me wonder how he'd become that way. If I dug too deep, I might discover something I wouldn't like.

Whatever. We'd probably be dead in the next ten minutes anyway.

His fingers lingered on my chin, and I wanted to rest my cheek in his palm, close my eyes, let him kiss me goodbye. I wanted to slam his head into the wall so hard his teeth shattered.

I jammed the atomflash in my pistol holster and walked stiffly to the console. "You want a go at that voice system?"

"Yes. But show me surveillance first. I want to know where they are."

He stepped up beside me, but he didn't try to touch me again.

I was grateful. I was angry. I didn't know what I was.

I brushed my finger over the screen. "Valet, show me the crew."

The display lit the air, divided into four this time. The bridge, where Spider lounged in the command chair, and Foxy and Lux threw virtual dice on the comms station display. The next screen showed Vish curled sleeping on a dark blue quilt like a pimply red-headed elf, his fingers tucked under his chin. The third screen, hash. And in the fourth, that empty corridor again, dappled in dark red shadow.

I peered closer, and my skin prickled. It wasn't the same corridor.

In the original image, the light had shone from the left, throwing the doorframes into sharp relief. In this one, the shadows definitely speared from the right, and in the image's corner, I spied the faint outline of a ladder.

It was the corridor outside this room.

And as I watched, movement glinted deep in the shadows. Elusive, like all those other shadows I'd been jumping at since I got here. My scalp tingled, and swiftly I checked the other screens. Spider, Lux, Foxy, Vish. All present and correct.

I glanced at Dragonfly. He glanced at me. And my stomach flipped cold.

Silently, I pulled out the atomflash. Powered it, a faint hiss. Tiptoed to the door.

Dragonfly wrapped his fingers around the locking handle, and when I jerked my head, he pulled it open. I whirled out and covered left, aiming two-handed into the dark.

A dark giggle, and a flash of wild black hair.

I fired. Heat flared, and the stink of charred hair stung my nose. I sprinted around the corner, but he—she?—had already fled.

I cursed, and my mind flashed back to that dirty corridor on Vyachesgrad. Foxy and Lux pinning Dragonfly to the wall. Spider stalking from the shadows. And someone hitting me. From behind.

It wasn't Vish. He'd stayed behind to flash us back to the battleship. I'd known all along, and I'd just been too dumb to realize it. There was a fifth crew member on *LightBringer.*

And he'd just heard everything we'd said.

25

"Shit." I wiped my brow with my forearm. "Who the hell was that?"

"No idea. Does it matter? We just lost our surprise." Dragonfly held out his hand. "Give me that. We'll blow the door."

I flipped the handgun butt-first for him to take, and we ran back to Natasha's cabin. Whoever Asshole Number Five was, no doubt he'd scuttled straight for a comms unit to tell Spider our plan. We had minutes. Seconds, maybe.

"Guess it doesn't matter if we make noise now," I said.

"Like we've got a choice. Shield your eyes." He fired rapidly down the corridor, the pure white flashes dazzling me. Ten or fifteen shots at nothing in particular to drain the charge. Then he put a single shot into the doorframe beside the lock at point-blank. The white plastic coating vaporized. Metal hissed and popped, electricity zapping from a melted conduit. A security alarm screeched. The air sizzled with charge, and hair lifted on my arms.

"Cable," he snapped.

I tore off a piece of the broken conduit, my fingers singeing, and handed it to him.

"Natasha, get back," I yelled. "We're gonna blow the door."

Swiftly he stripped the superconducting wire clean, and jammed both raw ends under the atomflash contacts. A feedback circuit. He fired the flash, and the wire glowed hot. "Something to tie it with."

I yanked the shrinkband from my hair. "Good enough?"

"*Es perfecto.*" He wrapped the elastic rubber around the trigger and yanked it tight. The wire sizzled, and he jammed the makeshift bomb into the broken plastic beside the door.

We both dived for cover just in time.

Boom. The walls shuddered, and we hit the floor together. Molten metal splashed. He covered me, shielding me from the radiant heat, but my hair still singed and stank and my bare skin stung like sunburn with tiny shrapnel.

Hot metal dust clouded and settled. I pushed him off me and scrambled up, wiping soot from my eyes. A ragged hole gaped in the wall, exposing the entire cabin and half the one next to it. Smoke billowed. Flames licked the plastic walls, the brown stink of burning polymer like acid in my mouth. And in the corner, under the table, cowered Natasha, streaked in soot and speckled with blood. If he hadn't fired the flash half-empty first, she'd probably be dead.

Tears striped her dirty face, and she crunched shaking fists in her ruined nightgown. "Don't hurt me. Please."

Dragonfly crawled over to her, coated in dust and dirt, and split her cuffs with a tiny plastic disruptor. More surprises. Had he stolen that from Foxy, or did he have it all along?

"Come on. We have to run now," he told her. "Stand up."

She shrank away, and I crouched before her, frustrated. We didn't have time for this. "Told you I'd come for you, didn't I? Well, here I am. Sasha will help us. Just do as we say and everything will be fine."

Her chin firmed. "Okay." She stumbled up, gripping his hand, her legs shaky.

He steadied her. "Elevator, Lazuli. Before they get it. Go."

My mind raced as I hurtled around the corner through acrid smoke. We'd melted our only handgun; we were weaponless.

As I skidded to a halt in front of the elevator, my heart sank. Lights shifted along the panel above the door. Spider's crew were already on their way down, and there was only one elevator in this section. And even if we found another, we'd never get all the way down to the shuttlecraft bay before them.

I ran back to the corner and collided with Dragonfly and Natasha. "Too late," I panted. "Ladder."

I skidded down the ladder on my hands, plastic scorching my palms. Next level was battle systems. Lights blinked on rows of dark green neuropanels, the air damp and heavy. Green neon plasma conduits rippled beneath the black grille floor, and the lights shone blue, the longer wavelengths filtered out. Somewhere here lay the virtual weaponspace, a black cocoon where tech-sharpened operators fed masses of battle data directly from the sensors to their brains with savage electrodes that left no room for error or distraction. Battleship weaponeers were a sought-after breed, highly intuitive and borderline psychotic. When they jacked into one fight too many, their conscious minds sloughed away into the machine and they emerged as drooling vegetables. They said that if you listened carefully on a silent night in the weaponspace, you could hear them screaming.

Who was the weaponeer on Spider's crew? Not Foxy. Vish was the pilot, Spider the captain. That left Lux, with his creepy premonitions. Or the mysterious Asshole Number Five. Either way, the psychosis quotient on this ship had just spiked. Great.

Natasha started to climb down carefully, clutching the ladder tightly. I yanked her ankle, tumbling her into my arms.

Dragonfly vaulted down beside her and sprinted for a console, dust drifting from his hair. "*Un momento.*"

"Ten minutes, you say?"

"Plus or minus." He jammed his hyperchip into the slot, fingertips racing over the touchscreen.

A black storage compartment hung bolted to the wall beside the console, locked with a virtual combo. It looked like a gun locker. I pushed Natasha aside, and attacked it with my best roundhouse kick, a yell bursting from my lips. Metal crunched and folded, and the flimsy lock broke. I tore the buckled cover away, hinges screeching.

Plasma pistols, shiny and black, a small model but still deadly. Little cylindrical charges already inserted, lightstrip glowing to show they were full, or close enough.

I ripped a pair from their hinges and stuffed a handful of extra charges into my shorts. "We have guns," I called.

"Excellent." Dragonfly popped his chip and caught the pistol I tossed him. "One for her?"

"You shitting me? She'll set her own hair on fire."

"I can shoot." Natasha's voice quavered, but she kept it steady.

She was doing okay, I admitted grudgingly, for a schoolgirl who'd never gotten her nails dirty.

Dragonfly quirked his eyebrows. "Would you want to do this unarmed?"

I didn't have time to argue. I grabbed another pistol and thrust it into her hands. "Pay attention. Safety, power, trigger. Point and squeeze. Don't close your eyes when you fire, and if you aim it at me, I'll blow your head off. Got it?"

She swallowed, and fumbled the safety off. At least she knew that much.

We ran, the hard floor clanging under our feet. No shock protection here. The black walls gleamed with red-lit instruments. Glittering cyberware was molded into twisted green neuroflesh, metal and skin contorted like a beast in pain. Here and there, dead synapses rotted, stinking, the excess organics no longer trimmed by careful Imperial maintenance crews, and in one corner I thought I saw an aborted attempt at a limb. Neuroflesh was alive and melancholy with half-remembered genetic instinct, and if you left it alone, it grew.

Another ladder down, this time to the reactor level, a massive open space where the slipspace drive flavored its quarks and charged its photons and plied whatever other quantum black arts were necessary to warp the fragile cosmic fabric to its will. We sprinted along under a metal catwalk, past the long shiny cylinder of the starboard particle accelerator, our reflections bulging monstrous in the dim purple light.

Dragonfly ran beside me, Natasha close behind, as we approached a T-junction where the accelerator curved to the right.

"I assume you know where you're going?" he said.

I panted, my breath light but strong. Times like these, I was even more thankful for the ultragym. "Now why would you assume that?"

"Stubbornness? No, wait. Denial that we're about to die?"

Or had he already mined the dataspace for info about Lazuli, secretly-ex-military rebel wannabe? I didn't have time to allay his suspicions. We needed to get out of here. "Deny away then. Should be another set of elevators beyond this junction—"

Bright plasma rounds sizzled into the floor as we hurtled into the corridor. Hot metal splashed my boots and I skidded to a halt, off balance.

Dragonfly yanked me back. Natasha collided with us, and we thudded into the wall for cover.

Distant laughter drifted from the left. "Told you so," sang Lux, ripe with giggles, and more plasma fire skipped across the floor like a rock on water, leaving molten holes in its wake.

At least two guns, maybe three. I gritted my teeth. They'd known just where to find us. Little bastard really did think like other people.

Natasha huddled against the wall, her knuckles white as she gripped her pistol. "That spiky-haired one's a freak," she muttered. "Your friends really suck."

Dragonfly touched her chin. "Hey. You're doing well. Just a little further."

She jerked away, but not before she blushed, and I had to grin. Little schoolgirl had a crush. Not that I could blame her. He looked dangerous and piratical, dusty chocolate hair spilling loose, bare arms coated in soot and sweat. Just like a dirty rebel scumbag, in fact, for the first time since I'd met him. The irony didn't escape me.

"Shuttlebay is still three levels down," I whispered. "They're in the way. Like our chances of winning a shootout?"

"No." Dragonfly's gaze was dark, candid. If he'd lied before, he wasn't lying now. Refreshing.

I adjusted my sweating grip. "Okay. Thorn tubes are next level, down to the right. It's our only option."

"You want to jack into a neuroware fighter? You'll fry your brain."

More shots, the floor catching fire. I risked a look around the corner, and dodged back from the barrage of plasma rounds that greeted me. Long narrow corridor, Spider up on the catwalk, Foxy and Lux at ground level. Vish must have stayed on the bridge. No sign of Asshole Number Five.

I crouched, ready to jump. "They'd be stupid to follow us, wouldn't they? I'll fly it without neural contact. We'll just have no weapons. You got a better idea?"

"Actually, I do."

Dragonfly wrapped his hand in my hair, dragged me close and planted his lips on mine. Hot, alive, dangerous. Addictive. A thrill junkie, just like me. I wanted to open my mouth, wrap my wrists around his neck, press my body against him until we burned.

I jerked back, my pulse stumbling.

He grinned, devastating. "You didn't say it had to be a *helpful* idea."

"Oh, please," muttered Natasha, rolling her eyes. "You guys are way too old."

I glared at him, and hefted my weapon meaningfully. "There's something seriously wrong with you."

"You noticed. Ready?"

"Readier than you." I jumped up, and we danced out into the arc of fire.

***

I ran backward and laid down rapid fire, holding the recharge lever back with my left hand to shoot faster. Lux hit the deck, spraying his fire, and Foxy dived for cover in a doorway. My shots sputtered. I released the lever and the recharge kicked in with a hiss. I switched my aim to Spider up on the catwalk, and metal splashed as my shots sizzled into the handrail. Behind me, Dragonfly, with Natasha, sprinted for the ladder at the far end, firing as he ran, his plasma bolts *schlupping* over my right shoulder. Ozone and hot metal stung my nose, the familiar stink of battle. My pulse banged harder, hotter, slicing my nerves to a fine fighting edge.

Spider shot at Dragonfly, missed and cursed colorfully. "Fine," he called. "Leave. It's what you're good at. You coulda said goodbye this time."

I fired another barrage at him, and the panel behind him burst into flames.

We reached the ladder, and Dragonfly shoved Natasha down one-handed. I covered, crouching low. He dragged me back, and together we stumbled down to another steel floor, noisy with the rush of coolant through thick white pipes bolted to the ceiling.

“This way.” I dragged him up the corridor to where the wall was riddled with man-sized holes like cocoons. Fighter tubes, a quick-release system for pilots. Drop in, lock out, depart.

Boots clattered behind us on the ladder, and shots carved molten holes in the floor.

We pushed Natasha into the tube first. She squealed as she slipped down the slide. I shoved Dragonfly forward, but he hung back, and I gave up and vaulted into the tube. I slid down the plastic-smoothed steel on my butt, my sweaty thighs catching, and landed in a pile of torn nightgown and soft bruised limbs. I dragged us both to our feet on the fighter’s tiny deck.

No room to walk. Just a square meter of flat white deck between two steeply tiered seats, dark clearviews slanting down above a glass instrument panel and a virtual display that kicked on as I entered and filled the air with diagnostics and navspace data in fine green detail.

I pushed Natasha up into the weapons chair, holstered my pistol and vaulted down into the pilot’s seat, pulling the harness over my shoulders and clipping it tight.

Above us, plasma sizzled, and Dragonfly dropped to the deck. He jumped behind me into weapons and dragged Natasha into his lap, yanking the harness on over both of them. “In. Let’s go.”

Already I’d primed the slipspace drive to howling. I cut contact and slammed my palm on the airlock release. Air hissed, and plastic slammed shut, and with a clunk of releasing magclamps and a rich arcfuel spray, we shot out into blackness.

26

Eighty-seven minutes and thirty-two seconds later by the clock, the clearview shimmered blue, and we dropped out into real space, the light-sprinkled sphere of Vyachesgrad outpost glittering in the clearview.

After leaving *LightBringer*, we'd locked onto the nearest slipspace beacon, and by the time Vish (or whoever) repaired the mess Dragonfly's magic chip had made of their navspace, we were long gone. It was simple to navigate via the slipspace beaconweb back to Vyachesgrad. Whatever stealthy trajectory *LightBringer* was flying, it hadn't taken us far from the station.

I rolled my shoulders, tense, the display painting green and red streaks onto my body. Escape from the psycho rebels: check. But now we had to return the admiral's daughter and retrieve *Ladrona*, and Vyachesgrad would be on high alert.

The station loomed closer, its docking arms gleaming with floodlights. I twisted a virtual knob, and the gammaspace filter stained the clearview scarlet. The approach grid popped up. All the vectors were outlined in yellow, except for one narrow arc.

"Well, look at that," I said. "They're closed for approach."

"What are the chances?"

Pretty much the first thing Dragonfly had said for the whole trip. Not that I'd been the queen of conversation either. My nerves still stretched sharp from the firefight, and my thoughts kept lurching back to how he'd kissed me, to the hot weight of his body pressing mine into the floor outside Natasha's cabin, and what it'd be like if he did both at once. It wasn't a subject I wanted to discuss.

Natasha had crawled from the harness as soon as he let her, and now she curled in the tiny deck area between the seats, her face pale under the soot. He'd reclaimed her pistol. She didn't look happy.

I craned my neck to eye him. "We could call them up and tell them we've got her on board."

He laughed. "Nice idea. If you want them to shoot us as soon as we step off the ship."

"Then what do you suggest, smart-ass?"

"I think our etherwave just went offline." He touched a pulsing light in the display above my head, and the red stripe indicating transmitter power slipped to zero.

"O-kaay."

"Turn the gammaspace off. It's vector zero-six-zero arc three, or thereabouts. Just fly us in like you've got no comms, and we'll deal when we get there."

"And they won't send their Slivers to intercept us because?"

"Maybe it'll be our lucky day. You got a better idea?"

I shrugged, tense, and reached for the arc rockets, rocking the ship from side to side in the universal signal for *I can't hear you.*

As I reached the approach grid boundary, etherwave crackled. "Thorn on zero-six-three, this is Vyachesgrad Black, identify."

Black was the marine control callsign. The station was on security lockdown. I snorted, safe with our transmitter switched off. "Idiots."

Closer and closer we came.

"Thorn, the station is in secure lockdown. Identify or we will launch interceptors."

"Sure, why not? We're a pair of crazy rebels bringing back your admiral's daughter. Why don't you come kill us?"

"I hope they do!" Natasha's girlish voice stung harsh. "I hope they come in their ships and blow you out of the sky!"

"Shut up, party girl." I shot her a scowl. "There's gratitude for you."

"Thorn, this is Vyachesgrad. Respond—"

"And you can shut up too." I flicked the receiver off, but my hands jittered on the controls. They hadn't launched interceptors. Why not? What were they up to?

"Relax. They won't scramble an attack." Dragonfly spoke softly, calm.

I was neither. "Why not?"

"Because Lukas told them not to, remember? For all they know, he's right here, ready to flash out of slipspace and blow them all to oblivion." Metal clicked as he jammed a new charge into his pistol. "Try the vertical docking ring, close to *Ladrona.* I don't want to have to blast my way out. And get ready to run."

"Already on the way."

I cozied the ship up to an empty slot on the docking ring—not as stylish an approach as Dragonfly's, but close—and the automatic airlock extended, clunking against the hull and attaching itself to the outer hatch with an electric crunch of magnets. Even the Imperial security lockdown hadn't overridden the docking safety protocols. Maybe Verenski was still hoping Spider would return his daughter alive. Lucky for him we'd taken matters into our own hands.

We had seconds before marines were on top of us. My fingers fumbled unclipping my harness, and I cursed, forcing myself to slow down. Finally I peeled the straps off and climbed from the chair. Dragonfly was already up, and for a moment all three of us crowded into the tiny deck space.

I sucked in a spice-scented breath and flushed. Damn. Thinking was difficult with my breasts jammed up against his chest. "What do you think? Human shield?"

"Untidy." He jammed his hand between us and came up with a coiled silver smartcuff. "How about this?"

Natasha squealed and scrambled for the airlock tunnel. "Get that thing away from m—ugh!"

We grabbed a thrashing ankle each, dragged her down and tossed her into the pilot's chair. Efficiently, Dragonfly cuffed her wrists to the seat post.

"This is your second chance," he told her, his tone sharp. "You might not get another. Better make sure the rest of your life means something."

And without waiting for me, he climbed up the ladder beside the slippery slide and popped the airlock open.

Silence. Only hissing air, the distant whirr of gravity engines, and Natasha's sputtering curses.

I hauled myself up the ladder and grabbed his hand, and together we climbed out through horizontal glass doors onto the docking arm floor. The black rubber was littered with dirt and metal fragments. Icelights glared. Above us, thick windows warped the starfield, floodlights shining in.

I whipped out my pistol, covering left and right along the docking arm's vast length. Dragonfly did the same. No one. We'd gotten here before the security team. Forty-three seconds from the garrison to Natasha's quarters, I remembered, and we were further away than that.

But not too much further. Boots thudded on rubber, and at the far end a shout rang out.

We sprinted, hurdling tools, lengths of pipe, a laser cutter left unpacked. Past a small freighter, its rad-shields cut loose to expose the curling sensor array. Then a battered marine dropship half-coated in pink rust primer. My lungs burned cold in the thin air. *Ladrona* lay between us and them. We were running toward a firefight. Not one of our better plans.

Just as we reached the airlock, the first plasma shots whizzed over our heads, and a harsh voice yelled out, "Stop, or we'll shoot!"

"You already did, idiot." I fired a heavy barrage just above head height, making him duck for cover.

More armed marines spilled around the corner, their tight black armor gleaming, taking up defensive positions in doorways and behind bulkheads. Dragonfly punched in the airlock code, his fingers a blur, and I covered, picking my shots carefully. Behind us on the Thorn, Natasha still yelled and cursed faintly, her voice swallowed by metal.

The glass airlock snapped open. I backed up. The marine sergeant darted out and fired at me, missing by centimeters. I couldn't help but gasp and sway to one side, and a bolt from some random gun glanced into my ribs. Acid fire splashed deep. I screamed and clutched at it, the burn spreading. Fuck me, it hurt.

Tears stung my eyes, and my pistol hand shook as I fired. I retreated into the pain, nothing but the corridor and the shimmering starfield filling my vision. In my mind, I was a soldier again, Corporal Thatcher, field stripes heavy on my shoulder, dragging my half-dead platoon to safety on my most basic instincts. *Shoot. Run. Don't fall. Repeat.*

Warm hands on my shoulders, the spicy smell of his hair. A whisper in my ear, or a yell: "Lazuli. You're hit."

I snapped to, my own crusted flesh crunching under my palm. I didn't want him to see. "I'm okay." My voice echoed distantly in my head. A sick laugh crippled me. I'd survived Spider's lunatic hospitality, escaped *LightBringer* unharmed, returned that silly girl to safety. And now I had to get shot by my own side, and rescued by a rebel.

Dragonfly dragged me back, and together we stumbled onto *Ladrona* in a trail of sweat and burned blood.

27

Dragonfly hauled me up the stairs to the saloon deck, his arm cool around my fiery ribs. Sickness gripped my guts: *Ladrona*'s security biochem kicking in. I barely noticed. Sweat dripped over my hair, my skin, my weeping burn, and it stung like a poisondart. I stumbled and the burned skin ripped, laying my muscle bare. Pain sheeted. I crunched my teeth on a yell. Don't let him see. For god's sake, don't let him care.

He laid me on the soft black sunken lounge, where, what seemed like years before, he'd stolen his hyperchip from my shorts while I slept. Remnants of his gammaspace link still littered the floor, stripped wire and solder and slivers of glass.

I tried to stand, my legs weak. He pushed me back down. "Stay there," he ordered, his voice stressed like I'd never heard it before.

I stayed, gritting my teeth on the pain. I didn't look at my ribs. Didn't want to see. God, I hated getting shot.

Dragonfly ran to his console, and in moments the luminous green biochem fizzled away, the clearview shutters snapped open and *Ladrona* lurched to port and dived away from Vyachesgrad, arc rockets howling as they accelerated. The stardrive kicked in, jerking us forward in a smear of stars, accelerating toward slip velocity. Almost before the slipspace coil warmed up, he hit the contact. The ship shuddered in protest, visible light tearing apart into prisms like falling jewels, but then the familiar redshift shimmer erupted and the clearview blanked out.

The sudden lack of motion rocked me forward, lighting fresh agony. Slipspace. We'd escaped.

Urgently, Dragonfly sketched route details into the navspace and tapped impatient nails on the glass, his mouth tight. "Today, you stupid ... Fuck. My brain works faster than this thing."

"Where are we going?" My dry voice cracked dully. I didn't really care. I just wanted to think about something other than pain.

He skidded to his knees at my feet. "Never mind that. Let me see."

I shuffled away. I didn't want him to see. Didn't want him touching me. My shell had remained intact, barely, while we'd fought and lied and run together on the battleship. Now, with the pain—with adrenaline and endorphins and god knows what else sprinting around in my blood—I didn't know if I could keep him out.

I covered myself with one arm pressed to my screaming side. "I'm okay. Just give me the medkit—"

"Let me see." He pulled my arm away, gentle but inescapable, and his soot-streaked face shone pale. "*Madre de dios.* You're coming upstairs." And he unstrapped my pistol and reached for my hand.

"No."

I pulled away, pain and fear tumbling over in my mind like bolts in a falling glass jar. I knew it was irrational, but I couldn't let him touch me. Couldn't let him heal me. I had to heal myself.

But he just swept me up in his arms and carried me up the flimsy white steps, plastic creaking under our weight. He turned sideways, my feet brushing the white plastic walls, and laid me on his bed.

"Hold on. Just stay awake."

Distantly I registered that the sheet was soft, cool on my fevered skin. But I wasn't feeling much of anything except pain and thirst. I hoped he didn't mind if I vomited on his pillow.

He ducked into the tiny bathroom and came out with a cup of water and a clear fragplastic case. Shipboard medkit, designed to withstand slipshock in an emergency. If he had pain meds, I'd be his friend forever.

He pressed the cup into my hands and I gulped, grateful, even though my guts ached and my murderous thirst devoured the cool water without trace.

He kneeled on the floor and opened the medkit. Gently, he pressed me onto my back and gingerly explored the edges of my wound with his fingertips. "It's not deep. Just the skin. You're lucky."

Did his voice shake, or was that my imagination? I gave a weak laugh. "Doesn't feel too lucky."

"I'll bet. Just keep still."

A soft hiss, and I felt cool antibiotic spray, mixed with anesthetic, tingling and soothing at the same time. I sighed, relief shivering my aching muscles.

"Is it sad if I say that feels really good?"

"More?"

"Yes, please. Mmm."

The aerosol drug seeped into my flesh, and the pain relaxed and faded, still uncomfortable but distant and bearable. I wanted to stretch out and sleep, but my mind clanged a warning. I'd used enough of that spray over my career to know it had a nerve relaxant in it. I should tell him to stop. But it felt so good.

I closed my eyes. Plastic wrap crackled, and dimly I felt him apply the cool nanoskin, a thin layer of moisture and synthetic skin cells that would mold to my wound and rebuild the layers. I probably wouldn't even have a scar. Pity the new skin wouldn't match the tan I'd got at Vostok. When this was over, I'd go back there and lie on the beach for a month. The nanobots itched as they crawled invisibly over the ruined skin in the curve of my waist. They tickled, and his fingers weren't helping, prodding me gently, pressing the synthetic dermis over the wound. My skin tingled, lulled.

"Keep still." He smoothed it over my lower ribs beneath my breast, lingering. "There."

I sat up, flexing my side gingerly. The growing skin pulled under its square plastic coating, but held. Soon I'd be able to peel the plastic off.

I glanced up at him, wary. "Thanks."

"*De nada.*" Tense. Hard. Almost too softly for me to hear.

His eyes mesmerized me, and I had to tear my gaze away.

His hands were burned, I noticed, a couple of fingertips scorched and a blister on one knuckle. It made me angry. Such beautiful hands, such a delicate touch. I'd seen him, stroking the Esperanza neurospace into submission, lulling the dumb creature with that hypnotic caress. Now I knew what that felt like. Suddenly, sitting so close to him didn't seem okay at all.

He leaned in and brushed his lips across my bruised ribs. The faintest touch, and it spiraled shivers deep into my belly.

I swallowed, dry. "What was that for?"

"Same thing this is for," he whispered, and kissed my mouth.

A single, hot, gut-melting kiss.

I gasped, and he pulled back, giving me time to get away. But I slid my arms around his neck and sought his mouth with mine. Hot, hungry, like we'd kissed on Esperanza, only this time it hurt, deep inside where my flesh yearned for his touch. My torn side throbbed, but I ignored it. He murmured and kissed me harder, and I couldn't help but inhale, tasting him, opening my mouth to get more of him into me.

God, what was I doing? He was a rebel, a murderer who'd lied to me in so many ways. Guilt stung my throat, but it was too late. I'd wanted to touch him ever since I'd laid eyes on him, and I was too tired and too drugged up and too damn sick of denying what I wanted to push him away now.

He averted his face, breathing hard. "Um. Look, I'm—"

"Don't talk. Just kiss me." I sought his lips again, and this time I didn't let him go.

We fell onto the bed, and I arched into him, folding my bare leg over his hip. I could feel how much he wanted me, how hard he was for me, and that hot pressure between my legs made me ache. He slid his fingers inside my shorts, caressing my ass, pulling me in tighter. He smelled of hot plasma and sweat, and his kiss tasted of warm metal and that piquant edge I remembered.

He nudged my chin up to kiss my throat, and hot desire shivered me electric. My fingers curled in his hair and pulled him on. I struggled to think clearly, to think of anything but the way his lips teased my skin, his tongue flicking my collarbone, that sly sting of his teeth that lit me up like arcfuel. I wanted him all over me, inside me, his taste filling my mouth, the heat of his naked skin covering me.

Dimly, my brain fumbled. Think, Carrie. Weigh up the facts. He's a terrorist. You're a terrorist hunter. He murdered your friends. Are you fucking insane?

But it didn't feel insane, his hands and his mouth and his body hot on mine. More like sweet starfire in my blood.

He caressed the crease of my hip with his thumb, and his lips crushed mine again, breathless. "You're so alone," he whispered into kisses. "Let me be with you."

My desire scorched deep. I wanted him to slide that thumb deeper, peel me naked, make me sigh and shiver. Even as enemies, we were so alike. We both walked alone, unquiet ghosts in our wake. Surely we could find some peace together.

But denial rippled me cold. I wasn't Lazuli, this sassy rebel thief who burned for him. And this beautiful man who seduced me with his touch and his clever words and his gentle, maddening smile wasn't Dragonfly. He couldn't be. Touching him felt too right.

This was all a lie.

My mouth stung, sour like betrayal. "No. Stop it." I pushed him off and staggered to my feet.

He raked knotted hair back in both hands, struggling to catch his breath. "Shit. Listen, I was out of line. I'm sorry. I didn't mean—"

"Just stay away from me."

Thirst dizzied me, and I swayed on buckling knees. This was stupid. I should go to him. Be his lover, seduce my way into his trust. The mission demanded it.

But it wasn't right. He'd killed my friends. He'd ruined my life. I didn't want him like this. I couldn't. Guilt and self-disgust watered my guts. To admit my stupid physical attraction was one thing. To act on it was entirely another.

He gazed up at me with those hot chocolate eyes, dark hair tousled, and he was so beautiful it hurt. "Okay. I won't do it again. Unless you want me to."

And the truth blinded me like rocketfire.

I wasn't the only one on a mission. This was all just business to him. He needed to find out who I was and what I wanted from him, and I'd resisted curiosity, so he'd resorted to sex. Turned a dangerous situation to his advantage. He'd nothing to lose by trying, and if he got himself laid in the meantime, so much the better for him.

My thoughts reeled, poisoned. He'd challenged me at my own game, and I'd played into his hands like an amateur.

Embarrassment burned my skin like a plasma shot all over again. My voice cracked sharp. "You've got to be kidding me. Don't you ever touch me again."

And I swallowed hot bile and fled.

28

I flung myself onto the sunken lounge. My blood burned. My nerves strung tight. Damn it. I could still feel him under my hands, his lips on mine, hot and relentless. His hands on my body, luring me, my defenses stripping away under the raw honesty of his desire.

The fuck it was honest. He'd tricked me.

I jumped up and paced, my boots too loud on the plastic deck. He'd hear me. I didn't care. I ripped the plastic off my burn, yelping at the sting. The pink skin underneath was healing perfectly. He'd done a good job and it only maddened me more.

My fists clenched, and I grabbed his empty mocha flask and hurled it at the clearview. It bounced off, undented, and I relapsed onto the lounge and slammed my head into the cushion, fuming. The ceiling glared down at me. I glared back. I couldn't hear anything from upstairs. Likely he'd shrugged it off and fallen asleep.

At the thought, fatigue clawed me. I hadn't slept for two days, not since before Vyachesgrad, and my body ached. I'd never sleep now. I was too furious—at him and at myself.

But I must have drifted off at last, because next thing I knew his hand lay warm on my shoulder.

I jerked up and shoved him away, grit blurring my eyes. "Get off me."

He lifted his hands and backed off. "Relax. You wanted to know where we're going."

I registered the slower vibrations under the floor and the absence of the tiny whistle from the gyros. We hadn't merely jumped out of slipspace. We'd stopped.

My guts wriggled, warm. How could I face him, after last night? I'd revealed far too much. If he said anything, I'd die of embarrassment. I had to keep to the plan. Pretend it was nothing. Get him back on the defensive.

It wasn't such a disaster, now I thought about it. He'd tasted me now, and liked it. Maybe he'd want more. I could use this to my advantage, so long as I could keep from punching him.

I sucked in a calming breath and took a moment to slot my thoughts back into mission mode. Forget Spider and *LightBringer* and Vyachesgrad. Forget kissing my enemy. Surov the cat-man had screwed me. I needed to keep Dragonfly alive, at least until I knew I had Director Renko's support. A billion rubles, locked in the vault at Esperanza. How would he get them out? And what was he really up to?

I stood and scraped my loose hair back, wishing I could shower or at least wash my face, but Dragonfly had already hopped down the steps to the airlock. He'd shut the console down and shuttered the clear-view, so I couldn't glimpse any coordinates or see outside. I couldn't even guess with much accuracy how far we'd traveled from Vyachesgrad. Guess I'd just have to ask for directions. I checked that my ESE was safely hidden, reholstered my pistol and followed him out.

Bright reddish sunlight streamed through the plastic airlock, dazzling me for a moment. I heard one door slide and Dragonfly tugged me forward. Cold air hissed in, repressurizing, and by the time my eyes adjusted the lock had opened.

The sun shone small and scarlet, the pale sky bleeding pink and deepening toward a bleak desert horizon broken by blackened buildings and towers. A massive ring-streaked crescent planet loomed, close enough to touch. A cold wind blew, and red dust thickened my nostrils with the smell of rust and crushed concrete. Dead vegetation skittered in tangles across the barren ground, tossed into dancing motion by aimless dust devils. Bumps broke out on my skin in the chill. I'd visited nicer places.

He'd put *Ladrona* down on a cracked bitumen hardstand, her four steel legs biting into the softened tar. Must have been a soft landing if I hadn't even woken up. Next to us squatted a fat frog-like moonhopper, its bubble hull dented and tarnished under a coating of dust; and across the hardstand hulked a heavy freight variant Wolf-class utility, small and ancient, its broken steel bulkheads half-repaired with rivets and misshapen scrap metal.

Dragonfly kicked open a set of black plastic steps and swung down, holding his hand out for me. I glanced coolly at him and climbed down on my own, my boots hitting the tarmac with a sticky thud. The gravity felt weak, less than I'd expected, and for a moment my balance lurched, adjusting.

"So where are we?"

He wouldn't look at me as we circled the ship in its pale shadow and headed toward what remained of the flight line, a dented row of square iron buildings and a hangar with the door missing. "This is where I live. Don't ask too many questions."

Dust coated my lips and I wiped it away roughly. "Hey, you brought me here."

"Because I don't know what else to do with you. Okay?" He rounded on me, and I nearly ran into him. "Believe me, I'd rather get rid of you, but there's no time to take you anywhere else. Just stop asking questions."

His arrogance made me bristle. *He* was shitty with *me*? He was the one who'd brought kissing into it. "Get *rid* of me? Why didn't you just leave me on *LightBringer* then?"

"You want the truth?"

"Ha. That'd be a change."

"Because I don't want your death on my conscience. That doesn't mean I want you following me around."

"Don't go out of your way, hero. First chance I get, I'm out of here."

I pushed past him, resisting the temptation to elbow him in the guts. Like a jungle fungus under my skin, the bastard just kept itching.

He touched my shoulder, and grudgingly I halted. "What?"

He sighed. "Look. I'm sorry you had to get into this. Once it's over you can go. I just don't want you to ..."

I swallowed. That looked like guilt in his eyes. "Don't want me to what?"

He gritted his teeth. "Forget it. Come on."

The concrete hangar floor was marred with old oil stains and stacks of rusty junk. Dust crusted the clear ceiling panels designed to let in light, and in the shadowy steel rafters, clumps of soft little grey animals hung by their feet, long jointed limbs twisted together. Space bats: vermin that lived in the bowels of freighters, feeding on the cargo and spreading to every inhabited world. A flat-pallet loading truck sat in the corner out of the weather, its tires fat and clean and the windows wiped free from dust.

Opposite us, a door opened, and a man and a small woman emerged. The man was tall, thin, older than I was, his grey coverall smeared and patched with silver duct tape. The woman wore a long, soft black dress and boots, with a thick midnight blue wrap around her slender shoulders. They carried no weapons that I could discern.

Dragonfly grinned and quickened his pace to meet them, touching hands briefly with the man and folding the woman into a tight hug.

I hung back, watching, the man's suspicious stare crawling my nerves. The woman had smooth brown skin and curly black hair forced into a thick braid, and she smiled and closed her eyes as Dragonfly kissed her. I chewed my lip, wishing I wore normal clothes instead of showing off everything I had in sweaty skintight black. Was she his girlfriend? He sure hadn't acted taken.

The man touched his arm, pointing to me, murmuring something in rapid Espan. Dragonfly's mouth tightened, and he replied with a headshake and a dark glance in my direction. I strained my ears, but my Espan's not that good and I couldn't catch it. The woman squeezed his hand and gestured to the door, and the two men walked away, leaving us alone.

She approached me with a toothy grin, her brown eyes glinting with amber highlights. Beautiful eyes, more so than mine. Her breasts looked bigger than mine too. I caught myself checking out her ass, just to see, and gave myself a hard mental smack over the head.

Mine was better, though.

She gave me a little wave. "*Hola. Soy* Isabel. Jandro say I make you out of his way."

Inwardly I winced, wishing I'd blocked my ears. So his name really was Sasha. Alex in Brit; Alejandro in Espan. Way, way too much information. I wondered how much Isabel knew about what he did for a living.

"*Lo siento*," I said, exhausting much of my polite Espan. "I don't want to be any trouble. I just hitched a ride."

"Is no problem. Come, eat, rest. Jandro make you awake *toda la noche*, huh? He make all us awake. Madman." She smiled fondly and ushered me toward the door.

Outside, cheerless red sunshine lit a dusty road that was separated from barren, rock-strewn ground by a chainlink fence lined with weeds. In the distance, buildings clustered, maybe a town.

Isabel yanked her pick-up truck's passenger door open with a screech, and I climbed in. Springs poked into my behind from the worn seat. I couldn't see the others. Perhaps they had another vehicle. She revved the engine, grinding the gears in, and we rattled off. Dust clouds puffed through the missing passenger window, making me sneeze.

"So," she said as we left the hardstand behind and passed a scrapmetal yard filled with exhausted spaceship and vehicle parts and vast knots of barbed wire, "you like *Ladrona*, eh? Good ship, good name." She shot me a sidelong glance.

I wondered what she was insinuating. I didn't know what Dragonfly had told her about me. "There's no shame in it. We all have to make a living."

"*Allí*," she said, as if she hadn't heard me, and pointing to a massive rusted water tower concreted into the dirt. "How to say? For sick water?"

"Purifier."

"*Sí*, purifier. Empire shit, him no work any more. We pay to fix, him work. Money no grow from dirt. We got hospital now too. No doctor, but we learn."

So Dragonfly didn't steal for personal gain. But I already knew that. I'd watched him gamble away half a million sols at tarocchi, and even a bunch of fight-for-fighting's-sake psychos like Spider's crew weren't rolling in cash. Still, Dragonfly could have fixed a lot of water purifiers for what it cost him to steal those Esperanza grav schematics. I guess he thought the billion rubles in the vault were worth taking a few risks for, and I wondered if the people who drank this water thought the same.

It occurred to me that the money Nikita and I had won from Dragonfly still sat on *RapidFire*. We'd cashed the chips, and Nikita would probably take the money before long, spend it on oblivion crystals or random gifts for people he wanted to impress, or gamble it on a single faro hand to get off, or even give it back to Axis on a whim. It all seemed shallow, compared to cleaning up a colony's drinking water.

I swallowed, my throat tight and dusty. When had I grown a conscience? And the memory of Dragonfly's insult still riled me: *Too bad you think so small.* What was small about a billion sols? He'd practically dismissed it, almost as if …

As if it wasn't Esperanza's vault he was after.

My guts tightened, warm despite the chill. Even after all that had happened, I'd gotten nowhere with figuring out what was really on his mind. What was he really doing with those grav schematics? What if the heist was a decoy?

We turned onto a rubble-strewn street between rows of two-story buildings, their cracked concrete walls pink with dust. The low-rising red sun slanted across dirt and gravel patches. More fat grey bats roosted under the buildings' eaves and little guano piles lined the ground beneath. Somewhere, distant machinery buzzed—maybe an old carbon fuel generator. I studied the streetscape with an experienced eye. No blast damage, no flash-seared edges, no bomb craters gleaming with melted silicon. If Imperial colonists had been here—maybe an abandoned mining project?—they'd left without a fight.

Isabel pulled up with a squeak of brakes before a narrow steel door in a line of old tenements. Dust clouds puffed as we climbed out. I rubbed my arms to warm them, a shiver rattling my teeth. She led the way inside, into a narrow corridor that smelled of sour detergent. Plastic pinboards lined the walls, their papers bright with the fingerpaint smears of tiny hands, and the high-pitched rattle of childish voices and laughter drifted toward us. I stretched my cold limbs, uncomfortable. Was this her idea of keeping me out of Dragonfly's way? I'd never had much to do with children.

She pulled a soft blue coat from a hook behind the door. "*Aquí.* You cold?"

"Thanks." I shrugged into it gratefully, reveling in the warmth. It covered me to mid-thigh. A familiar, spicy scent rose from it, a sharp reminder of his body on mine. I wanted to rip the coat off and toss it away, but I wanted to wrap up in it too. I cursed inwardly, hoping I wasn't blushing. "Are you a teacher?"

Isabel shrugged. "We make them be kids as long as they can. One day, they learn Empire. Not yet." She grinned, waving a warning finger. "No curse," she chided, and pushed open the glass-paned door.

The noise level rose to ear-splitting, and I had to hide gritted teeth. Tiny children zoomed around at knee height, shrieking and scattering pastels and thin cyberpaper on the torn carpet, while larger ones banged plastic books on the homemade wooden desks or screeched colored chalk on the blackboard or laughed their heads off at one another.

The room reminded me of the chilly basement where I'd gone to school: dirty, low-tech and cheap, with none of the fancy consoles and virtual kit the Imperials had. Our Mrs. Wilson wasn't a real teacher, just the best we had, and picture book downloads were censored and expensive, so she spent hours telling us stories, her tired face animated as she described feisty little girls fighting monstrous aliens and escaping evil black-suited soldiers with the help of brave rebel heroes in ultraglass armor. One day, she didn't show up, and the whisper was that those black-suited soldiers had come for her in the night. We never saw her again.

I sniffed, the scene before me uncomfortably evocative of those dusty memories. This was where Dragonfly lived? I'd imagined him more like Spider, cruising around the galaxy raising hell. I hadn't expected him to be so ... normal.

I didn't want him to be like me.

Isabel yelled something in Espan, raising her hands. Gradually the noise subsided and the kids ground to a halt, confining themselves to rolling on the carpet or swinging on their grubby plastic chairs.

As Isabel spoke again, I studied them. Dirty, sure, skinny, poor, their hair ratty with lice and their second-hand clothes patched, but at least they weren't hiding in the street covered in cam paint with laser rifles too heavy in their hands. I wondered if any of them were hers—theirs?—and I bit my lip. Would it make the horrid things he'd done better, or worse?

Isabel ended her speech with a big grin. A bubbling cheer arose, and the little ones tumbled to the front of the room in a rolling clump, ready for story time or pin the bruise on the marine or whatever little rebel kids liked these days. The bigger ones hung back, chewing pencils, kicking idly at table legs, twisting greasy curls around bony fingers.

Isabel sat cross-legged on the floor with a book and winked up at me. "Jandro say you do good math. Want try?"

I looked at the bigger kids. They stared back at me, dull-eyed.

I smiled weakly. I preferred it when marines were shooting at me. I'd get him back for this.

"Who likes fractions then?"

***

Three hours later, I was kneeling on the floor, cuddled in Dragonfly's warm coat, trying to explain quantum superposition to a bunch of seven year olds with the reluctant school cat trapped beneath an upturned plastic crate.

"Alive *and* dead, see? *Gato muerto y gato vivo. Los dos.*"

The kids didn't look convinced.

"*Es vivo,*" insisted one, and banged on the crate with his sticky fist.

The cat responded with a disobliging scuffle, and I had to scrabble the crate down to keep it from getting out, which sent the kids into gales of laughter all over again. I laughed too. We'd quickly gotten beyond the boring stuff they were supposed to be doing, and I wasn't sure if this was what Isabel had in mind, but I was having fun and, from their cheeky grins and bright eyes, they were too. They'd proven more interesting than I'd expected, even if my Espan was broken and their Rus was missing in action. Funny, charming, mischievous, inquisitive—just like small versions of real people, except better, because they didn't judge or pretend or deceive.

"*Es vivo,*" I admitted, and lifted the crate's corner.

The long-suffering beast slithered out, its orange tail twitching, and speared across the room with an indignant miaow, stretching its head up to be petted.

Dragonfly bent to stroke the cat under the chin and watched me with that sweet, maddening smile. I swallowed, my skin suddenly warm and alive. How long had he been standing there? I forced myself to smile back, though I couldn't hold my gaze quite steady. I was used to action, danger, deception, the rarified air of operations. I didn't know how to face him like this. Not in the real world, doing normal stuff. It felt wrong. Disorienting. Frightening.

Isabel clapped her hands and broke the class up, and the kids disappeared out the door like a swarm of bees. The mess they left behind showered down like leaves after a storm, drifting slowly to silence. Isabel began straightening the tables, picking up scattered chairs and stacking them in rows. I picked up the crate and collected discarded paper scraps, pens, broken bits of plastic, and soggy cheese fragments with miniature teeth marks still showing.

Dragonfly helped, straightening the carpet and pushing picture books into a neat pile. The cyberpaper flickered and erased its text and pictures, resetting itself for another download, but the pages were old and gray and letters and image fragments still showed. The cat rubbed against his ankles.

"You're good with kids," he said. "Got any of your own?"

The chill stung my legs, and I pulled my borrowed coat tighter. Mishka had said he wanted kids someday, because he knew he wouldn't live forever. To me, that seemed the perfect reason not to have them. It was one of those conversations where he'd eyed me strangely, confused, like we'd spoken a different language.

"Umm ... no. Never had time, I guess."

"Uh-huh." He studied one of the books, its cover showing a bright yellow sun in a black star-studded sky and a cartoon spaceship with flowerpots in the window. "Too busy cracking crypto or drinking martinis at Esperanza?"

I dropped the crate on a pile of chairs with a clunk. "What the hell is that supposed to mean? A woman belongs in the home?"

My fingers itched to slap him. He was a vicious murderer. Who the hell did he think he was to judge me on the life I'd chosen? The fact that he thought he was talking to Lazuli, cyberthief and killer, only made me madder. From the corner of my eye I spied Isabel making a hasty exit and spun to follow her.

He grabbed my elbow and pulled me back. "You're smarter than that. Look, I know it's none of my business. But why are you really here, Lazuli? Why do you want this life?"

I shook him off, yanked my coat straight. "Carrie. It's Carrie, okay? And you're right. It's none of your bloody business, Sasha, or Alejandro, or whatever you want to be called."

But I couldn't meet his eye. His question had hit me hard. *Why do you want this life*? I'd asked myself the same thing after Mishka died, and I still didn't have an answer other than *I don't know what else to do.*

"Sorry, but you're in my house, and that makes you my concern. I won't be responsible for the dumbest decision you ever make." He kept his tone low, but his eyes darkened, frustrated, or concerned.

Comprehension dawned like a winter sunrise, and I resisted a shiver. He believed my lies, and wanted to talk me out of a life of crime. He cared whether Lazuli lived or died.

I steeled myself against sympathy and turned again to leave. "Thanks very much, but I can take care of myself."

He grabbed my shoulder, and this time he didn't let go. "Why are you always walking away? Listen to me. Are you listening?"

Frustrated, I nodded.

"You're young, talented, intelligent. You could do anything, have any life you want. Why choose this? You saw what it's like on *LightBringer*. Always running, always sleeping with a gun in your hand. We all end up in prison or dead, and those around us die first. Why would you want that, when you can have so much more?"

I'd wondered the same thing about him on Esperanza. His dark gaze burned into mine, his fingers somehow warm on my skin through the thick coat. Damn, he sounded so sincere. And in truth his questions applied just as much to my career with Axis as they did to a life of insurrection and thievery.

"If you're so high-minded, why don't you give it up?"

He didn't hesitate. "Because it's bigger than me now. Too many people rely on me." He shrugged darkly and dropped his hand. "I used to be like you. It was all so exciting when I still believed I could change the world. You'll go far. Just be sure it's where you want to go."

I remembered the girl I'd been when I first made it into Axis: fresh, determined, full of zeal for a better, bigger, richer Empire. I chewed my lip, self-conscious. What had I achieved, besides a few dead insurrectionists and a twice-broken heart? What had I sacrificed? Could I leave even if I wanted to?

He gently straightened my coat where he'd pulled it awry, and lifted his hand to tuck my hair back, but changed his mind and let it drop. "Look, I'm sorry I snapped at you before. Of course you're welcome here. Stay as long as you want. But take my advice, Carrie, if what I say means anything to you: kill it while it's still small, while you can still control it. Don't let it swallow you."

"And if it's already swallowed me?"

My voice sounded small, afraid. Shit. No fair that he understood me when I still had no clue what was really on his mind.

He gave a little headshake and a smile, as if he didn't believe it. "You still don't understand. Come with me tomorrow and I'll show you what we do here."

My stomach tightened. At last, I'd learn what he was up to. I should have been triumphant. But cold reluctance wormed under my skin, and I tucked my hands in my pockets and turned away.

29

I ate dinner with them that night—Dragonfly and Isabel and the other man. Their kitchen lay upstairs from the schoolroom, a cold and cluttered space, the knife-scarred plastic table filling most of it, with a stained laminate sink and an electromag cooker that looked like they'd cannibalized it from an ancient spaceship wreck. Only pale remnants of daylight remained, and a dim lightbulb buzzed overhead, mutant insects dancing around it on oversized wings. Isabel's cooking, though, made up for it all. I hadn't eaten properly since Esperanza—dead furry animal and marine freezepacks are not real food—and my mouth watered at the smell of frying shellfish and paprika.

I'm inventive with ration packs and room service, but in a real kitchen I'm clueless. To my relief, Isabel had good-naturedly shooed me away when I offered to help. She had only frozen or freeze-dried ingredients, except for a fresh green herb bunch that Dragonfly had evidently brought her on this latest trip, but produced a steaming *paella* as if by magic. I watched the others a moment, unsure, but when they stuffed themselves like they hadn't eaten for a week, I did too, relishing the heavenly flavors of seafood, herbs and rice.

The other man, whose name was Paco, glared at me constantly, like I might grow a second head or disappear, until Isabel taunted him for it a few times, after which he subsided into ignoring me. Their Espan flowed too fast and complicated for me, and I stumbled along as best I could whenever I thought I knew something to say. They never corrected me or showed displeasure at the way I mangled their language, just grinned and replied as if I'd gotten it right.

It felt weird. In the Imperial forces, mistakes in your Rus earn you swift derision and a month's worth of shitty jobs before they'll trust you again. I'd learned that the hard way as a junior lieutenant, when my vowels still smacked of a Victorian colony, the kind of place where we still said *hell* and *damn* even though the Empire didn't officially allow religion. By the time General Shadrin chose me to work for him, I'd sounded like some New Moskva billionaire's resort-finished daughter. I made sure of it. I'd yearned so desperately to be one of the chosen.

Well, here I was, the Empire's best and brightest, and the simple way these people accepted me shamed me to the core.

It made me think of my father, the way he'd cursed me when I'd said I wanted to leave. The agricultural planet I came from was battered and torn from futile secessionist uprisings, but many ordinary civilians still supported the insurrection against the Imperial garrison that, they said, was bleeding our land dry. My father would sneak out of the ghetto to secret midnight meetings, thin shoulders huddled in his worn plastic coat; and my mother baked the Imperial soldiers' loaves short, making up the weight with sawdust and hiding her secret grain stash under a brick in the crumbling outhouse. But principles don't mean much to a hungry little girl. The Imperials were well-fed and sheltered while we starved and froze. They were educated and tech-savvy while my parents couldn't afford to send me to high school. And I knew some of the Imperial kids. I sneaked into the barbed-wire compound and played with them in secret, the garrison sergeant's pale-haired boy and his sister, until their mother saw me and chased me away. They had a funny accent I tried to copy, and they never got sparrow pox or footrot or had infected grass seeds stuck under their fingernails. I envied their warm clothes, their haircuts, their big house and safe neighborhood, and I wondered: why them and not me?

My father scolded me in that provincial accent I'd become ashamed of. *Keep from them, Caroline. They inna like us. They ken they're better than you.*

News flash, Dad. They are.

I burned a lot of bridges when I ran away to enlist. My family wouldn't answer my calls or take my money, and after a while I gave up.

For years I'd told myself I didn't care, during tour after tour on troop carriers and battleships, storming star systems and cleansing rebellious colonies so Imperial civilization could spread unchecked. Sure, our ways might step on a few toes every now and then, but on Imperial worlds, people don't starve in the streets or die raving of Kirov swamp fever. We have the best health care, the greatest statesmen, the most vibrant culture. I've been on enough so-called "free" worlds to know that they're invariably dark, dirty, lawless slums, bereft of order or hope. The choice—civilization with a few rules, or petty freedoms in poverty—always seemed a simple one to me. But some people just have to be beaten into doing what's good for them.

So sixteen-year-old Private Thatcher got to see the galaxy, and never went hungry. I liked the guns, the techie hardware, the predictability of it all. I was diligent and clever and always followed orders, so they made me a corporal. When I got a field promotion to second lieutenant, one blood-soaked night in a broken city aflame with rebellion, I dragged what was left of my platoon out alive and the higher-ups let me keep my rank. I was twenty-two and I got an officer's education, friends, a life beyond repairing harvesters and scraping for food every day. I kept people alive. I was making a difference.

Of course, I knew now that my father was right. The Empire overused our soil, poisoned our land with skin-rotting pesticides until nothing would grow—I'd seen it on countless worlds. But civilization always has a cost. Resources have to come from somewhere. And when you're commanding a company of exhausted shock troops, hunting terrorist guerillas through a toxic tropical swamp two hundred million klicks from safety, you don't care too much where the food in your dwindling ration packs came from.

My family were probably dead by now. They'd either got themselves shot as traitors before the Imperials left, or had starved to death afterward because they wouldn't submit and ask the Empire for help, not even to stay alive. I'd never admired them for it. Principles are no good if you're dead. I'd gotten out while the writing was fresh on the wall. It wasn't my fault they were too proud to do the same.

I always said the Empire was my family now. For a while—until I met Nikita—I'd even believed it. And tonight, here I was, eating *paella* with the enemy. Making friends with people who thought those empty principles were worth stealing and killing and dying for. To say I felt awkward was like saying Dragonfly was okay at sums. If a black hole could open in the floor and crush me, it'd be a relief.

Dragonfly—damned if I'd call him by his real name—leaned over to whisper to me in Rus, maybe to make me feel at home. I swallowed. He'd been doing it all night: murmuring in my ear, making me blush with a candid glance from those magnetic brown eyes. Teasing me. Making me laugh. Letting his fingers touch mine as he reached for something on the table. I wanted to scream, because I liked it. It made my stomach all hot and fluttery, and it maddened me. I could handle some meaningless flirting if it got me closer to the information I needed to bring him down. But when had I started seeking out his smile, letting eye contact linger, imagining his touch?

Right after I realized he was a person, not an idea.

I ate in tense silence until the meal finished. We crowded into the little kitchen to clear the mess, saving the scraps and emptying the dishes into the stained sink. I avoided looking at him as he filled the tub with hot, frothing water, but I could feel his gaze on me. For once, he was transparent like a clearview window. He was about to ask me out—as far as "out" went on this forsaken rock—to help him crack some crypto, or check his group theory, or maybe even take a walk outside. What I didn't understand was why. Lazuli wasn't a nice girl. She wasn't a good girl. She hadn't even acted like a particularly smart girl.

Only one explanation fit the facts: he didn't mean any of it. He was just trying to break down my defenses. And what maddened me the most was that I cared.

Soap suds dripped over his forearms as he stacked wet dishes, bubbles sliding on those elegant fingers. My palms sweated as I wiped the plates dry. I didn't want to be alone with him. I could see our future too clearly. Glances, blushes, uncomfortable silences; excuses to brush past him, touch hands, sit too close. I'd start thinking about how he tasted, how his lips had tempted mine last night, how I'd wanted him. And then, no doubt, he'd come to his senses and humiliate me.

My stomach coiled, even as his smile warmed my heart. I'd been attracted to murderers before. In my line of work, I rarely meet a man who isn't one. Mishka was an ice-blooded killer when it suited him, and I've done my share too. I just didn't want to be attracted to *this* murderer. It was unconscionable.

He finished, and dried his hands on my tea towel, trapping me between him and the sink. I wanted to slide my fingers between his, tug him closer, meet his secret smile with my own. I wanted to wriggle away from him and run. My mouth parched, and I licked my sticky lips.

Isabel glanced from me to Dragonfly and back again, and came to my rescue. "You tired, miss? You sleep. I find you room."

Gratitude washed over me like cool relief, and I faked a yawn. "*Gracias.* That's kind of you."

"You sleep," she directed firmly, sending him a warning glare. "I find you room, away from man make awake on computer *toda la noche*."

She pulled me aside before he could say anything, and I followed her down a glass-lined corridor that looked out over bare ground to the hardstand. Stupidly, I wanted to look back. Damn it if I didn't feel bad about hurting him.

Whatever. Snap out of it, Aragon. This was all a game. He didn't care about me, not really. He just wanted me off my guard, and it was working.

I paused by an open window, the evening breeze fresh and cold. The shadows of *Ladrona* and the other ships made a lumpy line above the black tarmac. Stars emerged into the blackening sky, and the crescent planet had set halfway, shedding a pale pink path to the horizon. No traffic queues carved the sky, no glowing advertising, no garish beacons flashing to wreck your night vision. Beautiful.

I wondered if he saw beauty here, or merely another thing that needed protection. If he'd been here to share it with me, I'd have asked him. For a moment my heart ached that he wasn't, and I huddled closer in his coat.

A scuffle pricked my ears, and I found Isabel in a tiny room lined with bookshelves, where she'd already arranged cushions on the floor for a mattress and a heap of fat blankets that looked dusty but warm. She flipped on an old incandescent light that buzzed and flickered.

"You want things, you ask me. My room *a la derecha*, bath also."

"You live up here?" I knew his room was downstairs, and I couldn't help asking, though it made me cringe and flush yet again. "You mean, you're not ...?"

Damn it. If I'd flirted with him in front of his woman, I wasn't the only one who'd be sorry for it. If they were together, she deserved better than the act he put on.

Isabel laughed knowingly. "I wonder when you ask. No way. Is never here. No point, eh? No make sense too, machine, computer, *matemáticas. No entiendo.*" Her brown eyes glinted. "Jandro never bring a lady like you before. I say, good. Is too old soon."

She winked, mischievous, and walked out.

I stood for a moment, bewildered. So what was his game? Lazuli had nothing to offer him except a poor talent for pure math, weak and stuttering compared to his own. Why waste his time with her?

Weariness ached my bones, and I arranged the blankets over the cushions to make a warm fluffy cocoon. I longed to curl up inside it and forget about everything; to lie there and think about what I could have been doing with him—crunching a set of vector spaces, or stripping some code, or even just kissing, slow and hot and delicious, my fingers in his hair ... But I couldn't yet. Instead I waited, listening, my hands stuffed into warm pockets, until I knew Isabel was gone, then slipped into the corridor.

I pushed the window open further to get a clear view of the sky. A fat grey bat shuffled aside with a snort, folding rubbery wings as it swung upside down from the eaves. I took a slow still and date-time of the stars with my ESE, then I shut myself into my new bedroom and sat cross-legged on the bed to call Nikita.

"Aragon. I was just thinking about you."

Languid pleasure glittered in his voice, a slick high I recognized. He was doing oblivion crystals again, likely out of boredom. It's part of his curse that nothing keeps him interested for very long. The poor darling, left on Esperanza with a pile of cash, countless beautiful women and nothing else to do. Life was so much easier when you didn't give a shit. For a moment, I envied him, which in turn made me angry.

I let the anger ring down the sub-ether line. In my current mood, I didn't care what he thought. "I don't have much time. Any update on the Surov situation?"

If black ops goons were after me, I'd prefer to know about it.

A short crackle of delay. "Nothing, sweetheart. Renko hasn't figured it out yet. But if I were you, I'd get the Dragonfly thing done ASAP. What's new?"

A dark shudder rippled my bones. and I knew it meant he was lying. But about what?

"We got off the battleship no problem. I'll debrief the Spider situation later. But get this: Dragonfly's taken me to his home planet."

Nikita's smile shivered over me like stardust. "The monster's lair. I'm impressed. Get as much intel as you can. And do try not to fuck this one up."

I flicked him the star shot I'd taken. "Here's our location. It's small, maybe not even a primary system satellite. Some abandoned mining op is my guess. Looks like colony level two infrastructure, just the basics, about fifty years old."

"I'll put it through charts. Anything else new?"

Soft tactile pleasure, a caress or a kiss at the other end. Of course, he wasn't getting shattered alone. My skin tingled, eerily pleasant, and I shook it off.

"Nothing extraordinary." A usefully opaque lie. The things I'd learned were all too ordinary—dangerously so—and I didn't feel like sharing. I didn't want Nikita to know that my enemy confused me. "My cover's still good. I'll see what I can get from his people here. Someone must know what he's up to."

"Any luck with that data you stole from Esperanza?"

I'd forgotten I hadn't had time to update him. "Yes. He decrypted it like it was a baby's jigsaw puzzle. It's grav schematics for the station. I didn't see what else."

A gentle glow of surprise, maybe admiration. "Ambitious, for a thief."

"That's what I thought. I mentioned vault integrity and he practically laughed at me." I hesitated. "What if it isn't the vault he's after? What if he's thinking bigger?"

A few silent seconds, with nothing but cold subether noise to warm them. "Like what?"

"I have no idea." My nerves itched. "It's just this feeling I have."

"Think about it, Aragon. Why rob a casino if not for money?"

"He's an insurrectionist and he's clever. From the look of this place, the Empire has done him no favors."

Nikita laughed, languid with oblivion. "There are plenty of easier places to play anarchist without taking on the Esperanza mob. Besides, the surrender negotiation is a done deal. The colony's guy Alvarado and his administration are in it up to their greedy eyeballs, and your boyfriend General Shadrin's just squeezing out the last drop of kickback. Even if the insurrectionists blow the entire station to static and splinters, the annexation will still go ahead."

Sickness crawled cold in my guts. Static and splinters. Blow the entire station. *Too bad you think so small.* Shit. For all my supposed skills at subterfuge, I just couldn't figure Dragonfly out from one day to the next. Had I let my attraction to him smear my judgment? He seemed so matter-of-fact and kind-hearted. Hard to believe he'd rip Esperanza open and kill thousands of people for sheer chaos's sake.

Mishka and my murdered friends would disagree.

"Aragon? Something wrong?" A sour, cynical twinge ruined Nikita's perfect concern.

"No. You're right, there must be something else on that chip. I'll see what I can find."

I broke the connection and burrowed under the blankets, shivering.

30

The cloudless sky glowed pale pink, fading to white overhead. The line of buildings cast long red shadows across the dirt, and smudge-faced kids chased each other around piles of rubble. A chill morning breeze tossed knots of dry grass along the street, and I huddled into my coat, glad I'd borrowed some trousers from Isabel. They ended a little short, but I'd tucked them into my boots. I had a warm scarf wrapped around my throat, and a fluffy sweater of hers beneath my coat. I'd taken a wonderful hot shower, once Isabel had showed me how to work the little electric heater on the wall. With that, a fresh tie for my clean hair, and a hot sweet chocolate drink for breakfast, I felt seriously human for the first time since the Esperanza neurospace.

Despite that, Dragonfly's promise to show me around carved a tiny hollow in my stomach. Thinking of him prickled my nerves, and I flushed again that I'd nearly fallen for his tricks last night. I forced myself to concentrate on business. Would I find out what he was up to at last? Would he let me in on his secrets to convince me to give up thieving?

This colony didn't act like a hotbed of insurrection, just ordinary people going about their dull little lives. But I knew from experience that the most innocent-looking people often proved the most dangerous. Maybe I should play on his sympathy, make him think me more stubborn and determined, so he'd show me everything in an effort to put me off.

My stomach twisted tighter. I didn't like lying to him, even though he sure didn't have any problem lying to me. Pretending he cared what I did, when he only wanted to get rid of me so he could get on with it, whatever it was.

The faint roar of rapid arcfuel descent attracted my attention. A broad wake shimmered in the sky, leading down toward the hardstand, and atmosphere buffers hissed and crackled as the craft landed out of sight. We had visitors. A supply ship? Friends? Or someone more interesting?

The school building's door creaked open and the orange cat darted out, then sat on the doorstep in a weak sunny patch to wash its face. Dragonfly followed, tugging Isabel's wrap around himself, his dark hair falling over the midnight folds. He'd changed clothes, I couldn't help noticing, from hot-and-dirty rebel scumbag back to casual-but-stylish cyberthief. Clearly, he'd been absent the day they taught mild-mannered secret identities, because he looked way too sexy and mysterious in that simple blue shirt and pants.

Strain showed around his eyes, as if he hadn't slept much, but he still managed a smile for me. I smiled back, my pulse glimmering uneasily. He wouldn't look away. As if he didn't care that I'd brushed him off last night, and the night before. Like he hadn't given up. I didn't know whether to be flattered or terrified.

He nodded toward the fading arcfuel wake. "That's for us. Coming?"

"I'm wearing your overcoat." I slipped from it and held it out to him, self-conscious. "Here."

"It's okay."

"No, really. Take it."

"Are you sure? I'll swap with you."

He folded the coat over his elbow, unfurled the wrap and arranged it around me, tugging my ponytail free and tucking in my scarf. I watched him but he didn't meet my eye, and suddenly I didn't know what to do, how to react. If Nikita did something like this, I'd assume he was trying to impress me with his manners. Mishka would do it because someone had told him that's how he should treat a lady. Dragonfly seemed just to care that I might be cold.

Had I been with Axis so long I'd forgotten how to deal with real people?

He tucked in the last corner and stepped away. The wrap was warm from his body, fragrant, delightful.

"Thanks," I said at last, because I needed to say something. I didn't want him thinking me even more ungrateful and standoffish. Damn, when had this gotten so complicated?

He put his coat on, stuck his hands in the pockets and grinned. "It's already warm. Thanks, yourself. We'll walk, if it's okay with you. I want to show you a few things along the way."

"Sure." I fell into step alongside him, glad to be moving. The cat trotted after us a short distance, then plopped its fluffy behind down in the dusty street to await his return. "Who's the visitor?"

"You'll see."

He walked casually but with purpose, seeming not to mind the cold breeze that tossed his hair and swirled grit in his eyes. He looked as comfortable here as he had losing half a million sols at the tarocchi table, sweating in green plasmalight over a hostile neurospace, or dodging plasma rounds on Spider's dirty battleship. Ease with yourself is either a talent or an act, and from the way he'd behaved with me I'd imagined the latter. I didn't want to think about what it meant if I was wrong. If he believed all that stuff about killing my problems while they were still small, and not letting them take over my life. If he'd meant what he said and did last night, and I'd shaken it off like a lie.

A voice called from a dusty screen door and a bent old man emerged. He hobbled over to touch hands with Dragonfly, who grinned and clapped the old guy's thin shoulder like they'd known each other for years. A rapid conversation in Espan ensued, before Dragonfly nodded and moved on.

I cocked an eyebrow in question, and he shrugged sheepishly, stuffing his hands back into his pockets. "He wants me to take a look at his alphaspace link. Says he can't get the sports syndication. I told him I'd be by later."

I laughed, though in truth his bleeding heart kind of impressed me. "That old guy sure saw you coming. You ever hear of saying *no* to people?"

His eyes shadowed, defensive. "They've given me a lot. I can do things they can't, so I help out where I can."

More people filled the street now: mothers trailing children, young men in groups of three or four, an old woman with a walking stick and a wheeled basket, the occasional rusty motorbike rattling past in a cloud of dust and oily smoke. All of them knew Dragonfly and wanted to talk to him or touch his hand or even just return his smile. He took his time with everyone, stopping to chat, play with the kids, make a sullen teenage girl laugh. Clearly he had somewhere to be—long minutes had passed since the visiting ship landed—but not once did he show impatience or brush someone aside. His smile flashed readily, his eyes were shining and direct, his conversation animated. Either he was a consummate politician, or he genuinely gave a shit.

I watched a dark-haired young woman lift her toddler up for him to hold, and I wasn't sure if I was touched or horrified. Had he engineered a little anti-Imperial personality cult here? They all sought him out, deferred to him, wanted to touch him. Maybe they just liked him because he could fix their pirate alphaspace array. Or maybe they respected him, this man who risked his life to get their kids clean water and a hospital, who could have any life he wanted but chose this.

He glanced up, and I ripped my gaze away, but too late. My cheeks burned. He kissed the little girl's dirty cheek softly before returning her to her mother with a smile and a *gracias.*

I hugged my wrap tighter as we walked on. "They look up to you."

He shrugged, but his gaze slipped. "Like I said. It's bigger than me now. Walking away from this isn't an option for me."

"Not now. But before?"

"You're asking whether I sought this out? Saw it coming? No. Would I have done things differently had I known? Honestly, I have no idea."

"But doesn't it bother you? The way they ... you know." I squirmed.

A fleeting smile. "Yes. But I've got so much they don't have, Carrie. I'm educated, I'm practical, I know how to get things done. They're just simple people. If I don't do it, who will?"

I glanced at the broken shopfronts, mended with jagged weld and rivets; the cracked icelights on poles, the missing ones replaced with electric tubes wired by hand. I remembered the water purifier, leaching heavy metals from the ground supply and alien spores from the storage tanks. This forsaken rock had nothing. No resources, no saleable commodities. They couldn't even grow anything here. Without him—without the money he made, fair or foul—lives would be poorer.

Could I say the same about myself? Nikita? Mishka? Anyone I knew, in fact?

I'd always thought I could. I'd left General Shadrin's employ for Axis secure in the certainty that the Empire brought order to chaos, and that without Axis, the Empire would crumble. I needed to do all I could to shore it up in the face of mindless anarchy, and beavering away at obscure encryptions in military intelligence just wasn't close enough to the edge for me any more. But the Empire had done precious little for the people here—it had simply abandoned them when the mining stock fell—and it had taken an anarchist, far from mindless, to set things right and make their lives worth living once more. What difference had Axis ever made to them?

I kicked at a loose rock, skipping it across the dust. "We all end up in prison or dead, right? Isn't that what you said? What happens to them when one day you don't come back?"

He scraped wind-mussed hair from his face. "I don't know. I don't like to think about it. Do you?"

I looked away, my throat tight. I'd never had to worry. All that would happen if I didn't live up to Aragon's legend was that I'd die. He had so much more at stake than I did.

We turned the corner down an alley leading toward the hardstand. "Wasn't there something you wanted to show me?"

He gave a little laugh, clearly not amused. "That was it. Haven't you seen enough?"

We walked the rest of the way in silence.

***

Chilly wind blew across the black hardstand, dry grass tumbling. I shivered, bumps rising on my scalp. The new ship was a mid-range Pharaoh class, a flat steel trapezoid with six blunt landing legs and massive arc-fuel boosters on each side, built for heavy freight and atmospheric tug work. The gangway gleamed dully in the bleak red sun, marred by scratches and gouge marks from countless loadings and unloadings. Inside, I saw rows of steel crateholders, stacked to the ceiling with white plastic freezeboxes.

From between the crates squeezed Fat Bastie, sucking in his extensive gut to ooze down the narrow aisle. He popped out with a squelch and a curse, rubbing his unshaven chin.

"Sash, ya stinky rebel," he boomed in his Brit-flavored Rus, his bald scalp spraying sweat even in the chill. "Whatever you're paying me to drag ass out to this forsaken shithole, it ain't enough."

My interest was piqued. The mysterious cargo from Vyachesgrad. Would I find out at last?

"It's more than you're worth, Sebastian." Dragonfly hopped lightly up onto the gangway to meet him and got a cuff over the head for his trouble. He ducked, shaking his hair back. "Did you bring what I asked for this time?"

Bastie stuck out his greasy bottom lip. "To the core, my friend, to the very core. Of course what you asked for. Come see." He shot me a grin. "Hello, lady friend. You've lasted forty-eight hours with him? Congratulations. When's the wedding?"

I winked at him to cover my blush. "Like you'd be invited."

Dragonfly held out his hand to me, and I took it and climbed up onto the gangway. His hand felt warm in mine despite the chill, and I didn't want to let go. He squeezed, almost imperceptibly, before he pulled away. Damn. He could read me like a plaintext dataflow.

Bastie rubbed stained hands on his stretched flight suit and leered at me. "Helping us unload, tough girl?"

"Sure." If it got me a look at whatever Dragonfly was hiding in this shipment, I'd heave a few crates. I tugged off the woolly wrap, wrapping it over the gangway rail so it wouldn't blow away.

"Capital. This way, darlin'. Mind your head."

Bastie jammed his fat bulk between the crates again, squeezing through to the main cargo bay, which had septurium alloy bulkheads and blue icelights denting the flat ceiling. Crates and piles of stuff were stacked up the walls, leaving a narrow path along one side that was cluttered with tools hanging from hooks and the long burned nozzle of an old handheld fusion welder.

The hydraulic loader—a fat steel plate set flush with the floor—was already stacked with pallets of ion drive parts, their weird metal shapes strapped under steelcore plastic nets. The weight alarm bolted to the loader still flashed blue, and Bastie's offsider was shoving crates on beside the pallets one by one. Curiosity tugged at me. Dragonfly's stuff. But what?

Bastie wiped his sweaty forehead. "Maxim, my boy, it's your lucky day. Told ya this job was fun."

The lights on the weight alarm flickered, and Maxim surveyed me with pale blue eyes. I remembered Bastie saying he'd take on crew at Vyachesgrad. Black-haired, he looked fit in his smudged flight suit; like countless other flyboys in space haulage, he was probably a pilot as well as a back-ender. He heaved the last crate into place, his suit pulling taut over an unnatural angular shape against his ribcage. A short-range atomflash handgun, from the triple corners. Looked like Max did more for Bastie than ping the autopilot and kick crates around.

"Hop on," Max said, and I jammed my foot in beside a pallet and grabbed the steelcore net for balance. The old hydraulics groaned, and with a tart whiff of leaking fluid we rode the loader down, the steel juddering beneath my feet. I saw him steal a professionally appraising glance at me when he thought I wasn't looking. Women have better peripheral vision than men. Sweet young Max should remember that.

Chilly wind gusted into the gap as the loader descended inside the ring of the ship's landing legs, fat hydraulic arms creaking as they elongated. Dragonfly had fetched the truck from the hangar, its tire tracks in the dust already blowing away across the hardstand. Max eased the platform to a stop level with the tray, red sun glinting on the steel. We each kicked a floating lever at a pallet's base, lifting the weight onto the slides, and shoved together, sending the pallet skidding with a screech onto the back of the truck.

The second pallet soon followed the first. Next came the crates, the sharp white ultraplastic freezeboxes digging into my hands as we swung them off. The molded lid of the last but one had been pressured loose in transit, and I stole a look. Airtight foil packages, jammed in like shells in a magazine. Freezedried food, most likely, or pharmo for the hospital.

The last crate felt heavier. I let it slip from my fingers on purpose, and it slapped onto the truck bed with a satisfying crack as the lid popped free.

"Sorry." I sucked an imaginary cut on my palm. Already dust collected on the freshly exposed plastic from the sharp wind.

"No mind. Watch yourself." Max rubbed his own palm with his thumb, his white skin reddened from lifting.

He turned away to hop back onto the loader, and I glanced up to make sure Dragonfly wasn't watching, then swiftly inched the crate lid aside.

An array of shiny black metal oblongs gleamed up at me, stacked in a clear plastic framework to stop them rattling together. A micro-ether receiver was soldered neatly on the side of each. Like sinister beetles with short crablike legs, but the diode where the beetle's eyes should have been was dull and dead.

Sub-band detonators, rigged for chain reaction. Sixty-four in this crate alone. Perfect for ripping apart a semi-sedentary deep-space structure like Esperanza, so long as you had enough explosive and knew where to put it to exert the correct force.

And Dragonfly knew exactly where to put it, and how much force he'd need. I'd helped him steal the grav schematics.

Chill settled in my blood, my fingers stinging. I didn't want it to be true. I'd liked him better when he just wanted the money; and I realized I didn't care about the billion sols any more. I'd let him steal it from under Shadrin's nose, let the Empire lose face, let Renko's superiors itch until their skin peeled off if it meant Dragonfly's people could live their forgotten lives in peace. But this was very different.

Hydraulics hissed behind me as Max activated the loader lift, and quickly I snapped the crate lid back on and grabbed the loader pole to ascend. It still didn't add up. What was in it for Dragonfly? What point was so important that he needed to kill so many people—innocent people, as far as complacent Imperial citizens could ever be innocent—to prove it?

I just didn't buy it. The Dragonfly I knew—the one who'd rescued Natasha from *LightBringer*, who'd kissed me in Esperanza's docking ring when he could have just shot someone—wasn't that kind of criminal.

Maybe Nikita was right. The detonators were for something else, and I'd missed the point entirely. Or maybe, I just saw what I wanted to see. What Dragonfly wanted me to see. Damn, when had this gotten so difficult? Curse him for being so attractive, for being human. Hating him had been so much easier from a distance.

The sun filtered out again as the loader slotted up into the cargo bay, and I sighed, checking it so Max wouldn't question me. Maybe I just didn't have enough hate in my heart. Now there's something to scribble under "Personality" in my security file. Hatred is practically the Axis virtue.

If Nikita was here, he'd scoff and taunt me into doing what he thought needed to be done. Mishka would smile, ruffle my hair with his big gentle hand, and shoot Dragonfly for me before I could change my mind.

From beside the loader, where he and Bastie unpiled crates under pale blue icelights, Dragonfly glanced at me with that little smile I'd become so used to, and my insides warmed, making up my mind. I wasn't Nikita or Mishka, and I'd blindly believed the line Axis had fed me for long enough. I'd get to the bottom of this my own way; make sure of all the facts before I did something that couldn't be undone. And if that meant failing Director Renko's test, I didn't give a shit.

31

Scarlet midday sun slanted through the downstairs window, and dust motes swirled on the breeze, bringing the smell of warm dirt and rust into Dragonfly's cluttered study. He kicked a stack of old laser viewscreens aside and I dropped the crate with a sigh, puffing loose strands from my face. "That where you want it?"

"Good enough." He put down his end and eyed me warily, wiping his dusty hands on his coat. I watched him back, awkward, wanting to bite my lip. He wasn't stupid. He knew I'd seen what the crate contained, and I waited for him to shrug, offer some excuse, make up some story about why he needed sixty-four sub-band detonators to fix some guy's alphaspace array.

The cat scooted in, tail sparking, and wrapped around his ankles in a puff of orange fur.

"So ... want to help me with this?" he said.

I swallowed. "What?"

He tossed his golden hyperchip into the air and caught it, flipping it over his knuckles. "I've still got data to sort, a game space to build." His eyes twinkled, betraying that inner puzzle obsessive I'd connected with on *Ladrona*. "We'll make a mocha and some *churros*, sit up all night, invent a few new vector geometries. It'll be just like high school."

I shifted, edgy. "I shouldn't."

"Come on, I could use the help." He flicked stray hair from my face, lingering. "I'd very much like the company too."

I wanted to smile, but I couldn't. I wanted to cry, too. Intuition, talent, charm, smarts that made it out of his head, that maddening scent that lingered everywhere I went. He even owned a cat. Truth was, he was too damn perfect. I'd searched my whole life for a man like this. I'd thought I'd found him once, but that was Nikita; and though Mishka had captured my heart, there'd always been a barrier between us, deep inside, and for the first time I realized what it was.

Mishka was a true believer, Imperial to his core. But in the depths of my dirty-backwater-planet soul lurked a dark whisper of doubt.

And as I looked at Dragonfly, that whisper grew louder.

But I couldn't let my weakness confuse me. This was about more than the two of us. He was about to kill thousands of people. The fact that he didn't seem like an evil person didn't make that right.

I tilted my face away, the movement slight but definite. "Umm ... no, thanks."

"Suit yourself."

He shrugged, but I could tell I'd hurt him from the tension around his eyes. My heart stung, and I wanted to reach out to him, but he'd already turned away. Damn it. This was ridiculous. I had to back off, calm down, get rational before I gave myself away.

He tossed his coat onto the sofa and sat on a stool at his dented plastic console. The hardware on *Ladrona* was newer, more powerful; this one looked old, the display worn and flickering.

The cat hopped onto the console and curled up on a data readout, purring. I hunched on the soft gray sofa, rubbing my sore hands on my trousers and looking anywhere but at him. The study looked shambolic: tables stacked with electromag components, data printouts; datashelves crammed with chip cases and old text viewers and piles of burned-out console hardware. And that damn crate of detonators, sitting quietly on the carpet like it wasn't the death of a few thousand filthy rich gamblers and Shadrin's entire negotiation team.

The sofa beckoned, deep and comfortable, and my body sank into the seductive, velvety cushions, but worry hacked at my nerves and I couldn't relax. I didn't know what to do.

Across the corridor, Isabel was busy with her class, childish laughter bubbling out. I could go to help her. I could call Nikita and tell him to put Esperanza on alert. I could forget about the whole thing and carry on as Director Renko had ordered me: follow Dragonfly back to Esperanza and betray him to Axis with his murdering finger on the button.

But I couldn't make myself do it, and my failure itched under my skin like a bad oblivion comedown. Something about this whole deal still didn't feel right, and it wasn't just that I'd somehow convinced myself that the man who'd been my sworn enemy for three years wasn't a killer.

I wriggled my fingers, wincing as they stung. I wasn't accustomed to lifting heavy loads in the cold, even for such a short time. I should have worn gloves. Fidgeting, I studied my palm where I'd pretended to cut it on the crate. No cut, though I had calluses along my right index finger and in the indent of my thumb from too much shooting practice. Some on the left hand too, though not so pronounced.

An image sparked of Max, rubbing his hand in the cargo bay, as if his palm hurt. As if he wasn't used to lifting either. Strange that a career trash-hauler like Bastie wouldn't hire more experienced help.

I recalled the angles of Max's atomflash, tight against his ribcage, his innocuously pale eyes giving me the once-over for weapons. Rubbing his hand, those same pale calluses ringing his thumb and forefinger.

Hot bile churned my stomach, and with a sick jolt I remembered where I'd seen sweet young Max before.

My pleasure, he'd said. The omega brief. Floor thirteen. Max was Axis.

I sat up, urgency twitching my muscles. I'd only sent Nikita that starshot last night. Surely they couldn't find us this fast.

"Sasha, where's Bastie?"

Dragonfly glanced over his shoulder at me, and the data streaming across his display paused. "What?"

My voice strained, harsh. "Bastie. Where is he?"

Across the corridor, Isabel screamed, and abruptly the air stung with the dirty static hiss of atomflash. The cat darted under the console, bristling. Dragonfly and I looked at each other and leaped up as one.

Furniture crashed in the classroom as we hurtled into the corridor. Children squealed and sobbed. Isabel's voice carried over the din, frantic.

A male voice cut across her in harsh Rus. "Talk properly, bitch."

We hit the wall, our backs thudding into the plastic pinboards.

Dragonfly cursed. "That's Bastie's new flyboy. What does he want?"

I sidled along the wall to risk a peek through the glass door. Atomflash crackled, and the glass vaporized, searing my face with a burning rush of air. I jerked back with a curse, singed hair stinking. The bastard was quick and accurate. Not just some spook from floor thirteen. More likely a black ops man.

An assassin. Excellent. But was he here for Dragonfly? Or for me?

"You okay?" Dragonfly touched my chin.

"Yeah, just the heat." I turned my face away, my cheek already swelling. The scald stung like fire, but I could manage the pain. I just didn't want him to see. "He's in the left corner, low. Kids are on the floor. He's got Isabel with him."

He banged his head back against the wall, frustrated. "Weapons?"

"Just the flash. I couldn't see anything else." I thought furiously. No way could Nikita have called Max—or whatever his real name was—onto me so quickly. And Bastie had only signed Max on as crew at Vyachesgrad. No, Nikita had nothing to do with it. This was Surov the cat-man's doing. Either Bastie was in on it, or they'd tricked him too. Surov wanted Dragonfly dead. And Max wouldn't think twice about killing me if I got in the way.

Dragonfly wiped his damp forehead. "What do you want?" he called.

"You," came the reply. "Alive. Alone. No weapons, no tricks, no help from your little girlfriend. I've got a story to tell you about her too."

I swallowed, dry. Max knew who I was. But why would he give me away? I was supposed to be on his side. It struck me that maybe this was Agent Electra's way of eliminating her competition for the A-D job: send Max out here with orders to kill us both. Hell, for all I knew, Max was just doing it for fun.

Dragonfly licked his lips. "Or what?"

"Or I count to five and another of your cute little friends goes 'poof'." A little girl screamed and Max laughed. "One, two, three—"

Atomflash spat. The screams cut off abruptly, and Isabel wailed.

"Shit," called Max cheerfully. "Sorry about that. Guess you'd better get in here, you mind-fucked anarchist son of a bitch."

The stink of burned flesh made me gag, and my muscles rippled tight and angry. Black ops collects the kind of twitchy, hyper-aware psychos for whom criminal insanity is just an occupational hazard. Nikita has nothing on these sick fuckers. To think I'd imagined I'd ever fit in there.

Dragonfly closed his eyes, clenching his jaw. I grabbed his arm and pulled him back against the wall. His muscles bunched, tense. I kept my voice low, but my hands quivered as I realized I'd made my decision. I didn't want him dead, not any more. And that meant we were in this together.

"What are you doing?" I whispered. "You can't go in there."

"What else can I do?" His dark eyes shimmered. "I've outlived my usefulness. I'm not helping them any more. At least this way they might live."

My heart clenched. He had more faith in Max than I did. And this was my fault, not his. I wouldn't let him kill himself for me.

I chewed my lip and thought fast. "There's another way. Give me your pistol, I'm a better shot than you."

He looked at me blankly, shaking his head.

Frustration and sorrow clawed at my insides. I wanted to shake sense into him, make him understand he hadn't come all this way to have his people die. That he hadn't done so many ugly things for nothing.

"Pistol, Sasha, before he vaporizes another kid. You know some people actually give a shit if you live or die?"

Our gazes locked. Slowly he reached beneath his coat and unholstered, handing it to me grip first. Not the new pistol from *LightBringer;* this was his own, worn and dented with use.

"You got a plan?" he said.

I flicked the energy up to maximum and wrapped my fingers around the warm black metal, managing half a grin. "Yeah. Look too dumb to be a threat."

The ghost of a smile haunted his face. "Worked well last time."

"Yeah, it did."

I squeezed his hand one last time, and concentrated on the plasma pistol's weight in my sweaty grip. I breathed deeply, trying to quiet my heartbeat. I'd done this maneuver before a couple times, but always in a team, and Mishka always took the shot. Mishka had joined Axis from special forces, and he never missed. I didn't even have time to adjust the pistol's sights. And Max was black ops, his reflexes wired, his vision likely primed with laser targeting. No way I could beat him. But I had to try.

"Get on with it, dickhead," Max yelled above squealing kids. "I'm in a counting mood."

Asshole.

I thought back to Esperanza, the krypton light exploding above our heads when Dragonfly shot it out. The corridor on *LightBringer* where we'd fought, plasma exploding left and right. I lowered my voice, barely audible. "You fire high and to the left?"

Dragonfly nodded, and swapped places with me without me telling him. We thought alike. It warmed me and maddened me at the same time.

"Trigger pressure?"

He held up four fingers.

Sweat trickled down my temple, and I wiped it away. "Okay. You go in hands free. Close the door, head right two-thirty, two paces past the carpet's edge and hit the floor. If I miss, use your imagination."

He brushed damp hair from my cheek in a swift, affectionate caress, and warmth stole into my heart. He cared so deeply. I longed to explain, to tell him I was sorry for my lies, but before I could say anything he turned and gripped the doorframe.

"Hold your fire, genius," he yelled. "I'm coming in."

I sidled up behind him against the wall, and he inched the handle down and pushed the door open, glinting glass motes drifting. I edged up to the doorframe and closed my eyes, trying to visualize the room as I'd glimpsed it through glass that was no longer there. Max, in a few meters from the far left corner. Isabel on her knees before him. Kids huddled on the carpet.

Fuck. Surely, I was about to die.

Surprise might be my only advantage. Max knew I was from counter-insurrection and, like all black ops guys, he probably thought that meant I was soft. He'd be cocky, confident of success. He might not be expecting this.

I heard Dragonfly step inside. The door clicked softly shut. I gripped the pistol in both hands, sensing it, testing its balance. My pulse pounded, the sound obliterating everything but my shallow breathing. I pressed my forehead to the pistol's warm barrel and counted, the closest thing I'd ever done to a prayer.

One step. Two. Three.

I curled my slick finger inside the trigger guard. Far left corner. High and to the left. Hope the bastard hadn't moved too much.

Look left. Four. Five. Carpet's edge.

I tightened my finger, pulling two pounds, then three.

Six. Seven. Look right.

"Oh, goody." Max's sarcastic voice, distant in my concentration. "Now let me tell you about your little lady friend before I melt your stupid rebel head off."

I held my breath.

Now.

I twisted, kicking out with my right foot, the momentum spinning me into the doorway, my aim straight and level. My vision melted into a colored blur and I cocked my left wrist down a fraction and fired.

Hot scarlet plasma sizzled. Isabel screamed. I thudded into the locker opposite, the hard plastic bruising my shoulder. Pain mushroomed, and my breath hurt my lungs. I'd heard multiple shots. But I wasn't dead.

I blinked, trying to see. Slowly, my pulse receded, and dimly I heard the kids screaming, Isabel sobbing in Espan. My vision cleared. I saw Dragonfly picking himself up off the floor. Max's charred body was slumped against the wall in a fading plasma vapor cloud, next to two little atomflash-melted shapes that didn't resemble children any more.

My shot had been accurate. I'd done it. Dragonfly lived, to go about his awful business at Esperanza. Agent Max was dead and could never tell him who I really was. Both our legends, intact.

Winning had never felt so wrong.

Carrie, Aragon, Lazuli—I was sick of legends and lies. I wanted to scream out the truth to anyone who'd listen: that I didn't know who the fuck I was any more.

I let my head fall back against the locker, and had to use my other hand to uncurl my stiff finger from the trigger.

"Carrie? You okay?"

I took a deep breath, flipped the pistol and held it out to him. I didn't want it.

Slowly, he took it. "Nice shot."

"Thanks."

Tears thickened my lashes, and I blinked them free. In my mind, he crushed me to him, warm and safe, his lips brushing my hair. Hot longing spread in my belly. I wanted to kiss him, feel his hair in my fingers, his skin on mine. But too many untruths mined the space between us.

He wiped my tears away, and his fingertips brushed my cheekbone, their touch so wonderful and warm yet somehow cold.

I wiped my face, pushing his hand away, and walked outside to let the chill wind scrub my skin clean.

32

By the time Dragonfly returned, the pale sun had slipped behind the shadowy streetscape and stars shone cold in the blackening sky.

Isabel had insisted on patching me up, once she'd sent her class home, though her hands still shook and her face shone sickly white. The salve she'd sprayed on my scorched face still tingled.

We'd found no sign of any other new arrivals. Max had come alone, and if Electra was indeed after me, she hadn't shown her face here. Bastie we'd found dead, his pale mass stuffed in next to a bulkhead on his ship. Maybe he'd sold Dragonfly out, maybe he hadn't. We'd never know. We'd crated his body for the freezer, in case he had a family.

Now, the darkness thickened. I wanted to go to my room and hide under the covers, but the silence between Dragonfly and me festered like an ulcer. If I didn't cut it out, it'd eat away at my guts forever. I retreated to his study instead, and flopped onto the puffy sofa in the glowing console's dim light, my limbs aching. I unstrapped my boots so I could curl my bare feet under me for comfort, even though the cool air bit my toes. I huddled in my wrap, rubbing my unbruised eye with a weary hand. My gun fingers hurt. I still didn't know how I'd done it. How I'd killed a black ops assassin who probably had cybernetic retinas and nanowires in his nerves. Maybe he'd gotten distracted at the vital moment. Maybe it was just my lucky day.

When Dragonfly came in, I almost didn't hear. He slipped off his coat and slid onto his console stool with a deep sigh, resting his forehead on the heel of his hand. His face was drawn, his dark hair stark against pale skin.

A lump swelled my throat, and I remembered Mishka's mother in tears the day I had to tell her he was gone. She'd hit me, her bitten fingernails tearing my cheek, and called me a whore for stealing her only son away. Her precious boy had probably killed more people than she'd had haircuts, but that hadn't mattered to her. And Dragonfly's dead were children, not soldiers.

"Are you okay?" I asked, then cursed myself. What a stupid question.

He glanced up, his gaze shadowed, and gave a little laugh as if he hadn't understood. "Carla—the little girl's mother—she couldn't talk. I told her, and her voice just disappeared. Compared to that, I'm just fine."

Compassion ripped my heart raw. All I could give him was understanding. If he'd never needed me before, he needed me now. I swallowed and went to him, awkwardness crawling on my skin. I touched his hand. It felt warm, tense, his tendons tight. I tried to squeeze it, to slip my fingers between his.

"It isn't your fault—"

"Then whose fault is it?" He pulled his hand away, his hot eyes accusing.

I squirmed, but there was nothing I could say.

He eyed me darkly. "I won't ask what he meant about you. I don't care, okay? For all I know, you're both lying."

I searched for something comforting, to ease into it, but I couldn't find a gentle way. "You're going to blow Esperanza apart."

"Only if I must."

I opened my mouth ready to argue before I realized he hadn't said what I'd expected. "If you must?" I repeated stupidly. An extortion plot then? Or a hijacking?

He shook his head, weary. "Haven't you figured it out yet? Do you even know where we are?"

"What's that got to do with it?"

Silently, he activated his console and flicked up a dimensional navplot. A diagrammatic representation of stars, orbits and ecliptics glimmered in the air, complete with designations. Imperial space was shown crosshatched with red, the controlled spaceways in pale white strips. He zoomed in and rotated, pointing at the display so I could see. An area of unannexed space, empty but for a few small systems, one minor planet highlighted. He moved his finger and selected another, larger one in the adjacent system, only a few declension arcs away. "Look for yourself."

I peered closer. The smaller planet was marked as uninhabited, its designation a code number that meant nothing to me. The larger's information block spilled open as I touched it: reams of information on climate, resources, atmospherics, all headed with a different code number and the words COLONY SANTA MARIA.

Dragonfly's little isolationist rock lay right next to the surrendering rebel colony.

Truth thudded into my guts like a fist. He wasn't destroying Esperanza just for kicks. He didn't even care about the billion new rubles—for all I knew, breaking the vault really was impossible. He cared that the home for which he'd sacrificed so much was about to appear smack in the middle of controlled Imperial space.

"Do you see?" His knuckles whitened. "I can't just let this lie. I have to try. And if that bastard Shadrin won't listen this time, then I'll do what I must."

His gaze dropped, avoiding me.

Suspicion prickled. How did he know Shadrin was heading the negotiation team? I'd only gotten that action message myself from Nikita a few days ago.

"You've met Shadrin before?" I asked.

He smiled grimly at the console. "Oh, yes. He's the genesis of the most famous Dragonfly myth. I'm surprised you've not heard it. He and I disagreed over the surrender of a place called Urumki Mor."

My guts churned. Urumki Mor. Mishka. I hadn't known Shadrin was in charge.

I almost couldn't bear to ask, but the need to know flared within me, burning, consuming. "What happened?"

"I was running guns to a bunch of separatists, and it escalated. They needed a tactician—"

"You were a mercenary?"

"Call it that if you want. I did it for nothing. It's hard to have talents and not use them when people are dying. You should know that."

I swallowed. I'd never had any trouble. "Go on."

"The Empire were arrogant, under-resourced, Shadrin had diverted half his battle group and couldn't get it back in time. We were winning, they couldn't infiltrate our command and control. Shadrin lost his head and shattered half the city from orbit so no one would find out how he'd screwed up. Must have wiped out hundreds of his own people. He put it out that they'd been on the brink of victory and I'd done it so I could escape."

Sickness welled in my stomach, and I nearly choked on bile. I didn't doubt him for a millisecond.

They'd lied to me. Axis. Director Renko. Everyone. Let me think some faceless criminal had murdered my friends when all the time they'd done it themselves. And Dragonfly would be hunted for the rest of his life for something he hadn't done.

I'd known Axis couldn't be trusted. I knew their methods—our methods—too well. But Shadrin was different. He was decent, incorruptible. He was the reason making it all worthwhile. And now he'd betrayed me too. He'd sacrificed his own people to save face, covered up mass murder by publicly destroying an innocent man. Shadrin was Imperial to the core, and that core stank rotten.

And it made me as bad as the rest.

My nerves twisted, and I wanted to scream. I felt brainwashed. I burned to confront Shadrin, to ask him to his face why he'd lied to me, to watch him stammer and flinch. To put a bullet in his cold, scheming heart. But I wouldn't get the chance, not if Dragonfly had his way.

"There must be another option," I said.

"There isn't. I've talked to Luis Alvarado. There's nothing he can do."

But there was. I remembered Nikita's words—*in it up to their greedy eyeballs*—and my blood boiled. Dragonfly's mistake was to think everyone was as good-hearted as he was. But I couldn't tell him that this Alvarado guy was corrupt. He'd ask how I knew, and then he'd hate me forever.

"So, what—you'll blow them all to hell?"

The despair shadowing his eyes clawed at my soul. "The people here die for me. Their children die because of me. What if everything you'd ever promised the people who rely on you was about to be swept away for small change? What would you do?"

I swallowed. My promises were to the Empire, and I'd always taken Imperial word on what was corrupt and what wasn't. I'd been itching to destroy Dragonfly, the way he planned to destroy Shadrin and Esperanza. But it was all a dirty lie.

Sourness stung my throat. Including Nikita, this was the second time I'd let them deceive me utterly. I needed to start thinking for myself.

"I think I'd blow them all to hell," I said finally.

"Could you? Really?"

He stared at me, fierce, and I realized this was a test. I owed him nothing less than abject honesty.

"Yes," I said steadily, though my throat ached, "if it meant someone I cared about didn't have to."

My heart clenched. I'd told myself this so many times—that I did it all to protect the innocent—but it didn't make the killing any easier. It didn't make the guilt go away. I'd always imagined that to be the difference between me and a terrorist. Until I'd met this one, whose sense of proportion shamed me to my heart even as it drew me inexorably to him.

I wanted to know him so badly it hurt, but how could he ever want me? He could never know who I really was, because I was pretending to be someone else. I was lying to him, exactly the same way Nikita and the Empire lied to me.

Tears misted, and I dropped my head, my face burning.

"Don't. Look at me." He lifted my chin, caressing my cheek, and the intimacy tingled warmth over my body. "You understand so much," he whispered. "Who are these people you're destroying yourself for? Don't they care about you? Why are you so alone?"

"Because I deserve to be."

I pressed my cheek into his hot palm, closing my eyes. Tears trickled, stinging my flashburned skin, and I squirmed. I never cried.

His cheek brushed mine, his scent on my lips making me quiver. "I can't believe that. Why won't you let me trust you? At least pretend you're not hiding anything from me, just for a moment. Please."

I inhaled, tasting him, and imagined I'd told him everything—Axis, the mission, Nikita, Mishka, that not only was Lazuli a fabrication but Aragon was too. And I imagined he didn't care, because he'd seen through it all and still wanted me. Me. Carrie.

Longing struck me so hard, my flesh ached. I couldn't help staring at his lips, so close, so perfect. My mouth dried. I wanted to taste him again, feel his tongue on mine, swallow on him, bring him into me. His eyes gleamed in the console's soft light, so beautiful, his lashes dark and curling. I could feel myself sinking into their warm depths, my insides melting, and I didn't want to struggle.

It's true, what they say about drowning. Once you give in, it's beautiful.

I slid my wrists around his neck, leaning into him. His body felt tight and lean against me, his hands trembling on my face as he brought his lips to mine.

For a heartbeat, our kiss was gentle, sweet, hesitant

with sorrow. Then he clenched his fingers in my hair and dragged my head back to devour me. His lips demanded my surrender and I'd never given it more willingly. His scent filled my head like the first sweet rush of oblivion, my every nerve ending awakening in a delicious shiver that sparkled over my skin like starshine.

Our tongues searched and entwined, burning. He tasted of the salt and blood of his bitter sorrow, and I swallowed, drawing his essence into me. He gripped my hips with strong, insistent hands and lifted me onto the console so I could wrap my legs around him. My thighs ached at the contact, and I pressed tighter, sucking on his tongue to taste more of him. Damn, he felt good there. I wanted him naked so I could pin him down on the sofa and climb on top. But I wanted more than the thrill of feeling him inside me. I wanted to sob with pleasure in his embrace, own him, let him own me, wake up the next morning and find him still there, our limbs still entangled.

He groaned and buried his face in my shoulder, his breath ragged. "I can't," he whispered, though he clearly could, and hungered to, from the hardness burning against me and the tension in his hands grinding my hips against him. "It's all or nothing, Carrie. This doesn't finish here."

I didn't want it to finish here either. I wanted to keep him forever, to forget the mess I'd made of my life and start again.

I trailed my lips through his fragrant hair, longing for his mouth again, desperate not to break this spell between us. "Don't hold back. Not now. Let me have it all."

He was still for a moment but for his rapid breathing. “Everything?”

“Everything.”

He pushed away, that sweet smile turning his lips, but now his eyes smoldered with desire, dark with sensual intent. Slowly he untucked the corners of my wrap, pulling it from around me.

“All right. You asked for it. I’m in awe of you. You’re the most maddening woman I’ve ever met. You make me rethink myself at every turn. You’re the only person who sees through me like glass. I can’t hide anything from you.”

He’d already found my sweater’s ziplocks and parted the soft fabric swiftly. Cool air washed my burning skin, raising tantalizing bumps and making my nipples ache and harden.

I gasped a laugh. “You’re kidding, right? I could have said the same about you.”

“Carrie, I have a hard time seeing anything except how beautiful you are.” He brushed his knuckles along the curve of my waist, where he’d kissed me that night on *Ladrona*, and I sucked back a gasp. My breasts hurt, I wanted so much for him to touch me. “Every trick you’ve tried on me has worked, you know that? I wanted you from the moment you called my gambit at Esperanza. I had a hard-on for five tarocchi hands just from thinking about your legs, and the thrashing you gave me only made it worse.”

“Go on.” I laughed, breathless, and it turned into a moan as he caressed me through the broad skintight strap that encased my breasts, grazing my swollen nipples with his palms. Sensation fired deep into me, shooting straight between my legs.

“Shall I? Let’s see. After you kissed me in the docking ring, I couldn't sleep with you on my ship—"

"You could so," I teased, arching my back to press into his hands. "I watched you."

"I know. I wasn't asleep. I was fantasizing about the things you could do to me with that wicked mouth of yours, and beating myself up for wanting to corrupt an innocent young woman." He kissed me, hungry, biting my bottom lip softly, and I cried out into his mouth, helpless. "When you solved that factor construct in your head, I nearly bent you over that console and took you right there."

The memory inflamed me, how he'd teased me into competing with him. "I wanted you to."

"I know. That's what scared me."

He lifted me down so he could slide my pants and underwear from my hips, and I wriggled them off swiftly so I could get back up there and pull him to me again. But he caressed my bare ankle, a shock shivering all the way up to my thigh, and pushed me down against the warm plastic. A diode flashed violet near my elbow and I fumbled to turn the console off before I broke something, but he brushed my hand away. "Leave it."

He lifted my ankle, arcing arc hot, wet kisses up the inside of my calf, and I shuddered with urgency, my blood coursing. He licked his way up my thigh, teasing me, and I crushed his warm dark hair in my fingers so he couldn't leave off.

"Then Lukas pointed that atomflash at you and I knew," he whispered, nibbling at my inner thigh. "I tried to stay away from you, but I can't. I craved you when I thought you were just a clever thief. Now I don't know what you are, and it drives me wild. I think I'm in love with you, Carrie."

Just hearing him say that burned my blood, the air itself sweet friction on my flesh for having him near. He dipped his head and drew his tongue up my slit, a single lick of flame. Pleasure seared through me like a plasma bolt, sharp, crisp and hot. He tasted me, exploring my shapes, and then he moved to suck me, teasing me with the tip of his tongue in just the right spot.

"Oh, god, Sasha." I was so close to losing it already, and I wanted to come with him inside me. But each determined stroke of his tongue spiraled tension up within me, filling me tighter and tighter until I screamed and came apart like liquid shatterglass, explosive, prolonged ripples of pleasure weakening my limbs.

He kissed my shivering skin as I caught my breath, trailing his lips over my belly, and I felt him smile. "Well, I guess everyone heard that."

"Yeah, I guess they did." I knotted my fingers in his hair and pulled him up to kiss me, my wet lips sliding on his. Tasting myself in his mouth made my pulse race again, his lean body against mine an even sweeter torture now he'd almost undressed me. I wasn't done. I still wanted more of him, and I didn't care who knew.

The console creaked under our weight, and I laughed, his soft hair tickling my face. "Look, I love antique virtual kit as much as the next girl, but don't you have something more comfortable?"

He pulled me up and swept me astride his lap on the console stool. "Better?" he murmured, slipping his hands inside my open sweater.

"Much."

My taut nipples already yearned for his mouth. I let my head fall back, arching my spine. He peeled the fabric away and captured a nipple in his mouth, his hot hand cupping my breast. The pleasure seared like atomflash, dizzying, my desire flowering under his touch as if I'd never been touched before.

I couldn't keep my lips from his a moment longer. I pulled him away, my breast wet and shiny and my nipple swollen from his attention. He tilted his head back for my kiss, letting me lead him. Urgently I unfastened his shirt. His body was all muscle, lean and compact, so smooth as I ran my fingertips over his chest. His skin seared mine when I pulled him against me, making me ache all over again, and I could feel the hot moisture between my legs seeping onto his clothes.

Dizziness and desire rocked me. I wanted to eat him, swallow him, consume his body and his soul and become what he was. This was beyond lust. This was possession, intoxication, crushing compulsion. I'd never felt like this with anyone.

I needed him now, before the spell broke. My fingers fumbled and shook as I tried to unfasten his pants. He helped me, and groaned and sank his teeth helplessly into my collarbone as I touched him, his breath hissing hot. The sting of pain only sparked my senses more alive, and desperately I yanked the fabric aside and took him in my hand, demanding, guiding him to my swollen entrance.

Oh. My. God.

The heat of his entry scorched me. I cried out, shuddering, and he dug his fingers into my hips, slamming me down, forcing himself deeper.

I braced my hands on his shoulders so I could

move, but he held me still. "Let me look at you."

My muscles pulsed around him, drawing on him, tension welling forth to grip me. I struggled to remain still, but his beautiful dark eyes captured me, so deep and warm and infatuated I couldn't look away. Slowly, inexorably, I leaned closer, until his hair tangled with mine. His lips brushed mine, our breath mingling as one, and we made love with our eyes open, drinking in this wondrous new thing, unable to get enough before we came together, gasping our pleasure into a kiss.

33

When I awoke, he wasn't there.

I sat up in bed, dragging knotted hair from my face. I slipped my hand under the sheets. His half was cold.

We'd moved to his bed once our limbs had recovered enough strength, and now the night was fully dark, wind hissing in the dusty street outside. A krypton nightlight glowed on the bedside table, violet light gleaming on overstuffed shelves, a smudged glass bookreader on the floor on his side. A handful of plasma charges scattered on the dressing table, their reflections dim in the scarf-draped mirror.

I arose, legs still wobbly, and plucked a shirt of his from the chair's back to wear until I found my clothes. The black cloth whispered on my skin, his scent drifting, and I smiled as I tiptoed out into the study. He sat at his console in the dark, the glowing display tarnishing his face in shadow.

I slipped my arms around his neck, resting my chin on his shoulder. "Can't sleep?"

He didn't answer, his gaze still on the display. It showed his message system, encryption off. He'd unwrapped a data block and text spread across the screen. The sender was Lukas, and the header read *Told you so ...*

My guts coiled, crushing my contentment. A message from Spider. And it was about me. A page of information about my life. Where I grew up, my time in the military, why I'd left, everything I'd done since.

Or so he thought.

Spider had found Lazuli's invented past, right where Axis's intelligence division had left it for him, information snippets scattered throughout any number of obscure databases he'd no doubt spent hours breaking into.

A lump swelled my throat. I'd wanted so much for the lies to dissolve between us that, for a sweet short while, I'd believed they had. And now here they were, in infallible digital. A sick chill fingered my spine, and I straightened, letting my hands slip away from him.

"You were in the marines." Toneless, as if he was sleepwalking. He didn't look at me.

Axis like to keep our covers simple, and as close to the truth as possible so we don't forget. But my truth was so much worse than the lie.

"Umm ... yeah. I had to get off my cesspit of a planet somehow. So what?"

He spun around at last. "When did you plan to tell me?"

I turned away from the pain glossing his eyes. Seeing him disappointed in me was more than I could bear. I hunted for my pants and boots, pulled them on and fastened them with sour spit welling in my mouth. "What was I supposed to say? That I'm ex-military but it's okay now, I've come to my senses? Why does it matter, Sasha? I got what I wanted out of them. The past is the past."

"No, it isn't." He shut the console off with a rough slap of his hand. "The past is *not* the past in this business and you know it. I don't care what you did or when, Carrie. I care that you lied to me."

"You never asked me!"

"I don't mean about that! You knew about Urumki Mor, didn't you?"

My nerves screamed, and I wanted to do the same. I wanted to tell him everything, about Axis and how I'd believed their lies, but terror that I'd lose him spiked me like a poisongun. I couldn't bear him looking at me like that. Not after the things we'd said, the things we'd done. "So what if I did? You said yourself it's a myth."

"A myth you believed!" Color burned in his cheeks. His lashes glistened, and he wiped them roughly. "You believed it because you believed in the Empire, and you damn well still do."

My heart stung. "What? What else did Spider say? You really gonna trust him, after what he did?"

"Lukas has watched my back more times than I can count. You ... Well, you're very clever, Lazuli, but you slipped up." His gaze shone frigid, hard. "I just didn't realize until now. And that bastard you killed in the classroom confirmed it."

"You can't be serious. The creep was just winding you up!"

"No. It's all true, isn't it? Yesterday, when I mentioned Shadrin, you said, 'you've met him before?'"

My insides heated like a naughty schoolgirl's. The way I felt about Sasha had put me off my guard, made me careless. I didn't need to hear what came next.

"What you *didn't* say was, 'who's Shadrin?' Or even, 'shit, I didn't know he was on the negotiation team'." Sasha yanked his tangled hair, edgy. "Do you know how much that information cost me? How long it took me to find that out? How could you know it if you're just a simple thief?"

I was digging myself deeper, but I couldn't stop. "That means nothing. I could have—"

"Stop lying to me, Carrie. Or whatever the fuck your name is. They sent you for me, didn't they?"

Bitter guilt strangled my throat. I couldn't find a single thing to say.

He laughed, empty. "No wonder you're so perfect. Mother of god, I've been so *stupid.* I can't believe I made love to you, told you I ... Fuck. You're good. I really thought you meant it."

I stared, my heart bleeding. *No wonder you're so perfect.* No wonder indeed. We had so much in common, we'd clicked like magnets. Axis had hand-picked me for the job, and only one agent knew me that well.

This had Nikita's malicious fingerprints all over it.

Tears swelled my eyelids, burning, and blindly I walked out.

***

I didn't know how long I walked the dark empty streets, huddled against the icy breeze, my tears drying warm and dusty on my face. Streetlights crackled overhead, shedding pools of white light in the darkness, and flabby grey bats sparred and cackled in the glare. Wind whistled through creaking tenements, stinging dirt and hair into my face and chilling my fingers stiff, but I didn't care. I already hurt too much inside.

Emptiness hollowed my heart, blacker than I knew how to deal with. This wasn't just an ordinary lovers' disagreement, where you cried your eyes out alone for a few days and then made up by begging for forgiveness. No, I'd done way better than that this time. I'd destroyed my one and only chance with the only man who'd ever seen me—not who I pretended to be, or wished I could be, but *me*—and I'd done it before I'd even met him.

I swallowed, tasting grit and tears. The sharpest barb ripping at my heart was that I'd no one to blame but myself. My Imperial bosses had lied, but I'd chosen to listen. I was no better than any of them. Not even Nikita, who at least had an excuse for his duplicity. If Sasha could ever have loved me, even for a moment, I didn't deserve it.

I walked past a rusted playground, chains swinging and squeaking in the wind. Through aching eyes I stared up beyond the tenements at the sky, where stars glared, careless. A fat white one gleamed larger than the rest, and listlessly I wondered if it was the Santa Maria colony. Beside it, a streak of arcfuel wake shimmered. An angular black shape arced in front of the stars, rising, and as the ship climbed into the upper atmosphere I caught the telltale glint of stealthplate shining in the vanished sun.

Ladrona. Sasha was leaving without me.

Sorrow gripped me again, but frustration squeezed my guts too. He'd destroy Esperanza and I'd never get the chance to confront Shadrin. He'd do it thinking I'd betrayed him, and here I was, stuck on this rock with no way to get off.

Except Bastie's Pharaoh.

Resolution seized me like a magclamp, and I whirled and broke into a run.

***

The hardstand lay deserted, unlit, the Pharaoh's ramp still down, its huge arcfuel boosters hulking. I leaped aboard, my boots clanging on metal, and smacked my fist onto the plastic panel just inside the hatchway. White icelights cracked on, sluggish insects lurching into flight, and the ramp juddered and retracted with a stiff hydraulic hiss.

The casket holding Bastie's weighty body still lay on the loader, a hastily modified freezebox powering the cryo. I sidled past as the ramp clanged shut behind me, squeezing alongside more crated goods he'd intended to deliver who knew where else, and hopped up the steel ladder into the cockpit.

The ancient-generation metal console sat dull and silent below a shuttered clearview. The low ceiling was claustrophobic, dangling with patched wires and weld-mended pipes. I scraped my finger cautiously over the nav computer's cracked plastic case. It itched, crawling. Biochem. Old, weak, not as immediate as *Ladrona*'s, but enough to lock me out of the controls and make me thoroughly sick and sorry in a few minutes.

On the other hand, first-generation biochem was imprecise. It could be fooled.

I glanced over my shoulder at the casket. A stunt like this would kill me on *Ladrona*. But it was worth a shot with old, sluggish biochem like this.

I climbed down and thumbed open the casket. Bastie'd been dead at least seven or eight hours now. The lid slid aside, revealing his white visage, ice crystallizing on his unshaven jaw. I surveyed his massive stiff body. No way could I drag him up the ladder into the cockpit. He was too heavy. But I didn't need his whole body to switch off the biochem.

My eyeballs swiveled to the slag-encrusted fusion welder hanging in the corner. Good thing Bastie was half-frozen. This could get messy.

I slipped on the purple anti-flash mask and arced the welder to life. It buzzed evilly in my hands, star-bright light crackling off the nozzle. As I wielded it, the stinking vapor hissing, I reflected that it was a pity the body wasn't sweet young Max's. I'd have enjoyed hacking off an extra limb or two in his case.

A few minutes later, I stowed Bastie's newly warm hand back in the casket, fired up the arcfuel boosters and set course on the ancient navset for Esperanza.

34

Interminable hours later, the Pharaoh jolted out of slipspace. I stumbled to the cockpit from where I'd been pacing in the cargo bay. Beneath the floor, the stardrive's hum intensified and the arcfuel rockets kicked in with a grinding jolt to slow the ship down. I blinked grit from my eyes as I checked the coordinates. At last, I'd arrived, and my body sparked despite my exhaustion.

I hadn't slept during the entire trip—useless even to try—and no doubt I looked like a starved raccoon, with black bruises under my eyes and creases pinching my mouth. My mind still tumbled over and over, spinning uselessly like shrapnel, and my muscles ached, my nerves juddering at every sound. I hadn't found any food on the ship, either, and my head pulsed and swam with hunger. A couple times, my ESE had signaled, a high-pitched squeal that pierced my eardrums like a skewer, but I'd ignored it. I didn't want to talk to Nikita, not in my current state. Maybe not ever.

The shutters slid aside with a crunch, and Esperanza loomed in the clearview, its tall spires glinting, lights gleaming from a thousand glittering windows. Approach beacons flashed red and yellow, ships cruising back and forth in intricate patterns, and beyond, the swirling blue Irkutsk nebulas filled half the hemisphere, eerie and silent.

I couldn't see *Ladrona* in the docking rings, and my lips tightened. Didn't mean he wasn't here. I scanned the rings for Nikita's modified Sliver class. Didn't mean he wasn't here either.

The console pinged as a channel opened, and an Espan-accented voice rang out in the cockpit. "Pharaoh on two-seven-four charlie, Esperanza control, *buenas dias.* Refresh your flight plan and retransmit."

"Control, this is *Nefertiti*, no plan on file. Request priority docking slot and expedite." I tried to hide my impatience. They were just doing their job.

A crackle; probably them holding their hand over the channel to laugh at me. Bastie's ancient ship didn't look like its owners could afford to breathe at Esperanza, let alone stay for any length of time.

"Negative, *Nefertiti.* Proceed to holding pattern echo, approach five. Will advise."

Idiots. I gritted my teeth. "Control, let me rephrase. This is Imperial warship *Nefertiti*, authorization Aragon delta phi four-seven epsilon. Let me the fuck into your airspace. Now."

A muffled snort, and silence. I guess I got their attention.

"Affirm, *Nefertiti*," the voice said, after an interval they'd surely spent riffling madly through security protocols to check my authent. "Slot delta seven, expedite."

"Delta seven, Control. Have a nice day."

I rolled *Nefertiti* to starboard, rockets howling, and a few minutes later the docking rig clunked into place.

I cranked the rusted airlock open, and the familiar, decadent smell of Esperanza flooded in, lights gleaming on the buffed metal floor. I finger-combed my hair and retied my ponytail as I waited for the blast doors to open, and fought to slow my breathing and calm my heartbeat as I walked as swiftly as I could without running toward the elevator and the alpha docking ring.

My body writhed in a contradictory mess, my senses pulling me in all directions at once. My nerves shouted at me to rip the station apart searching for Sasha, not to stop until I'd found him and explained everything. My trigger finger itched to go for Shadrin, blast my way into the Imperial quarters and blow his treacherous brains out. My stomach hankered for food, and my brain ached with fatigue, urging me to collapse in the first convenient corner and sleep until I died or woke up refreshed.

I didn't have time for any of that. Sasha had a big headstart, and *Ladrona* traveled a lot faster than *Nefertiti.* I didn't know how long he'd already had to finish his calculations, set his explosives, daisy-chain the detonators for effect, calibrate the remote control. I couldn't let him sink to those depths. I'd wallowed down there, and I knew what it was like. It would destroy him. Too much humanity still filled his heart.

I rubbed my face wearily as the elevator eased to a halt at alpha level. If I wanted to find Sasha, Shadrin was the key. I knew in my heart that Sasha had told me the truth, that he still thought he could change things, and he'd give Shadrin one last chance to back down on Santa Maria. If I found Shadrin first, then Sasha would come to me. But first I had to get in to see Shadrin.

I twisted the red steel handle, and the blast doors ground aside. I knew I wasn't really Aragon any more; I couldn't be. But she'd help me one last time, before Axis laid her to rest, hopefully not with a bullet in the skull.

With tense white fingers, I wound the chipped glass airlock open and climbed aboard *RapidFire.* She lay much as I'd left her: my rumpled bed unmade, the breakfast dishes undone and the warm, lingering smell of Nikita poisoning the air.

Swiftly I undressed, tossing the blue wrap and Isabel's trousers away, and pulled on a clean black silk flight suit, smooth and cool on my sweaty skin. I splashed my face, washing off grime and tearstains, and studied my singed self in the mirror. Dark circles blossomed under my eyes, and a horrible grey tinge sickened my skin. I even had pimples on my chin, angry purple ones just itching to spread.

God, I wanted a hot bath, a bed and a good night's sleep. Better still, a hot bath and a bed with Sasha in it, and then a good night's sleep. My body wept and pleaded just thinking about it, and I wiped my face on the hand towel, averting my gaze. I didn't want to look at myself any more.

The galley table slid aside when I touched the contact concealed beneath it, revealing Aragon's secret arms stash. I slipped my Axis ident into my suit's side pocket, and surveyed the array of weapons strapped to the side of the padded white compartment. The shatterjay would be no use this time. I needed something longer range, quick and accurate, but efficient at close quarters too. After a moment's consideration, I chose an under-powered atomflash with laser targeting for my shoulder holster, and a poison-cell plasma pistol for inside my suit, just in case. I didn't need to check the sights or the charges. They were already adjusted, already filled.

I slipped my black flight jacket over the top and shrugged to get comfortable. The guns' weight felt good. I still wore Aragon's skin pretty well, and I could still feel her come-and-get-it defiance burning in my heart when I thought about Shadrin. But I missed her confidence. All my truths had turned out to be lies, and I might never be certain about anything again.

I took a deep breath, letting it out slowly. Shadrin was a dead man, that was one thing I was certain of. But not before he'd answered my questions.

***

It was early evening on Esperanza, and the polished terraces were crowded with gamers, celebrities in gowns and jewels, out-of-uniform Imperial soldiers trying to look like regular people, Espan gangsters wearing sharp black suits or cocktail dresses with gold chains and etherwave earpieces. I shouldered through, and people noticed the sharp silver Axis flashes on my collar and let me pass, pretending they didn't see me.

I crossed the thick black carpet and stepped into an empty elevator. A couple followed me in, and quickly backed out again when they saw what I was. I smiled at them as the door phased solid, but my heart stung. Had it always been like this? Maybe I hadn't noticed how people feared and shunned us. Maybe I just hadn't cared. Maybe I'd liked it, being in charge. Being the one everyone else was afraid of instead of the frightened one.

Well, now I was mad as a slipspace rat. They were right to be afraid of me.

The elevator hissed upward, the floor numbers flashing in a blur. I knew where to find Shadrin. I knew all about the surrender negotiation team's arrangements from my omega brief.

Thirty-seven, and the numbers stopped. My pulse steadily quickened and my nerves tingled, exhilarating, reassuring. My vision seemed to sharpen, my hearing to intensify. This was what I'd trained for, what my whole career led me toward. And at long last, I stalked the real enemy.

The glass door dissolved, and I stepped through.

35

The black lobby gleamed under white calmlights. A shiny black partition behind the counter blocked my view of the inner sanctum. I flashed my ident at the black-uniformed sentry and she ushered me through with a sharp salute, which, not being military, I wasn't strictly entitled to. I resisted the urge to smack some sense into her, to show her where playing nice with Axis had landed me.

Beyond, the sanctum lay quiet in soft light. Pale curved desks and couches lined the dark carpet, and along one wall a clearview stretched from floor to ceiling, wisps of blue nebula misting the black starfield. A young blond lieutenant bent over a glowing glass console, absorbed in his work. Another riffled through a display, searching some cluttered dataspace. In the corner, an old Espan woman cleaned the carpet with a humming static filter, and lemon antivirals tainted the cool air.

At the far end, a broad white desk stood spotless, a tall, spare-fleshed man sitting behind it. An expressionless major in black marine uniform leaned around his high-backed chair, passing cyberpaper documents to him one by one. The general signed each with a digital authenticator after flicking his gaze briefly across the page, his long bony hands moving efficiently, without fuss. His silvering hair was cropped short, his face narrow and animated, his grey eyes sharp.

My throat tightened, and sweat trickled inside my flight suit.

His aide whispered into his ear as I approached.

He looked up, ident still in hand, and smiled, bright and genuine like he always had. "Major Thatcher. What a pleasant surprise."

I halted before his desk, my fingers twitching. Carrie Thatcher was unavailable, for the moment. "It's Aragon now."

Shadrin rose and came around the desk to meet me, his smooth black uniform spotless. "Yes. Yes, so I see. Wonderful. I knew you'd go far. It's good to see you." He held out his hand.

I didn't take it. "We need to have a chat."

He dropped his hand, watchful as he resumed his chair. "Of course. Have a seat. How can I help you?"

His aide stepped back politely, clasping her hands behind her.

I perched on the chair's soft edge, my thighs tense. "Talk to me about Urumki Mor."

Shadrin's brow creased, and he shook his head. "A terrible, wasteful business. I heard you were involved on the ground, in counter-insurrection? My condolences."

Smug bastard. Calmly, I reached under my jacket and drew my atomflash, placed it on the desk within reach. "It's not that kind of chat, Valodyi."

Shadrin's face drained, and his aide drew in a sharp breath.

"Leave us," Shadrin snapped.

Her hand strayed to the poisongun at her belt. "But—"

"Leave us. Clear the room. Now."

The aide marched away, her face carefully blank. She ushered the others out, and within half a minute we sat alone, only the buzz of the fans circulating lemon-scented air for company.

"What's the matter, Valodyi? Don't want them to hear what I've got to say about you?"

I reached across the desk console to thumb the lockdown contact. An alarm pealed two short high-pitched blasts, and steel shutters scraped down to cover the clearview and the sanctum door. I flipped open the emergency panel and hit the station evacuation alarm. Blue diodes flashed. I typed in Aragon's Axis ident.

"Authenticate it," I ordered.

"Why?"

"Because everyone on this station's about to die. Not that you care. Authenticate it."

"I can't do that—"

I slammed my palm on my atomflash, an unsubtle threat. "Authenticate, Valodyi, before I get impatient."

Slowly, he reached out, punched in his code and hit 'execute'.

Bright icelights snapped on, glaring on the white desk, and in the distance beyond the bulkheads the evacuation alarm shrieked. A blastproof panel near the doorway slid aside, revealing an emergency exit. I couldn't let Sasha kill them all. Now, he wouldn't be able to.

I eased my hand on the weapon. "Now. Urumki Mor. Talk."

"I've been through this with your people already." For the first time, fear shimmered in his voice. "All the questions. I told them what they wanted to know—"

"This isn't for Axis." My anger rose like a tide of blood. If Axis had already questioned him, then they knew everything and were in on the cover-up. "It's for me. I know what happened. I want to hear you say it."

He rose, awkward. "Why dredge up the past? We all know the insurrectionists play dirty. It's what we fight them for—"

"Shut up and sit down." I twitched up the flash, the metal warm and comforting in my hand, my aim swift and immediate. The old confidence coursed in my veins, and I welcomed it. I'd blown away Agent Max with a single blind shot at ten meters. No way would I miss this one.

Shadrin lifted his hands and returned to his seat, his gaze flickering. I could see the calculation, his narrowing eyes, the lines tightening around his mouth. He was wondering how much I knew. "The investigation was conclusive. A series of errors, miscalculations, poor intelligence, battlespace confusion—"

"An accident? Is that what you're telling me?" Sickness roiled inside me. He'd changed his story without so much as a blink. I leaned across the desk on one elbow, the flash steady in both hands. "You don't flood half a fucking city with shatterfire by accident. You killed my friends, my subordinates. If I hear any more bullshit Imperial spin from your mouth, I swear, I'll melt your lying head to mush. Tell me what really happened."

Sweat beaded on his temple. "Nonsense. Why all this rage? Your colleagues' deaths weren't your fault."

He sounded so calm, so fucking reasonable, like all those courses I'd done in hostage negotiation. It only maddened me more.

I stood and circled the table, lowering my aim to just a breath from his cheekbone. "Last chance. Tell me."

His knuckles whitened on his chair's arms. "Think about what you're doing—"

I pressed the flash's emitter into the hollow in his cheek and thumbed the charge with a hiss. It seared his skin, and he choked back a yelp.

"I want to hear you say it," I repeated, harsh. "Tell me."

"I had no choice!" Spit flecked between his clenched teeth. "The territory was lost. The battle was over. I did the only thing I could."

"The battle was not over!" Tears misted my vision, burning, and hot compulsion seared through my blood. I ached to fire. I didn't care about one more murder. I'd be shooting Imperial lies, not Shadrin. I'd be blowing away the bloody mess they'd made of my life. "The battle's not over until the last soldier's safe—isn't that what you taught me?"

"Grow up, Caroline!" He jerked his head around despite my weapon, malice flashing in his eyes. "The Empire uses you! It uses us all, and when it's finished it throws us away. What kind of adolescent arrogance makes you think you're any different?"

"This kind." I jabbed the flash back into his temple, kinking his neck to the side, and closed my eyes at the stink of burning hair. I tightened my thumb on the warm metal contact, feeling the spring tighten, the resistance increase. My pulse thudded in my ears, blotting out the shrieking alarm, strong, unstoppable, matching the thirst for justice that boiled in my soul.

Fuck. You.

***

"Carrie."

His soft voice penetrated my throbbing skull.

"Carrie, don't."

Gentle fingers wrapped my juddering forearm, trying to ease my aim away.

The evacuation alarm faded back in. I opened my eyes, hot tears spilling, blinding me. I tried to shake his hand off, still aiming at Shadrin's head.

"Go away, Sasha. I'm not done."

I didn't ask how he'd gotten in through the lockdown. He wasn't the insurrection's most infamous thief for nothing. I could see him now, his hair matted with sweat and grime, his lashes smudged with polymer dust from his explosives, his skin streaked with black dirt. His presence slashed at my heart, so close yet so far away, and my aim faltered.

He cupped my straining hands in his and steered them gently downward, levering the atomflash from my grip. "Let him go. Killing one man solves nothing."

I whirled away, frustration and grief burning my soul. "And killing a couple thousand does? Fine. Let's do it your way."

"That's up to him."

He flicked the contact to power the atomflash's charge down, and tossed a little round micro-ether transmitter onto the desk. Its silver contacts shone. A remote detonator. He'd set his explosives already.

Efficiently, he shackled Shadrin with smartcuffs, the living metal band wrapping the general's wrists and flicking out like a snake to fuse itself to the metal desk frame. Shadrin cursed at him, but Sasha ignored him.

"You set off the alarm," he accused me.

"Yes."

"Why?"

"Because I can't let you do it. You're better than they are. Don't sink to their level."

He glanced at the silver Axis stripes on my collar and didn't reply.

I hadn't wanted him to find out like this. Hot shame skewered my guts, and my mouth dried. "I'm sorry. I know you'll never forgive me. But—"

Metal bounced on the carpet. My throat corked tight. He'd dropped my atomflash in astonishment.

"Forgive you?" he said with a dumbfounded laugh. "Do you think I even care?"

My brain muddled wet. "What do you mean, you don't care?"

He bent to retrieve the flash and, to my surprise, handed it back to me. Automatically I reached for it, and he trapped my fingers in his, warm and damp.

"I trust you, Carrie. You. The real person I fell for in that neurospace. Not the person you're pretending to be."

"But—"

"Stop it. I don't care if you turn out to be the Emperor's daughter. I said I trusted you and I meant it, but you didn't believe it. *You* don't trust *me.* Not enough to tell me the truth." He sighed, weary. "I'm sorry for what I said back there. I've thought of nothing else since I left you and it's chewing me to bits. I just couldn't face it that you'd lied. I—"

He broke off when he saw more tears misting my eyes.

All those times he'd baffled me, when I'd wondered about his game. The answer was elementary, only I'd been too wrapped up in cruel Imperial intrigue to notice. His game was honesty. He simply meant every word he said.

I swallowed, wanting to sob with delight as well as terror. No way could I ever deserve this man. He was far too good for me.

"They sent me after you," I admitted at last, still holding his hands. "To kill you, or just to bring you back. I've been confused as hell over whether to betray you, help you or fall into bed with you. I guess I did all three." I shrugged, the strange sting of truth sweet in my mouth. "And now I can't go back to what I used to be. That's all I know."

Sasha brushed back my sweaty hair, cautious, but his eyes sparkled. "Thank you. It's nice to hear it. You're a good liar. I really thought you hated me for a while."

A smile curled my lips despite everything. I leaned into him, enjoying his touch on my face. "I wanted to," I whispered, and brushed my lips against his, sweet warmth. "But it's too hard. I give up."

I felt him smile, and then he kissed me, tangling my hair in his fingers so I couldn't get away.

Shadrin interrupted with a bitter laugh. "I should have known, Caroline. You didn't make up that bullshit on your own. You screwed it, and it poisoned you."

Sasha pulled away and leveled the atomflash at Shadrin, flicking the sizzling charge back on. "Let's talk about bullshit, shall we, General?"

I shoved my hands into my jacket pockets. Delight still bubbled through me, but an oily film of discomfort slimed the surface. Sasha couldn't win.

I recalled Nikita's words: *Even if they blow the station to static and splinters, the annexation will still go ahead ...*

Shadrin tugged uselessly at his bound wrists and glowered at Sasha, his face tight. "Whatever you people want, you can go to ob—"

"Tell him, Valodyi," I interrupted. "About you and Luis Alvarado. What's in the fix for you this time? Real estate? Resource stocks? A juicy cut of those billion sols?"

Shadrin frowned, doing his best to look mystified. "I've no idea what you're talking about."

"This entire negotiation is corrupt, isn't it? It was a done deal from the beginning. You get rich, Alvarado gets richer, plus his own personal Imperial protection force. And the lucky colonists get the Empire and no say in any of it. Right?"

"Think what you like." Shadrin's voice rang steady, but the cruel curl of his lip told me I was right.

Sasha stared, his face draining of color. "I know Luis," he said softly. "He's a decent man. He cares about his people—"

"You're not just a filthy terrorist," Shadrin interrupted, hate flashing in his eyes, "you're a fucking idiot. Everyone has their price. Luis Alvarado's was money. Offer enough and a man will screw anyone over. Don't you realize that yet?"

Sasha's gaze didn't fall. "Not me."

"You think not?" Shadrin sneered. "We'll see. Look to your lady friend, scumbag. A man will do all kinds of stupid shit when there's a woman involved. See how steelclad your principles are when she's screaming for her life."

My skin crept cold. Was I to be Sasha's weakness? Was a new vulnerability all he got for caring about me?

"Enough." Sasha jammed the atomflash under Shadrin's chin, leaving a scarlet welt. "Fact is, if I kill you now, nothing changes, does it?" His voice was gentle, dangerous. "The annexation can't be stopped?"

Shadrin shrugged as best he could, smug. "Not a chance."

"Wrong answer." Sasha leaned closer, his thumb caressing the contact.

My heart twisted. I could call out to him, beg him not to fire. But this decision he had to make on his own.

Shadrin averted his face, sweating, but Sasha dragged him back around by the hair, forcing him to keep eye contact. "See, your death does change things. If I kill you, I give your life meaning. Dead, you're a valiant Imperial warrior slain by the insurrection. Alive, you're just another greedy flunky on the take and you don't mean a damn thing."

Shadrin scowled, and Sasha shoved him away, powering the atomflash down once more. "I think I'll spend a while on the pirate newscasts instead. Make sure every last person on Santa Maria with a weapon and a grudge knows just what you've done. See how your career flourishes when your latest acquisition erupts in a howling rebellion."

I stared, breathless, but Sasha just shrugged wearily. "You were right. This is one battle we can't win." Despite his sorrow, that sweet little smile crept onto his smudged face. "Thank you."

"Oh, for fuck's sake. Will you just get on with it?"

The new voice prickled my spine, horridly familiar, and I spun around, scrabbling for my back-up pistol.

But a shot already rang out, and Shadrin's head imploded in a puff of scarlet steam.

36

Nikita stood in the doorway, grinning. He puffed an imaginary wisp of hair from his deep blue eyes, his aim unwavering as he switched it to me. "Never liked him anyway."

He looked gorgeous, elegant, flawless, his black Axis uniform fitting him like body paint. But it didn't stop me leveling my pistol at him.

He widened his eyes, pretending to be hurt. "What's the matter, Aragon? That's Axis money Shadrin was skimming to line his own pockets. Or have you gone totally soft?"

Beside me, Sasha tightened his fingers around the remote detonator's silver casing. "Perhaps we should play tarocchi for old times' sake," he murmured. "What's the matter with this guy?"

"Everything." I advanced, my aim steady. "Sasha, this is Nikita, codename Malachite. If you ever see him again, shoot first and ask later."

Nikita laughed. "Good advice, coming from you. Lyudmila was right," he added airily, cruel, daring me to ask what he meant.

I circled toward the emergency exit hatch, keeping him in my sights, but my stomach churned. "I don't care—"

"About Urumki, when your boyfriend bit it. She said you'd lost your nerve, wanted to cut you loose. I should have let her." He sighed. "Fuck. To think I told her this would never work. That Boy Genius here would never fall for it. I'll be buying her drinks for the rest of my life."

I wiped sweat from my temple, my nerves jittering. He never talked this much unless he'd planned something. "So what now?"

"You know that answer. I'll miss you, Aragon. We had good fun." He thumbed the power level on his pistol, increasing it to full heat, and flicked an icy blue glance at Sasha. "You can look away, if you like."

My blood jerked hot. I swallowed on a dry mouth, my hands shaking. Watery heat spilled through my intestines, and the alarm blared in my ears, uncaring. I could fire, but I wouldn't kill him before he shot me. And if Sasha fired, I was just as dead.

My legs weakened. I wasn't ready. So much more I wanted to do. Cruise the Minsk supernova fields, go solar-flare jumping, learn to cook. And Sasha.

A lump swelled my throat, stopping my breath, and I wanted to cry. Fuck.

Sasha flipped his remote slowly in his fingers, diodes flashing green. "Never."

Nikita raised his perfect eyebrows. "No? Suit yourself. Step back if you don't want her all over you."

He tilted his head to sight the shot, and I wanted to close my eyes, but I couldn't.

Sasha squeezed the remote softly, and the silver contacts flashed scarlet. He'd primed his detonators. "Two minutes. Or now. It's your choice, you fucked-up son of a bitch. Move that pretty finger and we all die."

Nikita glanced at Sasha's hand and laughed. "Micro-ether? Shit. I was having such a nice day. I suppose it's rigged to squeal if I melt it out of your grubby little hand?"

Sasha didn't blink. "Do it and find out."

Nikita swung his pistol to point at Sasha, his eyes burning frigid and empty. "Disarm it, or I melt your stubborn ass to mist."

"No." Sasha jerked his head toward Shadrin's emergency escape hatch. "Carrie, get out of here."

I blinked away stinging sweat, my thoughts racing. Shadrin had a ship, or at least a floating distress pod. Two minutes less small change might just be enough. But there was something I had to do first. And amid all the lies, there was one tiny fact about Agent Malachite that I could always rely on.

Nikita wanted desperately to live.

He was reckless and thrill-seeking, but unlike Spider, he wasn't suicidal. He firmly believed he was the most important thing in existence. He'd do anything to save his own life. And that meant he wouldn't shoot us. Not yet. Not while we had explosives in our grasp.

"Not me, Sasha." My steadiness surprised me. "You. Prep the ship—"

"It's a Shard-class chi variant," cut in Nikita slyly. "With a specially calibrated navset. You might not like where it takes you."

"He's bluffing. Give me the remote, Sasha. I can cover you. Prep the ship. I'll be there."

Silently, Sasha slid the remote into my hand, the metal hot and slick with his sweat. The heady comfort of his trust warmed me like sunshine, but I couldn't look away from my pistol sights and Nikita. Sasha's footsteps clanged on the metal escape gangway, and faded.

Nikita cocked his head, bemused, and lowered his weapon. His eyes glinted, appreciative. "Nice play. Guess I won't shoot you. Now disarm the fucking thing."

"I can't. It's encrypted."

My arm ached from holding the heavy pistol, but I didn't let it drop. I sidled toward the escape hatch, my boots catching in thick carpet, until I stood within the narrow blast door. Warning lights flashed red and white on its rim beside the twin sets of levers for blast and airlock, one set inside, one out. Sasha's remote buzzed quietly in my hand. One minute to go.

I inhaled, deep. "Come with us."

"What?" Nikita laughed, but strange softness kindled in his eyes. "You and Boy Genius in there? You've got to be kidding."

Compassion pierced my heart. It wasn't his fault he didn't understand, that he acted like this. For a while, he'd been my only friend, and he'd shown me the best time of my life. He deserved better. If I could save just one person from the Empire's deceit, the last six years might not have been wasted.

But seconds slipped by like fast-flowing plasma.

"Leave all this behind," I said desperately. "They lied about Urumki. They've lied about everything. You can be better than they are. I know it. Please, Nikita. Come with us."

He wandered up to me, thoughtful, and considered my pistol where I aimed it at his throat. His lips shone, and a soft, pale curl or two dropped over his eyes. For a moment, I remembered how much it hurt to love him, and my soul shrank.

For the smallest instant, recognition glimmered on his face, and then it died. "I'm sorry," he said softly. "I don't know the person you're talking to."

Tears made my eyes ache. I stepped back beyond the blast door, letting my aim fall to reach for its lever, the remote still clammy in my left hand. Last card in my game. Would he play?

"You'll die if you stay here."

He ruffled his hair and gave me that stunning, heart-shattering smile. "Didn't I tell you? I'm gonna live forever."

He flashed his hand out, but I couldn't halt my movement in time. I'd already operated the blast door and it slid shut with a hostile clunk, sealed for good. He'd closed the airlock, and I'd already sounded the evac alarm. The exit was in automatic emergency mode. Nikita had disengaged the ship.

My insides twisted, constricting my lungs to a tiny space, and I watched helplessly as first the blast and then the airlock warning light blinked out. I was stranded.

Sasha's remote control buzzed, tingling my palm. No way I could disarm it in the seconds I had left.

I sprinted to the sealed glass airlock, acid burning my lungs. Just in time to see the silver lozenge spin swiftly away, corners glinting, into a glittering starfield littered with departing spacecraft, emergency beacons flashing.

The remote buzzed faster, scalding my skin.

And then my skull smashed into the bulkhead, and the stars blinded me.

37

It took nine days for Axis to be done with me. Nine days in a shiny steel cell, my hair filthy and my skin caked with blood and grime, still wearing the same torn flight suit they'd pulled me from the wreckage in. That blast door had worked like a charm. When they'd scoured the sector for the missing bits of Esperanza, they'd found me in the still-sealed airlock, conserving oxygen with a makeshift carbon scrubber and hotwiring Sasha's micro-ether remote to the warning-light current to keep warm.

I held up pretty well in that cell. I got through the thirst, the pain, the psychological terror. I'm trained for that. Bully boys and their electric whips, hooded torturers, the mindfuck shrink with the fingernail needles. They don't scare me. What got me in the end was the sleep deprivation. When your vision's a hideous blur, your knees are cramping to your ribcage with nausea, and you think the walls are crawling with insectoid aliens that are chewing on your toes and crawling up between your legs to suck your insides out, you'll tell them anything if they'll only shut the fuck up and turn out the lights.

I don't doubt I told them everything. Who Sasha was, where he might have gone, how his console was calibrated, the objects on his shelves, the words he whispered to me as we loved. If I hadn't, I'd probably still be there now. They can keep prisoners alive for a very long time.

In the end, they never took me to Director Renko, or debriefed me, or officially terminated my Axis existence. I never saw Surov the cat-man, or Electra, his new A-D Ops. One day the goons just dragged me to the shower, shoved a clean pair of pants and a shirt at me, and emptied me out onto a dark New Moskva street next to a garbage compactor.

I knew I was bait. It didn't matter. I patched my bruises, biding my time. In a day I had a weapon, new clothes, a place to stay. In a week I had a ship, a rusty little Swallow-class hopper I named *Nikita*, and I went searching for Sasha. I knew they'd follow me, but I'm trained for that too, and by the time I got as far as the Ural spaceway I was alone.

When I reached Santa Maria, security beacons and traffic control already cluttered the space, and Sasha's little rock was deserted. I wandered along the empty street at dusk, the cold, dusty breeze lifting my hair, the planet's scarlet crescent shimmering overhead, but it wasn't the same. Even the air smelled different: emptier, less invigorating. Sasha was gone.

I searched the empty schoolhouse, in case he'd left me a clue. His room lay in shambles, overturned by searching Imperial hands, his console dismantled and useless. His blue coat lay heaped on the floor, the ripped seams ragged. I pulled it on, cuddling into his warmth. The unmade bed still smelled like him, faded but definite, and my heart ached.

I sat trailing my finger over the blanket, the dusty sheets, the pillow, remembering him, and faint green fluorescence blossomed under my touch. A biochemical clue, left just for me.

Stuffed deep inside the pillow, I found his golden hyperchip.

***

Twenty-seven days and innumerable spacials later, I set *Nikita* down on a windswept hardstand at midnight, the landing legs crunching in black ice. Buildings loomed dark and silent at the spaceport's edge: the silhouettes of empty cooling towers, abandoned scaffolding, the misshapen hump of a slagpile. Stars jeweled the blue-streaked sky, which was pure and uncluttered with traffic or signage, and a trio of blue-stained retro-orbit moons—like the one I'd landed on—twirled a silent cosmic slow-dance.

I'd decrypted his puzzle easily enough. He'd left it in Zykovski six-gen, a function he knew I could deconstruct, and the pages of slipbeacon data that unfolded had led me here: an abandoned energy plant on another mined-out rock somewhere in the cold backstretches of Imperial space.

I jumped down onto the concrete in darkness. My breath shimmered in the chill. I wrapped my coat tighter. Metaldust tickled my nose, and in the distance an animal howled. At the hardstand's edge, I could make out the hulking shadow of an old Wolf-class utility. Slowly my eyes adjusted, and I turned and walked toward the distant flame.

A tall hangar loomed. I bent aside a corrugated metal sheet and climbed under. Warmth greeted me, flickering firelight, the smells of sweat and cooking. They'd built a little shanty town from scrapmetal and wire, with partitions improvised from freight shrink-wrap. His people looked tired, hollow-eyed, cold, but they still joked and slept and took care of their kids.

A skinny boy with a pistol challenged me, hard-eyed, but backed down when I lifted my hands empty. I walked on, along a narrow path beside makeshift dwellings. Children played in the dirt at my feet, and curious eyes followed me. I spotted Isabel, crosslegged in the dust with a child on her knee, her long black hair braided over her shoulder. She smiled and waved and I smiled back.

"Is that for me?"

My spine prickled and I turned. I didn't know what this was, what we had. I didn't even know if I'd be welcome. Even if Sasha forgave me, the others here might not. But no point torturing myself. If he was going to reject me, I might as well take it now.

I lifted my gaze, and there he was. Dusty, dark and gorgeous, that silky hair I loved singed at the ends and unruly about his shoulders. Flashburn on his cheek, a ragged scar bright on his bare forearm. Wrapped in a stained green half-coat over dented black armor that hugged his muscles tight enough to make me hot. Pistol clipped to his thigh, atomflash jammed into his belt. A dirty rebel scumbag if I'd ever seen one. It was a really good look.

I swallowed, my face burning. "Hey, you."

"You made it." That little smile, the one that always sent me crazy. It still worked.

"Yeah."

I held out his hyperchip, firelight flashing it golden. He took it. Our fingers didn't touch.

I cleared my throat, dry. "Your entry regime really sucks. They let anyone into this dump." I moved closer, daring, and brushed my knuckles across his shoulder. "But now I'm here ..."

"Carrie, I am so sorry." He edged back, hands lifted, but his brittle tone cracked. "I wanted to come for you. It killed me. But ... Fuck, there's always a 'but', isn't there?" He dragged burned hair roughly behind his ears, and dirt smeared on his cheek. Tears. He wouldn't look at me. "I understand if you hate me. I dreamed of what they'd be doing to you. I lived it day and night. I just—"

"Sasha." Gently I pulled his hands down. "Look at me."

He forced his gaze down to mine, and my heart wrenched in sorrow. Such deep, hypnotic eyes, so bruised inside.

"I'm okay," I said softly. "I get it."

Because I was, and I did. I'd never have all of him. Not while these people depended on him. Not while the Empire chased us all across space like a mindless predator, hungry for the kill. And they always would. But I'd take whatever he could give me. I just hoped it'd be enough.

His fingers slid between mine and tightened. "Carrie—"

"It's all right, Sasha. We'll talk. I promise. Just ... come here."

I pressed my cheek into his chest, and after a rigid moment he folded me in his arms. Tears swelled, and I squeezed my eyes shut. Just the smell of him pushed all the hurt and bruises a little further into the distance. And the feel of his strong embrace, his living body against mine, made me warm and shivery like a pleasant fever. Damn it. The man was like a disease. I had a serious case of Sasha, and I'd be lucky if I lived through it.

I tilted my head up and he kissed me. Hot, deep, luscious, his hair curling crisp in my fingers. He tasted of dirt and tears. I didn't know how long we stood there, but when we broke apart, my lips stung swollen and my blood arced hot with need.

He took me to his corner, where coals glimmered red-hot in the firepit and blackmetal walls dripped ice. We had no privacy. I didn't care. I just wanted to be with him, drink up the sight of him, drown in him. Leave behind the hideous mistake that was my life and start afresh. I couldn't hope for forgiveness, not from myself. I could only forget.

I pulled him down on his blanket, hungry. Weapons clunked and I fumbled them aside. His armor peeled off in my urgent hands. Underneath, his body shone, hard and bruised like mine. His skin tingled my tongue with salt and metal, his hands on my body a sweet torture. When he stripped my shirt away, I didn't even feel the cold. My nipples ached tight in the sweet heat of his mouth, and when he pushed me down and spread my legs, tension already sparkled me breathless.

I winced when he entered me, and he paused, his mouth brushing mine. "Okay?"

"Always."

I arched and pushed harder, deeper, hotter. It hurt inside, deep where they'd done things to my body, but I didn't care. It was my flesh and I gifted it to him. Not them. Him. They'd have to do better to shame me into losing him.

He buried his face in my hair and dragged my thigh around him to take me deeper. I shuddered, pleasure rising. We moved hard, hot, angry, not at each other but at this dark, insane world that threatened to tear us apart. My nails bruised him. His kisses stung, and I tasted blood, and he held me down with fingers clenched in mine and we collided and ached and gasped and came and curled up together mixed in dirty sweat and love.

***

I jerked awake in the frigid dark to the sting of an alarm. Sasha still held me, close to his chest where it was warm. He didn't stir. No one did.

I sat up, dragging back my love-knotted hair.

The pinging in my head grew louder. Frost prickled my spine, and it wasn't just the chilly air.

I scrambled for my clothes, strewn in the dust where we'd left them. Pants, boots, socks, chassis, my coat. It was all new. I fumbled, searching, my pulse alive.

From a crease in my boot tumbled a tiny glass square. An ESE. And it was ringing.

I stared. This made no sense. Axis had stripped me of everything when they'd dumped me in that alley. I'd searched everything they'd left me. Unless ...

Unless they'd already found me. Bugged me, and let me run.

I glanced at Sasha. Still asleep, hair tumbling on his bruised cheek. Cautiously, I picked up the ESE. Thumbed the contact.

The pinging stopped.

Hash, like dirt on the surface of my mind. Nothing. Maybe I imagined it. But this could be a tracking device. I should decode it, jam the signal, send a false return to put them off the scent ...

A finger of amusement trailed an icy caress down my spine.

My skin tingled.

Laughter. Cold, false, angry laughter.

I swallowed, shaking. I knew that laugh. But it wasn't possible. Was it?

My voice cracked to a whisper. "Nikita?"

A smile, like a cold shadow on my heart. A hot brush of invisible lips on mine. And silence.

I dropped the ESE. Crushed it under my heel. Ground the splintered glass pieces into the dirt. It didn't make me feel safer.

I shivered. This wasn't over. Not by a starshot.

I curled back under the blanket and wriggled into Sasha's arms, but I couldn't sleep.

www.ingramcontent.com/pod-product-compliance
Lightning Source LLC
Chambersburg PA
CBHW021445240626
47153CB00001B/302

* 9 7 8 1 7 4 3 3 4 1 6 8 1 *